CW01113281

The Maker's Bloodline:

Land Rising

Michael-Israel Jarvis

All rights reserved; no part of this publication may be reproduced by any means, electronic, mechanical, photocopying or otherwise, without the prior permission of the publisher

First published in Great Britain in 2013 by
Taravatara Publishing
56 Chaucer Road, Great Yarmouth, NR30 4HA

Copyright © Michael-Israel Jarvis, 2013
Cover image copyright © Michael-Israel Jarvis, 2013

Michael-Israel Jarvis has asserted his moral rights

FIRST EDITION

Acknowledgements

There are so many people involved in one way or another with this book. Independent publishing is something of a misnomer: without the original readers of this book's first incarnation (the 0.5 Edition) the book would not exist in this revised form.

Thank you to my first readers, all of you. I hope you approve of what I have done to our book.

Thank you, as always to my wife, Katie. We are one, unhinged creature, and very happy. I love you.

Thank you, as always, to Daniel Stamp, my confidant and great supporter.

Thank you to Joseph Parsonage, whose polite yet keen criticisms improved this book a great deal.

Thank you to the McNerney clan, for being family, and to my own family, for your sanctuary and your food.

Lastly, thanks to you, for buying this book.
Unless you stole it, in which case, at least read it.

Prologue

Tara. Caimah.
Land and Sky.
They say that the winds, the breath of both Land and Sky, form a living bridge between the two. They say that man is bound to the earth, until the day he returns to it forever.
Yet, while he lives, it is the sky he breathes.

The column of soldiers breathed air thick with dust. All day it had stirred in clouds beneath their feet as they crossed the unwanted land, painting the trail of their passing against the blue sky. The end of the long march was coming, their last day of toiling in the heat.
Their last day before they joined that same dust. The veterans knew it. They had carried their own supplies down the slopes and through the fruitless fields, until the green had turned to dirt. No supply train followed them, and this confirmed suspicions beyond argument. Even small forces such as theirs were usually followed by wains, livestock and peasants, especially in times of famine. For many, war was the only provider once the harvests failed.
For this war, the soldiers marched alone.
Fox marched near the head of the column. He was surrounded on all sides by his honour guard, a group of grim-faced veterans who had known even before setting out that they were not supposed to survive the coming conflict.
Fox was no fool. He began to see it, even as the newly enlisted boys were beginning to understand; there was no returning from the dust of the East Waste. They had been sent to die. And he was beginning to understand why. He looked up, grey eyes narrowed against the sun.
'Branaghin...'
'Yes, your Highness?' Branaghin had a gentle voice for such a large man. The captain shortened his strides to walk beside Fox.
'This is all because of me.'
Branaghin closed his eyes for a moment, swallowing emotion. 'Yes, your Highness. It is because of you.'

Fox shook his head. He felt too numb for tears. 'Why would my father...' he broke off midsentence. The column halted. The horizon was no longer empty.

Time seemed to rush. Fox had nothing to do but stand beside Branaghin as the champions ordered the column into fighting groups. His heart was a-thunder and he was sweating. He was cold. It felt much like memories of being ill as a child. His skin prickled with expectancy.

'Too many,' Branaghin muttered. He watched the motionless ranks across the plain. The Ox troops outnumbered Fox's small army considerably. Even so, the lies about the enemy's number had not been the greatest of the Advisory Council's acts of sabotage. Fox had been given no specialist troops. Without archers, they had no offensive edge.

The yellow silk of the Ox pennants fluttered in the hot breeze.

Branaghin turned and put a hand on Fox's shoulder. The boy was trembling, his breathing coming in shallow gasps, his chest rising and falling beneath his lacquered cuirass. Branaghin shouted out an order to the honour guard. The shout and the squeeze Branaghin gave Fox's shoulder dragged the boy back into a better place. His panicked breathing slowed.

'Stake our colours on the rock!' Branaghin's order was followed at once. The company's flag bearer climbed a short outcrop of rock at the army's rear. Out in the dust, it seemed the only thing worth defending. The blue flag with the grey fox emblem fluttered in the wind.

Yellow silk, blue silk. Dust, sky.

The Ox troops began to move, and Fox took a great breath and bit down on his fear.

'They're coming,' he said.

Branaghin nodded. 'They are. They'll be in no rush. Their archers will loose before they charge. Now, listen to me! Do what I say, Your Highness. Draw your sword.'

Branaghin spoke with patient authority, like a mother cajoling a child. Fox had never known a mother. He drew his sword, eyes still wide and fixed on the approaching enemy. A chant and a banging of shields had begun. His heart seemed to be beating in time.

'Good. Keep it held. Do not let go of it! Do. Not. Let go.' Branaghin's hand closed around Fox's, around the hilt of the sword. 'When they come, after the arrows... concentrate on the first one that comes towards you. Don't stop, don't think, don't look at him, just step past his spear, and push this,' he gripped the boy's hand fiercely, so that the sword trembled, 'push this *in*. And don't let go!'

'Yes, Branaghin.'

'Remember one thing, my prince!' Branaghin unslung his shield and took it up on his left arm. 'We are for you! We will not leave you! To the death!' He lifted his spear and turned towards the front. The sky was filling up with arrows, rising through the air, their points turning earthward, dropping like rain...

Dust. Dust, caught between the Land and Sky. And when it ended, there was fire.

1
Ashes Of Defeat

The sun rose and gave colour to the blood-soaked earth.

A raven hopped disdainfully amongst the carnage, its careful feet picking a path around the dead. Its cruel beak knifed in and out, here and there, soiling the oily black feathers around its eyes.

In the dead stillness something moved. The raven ruffled its wings, alert. In its experience the dead rarely moved.

Moving cautiously, its head bobbing low, the raven picked its way towards the movement. As it stepped closer to the disturbance the raven began to feel warmth under its scaly pads. Ahead, there was a circle of clear space, blasted earth, with a body slouched in the centre. The raven stepped gingerly into the circle, feeling the heat under its feet.

The figure ahead moved slightly. It was breathing; painful, ragged breaths, arms crossed across its chest. It was a boy, charred remnants of cloth hanging from him. The bodies in the circle around him were horrifically burnt. The raven stopped suddenly, wary head held at an angle. The boy was stirring, lifting his head and opening his eyes. Alarmed, the raven shrieked at him and frantically clawed its way into the sky.

Fox climbed slowly to his feet, wincing. He looked around, gasping for breath. His mouth opened and shut, the arid air harsh in his throat.

'Fire.' The word came through cracked lips. 'Fire...I...' he nearly collapsed, tripping over part of a body. He stumbled towards the rock, over ground strewn with the destroyed bodies of the last stand. Fox reached out, falling against the stone. Waves of cooling energy began to flow up his arms, visible as a haze around his trembling figure.

Even as relief came, the stone began to steam and crumble beneath his hands. At last, a crack splintered across the rock and Fox pulled away, drawing in a deep breath. He slid down into a sitting position, his back against the hot stone.

Fox sat with his head in his hands, trying to reassemble his thoughts. He could remember the last defence, the soldiers fighting around this rock. They had been backed up here, surrounded by the enemy.

Standing, Fox looked up at the body of a boy about his age, lying across the top of the rock. The dead boy's fist was still clenched around the flagpole he had carried into battle. The flag hung from the spiked end of the pole, tattered, but still showing the Fox emblem.

He remembered their end now, under the Fox banner, against the rock. The flag boy had clambered on top. Enemy spearmen had pushed in, and the last surviving enemy archer loosed his final arrow. It had hit the flag boy in the eye and he had fallen, as the others fell to spear-thrusts, fighting in vain for their lives.

Fox turned and walked away.

He had thrown his sword at the bowman in his desperation. Here, Fox stopped by the body of the archer. His sword was in the dead man's throat, snapped near the hilt and useless. *What had happened then?* The whole thing was a painful blur.

Turning, he looked at the circle of burnt ground. He remembered the surge of flame. His rage and shame at the defeat of his men, rage at the death of his soldiers. *Soldiers dying to keep me from death.* He had seen the Fox family standard topple and he had lost control. He had destroyed twenty men with a word.

'Did I do this?'

The boy looked down at his hands. He had never expected anything like this. Never thought it possible. Hadn't he turned away from...from all that?

Fox turned and looked back at the outcrop.

So, the rock had saved him. The release of power from the stone into his lightly muscled frame had brought him back from the desperate edge of survival. He trembled still, less from exhaustion now than from his warring emotions and thoughts. The images of the dead remained burnt into his mind's eye, features and personality obliterated by his consuming fire. Maybe he should have died, fallen to the spears. But he couldn't have helped it. The fire had come completely naturally from him. It hadn't felt like sorcery.

His thoughts turned to his father, hundreds of leagues away in the Autumn Hills. Should he have died and left him sonless? Ended the Fox family line with his cousin? No. This... this would be dealt with later. Now he needed a plan. Word would need to be taken to his uncle.

The sun was high, beating down on Fox. He was wearing the banner boy's dilapidated breeches, the fox flag round his shoulders in place of his burnt clothing and armour. He followed a road leading north, away from the death and dust of the battlefield. Ahead, the land was beginning to level out, turning green and soft. To his right, the east, dense forest clawed at the edges of the road.

Fox looked into the dark between the trees, curious. No one travelled through the East Forest, in either direction. The trees grew all along the border of the Sacred Lands, a vast area of unexplored, unmapped mystery. They cut off the settled country of the Central Plains from the ocean, or, as some believed, protected the Lands from the Underworlds. Fox shuddered suddenly, but did not know why.

The nearby river cut through the green land and ran alongside the road, cooling the late summer air. For hours the road was almost straight, running through a valley, the setting sun's light playing across the idly stirring trees. The valley deepened suddenly, or rather the land rose on either side of the river, making a narrow gorge in between the steep slope on one side and the quiet forest on the other.

The shadows deepened. Fox carried on walking, feeling cold. He pulled the flag closer about his shoulders. Shivering, he turned towards the opposite bank.

It was not a good idea to try crossing the shallow river in the dark. The water made a soft, musical sound beneath the overhanging trees. A breeze set the branches moving above his head.

Behind him, in the shadow of the trees, a great flat stone loomed in the dark. As he went closer for shelter, the air became bitterly cold. Tired now beyond caring, Fox slid down against the bulk of the smooth rock, tightening the flag around his shoulders. With some effort he raised his arms and turned his palms inwards. Slowly the temperature around him began to rise. Oblivious again, Fox let his head drop to his chest and he fell asleep.

In his sleep he dreams, the night passing around him.

A hand reaches out for him through heavy shade, a claw hung with rot and creeping darkness. Black, hopeless fear clutches at his sleeping soul, searching for his end. A Death calls his name like a curse, a hidden name even he doesn't know. He begins to run down corridors he cannot see, desperately trying to find something, or someone, to save him. He cries out helplessly, the sob of a child lost in the dark, his enemy closing. Icy breath burns the back of his neck. He can feel his killer's joy as it senses victory.

'NO!' Fox woke and stumbled upright, pushing himself away from the stone, mind reeling. It was morning and bitterly cold.

Turning slowly, he looked back at the stone. A Carcer Stone. He recognised it now and the horror of it sent him stumbling back to the water's edge.

Splayed across the top of it, visible in the morning light, was a skeleton. It gleamed, oddly clean. He watched in frozen horror, as the bones nearest the centre of the slab began to crumble away. The area of dead grass around the base of the rock grew, tufts of green browning and curling. A pale glow wormed around the decimated bones. Behind the stone the closest tree died, branches twisting, the dead leaves spiralling to the ground.

Fox ran, nausea turning his empty stomach. He stumbled along the riverbank, searching for something to use as a weapon. He found what he was looking for in a tangle of long branches at the edge of the forest, where a straight length of wood sprouted from the trees.

A girl was at the shallow point of the river as Fox came back to cross, eyes averted from the foul rock. She looked about the same age, perhaps a little younger than him. A wooden pail lay discarded beside her on the opposite bank. Her dark hair concealed her face where she knelt, head bowed, shoulders trembling. She was crying. Fox stood still as she looked up at him. He said the first thing that came into his head.

'Are you all right? I'm... what happened here?' He glanced back to the stone. 'Who was...?'

The girl was backing away, afraid and angry. Her tears broke and she raised her head, showing her dark eyes. Her fists were clenched.

'My Ma. They killed her!'

She looked straight at him, then the bones on the stone, and choked in shock.

'She's gone!'

'Wait!'

Fox ran forwards into the shallow water, and caught hold of the girl's arm before she could run.

'Tell me who killed her.' A fury was in him now, burning against whoever had done this, and against the Carcer Stone that sat in fulsome dominion of the bank.

The girl looked into his eyes, her own burning with barely controlled rage to match his.

'They're soldiers. Ragged like you, come down the same road. They have my sisters at the house; they killed her in front of us! Threw her... threw her on the stone and left her... I have to take water to them, do what they say, or they'll kill... I can't...'

The girl covered her tears with her shaking hands.

'Keep away from the water.'

Fox pointed to the circle of death around the stone. The dry, dead grass was broken where the edge of the slow river lapped at the bank. A bad smell was beginning to come off the water. Fox stepped past the girl and picked up the pail.

'Take them the water. They've poisoned it, so let them drink.' He looked up the gorge, his expression grim.

The girl took the pail from him. She was shaking a little, but Fox saw more of her anger than her fear. It gave him hope. The girl lifted the pail to her hip and began to walk up the slope. Fox waited until she had reached the brink and then, gripping the length of wood he had torn from the forest, he went after her at a fast walk.

He reached the top of the slope just in time. Four rough, tired looking men were standing behind a fence in a beaten-earth yard. On the left were blocks of empty stables, and to the right, a long low building with a thatched roof. The men were drawing weapons, but they were not looking at Fox.

Another soldier, grasping at his own throat, stumbled through the open doorway. His fingers ripped at the leather armour around his neck, yellow silk spilling out as he tore his clothes. The man went into spasms, lying contorted on the ground, hands flapping in the dust. The girl with the raven hair ran through the door, almost tripping over him.

'Here!' Fox shouted quickly, as one of the soldiers turned his spear towards her. Fox vaulted the fence using the dark wood pole as an aid, rolling into a comfortable stance, the long straight branch held along the line of his forearm. A few buds of sprouting growth still showed along its length.

The first man to attack thrust forward a battered sword, trying to score a hit on Fox's left side. He reacted instantly. Holding the stick with both hands he brought it round to block the strike, his feet shifting in the dust of the yard. The other end of the pole came up into his attacker's face and down again across the wrist holding the sword. Fox finished his enemy with two more savage hits to the head and a spinning backhand to the neck. Something broke and the dead man dropped to his knees and fell forwards. The other three stood frozen with shock. Fox was fast. In a few heartbeats two were dead and another helpless. Broken.

The girl stood as transfixed as the soldiers had. She watched as Fox strode to the paralysed soldier, closing her eyes as he finished him with his dropped sword. Fox turned and looked at her, misunderstanding her revulsion.

'You said they killed your mother?'

'That one watched. He... yes. But...' Fox stared blankly at her, but anger was rising.

'He killed my men and hid under the dead when the fight went bad! He was a coward!' His voice trembled. After a moment of stillness he breathed out and started again in a softer tone.

'In war this is how it is done. It would be crueller to let him lie there until death finds him.' He attempted a smile to reassure her, but it came with difficulty to his lips.

She had not been joined by her sisters. The silence from the building behind her worried him.

'*Your* men? Who are you?' She whispered.

Her question triggered a learned response. He put his feet together and bowed from the waist. As he opened his mouth to speak, a voice rang out. Another man was stepping through the doorway of the inn, a naked sword in his hand.

'Crown Prince Fox!' The man strode into the yard. His armour was black, an officer's, branded with the yellow insignia of the Ox Family. The pommel of his sword was decorated with a tassel of blue-grey. Fox Family colours. The thought of this man wielding a stolen blade enraged Fox. He stepped forward, bringing his makeshift staff around in a gesture of challenge.

'Yes, I rather like Autumn Steel,' the man smiled grimly, glancing at the blade in his hand, 'it's got more bite than our weapons. I'll use it better than the man I took it from.' His voice was smooth. A look of fury crossed the Prince's face as the man continued.

'I liked your fire-play, your highness, what I could see of it. I felt it. The gathering of your strength. So much strength! So I thought I'd do better to play dead. After magic like that I imagine you're quite tired. Better use a spear when you fight me, eh? We won't use magic. Even I play fair. Some of the time.' His smile curved cruelly.

Prince Fox spat into the dirt and repeated his bow, this time to the new enemy. His eyes never broke contact as he spoke.

'I don't need a spear. I'll kill you with this stick, and I'll take that sword back and have you buried with it in your chest. A gift from its owner!'

The two faced each other across the yard. The girl sidestepped to the door and ran inside, calling the names of her sisters.

'No magic,' the black armoured man repeated, 'but before we fight, you should know your killer's name. I am Sirkor Wolf.'

Fox raised his head. 'What is a Wolf nobleman doing in the armour of the Ox family?'

'Helping out a relative. In search of wealth. And notoriety.' Sirkor Wolf grinned like his family's totem and moved suddenly, attacking on Fox's left. He used the security of the wall at his back to put strength into his attack, launching himself at the boy. Fox rolled forwards and Sirkor overbalanced. Rolling himself back to his feet, Fox moved next, feet scuffing the dust, the staff flicking out repeatedly at Sirkor's head and torso, forcing him away from the wall. Fox now pushed towards his enemy, varying his strikes. His frame was smaller than Sirkor's, and he was not muscled heavily, but hard training and recent experience had made a difference. Suddenly Sirkor went from comfortably deflecting attacks, to desperate defence; he stumbled backwards and yelled out, surprised by a body behind him.

Tripped onto his back, Sirkor scrambled backwards, warding off blows. Suddenly his guard was beaten aside. Fox punctuated every blow with an enraged yell.

Sirkor's eyes hardened in the last moment and his hand shot out, palm open, fingers rigid. Fox was smashed backwards by the simple movement and thrown to the ground. Sirkor hadn't touched him.

Both got hurriedly to their feet, readying their weapons. Fox's arm leapt forwards as he threw the branch. It glanced off Sirkor's chest, bruising him, and sprang back into Fox's waiting hand. Both took a moment to breathe, Fox leaning on his staff.

'Your sorcery broke the rules of our engagement!' Fox accused, sounding frustrated.

Sirkor shrugged. 'So did yours.'

Fox's fury returned. 'I don't...! I'm not a...! *I'm not like you!*' He shouted, biting out each word as he struggled to stay in control.

Sirkor's wordless, hateful snarl seemed to agree with him.

The girl returned, stepping through the doorway, holding a battered bow. An arrow was nocked on the bowstring. 'I'll kill you for what you did!' her voice shook as she raised the bow, hand also shaking as tears coursed down her cheeks.

Suddenly, Sirkor made a grabbing, twisting motion and the bow snapped, the tight strung bowstring whipping back with tremendous force and cutting a gash across the girl's cheek. Fox reacted instantly, jerking his staff forwards.

He found the movement in the staff and extended it. In his mind's eye he saw the energy of the staff's movement, leaping beyond the boundary of its physical shape, made real by his power, making horrible contact with Sirkor's throat.

Sirkor's neck crumpled. His hand went to his throat as the life began to leave his eyes. Fox ran forward, to where the enemy officer stood swaying, still upright. He tore the blue tasselled sword from Sirkor's hand. For a moment Fox stood, also unsteady on his feet. Then he let out a cry, burying the blade in Sirkor's chest. Transfixed by the blade, Sirkor fell for the last time, a confused look passing briefly across his features.

Fox felt hopelessly faint. The branch fell to the ground and he followed.

The rice Fox was eating was the last of the food in the lodge. The girl watched as he scraped the last grains from the bottom of the bowl.

'Thank you.' Fox passed the bowl back to the girl. The girl's elder sister took the bowl hurriedly. She was in shock, unable to come to terms with her trauma, and afraid to offend the prince.

The other sister had been disgraced and murdered by the Ox soldiers. She was wrapped in cloth now, in a back room. The older of the two surviving sisters was acting from habit, performing all the acts of courtesy and protocol that had been drilled into her from childhood, the daughter of an inn family serving their betters. Fox watched the poor woman's hands shaking as she bowed yet another time.

Fox felt horribly out of place. He was intruding on this family's grief, yet the elder sister was treating him in an apologetic manner, as if she had done something wrong. The younger sister sat in shocked fury, ignoring Fox and the bleeding gash that stood out vividly on her cheek. Fox felt more comfortable speaking to her. She seemed to have forgotten who he was, due to her grief. It simplified things: his title and place had not been important yesterday in the thick of battle, it should not matter here. This family had just lost their mother and sister in one day.

'I need to go to my uncle. I'd help you… but I have to go to my uncle. Thank you for the rice, I'll remember your family to my uncle, we'll reward you, send food. Until this war is over.'

If it ever will be.

The elder sister looked up as Fox spoke, and moved hurriedly to the table.

'Please, do as you will, Lord Prince. I'll bury…' she paused, grief tearing her composure, 'go to your uncle, to Lord Rice Fox, my lord, but please… please take Kesta with you.'

The woman stopped, shocked perhaps at her presumption. Fox did not speak, confused as he was, so she continued.

'She can be your travelling companion, my lord, you've seen her strength of mind, poisoning that man and, and wanting to fight when she saw Lia.' She choked over her dead sister's name, turning away.

'I… couldn't cope, my lord. I'm not strong like her. Please. Forgive me.'

She looked up fearfully from her pleading. Fox felt ill, worried he might have misunderstood. 'You want me to take on your sister as a servant?' He sounded incredulous, but the young woman was nodding. Fox stood. He opened his mouth to speak, but not knowing what to say, he bowed quickly and left the building. The young woman's cries of thanks rang after him.

The younger girl, Kesta, followed him out into the sun again. She was carrying a small bundle. She ran and picked up his staff and gave it to him, taking trouble to present it to him carefully.

Fox examined her face. She was the same age as him, certainly not younger than him by more than a year. She was strikingly attractive, despite the wound on her cheek and her malnourished state. People would talk, seeing the Crown Prince in the company of a young woman. Court etiquette told him that it was a risk to his already unstable reputation to let her come along. Yet he was drawn to her determination and her bravery. Her apparent ability to cope with the pain of her injury and her great loss, endeared her to him.

Fox looked back across the yard to the edge of the gorge, feeling a strange discomfort. In the yard Kesta's sister was beginning to drag Sirkor's body towards the brink.

'Don't go near the Carcer Stone!' Fox shouted suddenly. He had a horrible feeling that Kesta's sister, evidently a practical person, might try to use the properties of the stone to dispose of the bodies. The sister stopped guiltily, confirming Fox's worry. He turned and began to walk away from the inn, along the road that went on indefinitely across the flat land. He wished to get as far away from that evil rock as possible.

Kesta stared back at her sister a moment longer and then hurried to catch up with Fox. Her face was set. She was utterly determined.

They walked for hours. Now and then Kesta reached to wipe blood from the cut on her cheek. It stung sorely and she began to feel sick in the hot sun; it was about midday and they had no water. Fox walked without looking back, unwittingly making her feel out of place, unwanted. She wanted to cry for the first time since she was small, but knew how little that would accomplish. She tried to catch up with Fox but every step was beginning to hurt. Suddenly, stars were popping behind her eyes – the world seemed to slip sideways. She felt arms catching her, laying her down, not on the dust and dirt of the road, but on grass. *I haven't eaten in nearly three days,* she thought, blankly.

A hand brushed her cheek and then her forehead. The fire in her cheek froze over and the headache left her. When she looked up, Fox's hand was shielding her eyes from the sun. He looked worried.

'I'm so sorry. I wasn't thinking about you. I was thinking... I just forgot you were... I apologise. There is no excuse.' He paused guiltily, head bowed, before adding, 'Kesta, is it?'

Kesta sat up and touched her cheek gingerly. There was no blood. 'There's a scar,' Fox said hurriedly, 'but the cut's healed. The headache might come back though.' Kesta stared at him but decided not to ask how he had healed a bloody cut with a touch. She had heard of stranger things at the inn.

'I'm not a sorcerer,' Fox explained quietly, sitting back on the grass, 'I know that for certain. When I was younger they captured one - a sorcerer - on the borders. Normally they would have tried him and killed him, but my father had him brought to us to find out whether I was one of them.'

At this Kesta clearly looked bewildered, so Fox explained. 'I was adopted, Kesta. As far as my adoptive father knew, I could be the son of a sorcerer and Da... I mean, King Steel Fox, wanted to find out if it was true. The sorcerer set tests, asked me to do things. He didn't understand how I did what I could do. Where I got it from.

'I learnt how to make heat, flame, how to move things around at will. How to cause wounds without using a weapon, to break bones... He didn't teach me to heal though.' Here Fox reached as if to touch her painless cheek, though his hand stopped short. 'That came all by itself.'

Fox sat staring past Kesta, eyes turned to the west, lost in his memory.

'One day he set me a final test. He had been growing suspicious and it was to set his mind at ease. I was to "converse with the power within him". He wanted me to give control over to the power within me, so that they could... I don't know what. He called it the Rite of Rising and I couldn't do it. There was nothing there to give control to. Just me. It meant that his misgivings had been proved correct. He went berserk with rage before my father, screaming that I was no sorcerer.

'Of course, my father was delighted. The nobles, the Advisors... they had demanded my death before, but if even a sorcerer would not accuse me...

Well, before they took him away, the sorcerer called in some old language for my death, flung his hands out towards me. I don't know why, or what it was about me that angered him. I put up my own hands in defence. Just instinct. Nothing happened to me but... I saw his end.

'He lost control of his magic, I think; it turned on him, like some kind of living creature. I could see it like it was shadow, a worm. Eyes, perhaps. A mouth. It...devoured him from within. The hidden fee for his art.

'I don't know what my power is. I abhor sorcery. I'm no sorcerer.'

His gaze returned to her, his need to make her understand paramount.

Kesta had been sitting comfortably, listening to him. He was sitting close and his shadow fell across her, giving her shade.

'How many times have you told that story?' she asked, impressed by his eloquence. It sounded like a recital.

Fox smiled, a little embarrassed. 'I was raised in the Royal Court of the Autumn Citadel in the west, Kesta. We're taught how to tell stories properly. Stories are important, my father believes. You'll get used to things like that when we get to my uncle's castle.' Suddenly his brow furrowed. 'Actually, there are a lot of things you'll have to get used to. And quite a lot of it won't be good. I'm a champion in the army Kesta, though I haven't the experience to deserve the post. But my place is in battle, fighting my father's enemies. If you'd rather go home now, I won't blame you.'

Kesta considered in silence. He was sitting very close and was wearing ragged breeches and a flag for a shirt, clothing that belied his true position. She felt uncomfortable sitting so close to someone wearing practically nothing, particularly someone of his caste. She stood quickly. Fox remembered his state as well and blushed as he rose.

Kesta looked back down the road towards the East Forest and home. Then she turned slowly and looked on, towards a dangerous future. 'I'll come with you, sir.' She bowed awkwardly. Fox returned the bow a little more stylishly, smiling. Without a word they both walked on.

2
Fire And Nightmares

Fox sat on his bed in the village inn, looking out of the window. The sun left trails of red light on the paddy fields beyond the stockade wall. The East Forest was an indistinct smudge of black on the horizon.

Fox tore his gaze away from the woods and looked out at the straggling line of rice farmers moving along the raised earth at the edge of the fields. A breeze rose suddenly from the east. Fox pulled the shutters across.

'The weather's getting colder.'

Kesta glanced over from her bed on the other side of the room, where she was unpacking the few belongings she had brought. A small, brown leather pouch fell out onto the bed and she shoved it guiltily back into her bag.

Straightening up as if nothing had happened, she ran a hand through her long black hair and said 'It'll be an early winter this year. They're getting the harvest in now, I think, before the weather spoils it.'

Fox sat back, frowning. 'We'll need a better harvest next year, or a quick end to the war. Otherwise people are going to get a lot hungrier before the Ox kingdom falls.'

Kesta tossed the bag casually behind her bed and turned back to Fox. His knowledge surprised her. She had not expected a prince to understand the cares of peasants.

'Sir?'

'Yes, Kesta?'

'Why are we fighting King Rice Ox?'

Fox gave her a wry smile. 'Why do men ever fight? We have more land than him, I suppose, but he has all the fertile plain, surrounded by hills with regular rains, and the lakes, which means he can feed and supply his armies. I don't see that we have anything he would want, unless he just wants supremacy.' Fox looked up at the rafters, frowning as he spoke. 'We don't know how he's supporting his armies – they say his people hate him, so he can't be recruiting easily. Besides, he needs every peasant he can get to harvest his fields.

'Investigating why Sirkor Wolf was in the East Wastes might provide some answers, but I expect it will really mean more questions. I need to get to my uncle.' Fox tailed off with a sigh, speaking as much to himself as Kesta. He leaned back and opened the shutters a crack.

'It's nearly dark. I'm going to find a bath, but you should get some food brought up here. The meal's on Sirkor, is it not?' He smiled at her shocked expression.

'How did you know?' she pulled the leather pouch from behind her bed and offered it to him, shamefaced. Fox shrugged, a gentle smile reassuring her.

'I guessed.' He slid off his bed and walked over. Instead of taking the bag from her hand, he reached in and pulled out two gold coins. They were circular, unlike the square, holed coins used by the Fox nation traders.

'Look after the rest of it, please.' She nodded dumbly. He had just allowed her to keep more money than she had ever seen. She had been expecting punishment.

When Fox came back from the bathhouse, Kesta was asleep in the corner made by her bed and the wall, curled beneath her blanket. Fox was feeling closer to his true self than he had in weeks. Since setting out from Castle Rice Fox, down the slopes and onto the Central Plains, everything had been clouded by a pall of kicked up dust.

The week long march had been under an atmosphere of fear. Only the youngest, least experienced soldiers (and there were too many of them, Fox remembered) had feelings of excitement along the march to war. The day before the battle though, all patriotic fervour had died, along with the breeze under that blazing sun. Dust had settled as scouts reported the nature of the approaching enemy force. Now everyone knew that the Advisory Council had sentenced them to death in the East Wastes.

Fox remembered the despair. Knowing he about to die, knowing all his men would die too, wondering what offence they had committed to be consigned to such a fate. His mere existence and the circumstances of his birth had condemned them.

They had died. He had lived.

Fox sat down cross-legged on the wood floor and ate, thinking. His mind ran over a list of options open to Rice Ox, now that the East Wastes assault had failed. Fox finally felt able to experience some tainted satisfaction for the political effects of the battle, despite its tragedy. He was the only one left of the Rice Fox South Guard, but that still meant that the Crown Prince had survived, which was a blow to both Ox and the Fox Advisory Council who had wanted him dead.

There was no victory for either kingdom, despite his survival.

Fox remembered his three bodyguards clasping hands with him in turn. 'To the death.' He whispered the last words of Branaghin, captain of his royal guard, staring blankly into the memory. Branaghin had saluted as he spoke, strength and commitment burning in the face of a fear that had threatened to unman Fox.

Branaghin turned towards the rushing enemy, lifting his spear. He was struck down by the first flight of arrows, throwing himself in front of his prince. His shield had been dashed to splinters by the heavy, iron arrowheads.

Fox lifted his head, wondering how best to deal with the tears waiting behind his prickling eyes.

The room was lit now by one candle, flickering away on the windowsill. Fox stood and called to Kesta to wake her up. He pushed the empty bowls aside with his foot and waved at her with a false cheeriness.

'They're shutting the bathhouse in half an hour. I'll see you afterwards, if I'm not asleep.'

Kesta stumbled to her feet, her eyes bleary. Fox made a point of beginning to get ready for bed, waking her up properly. She went quickly to the door, hiding her embarrassment by rubbing at her tired eyes. Fox slid between his sheets and blew out the candle on the sill. Kesta paused in the doorway, her hand going to the scar on her cheek.

She hadn't thought about it much, but there would be other girls in the bathhouse. Girls with normal, pretty, unmarred faces. Kesta continued to hesitate in the doorway. She was a smart girl. Looks were vital to young women, let alone those without families; successful marriage was often the only way out of poverty. The alternative route was unthinkable.

'Don't worry about your scar, Kesta. It means nothing to who you are. Go get clean, before they close the doors!'

Fox's calm order caused Kesta to start, surprised and annoyed that he had known her thoughts. She went without replying.

The wind rose in the night. Fox's dreams were dark. They always were. But it was not he that kept crying himself awake. Kesta found herself again and again in the pitch dark, the wind howling over the rice flats on the other side of the thin wall, the voices from her dreams still with her.

The third time she woke the candle was relit. Fox was cupping his hands around it; the wind from the cracks in the shutters was making the flame gutter. His grey eyes were on her, full of thought and concern.

'How do the dreams go?' he asked seriously, shadows cast by the candle flame flickering on his face. She stared at him.

'Really,' he said sincerely, 'tell me what happens. If you can. It helps if you talk. I have... nightmares... myself.' *Madness and torture in the dark.* He shuddered. 'I know this pain too.' he smiled sadly.

'It was my Ma,' she started, still shaken, 'but...from before. She was trying to warn me about something, but a dark...hand clamped around her mouth to stop her from speaking. Then it dragged her back into this terrible hole and there were...screams, but not hers. Hundreds of voices. I've had it three times, the same dream. It sounds silly the way I say it...' She stopped to wipe the tears from her face, her expression of determination returning.

'What do you dream, sir?' She attempted to steady her voice. Fox looked blankly at the creaking shutters as if hadn't heard her.

'That, Kesta, I tell no one.'

'But you said...' Fox lifted a hand to stop Kesta from continuing.

'If I ever have a nightmare, one that I understand enough to talk about, I might tell someone about it. My curse is that my dreams are indescribable. I cannot, *I will not* talk about them. I do not have the words.' Fox fell silent and returned his troubled gaze to the creaking shutters.

For a moment it looked as if *he* might cry. It reminded Kesta that although she called him 'sir' he was only a little older than her. A child.

We're children, she thought suddenly. *We're children, and my family are dead and his made him go to war.*

Suddenly, a thought struck her. Her family weren't all of them dead, her oldest sister still lived. A chill feeling rose in her. Why had she just felt that she was alone?

'Lord Fox!' she called out, alarmed. He turned towards her. She took a deep breath to hold back more unwanted tears.

'I think my sister is dead.' the close memory of her mother's warning swum in her head. Fox was suddenly alert.

'That's what you dreamt, isn't it?' she asked desperately. Fox nodded slowly, although not in response to her question. A look somewhere between fear and anger crossed his face. For a tense moment there was silence.

'Open!' Fox was on his feet. The shutters slammed open, untouched by human hands. Outside, first light spread from the forest, ghostly pale. Mist wormed across the rice fields and Fox, staring at the forest road, turned and begun to pull on his tattered breeches.

Kesta had her head turned away for decency's sake but he shouted for her to wake the village watchman, fear-stung urgency in his voice. She ran and flung open the door, pausing only to grab the flag Fox had been wearing. She wrapped it around her shoulders to add another layer against the morning chill.

She ran along the landing. On her left was the rail, and one floor down the bar and long tables. She nearly fell down the stairs, pushing past two early rising rice-pickers. She burst through the double doors into the cold, turning and trying to think where the watchman might be.

The innkeeper came running out of the tavern behind her. He was shouting something about the cost of their stay, but a look at Kesta's face silenced him.

'Something wrong?' he asked.

'Yes. On the road! I don't know what... Get the watchman. Hurry!' Kesta answered breathlessly.

The man reacted immediately, running towards a little wooden watchtower at the gateway of the settlement, shouting 'Reddin! Wake up, man! Reddin!' at the top of his voice. Kesta followed, oblivious to the small sharp stones pricking her feet and the crisp morning air on her skin.

Reddin jumped to his feet on the platform as the landlord reached the ladder, still calling his name. He rubbed the sleep out of his eyes before yelling out in alarm. The publican was climbing the ladder and making the tower rock from side to side. Kesta came up the ladder behind him, but while he was still bent over, gasping for breath, she stood and looked at the road. Reddin followed her gaze.

'What's the emergency?' he grumbled. Kesta ignored him, trying to see through the thick mist down onto the road. Someone put a hand on her shoulder. It was Fox. They hadn't even heard him climbing the ladder.

Fox stretched out his other hand and murmured, 'Move.' Kesta thought he meant her, but there was nowhere to move to. The little bamboo pole tower was full, straining under all their weight. Kesta looked questioningly at Fox, but he nodded grimly towards the road.

The mist was clearing, but only over the roadway. Something was treading its way towards the opening in the stockade wall. Reddin suddenly looked as if he was about to be sick.

'Should I... close the gate then?' He looked as if he was having trouble standing, let alone able to climb down the unstable ladder.

'It won't do any good.' Fox said firmly. 'I'll wait for it in the square.' Kesta looked behind her at the village. It was arranged more in a circle than in a square, the inn central, surrounded by houses and workshops. She realised she was looking for somewhere to hide. But from what?

In the village, people were coming out of their houses; smoke was rising from the blacksmith's chimney. People were beginning to gather in a huddled group by the inn. It was obvious something was wrong.

'My wife!' the landlord clutched at one of the support poles, trembling. He didn't look as if his nerves could take the ladder either. A sense of palpable fear had risen to overcome all rationality.

Fox had no such problem. That look was on his face again, as if he was afraid of his anger, or angry at his fear. He stepped off the tower through the opening for the ladder, landing like a cat, both hands supporting him.

Kesta took one look back and followed Fox, climbing down the ladder. She didn't know what the thing on the road was, but Fox seemed ready to do something; she felt safer with him.

Fox ran past the staring villagers. A frightened murmur passed through them like a wave. Wisps of black mist were wrapping around the edges of the stockade wall. Kesta ran towards the confused huddle. To her shock her breath was visible, steam in the freezing air. She ran faster, afraid to look behind her.

Fox met her half way, running back again from the tavern wall, where he had left his staff on the way to the tower. He stopped suddenly, as if he had run into a wall, letting out a cry. Behind them one of the elder villagers crumpled in a dead faint. A small child clung to his terrified mother, crying. No one ran.

The beast stepped through the opening in the stockade wall. Rust appeared on the old hinges off the battered gate like a spreading disease. To the right of the gate, Reddin was desperately climbing down the ladder, but his hands were sticking painfully to the frost-ridden wood. The bamboo structure cracked and split. A moan came from the top of the tower, like the sound of an animal in pain. The innkeeper stumbled his way onto the rocking ladder, calling out the name of his wife, his voice masked by fear. Suddenly, inevitably, the tower buckled and lurched sideways, before falling back in on itself.

Reddin broke the innkeeper's fall. The landlord struggled to his feet as fast as he could. Something was wrong with his leg. Reddin took one look at him and terrible, trembling bravery rose in his face. He turned to the beast.

Its head was like the skull of a ram. Black, ridged horns curled up, around and down, framing the creature's face, the tips curling short of the beast's jaw. Teeth filled its mouth, a mish-mash of incisors, a horrible grey-yellow. It had no tongue, its strong broad neck ran into the broader, monstrous shoulders, and intent lurked murderously in the black pits of its eyes.

The creature's ribcage strained against the tight skin of its wide chest. The beast's waist was narrow, looking all wrong in comparison with its massive frame. The legs matched the monster's massive form, but the knees were jointed backwards like a camel's.

Long, three-toed feet blackened the ground as it approached, its long, muscled arms and rigid fingered hands swinging loose, ready. Across its entire gargantuan form there ran thick knotted veins, and all around it the thing dragged tangible shadow, like a second body.

Reddin's scream choked in his throat. He stood and pushed the innkeeper towards the crowd of petrified villagers, and like a madman, flung himself towards the beast. Lazily, eyes sparking with cruel malice, the creature swung its left arm back. Tendrils of shadow drifted speedily through the air like corrupt silk trailing from the beast's arm. The darkness swam over Reddin's flailing figure. He screamed very briefly. Blue fire rolled across him, and passed, leaving blackened, cracked earth and little else.

The landlord fell into his wife's arms behind Kesta and Fox. One of the older men was sprawled on the ground. A woman was crying over him.

Kesta looked at Fox, searching for something to trust in. Her fear was stealing energy from her resolve. He stood defiantly, facing the beast.

The shadow around it moved over the broad back, a concentration of darkness, seizing the heavy, bestial jaw. The creature's maw jerked open, between the teeth a black tongue, worm shadow, appeared like a snake coiling to strike. A great, cracked, dead voice sounded over the noise of sobbing.

'*I see you, Dreamer.*' The shadow forced the jaw to rise and fall around the words. The eyes rolled around to focus intently on Fox.

'**You remember me Dreamer? I struggled with your mind in the Carcer Stone – my prison. You fled me, Dreamer. I came so close to taking you. I chased you right to the border. Yet you escaped me. No mind is that strong, Dreamer. What are you?**'

Fox raised his staff.

'I am Crown Prince Fox, of the Fox Family, commander of the central army of my uncle, Prince Rice Fox, protector of the Sacred Lands put under me. I am a steward of the Land. Go back to your Carcer Stone, Shadow! Crawl back to the Underworld!'

His voice grew stronger as he spoke, lifting his head, staring proudly back at the beast. Despite the difference in their height, they were eye-to-eye.

Kesta looked on in amazement. Fox seemed transformed. He still had the same shape, his skin was the same fair colour and his hair still brown, but a cool, calm authority radiated from him as he gripped the staff firmly and stepped forwards. For a moment the shadow shrank back, the beast blinking under the intensity of Fox's blue-grey gaze.

Fox stood in the middle of the village, an island in the darkness, a lone sentinel between the shadow and the huddle of innocents.

'Come then!' He called out the challenge, and then, not waiting for an answer, sprinted towards the Carcer Beast. The shadow unfurled from the creature's head and flowed hurriedly along the beast's arms and legs. The creature flung out spools of it, like hands desperately trying to ward of a blow.

The blow came.

Fox kicked at the ground, and left it behind, sailing through the air towards the beast's torso. He went through the shadow like a summer dawn, the darkness peeling away before him. When he struck the creature its dark, fluid second form tore apart. Harsh red flame coursed along the length of the staff, and the narrow end drove into the chest of the monster.

The ribcage collapsed and the Beast's head fell in through the shoulders. Thick, black dust choked the air as the fire left the creature's eyes. The shadow melted away like pools of black ice, and Fox stood shaking, ankle deep in a soft mound of decomposition.

The sun cut through the mist like a knife and the villagers blinked under the sudden glare.

A full day's walk away, under the shade of the East Forest, a great, flat stone shattered in two. Thousands of years' worth of age and power leaked away, and the Carcer Stone crumbled to nothing. In the distance a sound like thunder rolled, a shudder in the land.

The village was dazed and bereaved. One old man's heart had given in during the ordeal.

Even so, Fox and Kesta were being treated like heroes. The tavern was packed full of fearful and gratified villagers. Fox sat next to Kesta, deep in thought despite the activity. He was tired but he was worried as well and he didn't want to go back to bed, although the village would have let him. They seemed to want him to address them, to say something.

Kesta sat in a mixture of shock and resolution. Her sense of justice had been satisfied; her sisters were avenged. She had seen the most potent evil she could imagine destroyed in front of her, by the person that she could now follow anywhere. It had struck home that she was now in the employ of the Crown Prince. And more than that.

Even so, she couldn't help noticing Fox's lack of enthusiasm. He was drawn in on himself, and he was beginning to look more troubled now than he had before.

The villagers dispersed throughout the morning, returning to the paddy fields. Fox, looking very tired, found out where the old man had lived, and stopped to offer his sympathy. Kesta made sure all of her meagre possessions were packed away. All Fox wanted to do was leave. Something more than simple urgency was driving him now. Kesta had noticed his constant glances towards the distant menace of the East Forest.

Fox came back to the inn bedroom at midday. He was wearing new clothes, slate blue silk wrapped three times around his torso, a high ranking soldier's garment. He was wearing grey military leathers as well, with steel studs and scales forming a breastplate. This shirt went to his knees and divided when it reached his waist, so that the flaps would protect his upper legs. He wore no helmet, but he had bought a leather belt for his shoulder, somewhere to wear his staff. He gave Kesta a suit of leather riding clothes, and a recurve bow.

'I bought a horse for us,' he said, glancing to the open window. 'From here we should be able to get to my uncle's castle in under four days, on horseback.'

Kesta looked over the rest of the provisions he had bought. 'Can the horse carry us both?' she asked. Fox nodded and passed her the quiver to go with her bow.

'He looks like a warhorse. I'm surprised he hasn't been requisitioned by the army. He's about sixteen hands, well muscled. Healthy coat, thick mane.' He smiled reassuringly. 'You can ride, can't you?' She nodded and ran her hand over the thick leather shirt he had given her.

'I can shoot as well. I learnt at the inn when the soldiers were using it as barracks, a few years ago.' Memories passed through her mind, of the man that had loved her mother, who had shown her how to draw back the bowstring, who had taught her not to listen to the grumblings that she was only a girl. She swallowed. War had taken him from her, from her mother. Forever.

A strange look came over Fox's face suddenly, his gaze jerked again to the open window and the East Forest. He turned and looked at Kesta, a frown creasing his forehead.

'Let's go.'

The horse was big, bigger than any Kesta had ever ridden. Fox went up the side of the animal with practised ease, settling comfortably into the saddle.

Kesta scrambled up as well, making the horse lift his head back and jitter to the right. Fox caught the reins and controlled him, and Kesta sat uncomfortably in the saddle behind him.

A few people who weren't working on the fields came out of their homes and shops to see them off. Fox sensed relief as well as regret from the people at his departure, someone like him was beyond them. Things would be simpler without him.

The horse seemed as eager to go as Fox, and when Fox slapped its shoulder and called out, 'Hai!' the horse leapt forward.

There were a few panicked moments for Kesta as the horse went from trot to canter, but as it settled into the rhythm of the gallop, she began to relax, loosening her hold around Fox's waist.

'Sorry, sir!' she called out as they sped between the uprights of the north gate. Fox turned in the saddle and grinned at her. 'Don't worry!' he yelled back. The tension from before was gone from his face. He laughed out loud and let go of the reins as they raced along the dirt road. Kesta lost her confidence and hurriedly tightened her grip on him.

The rice fields dried up the further they went, the irrigation channels un-maintained. A few lonely oak trees dotted the landscape, choked with ivy.

The sun was starting its descent when the horse slowed to a walk. Fox climbed out of the saddle and pulled down the bedrolls. He laid them out waterproof side down, and helped a weary Kesta down from the horse. Fox dropped down on to his knees and started to assemble food on a cloth.

'There's some dry grass, Kesta, over there. Pull some up for me, quickly, the horse is trying to eat it!' Kesta forced herself to move faster. There was an annoying ache in her back and shoulders, not to mention the more expected ache from sitting so long in the saddle. She was then asked to pull the faggots of dead wood out of the saddle roll so Fox could make a fire, and then to take off the horse's saddle and tack. Finally, exhausted, she sat down and gratefully accepted some water in a tin cup. Fox smiled as she drank.

'We've done well today. The horse is faster than I thought. We've gained nearly a day, I think.' He stood and looked out along the road. 'I think that we'll arrive the day after tomorrow.' He sat and shook out the blanket, ridding it of crumbs. He was just setting up his bed when Kesta stood.

'I'll get more wood for the night, Lord Fox.' Fox grinned at her approvingly.

'Good! I'll see you in the morning Kesta.'

The next day passed slowly, but peacefully. They walked for most of the day, giving the horse free rein. He trotted around them in a shaky circle, swinging back his head. He was, Fox said, the most obedient horse he'd ever travelled with. They spent most of the morning trying to decide on a name for him, while the flat land passed by lethargically. Kesta was in favour of naming the horse Silkriver, but Fox wrinkled his nose in disgust.

'He's a warhorse Kesta. Not a princess' mare. He needs something strong, energetic. River is good though.' Fox pulled a hunk of bread from the open saddlebag, as the horse brushed by him, nudging at him with his nose. Fox laughed.

'See? He nearly knocked me down!' he passed some of the bread to Kesta and continued, 'Riversteel. That's his name!'

They stopped momentarily for some more food. Kesta was pleased with the change in Fox, he had been so upbeat over the morning. It was preferable to the driven, fearful Fox that he had been before and after the Carcer Beast's attack.

She was beginning to find a good balance between providing entertaining company for Fox and being a dutiful servant. She could make him laugh, which surprised her because she had never thought of herself as funny.

At the same time, she sometimes felt shocked at the easiness that a witty reply came to her, so soon after the murder of her family. There was a steady gathering of tension as she ignored her grief, deadening her feelings. She pushed all inconvenient thoughts to the back of her mind.

They walked into the early hours of the evening, keeping Riversteel's saddle and tack on, for when their legs felt tired. Kesta was glad when they came to a complete stop. She was hungry, and wanted to test out the bow, to see if she could still shoot well. After preparing Riversteel and their camp for the night, Kesta began to practise shooting at one of the oaks, picking a patch to aim at that wasn't covered in ivy. Fox watched her avidly, a comfortable smile on his face.

'Control your breathing!' he called out after her first attempts glanced past her target. Kesta tried it, remembering that same advice from another voice years past, and scored a perfect hit. The lessons in those half-forgotten days before the real war had begun seemed to have paid off.

They didn't normally need to tether Riversteel. He never went far, but this night Kesta took the time to uncurl the long rope Fox had packed, and loosely tethered the horse, who was behaving a bit skittishly. Fox was already settled in. He asked her to pack again for him; replacing the water and all their food behind Riversteel's saddle. It was all they had for the next two days.

Packing meant putting Riversteel's saddle back on, and neither Kesta nor Riversteel were particularly happy about it. To top it all, Fox was fast asleep by the time she returned from the oak tree. She tried to make as much noise as possible as she got ready to sleep, but Fox remained peacefully slumbering. The evening was soured. Knowing that she should not resent her duties, Kesta fell asleep as well.

Fox, however, was feigning sleep. He was relishing the cool breeze and listening to Riversteel making horse noises as he settled down.

He was looking forward to another dream-free sleep. Last night had been amazing, not one dream of pain or death or sorrow. Just the ones he normally forgot, that had made him feel peaceful; home, his father, the mountains. As Fox slipped away into the night's sleep, he was happy that Kesta's presence had been added to his dreams.

Kesta slept for all of an hour. She woke, her head clear, to see something that made her heart jump for fear in her chest. Fox was writhing under his blanket as if in great pain, crying out, for his father, for an old friend, for her. The wind, biting, no longer a benign breeze, chilled the bare skin of her arms. An oppressive presence pushed down on her. The dark dreams were back.

3
Malice Pursues

Kesta screamed, overcome suddenly by a dreadful fear. Fox's eyes jerked open and he struggled free of the blanket like a wild thing. He stood but went down again almost immediately. His hand stretched out, shaking.

'He's here! Please, please help me Kesta, I can't fight him!' He struggled to stand, but seemed paralysed with fear. Kesta turned slowly, dreading what she might see.

She could make out nothing in the dark. The stars spread a dim light around them, but her eyes strained to see further into the gloom. Suddenly, a black light swam towards them, distorted through a shadowy mist. Something was coming.

Kesta gripped Fox around his shoulders. He was crying like a baby, repeating the same phrase over and over, that he couldn't do it; he wasn't strong enough. Kesta was moving too slowly, dragging Fox bodily towards the oak tree, where Riversteel was struggling to get free of his tether. His great liquid eyes were rolling in his head, he stood, legs splayed, torn between duty and terror. Kesta was sobbing with the effort by the time she reached him.

'You have to climb up!' Kesta shouted at Fox, pushing him against Riversteel's flank and grabbing hold of the reins. Fox scrabbled his way desperately into the saddle, screaming for her to get on. Kesta whipped her head around, acting on instinct, and her eyes widened in shock.

A man-like figure was tearing across the open space, his darkened face ridden with hate. Kesta stood, speechless and petrified for what seemed like an eternity. The rope suddenly snapped, and Kesta was mobilised into action. She mounted Riversteel faster than she had ever mounted a horse, fear driving her. Riversteel sprang away into a breakneck gallop.

Kesta stared behind her, over Fox's shoulder. The figure was dropping behind, but as they pulled into a good lead, it began to move faster, cutting off the sweeping curves in the road, leaving a dead trail in the grass behind him.

He – it could only be a he – was bearing down on them, sprinting faster than a horse, faster than Riversteel. Kesta stifled a horrified cry in her throat. Fox was gripping her so tightly it hurt. His eyes were tightly closed and it looked as though he was about to pass out.

Riversteel was running for his life. His ears were stretched out flat to his skull; his eyes were wide and staring as he pushed himself to the limit. The figure behind kept the pace, growing slowly closer. The road curved around towards the hills, leaving a great space of grass for the pursuer to cut through, space in which to intercept them.

The twisted shape behind put on a burst of speed. It became more vague and distorted the closer it came, and Kesta, her vision impaired, could only see the eyes. They flickered up to look at her as it came within arm's length, and the face split into a cruel grimace. Images flashed before Kesta's vision. A dying child, a red sky, a black flood covering burning fields, an open wound, Fox, dead. Spread across a Carcer Stone.

She slipped in the saddle, crying out as crippling pain seared through her head. The corrupted being snatched out at Fox suddenly, its groping fingers passing close behind. Fox moaned out, as if the creature had cut his back. Riversteel went into a kind of panicked sprint, his horse's scream tore the air. The figure fell behind. The last Kesta saw of it was its pitch silhouette, fists clenched, eyes smouldering, standing in the road.

Riversteel didn't stop. Foam was flying across his flanks and his muscles were burning, but the concentration of evil behind him drove him on like an infernal whip.

Kesta slumped forwards along the flowing line of Riversteel's neck, exhausted. Fox was passed out against her back and Kesta desperately grabbed his hands, keeping his arms around her waist. She fumbled with the strap on the saddlebag; food tumbled away beneath her as she tied the leather strap around Fox's wrists, looping it across her shoulders. She put all of her energy into securing the strap against Riversteel's mighty shoulders, and her bound hands slipped as she finished the binding. The panicked horse passed into the night.

Kesta woke slowly. Aching muscles. A thudding headache. She opened her eyes, blinking in the bright light. She was lying amongst the stubble of a barley field, a short distance from the road. The sun was directly above. Her bare arms and face felt burnt.

Fox was lying a short distance away. The leather strap of the saddlebag was strewn between them, indicating that they had slipped from the saddle rather than fallen. Kesta was not sure she could tell the difference though, she felt as if she had been physically beaten.

She crawled towards Fox, wincing as the broken stalks of barley brushed at her. Fox was stirring, letting out a moan of pain. She put a hand on his arm, making him start, beginning to roll away instinctively. The action made him gasp out and he stopped, blinking up into the bright sky.

'Lord Fox, are you all right?'

'Oh, Land and Sky that hurts...' He pushed against the ground with his arms, face screwed up with the effort as he sat up.

Tears welled in his eyes. At first it was just pain and then he found he couldn't stop; they kept coming, and he found himself trying to crush the sobs as they rose.

Kesta didn't need to ask what was wrong. She squeezed his arm in sympathy, lying back in the barley.

'You couldn't have done anything, sir,' she whispered, shading her eyes with one hand.

'Don't call me that! I don't deserve...' Fox bit down on the words, keeping them quiet to hold his anger inside himself. He turned away despite the pain it cost him to move.

'We're alive,' Kesta said quietly. 'We got away.'

'*You* got us away. I...' Fox clenched his fists and hit the stubbly ground uselessly. 'I destroy one day and can't even fight the next! Useless!'

Kesta sat up slowly, considering. Her eyes scanned the nearby road for sign of their pursuer. The still air and high blue sky gave no sign of evil following.

'My lord, why would you have to fight...'

'Be quiet! Just...just leave me alone!' Fox struggled to his feet. He stared back along the road, calming slowly as it became apparent nobody was coming. A whickering noise made him turn around to see Riversteel, trailing harness as he trod through the barley. Fox let out a sigh of relief.

'Something in me... like with the carcer stone beast...where I knew to fight it. I had to fight it and I did, and I killed it, and I still don't really know how, Kesta. There must be something wrong with me, it's like something else knows what it's doing when I don't: I change. I change.'

Fox slumped back down, shaking his head.

'It's all right.' Kesta got to her feet unsteadily, feeling as if she might throw up.

'We need to go,' Fox said, accepting Kesta's help up. 'We don't know if he's still behind us.'

'Who is he?' Kesta asked. Fox dropped the hand she had given him to help him to his feet. He gave her a look similar to the one she had received when she had asked him about his dreams.

'See if Riversteel is fit for riding.' He evaded her gaze.

Kesta went to the horse, greeting him gratefully; he had saved their lives. Riversteel was tired, but not in as desperate a shape as she had expected. His nose was damp and a waterweed had caught in his bit shank, showing that he must have strayed to a water source. A break in the line of barley a short distance away showed where the water must be, marked by a cloud of midges.

There was still water hanging behind Riversteel's saddle. Kesta brought it to Fox first, who accepted it wordlessly before she finished it, gulping hungrily at the warm liquid. There was no food but that mattered less. Neither of them felt as if they would be able to eat.

As they led Riversteel to the road, a running figure made them stop in their tracks. It came along the road in the opposite direction from which they had come. In the bright sun, it seemed to be a stark opposite to their pursuer from the night before. Pure white cloth flowed as the athletic man approached, coming to a halt and lifting his hand in greeting.

'Well met, Travellers! Are you well?'

'One of the Order,' Fox murmured to himself, eyes widening, 'Greetings, holy brother! I did not know there were Warriors near!'

The fair haired man peered at Fox for a moment, and then bowed formally.

'I recognise you from your woodcut, Your Highness. I am honoured, Lord Fox. We have a new tower to the southwest of the hill road leading up to Castle Rice Fox.'

'No, I am honoured, to meet a Son of Rashin.' Fox glanced back down the road. 'We are alive. I would not say we are well.'

'We serve the Land, my Lord. You are a steward, and thus I gladly serve you and your family. You came from the conflict in the south?'

Fox nodded. The man lifted a hand to wipe sweat from his brow, the gleam of mirror-bright armour showing where his white robe fell aside.

'I will make honest with you, my lord. I am sent to investigate a rumour that a nobleman, perhaps even yourself, destroyed a work of shadow in a village near the East Forest.'

'The beast from the carcer stone,' Fox said quietly, glancing again in the direction of the now long distant village.

'What did you say?' The holy warrior asked urgently, stepping forward.

'A sorcerer performed some kind of ritual on the carcer stone by the East Forest,' Fox started to explain with a nervous glance at Kesta, 'and shortly afterwards a monster came after us from the same direction. It claimed it was from the...'

'What kind of ritual? Forgive me, Your Highness, but it is important.' There was a fear on the holy warrior's face.

Kesta lifted her head, swallowed, 'My mother was killed on that stone.'

'Currency of blood...' the warrior breathed, horrified. He put a hand beneath his robe as if checking a weapon. 'You say a monster came?'

'Yes. Very large, horned, wrapped in a cloak like living shade. Nothing to cast the shadow, but that's what it was like.'

'The monster or the shadow, which was in control?' the holy warrior asked in a hushed whisper. Fox looked at Kesta and they both spoke together:

'The shadow.'

'Land save us. One of the...' The holy warrior covered his mouth with one hand. 'That's why you were in such a state? You've been trying to outrun it?'

'No.' Fox looked awkward. 'I destroyed it in the village, as you heard.'

A look of disbelief crossed the man's face, and then he bowed deeply. 'My lord. I cannot wait to tell the Order. Rashin himself will need to hear of this.'

'There's more. We are running from something worse.' Fox looked away down the road. 'Something man shaped.'

'Get on your horse!' The holy warrior pushed Fox towards Riversteel. 'Go! If it is still following you then it will not take long to catch up! I will go back to the tower and get Rashin, he is the only one there strong enough to even contemplate... What are you waiting for, Your Highness! GO!'

'It's as I feared?' Fox swallowed. 'Can Rashin turn him aside?'

'I don't know, we did not know that the Perversion was even risen! This is... you cannot wait any longer, go! I only pray you are wrong...'

The holy warrior left without further ceremony, running back the way he had come.

Fox climbed up behind Kesta. He patted Riversteel's flank and leaned forwards to speak to Kesta. 'Let's go.'

Riversteel started forward reluctantly. Fox didn't look back. He felt more confident now, the sun was high and hot and the feeling of menace was distant. His feeling of uselessness was growing, however; the happier he became at the apparent distance they had from their hunter, the more he felt a coward.

Kesta sat in front guiding the horse, and Fox didn't feel like challenging his servant over it. He sat behind her knowing that if their follower caught up with them, he would be unable to control Riversteel.

They did not travel at any great speed, allowing Riversteel to set the pace. Nonetheless, before long they passed the point where the holy warrior had left the road, his tracks leading off down a dust track through the sparse barley.

The land began to slope. Riversteel rode comfortably through increasingly overgrown barley fields, which were thinning out as they approached the foothills. The sun was hot on Fox's left shoulder and cheek. Gradually, he began to relax, feeling the breeze wash over his skin.

Kesta spoke for the first time in nearly an hour.

'What is he?' She turned in the saddle, adamant. Fox didn't need to ask who she meant. He looked back across the golden sea, to the swell of green rice in the distance. The road was still empty.

'I think...I think we are being chased by the Perversion of Light. You must have heard that name.'

'The Great Shadow,' Kesta murmured. Old stories, old beliefs. The progenitor of magic, of sorcery.

'Yes. He's why sorcerers are outlawed – their power comes from him, according to legend.'

Kesta swallowed. It was unbelievable, except that she had seen him, and he fitted the description.

'You have to remember that sorcerers themselves were children's tales only a little while ago. Then the massacre of the natives nearly seventeen years ago changed all that.' Fox shuddered. 'So many killed in such a short time.'

'The holy warrior the other mentioned...' Kesta started, forgetting the name.

'Rashin, I think he said. He has the same name as the one that started the Order in old times, so hopefully he will live up to it.'

'What can he do?' If Fox, who had destroyed the monster, could do nothing...

'There's something strange about the Holy Order. The Sons of Rashin have some deep natural protection, hidden rules that they have always said even the Great Shadow must conform to. If they stand in his path, he cannot hurt them, and he must face them, be turned aside or delayed.'

'At least, that's the legend. But it never says that they can defeat him.'

'The Great Shadow?' Kesta had never believed the tale.

Fox nodded. 'You know. He betrayed the Maker, or so they say. Betrayed the Land.'

Kesta felt the weight of long history and deeper myth pressing down on them. As the road wound upwards into steeper hills, she ran her mind back over the last few days. The carcer beast, its terrifying superior, the Great Shadow, Betrayer of the Land, Perversion of Light. And that was a strange name, was it not, for something so incredibly and fundamentally dark?

Thick grass pushed at the sides of the road, which had narrowed to a track. Riversteel trod contentedly in the soft sward, holding his head high, comfortable with the easy pace. Ahead, the landscape became rockier, boulders rising on either side to frame the trail. The sun was moving down now on the travellers' left, to the west, visible through the sinewy trees that were dotted across the slope, giving an interrupted shade. Everything was soaked in amber light.

'If we reach your uncle's castle, will we be safe?' Kesta asked suddenly. Fox smiled, resting a hand on her shoulder.

'Yes, if the legends are true. All the Land's old castles have been sanctified by the Holy Order, either recently or in the distant past. Buildings blessed by Rashin's Sons will not fail while people still live within the walls.'

'I apologise for earlier,' Fox added abruptly. Kesta turned in the saddle to look at him. 'I don't like to be in that position. In my dreams I am completely powerless and that's how he got to me.' Fox shuddered. 'The dreams are enough, but he was *in my head*. I think that's why we outran him – to attack my mind from even a short distance away...maybe it tired him.'

Riversteel bore his riders through a belt of mountain pine as the path led them higher. The trees gave way to stony ground, coarse grasses and scrubby bushes. Kesta reined Riversteel in on a shelf of stone overlooking the flat, fertile valley below. It stretched out like a sea, gold and green, broken here and there by a narrow river, flowing from the west. Kesta thought she could make out the village they had stopped at, but there were many small settlements peppered regularly amongst the paddy fields by the East Forest.

Fox followed the line of the river by the trees with his gaze, to where it thinned out: the East River under the branches of the East Forest. He knew instinctively where the carcer stone, and Kesta's old home, had been.

He felt the wind, stronger up on the heights, and looked up at the steadily rising mountainside. The castle was still ahead. Safety was still just out of reach.

'Come on Kesta. Let's go.'

Kesta took one last, long look at the East Forest and home, and turned the horse. Riversteel resumed his walk up the winding path. Fox put a gentle hand on his servant's shoulder. Kesta smiled through her sorrow. It was as if he was reading her mind again.

Darkness fell as if it had suddenly remembered its role. The sun dropped below the line of the mountain on Fox and Kesta's left, and the narrow, stony way was lit by nothing but the stars and a crescent moon. Some kind of wild dog, or a hill wolf, let out a mournful cry. The wind became mischievous, playing with Kesta's long, black hair.

Riversteel trotted along the narrow pathways of the mountain, cantering only when the road widened. He was heading for a pass between the two rounded peaks. The castle was near. Fox did not feel as afraid as he had done the previous night, *because the Great Shadow's power was limited on rocky ground.* A nagging thought came to prominence in Fox's mind. *How did he know this?*

Nevertheless he trusted the stones; bare rock meant an easy recharge of his power and energy. They were almost there!

Kesta stared ahead, straining her eyes. The road was widening and levelling. They had reached the pass. Ahead the ground flattened out and beyond the peaks that rose on either side it became a plateau. A great stone structure dominated the flat expanse of rock. Fox pointed, grinning.

'That's home! That's my uncle's castle, Kesta! Can you see the farms?'

Riversteel broke into a canter, heading for the lamplight above the gate. Kesta could see the farms as they drew nearer, enclosed by a wall spreading from the castle. The castle itself was a great square bulk of stone, blue grey under the moon, typical Fox colours.

It looked impenetrable to Kesta. The slope on the other side of the fortress seemed very steep.

'The northern approach is a cliff,' Fox explained, 'there's a zigzag road going down it, but otherwise there's no way up. If Ox wants to take this castle he'd better teach his soldiers to fly! And there's no fear of the Shadow now we're here!'

Riversteel came to a triumphant stop, aware of successfully completing his duty.

On the parapet above the gate, a watchman called down a challenge.

'Who comes here?'

Fox jumped down from Riversteel's back and called up, 'Prince Fox, back from the conflict on our southern border!'

He smiled to himself as the watchman panicked, yelling for the gate to be opened, and falling over himself with appropriate reverence. The gate swung open and Riversteel stepped regally through, bearing Kesta, with his master walking beside.

Kesta stared around her. The gateway led into a long courtyard, with parapets on the walls above their heads. The watchman stood there and saluted, his left hand balling into a fist and pressing smartly against his right shoulder, his head slightly bowed. His lord had returned.

Kesta watched, struck by the intense loyalty of the soldier, entranced by the proud joy in his eyes. She knew instinctively that this man would die for his Prince, and willingly. It both scared and impressed her at the same time.

They passed through another gate into a courtyard. The men and women carrying out their duties stopped what they were doing, often dropping what they were carrying before bowing deeply.

Fox took a deep breath of the clean mountain air and turned.

'I'm home!' He smiled warmly at Kesta, and she couldn't help but return it. Still smiling, she began to bow, but changed her mind and saluted smartly. Fox laughed out loud.

'Here, you!' he called out to a boy, who promptly dropped the bundle of clothes he was holding and stepped over. 'Take my horse, please.' Fox slapped Riversteel's side fondly, before turning back to Kesta.

'Raise you're a head a little. That's right. Now, the fist has to land a bit higher up the shoulder, so it sounds off the metal shoulder pad you'd wear if you were a soldier... Keep that head high! Good. Now do it again, but when you do, bring your feet apart, instead of together.' He smiled approvingly as she performed the salute correctly.

'Training a new recruit, Fox?' Fox turned. The speaker smiled affectionately. He was dressed in a dark blue ceremonial robe, marked with the Fox emblem. Behind him stood two people, a boy the same age as Fox, and a richly dressed man with a sharp, pinched looking face. The man who had spoken stepped forwards and enveloped Fox in a hug.

'Welcome back.' He drew away, tears glistening at the corners of his eyes. 'We thought you were dead!' Fox laughed at his uncle's show of emotion.

'I'm not, though it came close. More than once. I have to talk to you about some things, Uncle.' Fox whispered this last sentence so that only they could hear it.

'Later, later!' the man brushed the ambiguous request aside, 'first you must introduce your companion.' Fox nodded.

'Uncle, this is Kesta. She has kept me alive under the circumstances we will discuss later, and a better servant I have not had.' At this the man standing behind drew in a sharp breath of exaggerated outrage.

Fox continued, 'Kesta, this is my uncle, Lord Rice Fox, Regent of the rice fields and Prince in the East.'

Rice Fox shook Kesta's hand vigorously. 'Name anything, and it's yours, my girl! Anything at all!'

The man behind Lord Fox snorted derisively and turned away. Kesta ignored him, but Fox's eyes narrowed, staring at the man's back. Rice Fox waited eagerly for Kesta's answer.

'I want to stay in Fox's service.' She looked up, hope overcoming shyness. Fox smiled at her show of loyalty. 'I know it isn't considered…correct, my lord, but I want to carry on. Your Highness,' she added hurriedly. The king's brother grinned.

'Anything else?'

'Could I… I mean, could I please be trained? To fight? I'd like to be able to help, your highness. With the war. I'm no good otherwise.'

The man smiled warmly. 'Done! I'm afraid you're stuck with my nephew now.' Rice Fox turned back to Fox. 'Come, join me quickly to talk with me about your journey here. I must notify the kitchens…Trustan, Henshin.' He nodded to the two strangers and hurried away.

Fox and the other boy watched one another warily. Then Trustan spoke.

'I am pleased that you are alive, cousin.' His tone did not reflect the words. Fox nodded, eyes narrowed. He looked at the older man, who was trying to appear disinterested.

'I suppose you are also pleased, Henshin?' His voice supposed no such thing. The well dressed man grimaced.

'Of course. You must excuse me.' He walked quickly away.

'That was Henshin, the most influential member of the Fox Territories Advisory Council.' Fox murmured. Kesta sensed that he had left a lot of information unsaid.

'This is my cousin, Prince Trustan. He will show you to my chambers so that you can get things ready for when I have finished talking with my uncle.' Fox gestured to his cousin with a barely concealed expression of distaste. Trustan did not even bother to conceal his.

Fox hurried away as if he could not get away from Trustan fast enough.

'Well done,' her guide said dryly, 'you've successfully risen an entire caste. Most spend all their lives in the same way, and die as they were born. Even I will never rise, and I am of the ruling family…This way!

'Not that my royalty counts for much when my *precious* cousin is around.' He muttered, glancing at Kesta. 'I'm the prince who will never be king, in case you were wondering. At least *you'll* have to call me Your Highness.' He looked her up and down with disdain. 'I can be as pleasant as he is, I assure you.'

Kesta remembered Fox's attitude. She kept a polite silence as they walked down richly decorated corridors to Fox's rooms.

Fox's rooms were at the base of a great circular tower. There was an outer room, shaped like a crescent, with a bed in the tapering corner and a rack of weaponry hanging on the wall. The wall of the inner room bulged into the outer one. The door was thick and ornate, a deep red colour. There was a woven banner above the door, a steel-grey fox standing on a slate blue base, the tail curling around three objects. They were arranged on top of one another, a thin blue knife hanging above a spray of barley, followed by a rice shoot. The family's primary economic powers: steel, grain and rice.

Kesta opened the big double doors and stepped onto the thick carpet. She quickly took off her shoes and tossed them behind her onto the wooden floor of the outer quarters.

Prince Trustan said something unpleasant under his breath and left the room. Kesta put him out of her mind and walked around the room, enjoying the feeling of the soft, thick carpet under her feet.

Fox waited for his uncle to check that there was no possibility of being overheard. The expression on his face was now serious.

'You must hurry, Henshin and his colleagues will object to a secret briefing. They must be disappointed! You survived – thank the Land! – but how?'

Fox swallowed. 'All the soldiers died rather than let me fall, Uncle. I am the only survivor.'

Rice Fox's face fell. 'You were…defeated?'

'No. Both armies were defeated. They fought to our last man and then… I… they were likewise killed. No survivors under either banner. The ones that did flee the battlefield I came upon afterwards. They are dead now as well, but Uncle, one of them was of high blood. He was not of Ox, but Wolf. And worse – he was a sorcerer.'

Kesta stared around, loving the simple but luxurious surroundings.

The bed sat opposite the doorway against the wall, the headboard elaborately carved to fit the curve behind it. It was not as large as Kesta might've supposed a prince's bed would be, but the blue silk and rich embroidery on the covers spoke of long hours of skilled and dedicated work.

There was a desk with a simple chair, the table-top covered with professional and amateur maps. Kesta noticed the top parchments depicted the East Wastes.

A tiled, sunken area of the room appeared to be a bathing area, unlit candles lining the blue and grey walls. Kesta lit the lamps in the main area of the room, using a wick brought through from the outer room, where candles already burned.

As the light lifted, new details worked in gold and silver on drawer handles and fixtures began to glow. Kesta stared around, entranced.

'You'll get used to it.' Fox had arrived. He smiled wearily, closing the door behind him and removing his shoes.

'I've just had to fill uncle in on the journey. He's warned the watchmen to be vigilant. If the Great Shadow tries to enter he'll be met by a locked gate.'

For a moment they stood in awkward silence. Fox walked around the room, running his hand along the top of his drawers, checking personal possessions. He stopped at the desk, shuffled the maps and froze, seeing the East Wastes depicted in his own hand alongside the cartographer's version.

'Are you all right, my lord?' Kesta asked, watching him closely. Fox straightened slightly. He smoothly picked both maps up and folded them.

'Such a shame that there is no fireplace in here. My quarters are heated from beneath the floor. Never regretted that before.'

Kesta put out a hand. 'Would you like me to burn them, sir?'

'Yes, all right then. Don't burn anything else, please.'

'I'll do my best not to,' Kesta replied solemnly, making Fox smile again. The moment she took the maps out of his hand, he relaxed.

'Use a candle and the stone sill in your room.'

'The outer room?'

'Yes,' Fox nodded seriously, 'you're my shield bearer now. You sleep there so that if someone tries to get in here, he'll have to get through you.'

'As long as I wake up,' Kesta replied easily, looking through the doorway into her room.

'Do you sleep soundly then?' Fox asked, and then blushed.

'I might tonight,' Kesta said. The fatigue of the last few days was heavy on her. She walked to the door, trying to come to terms with her new responsibility.

'Kesta?'

'Yes, my lord?'

'Goodnight. And you don't have to call me lord anymore. Except in company. My guards don't have to observe that formality, not once I've got to know them.'

'Oh. Goodnight, Highness.'

'Kesta?'

'Yes sir?'

'My friends call me Fox. I hate 'Highness'. I hate 'sir' as well, come to that.'

They stood for a moment.

'Goodnight, Fox.'

'Goodnight, Kesta.'

Kesta stepped through the door and closed it behind her, overwhelmed by the day's events, but somehow, happy.

4
The Devil You Know

The sun rose. Light flooded the castle in the pass, the old blue stonework warming through, a glow spreading over the farmland held within the walls. Grapes growing on the south wall awaited picking, ripe in this last sunlight, the tail end of summer.

Slowly the castle began to wake. Messengers rode in and out of the great gates, news passed along the parapet from guard to guard. General chatter and gossip spread like fire through the soldiers in the cliff top barracks. The prince was back!

Kesta woke with sun on her face. The autumnal breeze passed over her, the window was un-shuttered and wide open behind her. Yawning, she rose and closed the shutters, looking around her. The room was patterned with intricate shafts of sunlight, streaming through the ornate apertures in the shutters, dust dancing in their bright paths.

Kesta stretched. The big doors leading to Fox's inner room were open. He must already have woken. Kesta looked through the wardrobe against the curved wall, choosing clothes in the Fox Family colours. Slate blue silk and grey leathers, combat clothes. The entire wardrobe was full of uniforms, meaning she could not forget her place. She was a royal guard now.

Feeling refreshed and comfortable, Kesta left the room, closing the doors behind her and using the little iron key that was in the lock to make the room secure. A soldier on watch duty nodded to her as she passed along the corridor the way she had come yesterday. At the last moment she changed her mind and took a left turn, taking the corridor towards the outer wall.

She came out onto the battlements. The two high, round peaks of the mountain were in front of her, framing the pass they had come through. Behind the peaks the sky was a crisp blue. It was definitely the good weather that came before the changing of the seasons. Summer was fading.

That afternoon, Fox introduced Kesta to a man called Haiken. He was a Champion in the Fox army, which meant that he was in charge of four high officers, their four under-officers, and their squads of men, ten men under each. Though Champions effectively commanded one-hundred-and-sixty men, Kesta, as royal guard, would have equal – if nominal – rank, which was a thought that terrified her. Thankfully she would not have to give orders.

Haiken was to teach her the basics of combat. Kesta liked him. He was the only person in a position of power who hadn't seemed appalled at Rice Fox's decision to appoint her as shield-maiden to Fox. He was a burly and rough looking man in middle age, a veteran of several conflicts, with his origins quite as common as Kesta's. His eyes were wrinkled from laughter and his brow furrowed from scowling. Once away from other soldiers, his speech became casual, putting Kesta at ease. He was quite talkative and Kesta soon learnt that Champion Haiken was in Fox's confidence almost as much as Rice Fox.

They were on the north plateau and it was the third day since Kesta and Fox's arrival. The sun was shining weakly, but the breeze from the north was cold. Haiken had brought a leather case with him; he put it on the ground between them. Fox murmured something to Haiken and gave Kesta an encouraging smile. He had to return to the castle.

Kesta watched him go, a lone figure running back towards the castle walls.

'Shield-maiden!' Haiken waved to get her attention. 'Mind on the task please, Kesta.'

'Yes, sir.'

Haiken bent and picked up the leather sheath. Dramatically, and watching Kesta out of the corner of his eye, he swept the leather away.

Gleaming in the sun were two identical weapons that Kesta had never seen before. They were broad bladed, shaped in a manner that was greatly reminiscent of a pair of narrow, curving wings. The edge was on the underside of each wing-sword, the blades of which had been finely etched with feather designs. The end of each sword came to a point, more than one in fact, although the secondary and tertiary points receded in length in comparison to the primary point. Each one was designed to look like a feather.

'Take them up, then.'

'Me?' Kesta stared at him in amazement.

'Well, there's no one else here.' He smiled, watching her appreciatively as she cautiously lifted them, gripping the hilts. A spur from the blade rose above her hand in a guard, again feather-etched. It was part of the upper edge of the weapon which was the stronger edge of the blade. It looked as though Kesta's arms had been extended with the glittering wings of an eagle, the pinion feathers of the wings standing out a bit less than a metre from Kesta's fists, which curled around the hilts with a feeling of surprising familiarity.

Kesta made an experimental sweep with both wings. They sang out keenly as they cut the air, the sunlight running rainbow patterns along their length.

'They're made from Autumn Steel, which is why they're so light,' Haiken explained enthusiastically, 'and the blades are broad – theoretically one should be able to use them to deflect arrows or other projectiles, although that level of training takes many years to attain. There are two stances. That stance with the blades held at full length is the "ranged" stance. Your ability to do great damage like that is limited, because your leading edge is the heavier, less keen edge – basically, you need to switch between the other stance – your "close" stance – and the ranged stance fluidly to make the most of them.'

Kesta swallowed, trying to picture how she should hold the wing-swords differently. Haiken showed her, letting the weight of the blade roll out of his grip before seizing the hilt again, so that the blade now pointed at the floor, the blunter edge of the weapon resting along his forearm, the blade extending beyond his elbow. With his fist held at eye-level the sword aligned diagonally across his body, offering a lot more protection. The hand guard could be effectively used for slashing out with punching movements.

Haiken did just that, his feet moving in a disciplined dance as he let the blades carry him across the dusty plateau. Kesta watched, awed, as he occasionally followed through a close stab by whipping the main blade out, extending his elbow to effect the blow. Now, he let the swords alternately slip from stance to stance, sometimes letting one protect his body in the closed stance while the other leapt and jabbed in the more conventional hold.

Finally he came to a stop, handing the blades back to Kesta with obvious, good natured envy.

'I have a feeling they will be very useful!'

'Sir!' Kesta sounded mortified. 'I can't do that!'

'Don't worry,' Haiken laughed, 'once I've taught you the basic discipline you can practice without further tuition. When I get opportunity to extend your repertoire to more advanced forms I will do so. Then, if it comes to combat, it's up to you to string together the appropriate motions according to the situation. A keen mind is more important than a keen blade.'

Kesta smiled nervously. As she set her stance, eyes on the swords, Haiken glanced away.

What was His Highness thinking? Dual weapons were not a soldier's choice. On the field of battle a shield was the fighting man's best friend, and dual blades removed that option. Worse, it implied that Kesta would be battle-bound in the future, a situation which Haiken doubted she could come through alive.

Fox walked around the top of the castle wall. If he looked out to his left, he would have been able to see the distant figures of Kesta and Haiken, training on the dusty plateau. Fox, however, was distracted. The regions owned by Rice Fox were on the brink of open and bloody war. To the northwest the Ox Family sat, every day gathering strength. Soldiers were marching on the rich plains beyond the horizon. Fox hesitated in the archway leading to the interior of the castle, before heading quickly for the throne room.

Rice Fox was deep in conversation with his chief advisor when Fox burst in. The prince glanced around the low table that dominated the room. Fifteen advisors looked back at him.

'Oh. I appear to be late.' It was not quite an apology, but Fox sat down hurriedly next to his uncle. Henshin looked down his nose at the young Prince.

'Oh, don't worry, Your Highness, we're quite used to it.'

'That will do, Henshin.' Rice Fox put up his hand to stop the arrogant man from continuing. 'This situation is deadly serious, and I won't have you two bickering!' He looked at both of them. Fox nodded curtly, Henshin indulged in a graceful bow.

'Good,' Rice Fox said, settling back on his cushion, 'let's get down to business.'

First came the facts, informed advisors and border spies delivering information in turn. Fox listened intently. This was the part that would be relevant to him. The Ox Family had enough raw resources to comfortably feed ten armies, without changing the way food was distributed through their territory. The actual number of soldiers available to Ox remained unknown, but preparations for battle were beginning, if supply movements were anything to go on.

Ox appeared to no longer be receiving trade from other regions. The Heron Family, who controlled all the main rivers, had taken the illegal crossing Ox had made as a breach of the ancient treaty against military river crossings. They were not only blocking trade with Ox, but also feeding information to the Fox Family. Ox's East Wastes assault had dealt serious ramifications.

Fox listened with interest. Heron's involvement was good, he was held to be a honourable and just man. If he was restricting information and trade to the Ox family then they were now completely shut off from the rest of the Sacred Lands. This could be useful.

On the other hand, the other Family of the Central Plains, to the northeast - a land consisting mainly of wooded mountains - had so far made no commitment to either side.

The Tiger Family had in years gone by been a steadfast ally of the Fox Family. The two families had drawn apart before Fox's birth. He was annoyed at the lack of optimism in getting help from them. He assumed that the advisors were only thinking about the size and might of the country. The Pine Hills region was weak in numbers and economically weak.

It was also possible that the advisory council were too proud to consider such an alliance. Tiger's royalty was not supposedly as pure blooded as Steel Fox's.

Fox, who was despised for the same reason, immediately felt a liking for the unknown northern king.

Then the bureaucracy began. The advisors all found different reasons for why, when, how and *if* they should attack. Only Fox and Henshin remained silent. Fox drifted off into his thoughts and Henshin just sat there, a small, secretive smile on his thin lips. Finally, Rice Fox turned towards him.

'Care to share your thoughts, Henshin?'

Henshin stood dramatically. He smiled and swept into an extravagant bow. 'I thought you'd never ask, my Lord. Allow me to call in the messenger who has been waiting so politely outside.'

He stood aside as the big double door opened. The man that came through was tall and dressed in yellow silk from head to foot. Ox colours. Henshin smiled pleasantly.

'I arranged for the beginning of diplomatic talks. This is a messenger from King Rice Ox's court. Well, isn't somebody going to greet our guest?' Henshin's eyes gleamed in the direction of the crown prince, whose duty it was.

Fox stood stiffly. 'Welcome,' he said dully, without sincerity. The Ox messenger nodded, and unrolled a scroll. He coughed, clearing his throat, and began.

'Greetings from King Danashalk, Rice Ox of the Lakes, to Prince Rice Fox, and Crown Prince...Trustan.'

The messenger paused, glancing at Fox to indicate, perhaps, that Ox was not aware that Fox had survived, remaining Crown Prince. Fox smiled widely up at him, enjoying the messenger's hesitation. *Interesting that Ox should have been aware that he had fought in the East Wastes...*

'Congratulations on your defeat of my troops in the East Wastes, your quick and surprising action has forced me to change my plans. I assure you, however, that any future engagements will not produce such a satisfactory outcome for your troops. I have many more men at my disposal. If you attempt to attack me I will crush you.

'However, I have a proposition for you. To the north of your lands are the Tiger Family. Insubstantial though their land may be, together we can take it, and form a lucrative alliance. If you are willing to throw away the memory of the past.'

A ripple of conversation went around the room, interest and trepidation in equal amounts.

'Thus, I wait for your reply, and trust it to be a sensible one. Land uphold you, and your family.

'Rice Ox of the Lakes.'

There was total silence in the dusty throne room. Muted conversation could be heard on the other side of the doors. Fox studied his uncle's broad, honest face for some reaction to the message. Rice Fox was musing over the information. Henshin, whose smile had faded during the threats, was now back in a good mood.

'My lord, how think you?'

'You didn't discuss this with me.' The king's brother replied with an answer that caused Henshin's face to fall. Rice Fox was barely restraining his anger.

'It must be for the best, my lord,' Henshin said hurriedly, 'if we can solve this with diplomacy, well, imagine the losses otherwise... they could be valuable allies...I...' Henshin looked down at his feet and finished lamely, 'it will not be good for us if we fight them, Lord. You know that.'

The messenger looked disdainfully at the Fox advisor, as if he agreed.

Fox stood, thinking quickly. Henshin had a point. Fighting the massive Ox armies in open warfare would be close to organising a mass suicide. However, Ox was a tyrant who held immense resources and still let his people starve. The peoples of both Tiger and Rice Fox were suffering in the food shortage but this was not the fault of the nations' respective Crowns. On the one side was a despot, on the other leaders attempting to rule fairly and justly. And Ox would play one off against the other.

The interests of the Fox Family and the people of the Central Plains were foremost in Fox's mind. Ox could not be trusted. This royal court should not suffer the derision of an enemy!

Fox stepped to his uncle's side and whispered in his ear, 'Let me give Ox an answer, Uncle. I'm certain you'll like it.' Rice Fox looked intrigued. He nodded, noticing his nephew's sly smile. Fox straightened up and faced the Ox messenger.

'Take a reply to your king, messenger.

'The Fox Kingdom greets you, with all *appropriate respect.* Your apparently generous offer for an alliance might indeed be attractive to us, considering our lack in numbers and resources. Yes, we understand that your force much outstrips ours. However, we will not be accepting your offer.'

At this Henshin groaned, covering his face with his hands in despair. The messenger looked at Fox in incredulity. A worried smile spread across Rice Fox's face but all the advisors looked on, their faces grim.

Fox continued. 'This is because we consider you to be a dishonest, unscrupulous man, whose treatment of his people is morally unacceptable. I am done with civility and politics in this matter!

'I declare that you are without honour! Your Lordship does nothing to deserve respect and so I offer none! Your messengers will be turned away and the only contact to take place between us will be at the point of a sword!

'Nevertheless, Land uphold you, and your family, until your time ends. Your steadfast adversary, Crown Prince Fox.'

Fox could not hide his pleasure in the dictation of the message and as he spoke the customary blessing to sign the message, sarcasm slipped into his tone. Rice Fox let out an exultant 'Hah!' both frightened and delighted by the strength of the message's tone. Even some of the advisors could not help but smile. The messenger stepped back, appalled. Henshin was hiding his face.

Fox bowed mockingly to the offended man. 'That, I think, will be all. Now, please get out.' A fire burned in Fox's eyes as he stared down the taller, older man. To the men seated around the table, with the exception of Henshin, whose head was still hidden in his arms, the six-foot messenger suddenly looked small in comparison to Fox. The man, dignity wounded, turned and stalked out of the room.

Fox sat down triumphantly, fists clenched on the tabletop. Rice Fox stood. 'Well said, Fox! You have just encapsulated everything I have been too afraid to say myself, in a single message. And did you see their messenger? If he'd a tail, it would have been between his legs. By the Land, that made my heart proud.'

Henshin looked up slowly. When he spoke, his voice was hollow. 'We are all going to be put to the sword, Your Highness. Congratulations. I am glad to know that you feel confident enough to consign us to the cold grip of death, for the sake of making a point. All of us here, we will die at the cut of an Ox blade.'

Fox rose again, coldly enraged. He strode up to the bitter advisor. There was a storm in his eyes now, defiant and dangerous. Fox seized the front of Henshin's robes as the man stood, and pulled him down to his level, so that they were eye to eye.

'Then you will die for the Fox Family, proudly and free of shame, you miserable coward! You will serve with honour! You should not fear me less than you fear death; you have nothing to fear from death if you do your duty! An honourable death would be nothing compared to what I would bring to a traitor!'

Fox pulled Henshin in closer, registering the fear in the Advisor's eyes. He spoke in a harsh whisper, so only he could hear him. 'There will come a time when you must decide who you serve, Henshin. Convenient, that you should be in contact with Ox, convenient that I should be chosen to lead a doomed force into battle, convenient that Ox should know I would be amongst the defenders!'

The advisor affected a look of confusion. Fox shook his head, disgusted. His voice returned to full strength, ringing with steel. 'You serve this Family with loyalty and love! Do you understand? Do you all understand?'

Fox's gaze swept around to take in the entire room. He looked at them with fierce conviction. His uncle stared proudly back, making eye contact. There were tears in his eyes, and to Fox's surprise there were advisors also lifting their eyes to meet his own, swearing an unspoken allegiance. The majority of the advisors looked away, ashamed of themselves. Try as they might, they did not possess the courage to meet his gaze.

Kesta listened as Fox explained the outcome of the meeting. They now had four more allies. Kesta was still getting used to the fact that the war was not a simple "them against us" problem, that there were people on their own side who could – or could not – be trusted.

Haiken could be trusted implicitly, and now there were four more that she would remember to think of as friends. They were Lannos, Renn, Daris and Tellik, four advisors who had been brought into fealty to Fox by his speech in the meeting room.

From the way Fox looked darkly at his cousin when he passed, Kesta had already established that Prince Trustan was not to be trusted.

She never asked Fox about Trustan's bitterness, and Fox did not seem keen to discuss his cousin at all. It was simply obvious that he was set against him as firmly as he was any enemy.

Kesta was introduced to the loyal advisors at a meeting Fox organised, in the barracks on the cliff top. The long, low building was packed, even with the bed pallets moved outside into the sun.

Kesta looked around the hot, dark room and wondered why it felt like a secret meeting. The four advisors were there, and the Champion of the Elite Sword. He sat listening quietly as Fox began to speak, his head tipped to one side, hands busy polishing the cold length of steel that made him his living.

'Thank you all for coming. I would like to thank the advisors here for making a commitment to our family. Before I begin, I want to introduce everyone fully. This is Renn, advisor to the Elite Sword Unit, and his Champion.' Kesta examined Renn closely, trying to evaluate his character from his looks. He had a scar on his left cheek, which implied past combat duty. He was mature looking, the short brown beard and the serious eyes building a picture in Kesta's mind of someone who preferred to make realistic choices. He bowed to Fox and Fox saluted.

The Champion looked up from his sword polishing and nodded. Leaning forward, he whispered in Renn's ear, 'Who is she? Why is she here?'

Fox lifted his hand. 'Kesta is my companion by circumstance, and now my shield maiden.' Nobody raised an objection, although Kesta wasn't sure whether they were holding back, or simply didn't mind her being present.

Tellik was the advisor for the vital work carried out in the quarries and mines. His colleague in the Autumn Hills was apparently more valued; there were few resources of that kind on the Central Plains and some thought of Tellik as redundant. He was brown haired like Renn, his brother, but he went clean-shaven and his jaw was narrower than Renn's.

The last of the advisors was Daris, an excitable young man who bowed deeply, and smiled charmingly at Kesta. He had been given his post as Advisor to the Archers due to petty political conflict; the archers of the Fox Forces were notoriously unwelcoming to advisors and his father had annoyed some important people.

Daris had shrugged off the reason for his posting and simply worked as hard as he could to build good relations between himself and the champion archer. Champion Koshra, one of the few female warriors serving at high rank in the Fox Army, sat behind Daris. She treated him a bit like a favourite student, and he listened to her avidly. Kesta identified with him easily.

The other champions and officers introduced themselves and Fox started to talk about the war. Everyone seemed to agree where to fight the initial battle; there was a pass in the hills where the borders of the Fox, Tiger and Ox territories met. Fox described it as two narrow, shallow valleys cutting through the line of hills, separated by a raised peninsula, that stuck out into a sea of grass.

Daris was interested by the details of the promontory, visualising archers standing their ground on the middle, able to loose into either of the two valleys.

Fox listened to this idea with interest. He stopped Daris to tell him that the middle hill had been used that way in the past; the natives had used it similarly against the invading Dragon Family over four hundred years ago. The Dragon Family had won the war but were defeated, despite their superior numbers, at the battle of the Twin Pass.

Renn spoke for the first time. 'It's a good idea. The problem is that we don't have that many men. At best we can hold one of the passes. Even if we hold the greater pass, Ox can flank us through the other. We'd be massacred.' There was a murmur of agreement. Daris looked crushed.

A few more ideas were brought into the open: if they couldn't use the twin valley pass, why not let Ox enter the kingdom? Why not let him exhaust his army against the cliff? Fox waved the idea aside. If Rice Ox entered the land, he wouldn't waste time attacking the castle. He would sweep across the fertile plains like yellow plague, laying waste the villages until the castle was an island surrounded by a sea of invaders. For a moment there was silence as everyone considered this. Did Ox truly have that many men at his command? The atmosphere in the meeting had become very subdued.

Kesta thought about what Fox had told her the last few days, since the meeting in the throne room. She watched Daris sympathetically. He had lost his confidence, and sat quietly, not joining in the debate as to where they should meet Ox. Suddenly, an idea came to her.

'Tiger!' she said loudly. The others turned to look at her, puzzled. 'We should get help from Tiger!' she added hurriedly, 'we could fill both valleys if he helped, couldn't we?' Daris raised his head, grinning.

'Yes! By the Land, she has it!' He jumped to his feet. His champion glanced at Fox, eyebrows raised as she asked a silent question.

Fox nodded. 'It could be done with King Tiger's aid, perhaps. Although we don't know how many men he has.'

He sat back, considering. He had almost forgotten about Tiger. The two families *had* once been partners in a very strong alliance. Maybe the partnership could be re-forged?

'I'll send a messenger, if you like,' said Tellik, rising to his feet. His brother shook his head and motioned for him to sit down.

'The other advisors have control over the messengers, brother. They could intercept it at their will.'

Fox looked to Renn. 'You think they'd do that?'

'Yes,' Renn nodded, expression dark. Fox looked down and shook his head.

'I didn't realise that Henshin had that much influence. He will do anything to keep us from conflict. What can we do then?' He looked around the room. Lannos, who had been silent for the most part, spoke up. 'You could go, Your Highness. If one of us tries to, they can vote against it and, having the majority, bring us back by force. However, they don't yet have that power over you.'

Fox sat, mulling the idea over. There wasn't really anything to think about, he would have to go, and that was that. But how? And when? He noticed Kesta watching him and smiled. He knew who he'd be going with. For a moment, an image of the Great Shadow flashed across his mind. If he went...

No. I will not be crippled by fear. He couldn't allow the mysterious enemy to stand in the way of his family's war against Ox.

Fox stood slowly, dismissing dark thoughts. There was no way Ox would be able to gather his armies inside of the month, so there would be time to worry over details later.

'I think we should leave it at that,' Fox said, looking around. Nothing could be planned until Tiger had been contacted. Talking amongst themselves, the officers and champions left, along with their advisors. Fox and Kesta followed them out.

It had clouded over, and as they walked back towards the castle, the first icy breath of the coming Autumn bit at their cheeks. Fox looked up towards the castle, then slowed his steps. A group of men were walking purposefully towards them, Henshin in front. He had recovered from despair, now he was furious. The other advisors walked behind him, their faces grim.

'What are you doing?' he began, brimming with outrage. 'When advisors meet, they all meet! This is a time-honoured law that none have *ever* dared break! Yet you choose to break it with this...this arrogant *prince*? Have you lost your minds?'

Renn and Tellik stepped to the front of Fox's group. The two brothers stood defiantly, facing their former chief.

'We are no longer under your law, Henshin. We bow to a different flag!' Renn scowled proudly as he said it.

His brother nodded and added, 'If you have concerns, take it up with the prince!'

Henshin barely hesitated. 'I intend to. Fox, explain yourself. If you please.'

'We had a meeting between friends. And do try to address me correctly, Henshin.'

'Oh! Be silent! Pretention! I've been an advisor since before you were left in the gateway, wrapped in a flag you had no right to wear! I've more royalty in me than you will ever claim to have! We've been here for centuries; we are a *foundation*, you little bastard!' There was an outbreak of outrage at this from the loyal advisors and some of the soldiers that stood nearby.

'The blood of the Dragon runs in *our* veins!' Henshin finished, spitting. Kesta clenched her fists.

Fox put a hand on her shoulder as she opened her mouth to curse Henshin. The advisor sneered down at her. Fox lifted his head and looked Henshin straight in the eyes.

'Watch your mouth, Henshin, or I'll break you! The men behind me chose this allegiance. There is nothing you can do to stop it. From now on, our plans are our own, I no longer consider you *my* Chief Advisor. I have no reverence for the Dragon Family, they are long dead, and their power with them. Now let us pass.'

Henshin stood aside. He spat on Renn's feet as he passed, but Renn ignored him. Daris looked down as he passed the hostile group of men, intimidated. Somehow, Kesta found the courage to meet the advisor's eyes. She hoped to make him look away as Fox had, but in the end she turned her gaze away, astonished at the intense hate she saw.

Fox and Kesta walked along the walltop in companionable silence. The clouds were heavy above them and thunder rolled, first in the dense, dark bank of cloud, and then in the earth a long way to the north.

Prince Trustan was standing on the walltop, leaning on the battlements. He was smiling to himself as he watched Fox and Kesta approach.

'Hello, cousin, dear! And your faithful servant, how pretty she looks today!' He pushed himself away from the battlements and stood legs apart, arms wide in mock welcome.

'Get out of my way,' Fox said coldly. Trustan's eyes widened.

'No need to be rude, cousin. Just because you've been having trouble with the advisors... there's no need to take it out on me.' He watched Fox's face eagerly for a reaction.

'How did you know...' Fox started forwards, annoyed. 'There's no way you could know!'

Trustan laughed.

'Unless, of course, I am somehow involved? I'll leave that up to your perceptive mind, Fox, or maybe that piece of pretty *flesh* next to you can do some detective work, prove she's not just big brown eyes, not to mention the rest of her.' He shot a disgusting look at Kesta that made her teeth clench.

Trustan laughed hysterically as Fox jumped forwards. Kesta didn't attempt to stop him. She had been called far worse before but she did not like Trustan. She was surprised – and pleased – at Fox's quick anger on her behalf.

Fox stopped himself from punching his cousin, just in time. Trustan jutted out his chin and shoved his face towards Fox's, still laughing, openly inviting violence and not caring.

'Raw nerve, cousin?' Trustan jeered, his laughs following Fox and Kesta as they hurried back the way they had come. The sky was dark and heavy above them, mirroring Fox's thunderous expression. All his fears and frustrations were weighing on him and Trustan's mistreatment of Kesta had made him angrier than he felt he had ever been.

They walked quickly through the corridors and courtyards of the castle towards the walled-in farms. Kesta hurried to keep up with him. She had no idea where he was going.

They came out through an open wooden gate onto a path made of wooden slats, which snaked away through a field of hemp. The dark green leaves surrounded them as Fox almost ran down the path. Suddenly he turned off the pathway into the greenery, and stopped, looking up at the mountain. Great, heavy drops of rain began to fall, making the leaves bounce as if they were nodding. The rain ran down the leaves and dropped from the tips, as it ran from Fox and Kesta's shoulders and hair. Fox opened his arms to embrace the driving water.

Kesta smiled, Fox had come here to cool his temper. She watched with a growing fondness as his face relaxed. The past week's events were running off him with the rainwater. He yelled out; she couldn't hear the words but they were strong and triumphant and sounded more like a thank you than a frustrated cry. His face was upturned and he stood completely open to the elements, feet rooted in the mud with the sky running off him. His face was a stark contrast from before, worry and anger were gone, replaced by something in between worship and pure joy. Or maybe they were one and the same. Kesta didn't know.

Fox opened his eyes and looked at Kesta's wonderment, smiling. 'It won't matter Kesta, he won't matter!' He held out his hand. 'Stand with me!'

Kesta laughed. 'I already am!'

'No, like I am! Take my hand.' His eyes went soft as he tried to speak above the drumming rain. Kesta met his gaze. She felt odd, excited and happy all at once, an emotion she couldn't describe. She took his hand and they both looked up into the tempestuous sky. Her hand was in his, but as she closed her eyes, feeling the rainwater run off her face, their fingers became intertwined.

Kesta tried to find what Fox had found in the rain. She felt happy, and that was it; maybe her capacity for what Fox was communing with was too small to feel anything more than happiness. Kesta found she didn't care. It just felt good to be holding his hand.

But now, thoughts ran through her mind. She remembered her place, who she was and the caste system that separated her from him. She felt ashamed to be holding his hand, unaware that the feeling was anything deeper than their difference in wealth and power.

Kesta looked down and let go of her prince's hand. He looked at her questioningly but she shook her head. 'I shouldn't be so familiar, we shouldn't, I'm your servant, or shield maiden, or whatever your uncle and you would have me be, but to the others I'm just a peasant, Fox. Just a peasant. I still feel that way.' She looked down and Fox looked away, disappointed.

'You're not...' he started, but Kesta pointed towards the castle and he stopped. A messenger was riding through the hemp towards them from the castle wall.

Kesta felt relieved that she had listened to her instincts. When the horseman arrived, all he saw was the prince and his shield-maiden, caught in the rain.

5
The Devil You Don't

The rain continued to thunder down all through the night as banks of heavy cloud broke over the mountain. The rain swept across the plains, washing away roads and unharvested rice fields. The castle and the plateau soaked up the rain like a dusty sponge. Lightning danced in the clouds and thunder crashed directly above, seeming to shake the stonework.

The kitchens were full of steam and shouting. The castle's peasantry were all working together, cooking, cleaning or just getting in the way of each other. In the hall above the kitchen, the heat was rising through the dark floorboards. The shutters banged high up in the wall, but the sounds of food being set on the long, low tables masked the clamour of the storm. Lamps were lit; the room glowed golden, ambient light flooding across the great, blue silk banners.

Fox was sitting in his rooms, his thoughts once again on the road. He felt trapped, his sanctuary spoilt by the workings of Henshin and his petty advisors. Any chance of victory lay north, out of reach, in Tiger's kingdom. Fox felt sure that the banquet was nothing more than a way of keeping him inside the castle. As the celebrations were in his honour, there was no chance he would be allowed to leave during them.

Kesta was also on Fox's mind. She had been uncomfortable with holding his hand and he worried he might have done something wrong. He liked her very much. She was his friend, above all other thoughts, and she had even saved his life. But now she saw herself as his servant.

It was not good enough. The realisation thudded in his chest. He wanted more.

Fox's hand closed, as if around the memory of her hand. She was beautiful. To him. Even the scar on her cheek pleased him. *He had healed that cut.*

Was it wrong to hope that she would end the distance between them? Fox frowned into space. He felt a frustration bordering on anger, but couldn't pin down why.

He went to his window. The rain hammered down on the other side of the shutters. He could see nothing in the dark; the way north was veiled by the torrents and the thick, black cloud.

Kesta called from the outer room. Fox sighed and closed the shutters. Kesta was in the doorway. She smiled. 'It makes a difference from your normal leather and steel! I've never seen you wear anything other than your fighting clothes. It suits you.'

Fox glanced down at his clothes. He was wearing the same blue and grey silk robes as his uncle, brought in at the waist with a sash. Fox wished he could be rid of it, armour up, force open the gates and march into the storm. He forced a smile for Kesta's benefit, but it didn't fool her.

'What's wrong, sir? Fox?' She put her hand on his arm, but he shrugged it off.

'We will be late,' Fox muttered, turning away. 'My uncle is waiting.' He walked out of the door and turned back to her, trying to make himself look relaxed. 'Come on, you'll enjoy it.' Kesta narrowed her eyes and put her hands on her hips.

'But you obviously won't! You don't need to lie about this! If you don't want to go, don't, I can just say you're sick, or you're tired. You don't have to go!'

Fox bit back an angry retort, unwilling to let himself admit to his deceit. 'I want to go,' he lied unconvincingly, 'and I'm not sick. Or tired. Now come on!' He turned away and began to walk towards the stairs, feeling bad. Why was he unable even to attempt to enjoy the night? Unable to tell the truth to the only one who cared enough to see his lies for what they were? *Unable, even, to find any real reason to tell the lie in the first place...*

On top of this, Fox didn't know how he could cope with a night of speeches and false friendship, with Henshin watching his every move, and Kesta angry with him.

The hall was loud with excited conversation when Fox and Kesta entered. Rice Fox rose, smiling. The whole room did the same, applauding their prince. Fox smiled, pausing in the doorway, his gaze panning around, from the honest faces of the peasants and tradesmen, to the false smiles and deliberate clapping of Henshin's advisors.

Fox looked down, his smile fading. He went quickly to his place beside his uncle. Kesta followed.

The room quietened as Rice Fox lifted his hands for silence. The people stayed on their feet as Rice Fox spoke, before repeating the final words of the salute. Fox could see Henshin watching him, casually invoking the Land over his raised cup, a shrewd smile on his thin lips.

There were more toasts by various members of the castle's community, all of which had to be honoured by a drink. As a result Fox was feeling slightly unsteady as proceedings began to wind down. Kesta never let more than a drop of the strong mountain wine pass her lips. She watched Fox vigilantly. He was obviously aware he was losing command over himself because he was discreetly watering down the contents of his glass each time a salute was called.

The chief of the silk workers rose to his feet, yet another speech ready on his lips. The crowded room resounded with cheers, which faded away as they waited for him to speak.

A sudden chill broke Fox's concentration. He passed his hand across his face, as if wiping something away. Suddenly, he seemed more controlled, more confident on his feet, but as he turned to speak to Kesta she could see the fear in his eyes.

He opened his mouth to speak but was cut off by the great *boom* of the massive doors. In the deafening silence, all eyes turned towards a soaked and frightened wall guard.

'My lord!' the man started forward, leaving wet footprints on the warm wood. 'My lord, there is someone at the gate. He asks for you, nay, he insists that you come to the wall top!' His face was deathly pale.

A few people spoke quietly in the silence. Fox closed his mouth, leaving his thoughts unsaid. It was clear from Kesta's expression that she had guessed the significance of the guard's arrival.

Rice Fox stood. 'Who asks for me?' The guard looked at Rice Fox, confused.

'Forgive me sire, it's not you he…it…asks for. It is my Lord the Crown Prince.' He looked over at Fox, who had already risen to his feet.

Fox nodded, controlling his fear. 'I'm coming. Don't open the gate!' he went around the back of his uncle's chair, pausing to whisper in his ear. A look of understanding came across Rice Fox's face. He stood and followed Fox to the door.

Kesta got up as well, reaching the door just ahead of Henshin. He gave her a foul look as she glanced over her shoulder. Kesta ignored him and ran down the corridor after Fox.

Fox stepped out onto the wall top. The rain hit him with battering force, stinging his cheeks and the backs of his hands. His brown hair was plastered against his skull and the wind dragged at the thick layers of his robes. Fox forced himself to the edge of the battlements, the now familiar fear rising in him. He welcomed the beating rain as if it were a cloak to conceal him.

Fox could hear two pairs of feet slapping against the wet stone, Rice Fox and Kesta had kicked off their soft leather shoes, afraid of slipping. Rice Fox looked over the edge first. He made a sound as if something was caught in his throat; doubling up he turned away from the edge.

Kesta forced herself to look down. Fox had his eyes closed, mustering his courage.

Below stood the Great Shadow.

His tortured face stared up, skin writhing. Worms of shadow coiled ceaselessly around him. Kesta felt nausea rise as his eyes narrowed on her.

Without warning or mercy his eyes burnt through her skull and into her mind in a dreadful assault. Kesta screamed out, her nails biting at the stonework under her hands, the strain of the attack blinding her.

Fox heard her scream. His eyes snapped open and he saw the unholy form below him, saw, in a heightened, second sight, the stream of raw darkness pounding against Kesta, shaking her body.

'LET HER GO!' His voice cut through the sounds of the storm, keenest steel through silk. He seized Kesta's arm, feeling her seized muscles, rock hard under his hand. He pulled as hard as he dared. Kesta dropped like a statue to the cold, wet stone.

The Great Shadow smiled like an open wound. The rain hissed away to nothing above his shape. Now Fox could see him truly. He could see the smile splitting the ghastly face, trickles of dark fire slipping between putrid lips, wriggling like live things down the dead face. Not once did the Great Shadow take a truly solid shape. The trails and wreaths of darkness danced around him like serpents.

'She is mine! Give her to me, Arisen One! I take what I claim, I kill what I take; let my shadow take away her pain! Give her to me!'

Fox's fear buzzed away at the back of his mind, but a new emotion was rushing through him in a surge of raw energy. An anger took him. He leaned forwards, confronting his enemy.

'This gate is not open to you! You will not enter! My friend will be free of you – your hate will not affect her! You have *NO power over her!*' Fox's face shook with emotion. He roared out the last words with the force of a command. Below Fox, the Great Shadow stepped back, surprised and enraged. Beside Fox, Kesta's eyes snapped open, her muscles still frozen. A brief but violent fight took place within her. The shadow that had been forced into her body broke, issuing from her mouth in a failing stream.

Through her confused eyes, she saw it; a shred of passing dark dissolving in the light surrounding Fox's body. Kesta breathed again, the air burning in her lungs as oxygen flooded back. Her muscles shook once more and released. Then she passed out with great relief, her dark hair spread around her head on the wet stone like a halo.

The man sat in the corner of the room, head bowed in thought. His pure white clothing surrounded him, covering the brilliantly polished steel armour that lay beneath. There was no sword on his dyed leather belt but the man still gave the impression of somebody who knew how to look after himself. He was unusually tall, with fair hair and striking blue eyes.

Fox sat beside his bed where Kesta lay, watching the man quietly, waiting anxiously for him to say something. Kesta lay still beneath the sheets. The healers had dressed her in a silk nightshirt for modesty's sake, but the cover was drawn to her chin anyway. She was shivering, although the temperature in the room was not that low.

At last, the man got to his feet. He walked to the other side of the bed and placed his hand on Kesta's forehead. His brow furrowed as he considered her state. For a moment the room felt cooler, more comfortable. Kesta shivered noticeably and the cold seemed to break. She relaxed beneath her blanket.

The man straightened up and smiled at Fox. 'The trauma is gone. The Shadow has been inside her mind, but at no point did her resistance weaken. You broke the shadow's power over her yourself, and just in time. It was a manifestation of the Perversion of Light, and would have gone to work quickly. Anyway,' the man sat back down in his chair and looked over at Kesta's sleeping form. 'She will be well. Congratulations on your victory.'

The man looked at Fox with great interest, not speaking his thoughts. Fox returned the man's gaze. He had thoughts of his own that he needed to explore.

'What is your name, friend? How did you know you would be needed here?' Fox waited for an answer. The man smiled.

'I am a Warrior of the Land's Holy Order. My name is Rashin.'

'I know of your order,' Fox confirmed. Rashin bowed slightly.

'I will tell you my story, which begins six days ago.' The Holy Warrior sat back and looked at the ceiling while he summoned up memories. Glancing across at the window, he began.

'Six days ago one of my Brothers came out of the stripped barley fields on the way back from some errand. He said that there was a great evil on the road, following the prince and his servant. As the most experienced of my order, I left immediately to attempt to stay whatever it might be. Night fell and with it came the Shadow. The Perversion of Light came with the going down of the sun. I knew him before he came into my sight. I was taught that I would know him. It is in my bloodline.' At this, he watched Fox's face carefully for a change in expression.

'I barred the road and prayed that the Land would aid me in my fight. He came out of the dark at speed until he slowed and came to stand in front of me. The Perversion himself stood in front of me! My fear almost made me run, but I have fought my fear before, and know how to defeat it.

'He challenged me for hours but he did not turn aside or attempt to go around. Finally he withdrew, his eyes on me all the way. When he had reached a suitable distance he set off west. I followed.

'For a day I followed the trail of dead grass he left in his wake. At the end of that day I came to a great stone – a carcer stone, the peasants call them - lit up with symbols I could not read. I would not sleep in the presence of the stone, but in travelling onwards a new problem presented itself.

'The trail of dead vegetation split. One went west still and was the trail of my unholy quarry, but another, larger path went northwest, towards the great river Lifeblood. In this trail, caused by the destructive effect of the shadow, were physical tracks, great, clawed footprints, alien to me in shape and size. This intrigued me and I followed this trail, knowing it to be slower and easier to follow.

'I followed the path for a second day, without food or rest. On the evening of that day I was rewarded: I saw the thing I was trailing. A great horned beast, walking as a man would, head bent with purpose. Shadow cloaked it, trailing before and behind. I felt ill to see it. I knew I was not protected from its physical form by the Land, as I am from the Perversion – he that you call the Great Shadow. I fell back, but the creature did not continue.

'At first I thought that the creature was aware of my presence but instead it seemed simply tired. The shadow pulled clear of the beast's mighty form and as the shadow forsook its host, the beast turned to thick, black dust, with teeth, horn and bone all rotted away. The shadow seemed stronger and faster, it continued the journey it had begun and soon I lost sight of it.

'I slept then, and ate. When I woke on the third day I knew that before reporting to my order, I must first tell the Shadow's original prey - that is, you, Lord Fox – of the events.

'I arrived here early this morning. In the mountains I again picked up the trail of the Perversion of Light. This worried me greatly. I arrived at the pass to once again be confronted by the Enemy.

'Another hour of battle I managed, before I passed out. When I regained consciousness, dawn was breaking and I made for the gate.'

Rashin spread his hands. 'And here I am, Lord Fox.' Fox stood. Kesta was stirring and Fox stopped what he'd been about to say, putting a hand on her arm to see if she would wake. Instead she rolled over, now sleeping completely naturally. Fox smiled, unable to hide his fondness.

Rashin smiled too. He leaned forward and said, 'Let her sleep, Lord Fox.' He paused for a moment, considering his next words carefully. 'You have feelings for her, but that is something you should hide from others who might also be able to perceive this. You know that you blush? Some look on such affections from a prince to a servant as a crime, a sin.' Fox looked away.

'I do know this, Warrior.' He sounded annoyed. 'Rashin, tell me; I have met two creatures of shadow now. One was the Perversion, the other the same as this second creature you tracked. Both of them spoke to me. I wonder if your experience would shed any light on what they said.'

Rashin gestured for him to go on. After Fox had recounted the words of the shadow, Rashin looked at him for a long time, as if he had just realised something incredible. Whatever that was, the Holy Warrior kept it to himself.

'I am afraid I have no wisdom for you, for the moment. Only to say that I know that the two are connected, from the same source. That is to say, the greater one is that source. That's all I can tell you. Perhaps things will become clearer with time.' The warrior rose, and the knowing look left his face. 'Perhaps I should see to your uncle now.'

Fox went to the door, holding it open for the holy warrior. He closed it behind the two of them, glancing back at Kesta before it shut. He had wanted to discuss the strange instances of knowledge he experienced in the face of danger, inspiration coming from he knew not where. But it could wait.

Kesta opened her eyes slowly, blinking in the light. She considered the information she had just heard, carefully. The memories of last night and the short, tortured sleep were blurred and painful. She sat up slowly. Her muscles ached, but whatever the holy warrior had done for her while she slept had helped.

Kesta slipped out of the bed, enjoying the refreshing feel of the cool air. She decided she wouldn't tell Fox she was awake yet. Instead, she wanted to go and find Haiken. Her fear of the Great Shadow was now coupled to a heated and righteous anger. She wanted to go and fight. Her mind had been violated. Her desire to learn how to protect herself and Fox was greater than ever before.

Kesta thought about what Fox and Rashin had said when she had been 'sleeping'. She was glad of it but would be happier if she didn't have to think about it for a few hours. Kesta remade Fox's bed and went out into her own room. She retrieved her wing-swords and set off for the northern plateau.

Haiken had never had such an eager student. Kesta was also a good learner: quick, but thorough. In the last three weeks she had developed an acrobatic ability which was coming through in her fighting. The wing-swords encouraged an original approach and she was rapidly developing her own style, elaborating on the basic movements and stances taught by Haiken.

Haiken was still comfortably defeating her when they sparred, but she was up quicker than before and was able to spar for longer without giving in. She was fitter now than she had ever been. The veteran warrior could barely believe her progress, it was something he had never seen before. It reminded him of Fox, who came to watch as many of her sessions as possible, occasionally joining in.

Haiken used a heavy, single-bladed sword. He had always been able to win against his first student before, when Fox used a practice blade, but now Fox seemed to have gained new heights of skill with the wooden staff.

Haiken found himself forced to the ground for a third time. Fox helped him up, laughing.

'Either I've improved, or you are less than you were when you taught me how to fight! Are you all right?' Haiken straightened, smiling and wincing at the same time.

'You *have* improved, Fox. But since I last sparred with you, you went through a terrible battle. And defeated this hidden enemy, twice. I've heard the whispers. I am not so ashamed as you might want me to be.'

Fox shrugged. 'I wouldn't want you to be ashamed.' He looked over to the castle.

'You have to leave soon,' Haiken interpreted Fox's faraway look. 'You are going to try to reach Tiger?'

'Yes. Henshin and his snakes still think they can stop this war through diplomacy. If I go and get Tiger involved they think that we're committed to the conflict. As if we weren't already.'

Fox looked north to where the plateau ended, a sharp edge against the soft greens of the wooded hills below.

Turning to Kesta, he smiled. 'We have been waiting around now for too long. Do you think Henshin would mind if we slipped off at some point today?'

Kesta smiled wickedly. 'Oh, he'll be enraged! He'll *try* to stop us, I think. What do you suppose he has planned?' Fox shrugged in answer.

'He can't do anything. I will go tell Uncle later today, that we plan to leave tomorrow morning. That will give me time to leave instructions. In fact, if we're all done here, Haiken, we could go to the castle now?' Haiken bowed.

'I would like to join you in the throne room, sir, if you don't mind.'

Fox nodded. His mind was already on the throne room and the Chief Advisor's reaction to his plans. The three of them set off towards the castle.

Rice Fox was arguing with his advisors. Tellik, Renn, Lannos and young Daris were sitting around their lord, faces stony and defiant. Henshin was standing, with the other advisors backing him up vocally. The doors opened and the main body of advisors hushed, turning to see who had entered. Henshin, however, continued.

'Furthermore, my lord, I will remind you that our powers, as direct descendants from the High Council of the Dragon family, include this rule: at any time, the Advisory Council may take up a vote on the subject of who is allowed onto the council. That, my lord, is the final word on the matter. Therefore there will be a vote on whether Daris is allowed to keep his post.'

Henshin sat down with a satisfied smile. All eyes but his turned to Fox, standing in the doorway. Kesta and Haiken were with him. In the corner of the room, Rashin, half hidden in the shadows, moved slightly. Slowly Fox began to walk down the line of the low table behind the advisors. Henshin continued to belligerently ignore him, tapping his long fingers on the table.

Fox walked round to stand in front of Henshin, who looked up with an expression of mock query. Fox paused, about to say something, but in the end he chose to simply give the smug advisor a disgusted look, turning to his uncle. Rice Fox leaned forwards to listen, a serious look on his face, already knowing the subject of the conversation.

Fox glanced over his shoulder at Henshin, smiling as he began to speak. 'Uncle, I am requesting your permission for my shield-maid and I to take a journey to the hall of King Rice Tiger. This would be so that our family could finally extend a new alliance to theirs, and in so doing, defeat the threat posed by Rice Ox. Do I have your permission?'

Rice Fox smiled and opened his mouth to answer, but his advisor cut him off. Henshin stood, shaking with anger and anticipation, unable to contain his indignation. 'We refuse you permission!' Henshin was almost shouting. 'The Advisory Council has already discussed this, and your permission is refused!'

A smile played over Fox's lips as he ignored the conceited advisor, and repeated his question. 'Do we have your permission?' Rice Fox met Fox's smile with one of his own but again Henshin's infuriated spluttering interrupted him. Henshin banged his fist down on the table.

'WE WILL NOT GRANT YOU PERMISSION! WE WILL NOT GRANT YOU PERMISSION! How dare you challenge our authority? How dare you?'

Rice Fox's amusement was tinged with irritation at Henshin's presumption now. Fox raised his eyebrows, still waiting for the answer. In the end, Rice Fox simply nodded.

'Thank you, Uncle. Please inform the Champion of the Archers that she has her orders: to send the archers into the northern hills for training, as I do not find Daris' replacement – whomever that might be – worthy of the post. I will send a messenger when I arrive at the castle of Rice Tiger.'

Fox nodded to Kesta and Haiken. He bowed once more and turned and walked to the door.

'No!' Henshin's rage was barely contained. 'Stop! Guards!' The door swung open. Two soldiers stood in the way. Fox carried on walking. The two men looked at Henshin, at each other, and finally saluted Fox and stood out of his way. The soldier on the left looked fiercely back at Henshin. For a moment the advisor met the soldier's eyes. The gaze he saw there was heavy with contempt and defiance. As the soldiers turned, Daris stood and followed them out of the room. Now Henshin saw the recurve bows on the backs of the soldiers.

A short time later, Fox and Kesta passed through the northern gateway, with Haiken, Rashin and Daris. The five of them slowly crossed the plateau, discussing the confrontation. In the castle, the meeting of the council must have finished, Renn and Tellik were coming down from the battlements, entering the courtyard behind them. The five stopped about halfway across the plateau, as a servant brought a horse around from the stables. It was Riversteel. Kesta greeted him enthusiastically.

Rashin turned to Fox. The holy warrior shared Fox's dislike of the advisory council and he had been smiling with the rest, but now his expression became serious.

'Good luck, Fox. If the Shadow finds you on your journey, run and don't look back. From what you say, you should be safe among the rocks.' Fox nodded to Rashin and gripped his hand for a moment in a strong gesture of friendship. For some reason, he felt a sense of kinship for the man.

Haiken handed Fox's staff up to him as he climbed into Riversteel's saddle. Former advisor Daris opened his mouth to say goodbye, but something caught his eye and instead he waved to a person who was coming out through the gate, behind the figures of Renn and his brother.

'Champion Koshra!' Daris called. The figure waved, and started to run, quickly overtaking Renn and Tellik. She was a middle-aged woman, lean and fitted out for combat – there was a bow on her back. She saluted both Fox and Daris.

'My Lord Fox, young master Daris. The archers have made their goodbyes. We are leaving, as was commanded by Your Highness. Do you have instructions for us?'

Through the gateway, a column of archers were marching, heading in the same direction that Fox and Kesta were to take. Fox smiled sadly.

'It is sad to see Fox soldiers forced to forsake their place. Yes, Champion, I have orders for you to carry out. Kesta, take the reins.'

Fox slid out of the saddle. Kesta nodded and climbed up onto Riversteel's back, not quite as clumsily as she had done weeks ago.

'Take your archers to the Twin Valley Ridge. The first sign of enemy activity, one of your soldiers must ride, ride as fast as they can to Tiger's castle to tell me. Then you must wait. We will come. It may be that we come to you before then.'

Koshra nodded, climbing into the saddle of a horse that Renn had brought for her. 'Thank you, my lord!'

'To me, to me!' She called out to her soldiers who were already filing by. She cantered away.

Fox turned back towards Renn and Tellik. He opened his mouth to speak, but was interrupted.

Tellik jerked suddenly, his hand going to his back, shock written across his face. His brother cried out. He could see the arrow that had suddenly stuck fast between Tellik's shoulder blades. Slowly and terribly, Tellik fell.

A lone figure stood on the battlements, smiling and swaying slightly from side to side. The bow fell from his hand as he laughed nervously, a twisted and almost confused grin on his face.

Fox stared, in shock, at the figure of his cousin, high up on the wall top. Suddenly a shout of pure, uncontrolled rage broke away from his throat. The masonry directly in front of Trustan shattered and fell away, but the murderous prince was unharmed. Trustan threw the bow from the wall and ran. Fox stared after him, shaking with fury. Tears ran down Kesta's cheeks, as Rashin knelt beside Tellik. The holy warrior's hand was on the advisor's shoulder, the other hand clenched in a fist.

A desperate weeping rose on the breeze as all the world seemed to fall silent for Renn's grief. He hugged his dying brother to his chest, afraid to look at his blinking, confused face. The moment Tellik died, they all knew. Renn cried out as if he had been stabbed.

Fox turned to Daris and spoke with urgency, still trembling with rage. 'Take Renn and Lannos away to the Twin Valley Ridge. Follow the archers. Convince Renn to leave the body. If it has not been graced by a proper burial when I return, I will kill everyone responsible with my bare hands! Go!'

Fox turned to Rashin. 'Go with them, Warrior, Brother. I will join you soon. Kesta? We must go as well. If I go back, I won't be allowed to leave. They will want me for the trial. We cannot stay, don't argue! We need to ride.' Fox climbed up behind her and whispered in her ear. 'Please. We have to go.' Kesta wiped her tears away furiously, shouting out, anger cutting through the shock. Lifting her head and gritting her teeth, she slapped the reins down on Riversteel's shoulders. 'Yah!'

6
Mud, Blood And Rain

The road was darkened ahead. Clouds rolled in, promising more rain, as thunder shook the western horizon; the haze of the wooded hills. Fox turned his gaze away. That way was an uncertain future, as overcast as the weather. The air smelt damp, and had a prickly, static feel. There would be another storm.

Kesta's tears had dried, but her mind was still on Advisor Tellik's death as the first, heavy drops of rain began to fall. Riversteel shook his head, blinking away the water. Neither Fox nor Kesta spoke as they dismounted, feet squelching in the saturated earth.

Fox lifted the oilskins off Riversteel's back. The horse stood patiently, as Fox draped the heavy sheet across his shoulders. Another went down onto the ground and the bags and weapons were laid on top of it. Kesta moved fast. The third sheet was propped up above the second, which although already a little damp, could still be used to lie on. Kesta and Fox wriggled underneath. The rain hammered down now, they could feel it drumming on the sheet above their heads.

Kesta was tired. They had been riding through the hills for most of the day. Outside, the sky was darkening with tempestuous gloom. Night was coming fast. There would be no more riding today. Kesta wanted desperately to be moving on, passing through the storm, mobile, safe. A doubt, tucked away in the back of her mind, was growing. The Great Shadow's remembered presence was haunting her.

The dark came on rapidly; soon it was almost pitch black. Kesta hugged herself, her fears tumbling over one another, all fighting for precedence in her mind. The images of both of the Shadow's attacks were returning. She had been pushing the memory away, ignoring it since it had happened. Now, in the dark and the storm, they would not be ignored. Kesta felt everything spilling out into her. She felt like crying out.

Fox watched her anxiously. She had been silent since the race down the treacherous cliff path, when they had left the castle behind. The murder, and the way that Fox had made Kesta run, had obviously not been left behind. When he had met Kesta, he had seen her emotional strength. Later he'd found a few weaknesses she hid. He could now see her unwillingness to give in, her defiant streak. She didn't like to run. Again Fox thought of the plains to the west, and Ox. If the forces met there, and he knew they would, there would be no running.

Kesta lay down. She was struggling to fight back the panic that was overtaking her. Closing her eyes didn't make it better, it simply locked her in her head, with formless dark wriggling around her. Opening her eyes, Kesta saw Fox lying opposite. His concern was obvious. Still, neither of them spoke. Kesta's eyes pleaded for help, yet she would not ask for it. She couldn't forgive him. He had made her run. And Tellik was dead, and Fox had done nothing.

Fox sighed and closed his eyes. Kesta immediately panicked. The eye-contact had been giving her strength against the visceral flow of terror that threatened to overthrow her.

Suddenly, a new wave of feeling went through her. The images of death and pain, her worries and fears, all melted away. Peace settled on her, her mind emptied. Fox frowned, his eyes still closed. His hand was held out towards her, now he let it rest again on the coarse oilskin. He resisted the urge to reach for her hand.

Fox opened his eyes slowly. The images that had been flooding Kesta's consciousness played through in his head, fading already, their potency lost. He had glimpsed worse in his dreams. Fox focused on Kesta's face. Her terror was over, the last fever of the sickness left by the enemy.

'I didn't know. You should have told me. I don't get visions anymore, not when I'm awake. Just what I see in my dreams.' Now Fox offered his hand. Kesta took it gratefully. For a moment she couldn't bring herself to say what she wanted to say.

'I'm sorry. I'm sorry I didn't ask for help. I know that we had to go and it wasn't your fault. I just... I just thought that you could have done something – I expected you to avenge him, to *do something*. I'm sorry.' Kesta flushed, uncomfortable with apologising.

'I can't do everything.' Fox said. Kesta nodded. The rain drummed above them. 'Anyway,' Fox said, frowning, 'smashing part of the battlement like I did was quite impressive, don't you think? I just...couldn't bring myself to kill the bastard.'

Kesta woke, expecting the stiffness that came with riding. She was pleasantly surprised to find that she felt rested. It was quite hot, stuffy beneath the oilskin, and when she peeled it back she enjoyed the feeling of the cold air against her sticky skin. Light clouds scudded across the sky above her. The storm was utterly spent, the last heat of summer drained away. The cold, damp months would begin.

Kesta got to her feet, looking around for Fox. The place where they had slept was on a rise and all the rain from the previous night had run down into a nearby stream. It rushed by, heavy with water. Kesta walked down the slope to the stream, stretching her arms. Her feet, still in her riding boots, slipped a little on the wet grass and she trod carefully.

Reaching the water's edge, Kesta knelt, feeling the water bubbling up over the shallow bank to soak the knees of her riding breeches. She drank deeply, despite the cold.

Glancing up at the branches of a tree, something caught her eye. Behind where the slender branches swayed with the breeze, she could make out a haze of smoke, drifting across the long hill above where she and Fox had slept. At first Kesta barely thought about it. She went back up the slope to fetch one of the bottles they were using for water, when the thought struck her.

Smoke meant a fire. A fire meant people. People meant...

Kesta started to run, now looking for Fox in earnest. She slipped over as she reached the crown of the little hill, landing hard in the wet grass. Looking up, she could see Riversteel's proud outline against the sky. Fox was slipping out of the saddle, laughing, but not unkindly.

'In a hurry? I'd walk carefully if I was you, I can't have you breaking anything before anyone even lifts a battle-cry! Are you all right?' He helped her up, smiling warmly.

'I'm fine,' Kesta kept her voice hushed as she spoke, motioning for Fox to speak quietly. 'Fox, I think there's somebody just on the other side of this ridge. See?' She pointed at the faint clouds of smoke rising above the trees. The smoke was plainly visible behind the naked branches.

Fox's expression froze, and he pulled Riversteel in closer, whispering in the horse's ears for quiet. The patient beast put his head down, appearing to understand the command. In the silence that followed, the only noises were the birdsong and the stream. Then, very faintly, another sound could be heard. Both Fox and Kesta stiffened as they heard voices on the breeze.

For a moment Fox seemed to have become paralysed. His eyes glazed over as if he were somewhere else. A moment later he blinked and shook his head, shock registering on his face. The look was quickly taken over by a thoughtful smile, but still he raised his hand to keep the silence constant.

'There are five men on the other side of the ridge. They don't know we're here, but they are expecting travellers like us.' Fox grinned at Kesta's reaction to his words. 'I can see them in my head. I... stretched my mind out beyond the hill. I haven't done that before! What do you suppose they are doing?'

Kesta closed her gaping mouth, feeling foolish. She should be used to Fox's many abilities by now. She shrugged.

'Maybe they're refugees, or woodsmen. They could be Tiger's men, don't you think?'

Fox shook his head. 'We're not close enough to Tiger's castle for that. I think they are waiting for us.'

Kesta looked at the trailing smoke, puzzled. 'I thought you said they didn't know we were here?'

'I did.'

'I don't understand, why would they be waiting for us if they don't know about us?' She waited for his answer. Fox walked quietly over to their groundsheet. He crouched to pick up his staff and her bow.

'They've been told that we'll be using this road. Someone doesn't want us meeting with Tiger.'

Kesta paused in realisation. 'Ox spies?' she asked, her eyes roving across the outline of the ridge as she took her bow from Fox. Her heart began to beat faster. *Would she have to fight?*

Fox shrugged, straightening up. He began to walk up the slope, a hand out in case he slipped. Looking over his shoulder he whispered an answer. 'We'll soon find out!'

The five men were languishing around a fire they had built in the early hours of the morning. All of them were soaking wet and thoroughly miserable. They had not come out on this mission properly prepared for bad weather. Their leader wriggled closer to the fire, listening to the argument beginning amongst his men. Two of them were for turning back, their target had probably taken another road, and there was no point in waiting around in the damp.

The leader hated failure. He had come determined to bring back the head of the prince to his employer. Winter was almost upon them, he reflected, as he wrung out his wet sleeves. They would need the money if they were to outlast the snows that were inevitable in this part of the world. Looking up, he watched the trail of smoke rise into the grey sky.

'Put it out, you fools!' It was a dreadful mistake. The man cursed himself as his men hurriedly scattered the fire in different directions, throwing the soaked groundsheet they had slept on over the embers. 'If they've seen the smoke they will have taken another route!' The man pulled his sword from under the ground sheet, which lay steaming over the remnants of the fire. He slid it quickly onto his belt, looking around in disgust at the result of his blunder.

Waving for his men to follow, the mercenary wriggled over to the edge of the drop they had slept by. Below was the hill trail. The mud there was thick and the man saw with relief that there were no footprints or hoof prints in the damp soil. He would wait here all day if he had to.

'Chief!' One of the mercenaries wriggled up beside him. 'Chief, I'm sure I saw something just now. On the ridge behind us. Chief?' The leader turned quickly, looking up at the line of winter-bare trees on the ridge above them.

'There's nothing there, Falkin. Keep your eyes on the road!' They were too jumpy, he reflected. Next time he would choose his men more carefully.

Suddenly, Falkin pointed, restraining a cry that threatened to give them away. The scout's quick eyes had seen the boy, walking alone along the waterlogged path. The mercenary leader ducked reflexively, hiding his face behind the rock they were using as cover. He turned to his men, grinning with excitement.

'When I give the word, boys! One charge and we'll have him, wait for my word!' Falkin blanched, peering over the edge of the slope.

'Sir! He's only a boy, are you sure–'

'Hush!' The mercenary glanced over the edge himself. The boy was almost a stone's throw away. 'That's the prince, all right.

They described him well. Ready, boys?' The mercenaries tensed, readying themselves for the charge.

'Now!' As one, the men rose and surged forwards, running down the steep and slippery slope towards Fox. Behind her tree, looking down from the ridge, Kesta drew in a sharp intake of breath. Turning, and struggling to stop her hands from shaking, she drew back the bowstring, feeling the soft feather and hard wood between her fingers.

Pull back to your ear. Aim along the shaft. Deep breath... And release!

Falkin was the last to rise for the attack, and the first to fall. Kesta's arrow struck him hard; the shaft went straight through the back of his neck, the arrowhead protruding suddenly from his throat. The man gurgled horribly, confusion and realisation crossing his features as he began to die. The others didn't notice the death of their comrade, they rushed blindly on, lifting their swords to attack Fox, just a boy turning towards them, raising a stick in his defence.

Kesta's hand drew back a second time and a second time released an arrow. This time her aim was not as confident, shaken as she was by seeing a man die at her hands. The shaft hissed through the air with violent ease, sinking into another man's shoulder. He cried out with pain when the arrow bit into him, and again, when Fox brought his staff round with astonishing speed, slamming the hard wood into the side of his head.

The staff whirled, making contact again, meeting flesh and bone with horrible force. Another mercenary went down, his knees broken, a third, dead with a broken neck.

Two remained. One of them was their leader, unable to understand what had just happened. It should have been an easy kill. A young prince, the description had said, barely a man, travelling without the security of his guards, alone in the hills.

There had been no warning of this.

The leader had never seen such speed and efficient violence from someone so young; the rapidity with which his men had been dispatched was horrifying.

Fox lifted his staff above his head, spinning it gently from hand to hand. The men before him were backing away in terror. There was another hiss and a meaty thud as an arrow sailed down from above, driving with finality into the chest of one of the men. He had turned to run, his arms still pumping as he fell, still trying to escape.

The leader snarled like a cornered animal, tightening his grip on his sword hilt. Fox moved aside easily as the man lunged at him. The staff swung twice more, hits to the back of the man's legs and to his chin.

Kesta came down the slope. She was shaking, walking past the bodies of the men she had killed. One of the bodies in the mud around Fox moaned; the man with the broken kneecaps still lived. Kesta watched with horrified fascination as Fox rolled him over.

'Who sent you? Tell me who sent you to kill me!' Fox commanded, keeping his voice clear and even. The man answered through a haze of pain.

'I... Not to say... I... supposed to tell you... Ox.'

'I thought so.' Fox stood. His expression was grim and distant but he turned and smiled at Kesta. 'Good shooting. You remembered what I said. Go and get Riversteel and our gear, no reason to stay any longer.' Kesta nodded, biting her lip. She felt sick and tried not to look at the bodies as she walked back along the path to the hill where they had slept.

Riversteel stepped gingerly around the bodies, shaking his mane with disgust. Kesta understood the horse's feelings. Fox was riding in front now, allowing Riversteel to have his head as they stepped away from the dead mercenaries. Fox ignored the delirious cries of the injured man as they went by. He was not in a mind to kill him, now that the heat of the fight had faded.

There was always the chance that he would survive, Fox thought, aware that he was justifying himself.

As they rounded the next corner into a steep incline higher into the hills, Kesta slipped from the saddle. She staggered to the side of the path and was violently sick in the long wet grass. Fox watched sympathetically. The first time he had killed he had felt the same way. He remembered the hot blood that had flowed across his hand as his sword cut deep in that first desperate thrust, barely a month ago, in the battle of the East Wastes. He was cold now. Or perhaps distant. The deaths seemed to happen a long way away.

They went deeper into the hills as the day wore on. On the straighter stretches Fox allowed Riversteel to break into a gallop, only reigning him in when the path twisted and became loose and stony. The dark came on fast in the hills. There were plenty of great stones and boulders to cast shade, and the sun vanished quickly behind the tree-line, silencing the chattering birds.

Fox brought Riversteel to a stop beneath a slight overhang where a great boulder protruded from the side of the hill, providing a little cover from the wind. Fox and Kesta unpacked. Riversteel waited for them to finish, pulling up the long grass that grew below the rock-face.

Fox and Kesta sat down against the cool stone, letting Riversteel wander along the path a little so that he could find more grass. The air was full of the scent of damp moss.

'We should have brought some dry food for him.' Fox watched Riversteel munching on the damp grass. The horse, however, seemed unconcerned with the humidity of his food as he chewed on contentedly, his tail swishing from side to side.

'He looks all right to me,' Kesta said, turning over one of the bags to find some food, 'maybe we should have brought more for us. This won't last long.' Fox glanced down at the hard biscuits she was handing him and wrinkled his nose.

'Good point. I think we should do a little foraging tomorrow evening, before it gets dark. Thank you.'

He took the biscuits and the chewy, dried strips of beef, unable to successfully feign gratitude. Kesta laughed at his expression. 'Your eyebrow goes up when you're pretending. Sort of a quirky slant.' She smiled at him, before looking away, blushing. He grinned at her, only a little embarrassed by her personal observation.

Fox put his head on one side, studying her face. Kesta met his eyes. In the end he seemed to give up and simply said, 'Your cheeks are colouring.' Kesta shrugged.

'So are yours.' She pushed her hair back behind her ear, trying to find something to do with her hands.

'Ah! Got you! You play with your hair when you're embarrassed!'

'I'm not embarrassed,' she replied, her blush deepening. Fox laughed at her denial, pushing her away playfully.

'Liar!'

Kesta changed the subject, feeling uncomfortable. She glanced up at the sky. 'It's getting dark. We should probably try to sleep.'

Fox nodded, looking away. 'Agreed.'

'River! Come here River.' Riversteel wandered back to the rock face as if it had been his idea, still chewing on the long grass. Fox jumped up and whispered in the horse's ear as he tied him to the root of a young tree. Riversteel lay down obediently.

Fox returned to where the oilskin was laid down. Kesta was already tying up the second one, attaching it to the top of the overhang, then pegging it to the ground. Fox bent under the top sheet and sat down in the makeshift tent. Both of them lay down, using the blankets they had brought to keep the cold at bay.

'Goodnight,' Fox said, reaching for one of the bags to use as a pillow.

'Mmm.' Kesta was already half asleep.

Kesta's dreams took her back over the ridge where she had shot the two mercenaries. She dreamed that the men were calling to her, accusing her of murdering them. The dream passed quickly and their faces faded as she slept.

Fox's dreams were full of the usual torture, images he didn't understand and didn't want to. Blood and fear and darkness filled his mind, enough to drive a weaker person into madness.

Fox was not weak. He had learnt to cope with the nightly onslaught, although every night it became harder, the images more vivid, the fear more pressing and urgent.

A new dream entered Fox's head. This one was different from the usual rush of evil. It was a simple dream of anxiety. The dream was blurred and confused, it had something to do with Kesta, Kesta, in danger. He was wading through water, or mud. He was very afraid of death, but not his own – he felt the need to protect her.

Fox slept on, the night quiet around him, except for the distant sound of animals hunting.

The next morning neither of the two remembered their dreams. Together they finished the biscuits and beef, and changed their clothes, one at a time going up on top of the overhang for privacy. There was no stream nearby to wash at, and at any rate it was far too cold. The change of clothing was the best alternative.

Riversteel was eager to be untied, the morning was chilly and he wanted to move around. Kesta packed away the groundsheets while Fox changed. The sun still hadn't appeared in the eastern sky when they set off, still travelling north.

Riversteel trotted along the hill path. The cold had worn off since sun-up and Kesta had stopped shivering. She reached behind her, checking that her bow was still on her back. The path wound ahead, sometimes ascending, other times dropping into gullies. Now and then they passed streams. Kesta was sure some of them would not have been there before the rains had begun.

The day went slowly. Now and then Fox decided to give Riversteel a rest; he climbed down out of the saddle and he and Kesta walked beside the horse. There were more trees as they journeyed on, hardy, gnarly pines and spruces. That evening Fox foraged in a copse of the great evergreens, bringing back some edible mushrooms for them to stew. Kesta found the time to get out her wing-swords and practice with them, watched closely by Fox.

Over the next three days the journey continued in the same way. Fox managed to catch some rabbits to go with the mushrooms. On the sixth day of their journey the rain returned, storming in over the hills in great rolling banks of heavy cloud. They ate the last of the rabbit and mushroom stew sheltering in a pine forest at the top of one of the hills.

Kesta felt tired and wet, frustrated that they had not made better time. According to Fox they should have arrived at Tiger's castle that evening, but would now not be able to eat well or bathe until tomorrow. Kesta had used the two pairs of clothes she had with her three times now – one of the hemp shirts had torn climbing through brambles and all of her clothes were wet, dirty and decidedly unpleasant to wear. There were few ways in which her situation could be less comfortable.

Kesta was used to feeling hungry. Her family had run out of food before the Ox soldiers had arrived and killed her mother; since the beginning of the war she and her sisters had been hungry, giving most of their food to their mother when she had fallen ill.

Hugging herself tight against the rain that dripped from the branches above, Kesta thought about her dead family and felt like crying as the water ran down her neck.

Fox sat close beside her, the protective feeling from his dream on his mind. He couldn't remember the dream, but he recognised the feeling and put his arm around Kesta's shoulders. The wave of emotion in her broke and she cried desperately, the first time she had really mourned the death of her family. She leaned in against Fox's side, her body shaking as she wept.

In the forest a wolf howled.

Riversteel clambered to his feet, his eyes rolling with terror.

Fox stiffened. The howl came again but this time it was much closer, barely ten metres away. Riversteel neighed loudly and snapped his tether. Fox saw the horse disappear in a panic, going for the path. All Riversteel's ardent loyalty from the time of the chase seemed forgotten. Fox stood hurriedly, pulling Kesta to her feet, hating himself for doing it, but not willing to risk being set upon. Kesta stopped crying and fumbled for her bow. Looking around into the deepening gloom, Fox used the neck of her shirt to wipe away her tears, her own hands were busy stringing the bow, and he didn't want her to ruin the bowstring.

Fox lifted his hand. A glow rushed along his fingers towards the centre of his upraised palm. As the glowing lines met, a flame sprung up and gathered strength. Soon a fire too bright to look at blazed away on the palm of Fox's hand. He gritted his teeth, straining to keep the flame alive. Among the trees, several pairs of gleaming eyes reflected the fire. The lupine bodies behind the eyes slunk back, out of range of the light.

Fox swore and let the fire go out. In the sudden dark both he and Kesta blinked, unable to see anything but the vague shapes of trees. In the blackness one of the wolves moved, gliding forwards like a ghost, running low to the ground, ready to spring. Again the flame sparked into life in Fox's hand. The wolf froze, caught in the flood of light, before being sent tumbling with an arrow in its eye. Before the light faded again Fox and Kesta could see the wolves slinking away. The depths of winter were still to come, and none of the wolves were yet hungry enough to attack dangerous prey.

Fox listened to the sounds of the animals disappearing into the gloom with immense relief. If they had been great-wolves, the situation could have turned out very differently. He picked up the empty food satchels as Kesta slid back down into a sitting position, her back against the tree. She put her head in her hands, feeling desperately tired.

Fox made fire a third and final time, setting alight to the useless bags. By heaping pine needles onto the fledgling blaze he made a fire big enough to warm any wet branches he could find.

Watching the fire burn, Fox sat down and put his arm back around Kesta. She smiled sadly at him. 'I'm missing my ma, and my sisters. I don't think I'll ever see my home again.'

Fox tried to smile sympathetically, feeling more than a little useless. He opened his mouth to say something, but found he had nothing he could say. The fire burnt down slowly in front of the two, keeping the wolves away until daylight.

7
The Tigress

Kesta woke up coughing. She stumbled to her feet, leaning against the rough bark. There was an ugly taste of smoke in her mouth and her bare arms and the backs of her hands were sticky with smoke residue and smears of ash. The fire had burnt down to a little heap of grey and red embers. The rain was persisting; Kesta could feel it dripping down from the branches above.

The forest seemed less threatening in the daylight. To her great relief Kesta saw Riversteel standing amongst the trees, looking as doleful as herself. She walked stiffly over to him, certain that the wet weather had given her a cold. She patted Riversteel's neck, looking back at the tree, where Fox still lay asleep.

Kesta woke him by touching his arm. He jerked awake, looking around for the wolves that had hunted him in his dreams. The forest was quiet; the only sound was of water dripping from the evergreen branches above. Fox let Kesta help him to his feet. He felt tired. The body of the wolf they had killed lay a short distance away, Kesta's arrow protruding from its skull. Fox felt a sudden stab of regret for the wolf's necessary death. He smiled wearily at Kesta. 'Riversteel came back then.'

Tiger's castle was seated on a tor which rose from the sea of evergreens and bamboo. The trees grew all the way up to the walls of the castle, in some places brushing their branches up against the rough stone. The impressive rock heights formed the foundation of the castle's structure, while the upper levels were built from timber. A great triangular roof, stained a deep red, topped the castle. The upper structure, detailed partly with thick bamboo, was stained the same colour, as if it had run down the walls from the roof, giving a defined contrast between the red walls and the green forest surrounding it. Flying from the many gates was the Tiger flag, the simplistic shape of a leaping tiger, also in red, on a dark green fore.

The gate ahead was open. The impressive pair of doors were detailed with fighting tigers. The whole expanse of wood was heavily lacquered, making it fire resistant and very durable. Fox and Kesta glanced at one another in trepidation before leading Riversteel out from the tree line.

An argument was in full swing in the gateway as Fox and Kesta approached. A young rider was sitting in the saddle looking out into the forest, pointedly ignoring the robed man who was attempting to hold her back. The rider, who had long, thick, fiery red hair, rolled her eyes as the man tugged at her leg. She turned in the saddle to confront him.

'Please, Tigress, you went riding yesterday! Come in, come down please. Ouch!' The richly dressed man jumped back looking angry, the girl had just kicked out at him. Fox and Kesta could hear her forceful reply easily; behind them, pigeons took flight in alarm.

'Oh, be quiet, Hadran. Go back inside and get fat like the rest of your rat friends! If I want to go riding, I *will* go riding!' The girl shook back her fiery hair and pulled away, clucking soothingly to her nervous horse. The man grabbed at the reins, determined to make himself heard.

'Please, Tigress! Last time you went riding you didn't come back until the next day. Do you remember the time you spent three days out there? We were afraid you had been taken by the wolves.'

'Pah! Those dogs couldn't get near me if I was tied to a tree with my eyes blindfolded. I was fine.'

'Tigress! You came back with a broken wrist! It took months to heal fully, and then off you go again, another day in the forest, ruining our hard work. Please, come in and talk to your father.'

Fox glanced at Kesta with his eyebrows raised. Kesta struggled not to smile. The two of them stepped closer until they stood with Riversteel, squarely in the way of the girl and her horse. She turned to look at them and her thunderous expression changed instantly. Kesta drew back instinctively as the girl slid out of the saddle and came to meet them.

Fox began to bow but she seized his hand and shook it vigorously. She smiled, flashing near perfect teeth at the two of them. 'Good timing.' She looked around at the exasperated man behind her as she whispered to them, 'I don't know who you are, but now I have an excuse to get away from this fool.'

Fox smiled. 'Glad to be of help. I'm Crown Prince Fox, son of Steel Fox of the Autumn Hills. Your Highness.' The Tigress nodded as if he'd said something quite unremarkable. She looked at Kesta, her eyebrows raised questioningly.

'I'm Kesta. Prince Fox's shield-maid.' Kesta said. She glanced at Fox, wondering at the girl's brisk, informal manner. The girl grinned.

'I'm the Tigress Taneshka, but if you call me Tigress, I'll ignore you. You've never visited before!' She added brightly as she turned, walking with them back through the gate and signalling for the man to take the horses.

Fox and Kesta listened to the heir apparent of the Tiger family as they walked through the twisting inner roads leading to the keep, which rose forbiddingly out of the mist. The Tigress talked cheerfully and waved to passers-by, as if she were a villager on the way to market. A few people called out to her, with more familiarity than any peasant would have addressed Fox.

Taneshka was the only child in the Tiger family. Her mother had died giving birth to her. Taneshka talked about this in a simple, matter-of-fact way, comfortable despite the personal subject. She asked a lot of questions about the plains as they got closer to the keep; she had never left her region and spent most of her time doing the two things that Hadran and his fellow advisors hated most: learning to fight, and disappearing into the forests for long periods of time.

Fox listened intently, finding the conversation of great interest. When he asked why the advisors looked down on Taneshka's need to learn the arts of combat, she simply replied that they didn't want her to go to war and die on a battlefield. Fox thought that understandable, as she was the only heir. Taneshka smiled and explained that when her father died the family's land would be annexed to that of whichever Lord who could offer her a good marriage. The Advisory Council here refused to allow a woman to accede the throne.

The three walked along the ornate but worn corridors of Tiger's castle, Fox and Taneshka deep in conversation and Kesta listening, feeling slightly left out.

Taneshka led them into a large, cool room wherein a great rectangular table dominated the floor space. A man sat at the head, a man resembling Taneshka but not looking like the king Fox had expected.

He had red-brown hair and was dressed in leather working clothes. There was a bow lying on the table at his right hand. The man looked up when they entered, pushing aside a plate of cold meat and standing.

'I see Hadran dissuaded you from another sojourn in the forest, daughter of mine.'

Taneshka looked insulted. 'He did no such thing, Father. I decided to come back of my own accord.' She grinned cheekily at her father's disapproving expression. He broke into a smile at her impudence and turned to Fox and Kesta.

'Of course. After all you had to introduce our guests, am I right?' He extended a hand to Fox and then Kesta, using the same informal greeting as his daughter.

'I am Tiger of the Pine Hills.' He looked darkly to the west for a moment and then sat, gesturing for Fox and Kesta to do the same. Fox thought that the man looked a little tired, as if he had been sleeping badly.

Tiger passed his untouched plate of breakfast to them and smiled approvingly as they fell upon it hungrily, forgetting all etiquette. 'Don't tell me you got lost in our forests. The amount of visitors we lose to falls or the wolves, it's unthinkable. So. What is the purpose of your visit?'

Taneshka looked up at her father. She was playing idly with a knife from the tabletop and said in even tones: 'Father, this is Prince Fox.' Tiger's eyes widened. His expression of cheerful light-heartedness changed immediately and Fox could see at once that Rice Tiger had just dropped an act, one he must have found wearisome, because now he seemed relieved despite his concern. He leaned forward to look Fox in the eye.

'I have been waiting for months for your uncle to send word. I was dreadfully afraid that I am no longer considered a friend of your family, there has been no communication between us for so long.'

Fox nodded and apologised, 'I'm sorry, my king, but it could not be helped. It is not long since I was in the lines of battle in the south, it was only once I returned that I realised how much I had been kept in the dark.

'The advisors never wanted me to know about their plans, and thought to prevent me from seeing their purpose when I reappeared. I think they thought I was dead and now I am sure that is what they intended when they sent me into battle: the ancestors of the Dragon family are anxious that the ancient family's bloodlines are kept noble. I am, it seems, not noble enough for them.'

Tiger looked thoughtfully across at his daughter for a moment. 'My advisors are also claiming that the First Family would never have allowed a woman to rule. It shows their ignorance of course, one of the daughters of Dominago was a mighty general, and the favourite of King Dragon himself. But perhaps they have forgotten such inconvenient facts. After all, it was so long ago.'

Tiger smiled reassuringly at Fox. 'I believe there is more to nobility than lineage. The woman general I mentioned was a heartless killer, by all accounts. Not a noble virtue, yet she was as much a Dragon as her father, and her mother, who was his mother as well.' Tiger shuddered at the thought. Kesta had been reaching for another piece of the cold chicken, but now she withdrew her hand feeling slightly ill.

'No, there was little nobility amongst the "First Family."' Tiger looked back at Fox, smiling. 'I have no doubt that there is a peasant or two in my ancestry, and I am glad of it. You would be my choice to succeed Steel Fox, even if both your birth parents were pig keepers.'

'Thank you,' Fox said, and meant it, he had long dismissed the thought of his real mother and father from his mind, afraid of what it might mean.

'What is being done about Ox?' Taneshka pushed the point of the blade into the wood as she spoke, as if by doing so she could cause the faraway king an injury. Fox opened his mouth to answer, but at that moment three men came hurrying through the door at the end of the room. It was plain from the self-importance on their faces that they could only be advisors, even though they were not as richly dressed as Henshin and his associates.

Kesta felt herself sitting straighter in a kind of defiance at their presence and was pleased to see Taneshka do the same. The red haired Tigress was staring with fierce resentment at the three men. They ignored her, but Kesta sensed that none of them wanted to meet the young Tigress' eyes and instead moved towards the head of the table where Tiger sat. The one walking at the front was the man from the gate. Kesta wondered if he could be related to Henshin, as he had a similar look about him, but perhaps it was only the arrogance they shared.

'We didn't realise that there was a meeting, my lord Tiger. Naturally we came as soon as we could.' Hadran smiled and seated himself. The other two copied him, even down to his smile. Tiger seemed to be waiting for them to say something. 'Oh please, continue,' Hadran urged, 'I shall gladly advise you once I have listened to the conversation for a time. Act as if I weren't here.'

'If only you weren't,' Taneshka said pointedly. Hadran just laughed politely, as if the Tigress had made a joke. He smiled around the table pleasantly, hiding his impatience to hear their conversation. Fox paused, trying to think of what to say concerning Ox. In the end he looked up at Tiger and continued.

'Nothing has been done about Ox as yet. However, war is inevitable and the only choices we have are as to where and how we fight. And the time needed to make that choice is running out.'

Tiger nodded. 'I have been anxious to discuss this with someone from your uncle. I have little in the way of men and without a guarantee of a strong ally I would be foolish to send the troops I do have into battle. Ideally I would like to meet Ox at the Twin Valley Ridge, the promontory would be an excellent place to position my archers. Of course, without a lot more soldiers any attempt to hold the valleys is doomed.'

Tiger looked questioningly at Fox. Fox stood, his hands flat on the wooden surface of the table. 'I am here partly because Kesta suggested that we should ask for your help. I agree that the Twin Valley Ridge is the only place where we stand any chance of victory. My lord Tiger, will you ally yourself with us and commit men and resources to end the reign of Danashalk Ox?' He stood straight and asked the question that he would have dreaded being asked. Even now he was afraid of the answer, knowing that his fortunes and almost certainly his life hung in the balance.

Tiger stood too.

Hadran raised a hand to his face in a thoughtful manner, but it was obvious from his expression that he had made his mind up. 'I would consider it inadvisable to agree, my lord,' Hadran said calmly, not even looking at Fox.

Tiger seemed not to have heard his advisor. He stared at Fox with a searching intensity that would have turned down the gaze of most others.

'Renew the old alliance? Re-forge the partnership of our forefathers? Their weapons lie broken in their graves. It is said that the sword of your great grandfather lies entombed with my own grandfather, whose bow likewise lies in his ally's grave. They fought as brothers, and died as brothers, Fox and Tiger. Since their deaths the alliance has crumbled. But here! Here is a chance to resurrect it. My people are close to starvation. There could be no worse a time.'

Tiger looked at his daughter, glowing with melancholy pride and affection. 'There is no future for the Tiger family. Our flame dwindles. When I die they tell me that my name will cease to exist. They say that Tiger will be forgotten because his daughter will take the name of whoever she marries.' He looked up suddenly, meeting Fox's gaze with fierce pride. 'If the Tiger ends with me, it will end with teeth bared and claws out. It will die fighting! Everyone will see its end and remember. I will ally myself with you, Fox. I will meet Ox at the Twin Valley Ridge.'

The room Fox and Kesta had been given was a good size and like most of the interior sparsely but comfortably furnished. There were two beds, both side-on to the door. Kesta had taken the one closest to the door out of habit.

On the wall above the headboards was a tapestry showing a leaping tiger. It was made from good cloth but was very old; the colours were faded, but the tapestry was still beautiful to look at. Neither Fox or Kesta had ever seen a tiger, but the flowing muscles of the striped predator were stitched in brilliant detail and the creature seemed about to leap out of the weave.

The wall opposite the door was broken by a heavy bamboo curtain that led onto a balcony. Kesta went across to the curtain and swept it aside with her left hand, looking out onto the rippling sea of dark green trees. Kesta appreciated the bamboo screen; it was cold and likely to get colder.

Fox went through to breathe the fresh air on the balcony while Kesta unpacked their possessions. There were few things of importance or value left in the old saddlebag. After the tattered and filthy clothes that they had worn to pieces there was nothing for Kesta to unpack, apart from her weapons.

While checking her wing-swords, Kesta noticed a spear attached to the wall. In fact, it was hard to miss. It was very long, with a thick, strong shaft. Embossed tigers paced the length of the dark, polished wood. The spearhead was a long, leaf shaped blade, beautifully crafted from strong steel. One of its edges was serrated; the tiny teeth running along the curve of the blade looked ferociously sharp. The weapon was obviously battle ready and well looked after.

The door opened and the Tigress Taneshka walked casually into the room. Fox's head appeared through the bamboo curtain to check who it was as Kesta stood. Taneshka saw Kesta examining the spear.

'You found Tiger's Fang then.' Her eyes lit up as she went over to the wall, lifting the great spear down. It was too long to hold upright and even when horizontal the spear touched both walls. 'She's mine,' Taneshka said with quiet pride, 'Father gave her to me when I turned fourteen. I'm probably tall enough to use her now. If the advisors let me, damn them.'

She looked up and smiled brightly. 'I hope you like the room. It gets cold in the middle of winter but it should be all right for at least a month. I've brought some clothes for you both, because tomorrow I'm taking you hunting, whatever Hadran says. You can both shoot, of course?'

Fox nodded and frowned. 'Are you sure we have time? I thought there were things to do.' Taneshka looked at him for a moment and explained.

'The archers are still in the hills and won't be back until late tomorrow, so there isn't anything we can do yet. However, if we go hunting in the morning, in the afternoon we can walk to the Loop.' Kesta and Fox gave her bemused looks.

'It's a tributary of the river Lifeblood. It flows south but, well, makes a loop shape towards the north. Heron's trading boats use it to meet our traders. Not that we have much to trade.'

Fox came and sat down on the edge of his bed. 'I thought you made lacquer here.'

'Oh, yes, I suppose we do. We can make pretty much unlimited quantities of the stuff; the trees grow all throughout this region. We send a lot of it south, we trade it for their iron.' Taneshka sat down on Kesta's bed, resting Tiger's Fang against her shoulder. 'We lacquer a lot of our armour, same as you do. Arrows bounce off and you really need to make an effort to get a sword through. It costs though, because the lacquer we use for that can't be used in trade and half the time we spend our time bartering for rice and livestock. We've got nothing to eat but chickens and forest pigs up here.'

Taneshka talked about the little isolated villages that lay abandoned in the forests, left to the wolves. She described the mountains bordering Tiger country to the north, snow-capped and mighty, wreathed in cloud. She spoke quietly of a great lake between Rice Fox's territory and her father's, surrounded in mists. Fox and Kesta listened as the Tigress described all of her lands in fond detail. Outside the sun began to slide over the horizon, leaving its scarlet stain washed across the pale sky.

Kesta listened with her eyes closed and her head nodding as sleep reached out to embrace her. Taneshka kept talking until she could see Fox beginning to lose concentration due to tiredness. Then she stood and said goodnight, smiling good-humouredly as Kesta slipped backwards onto her pillow, completely asleep. She nodded to Fox as she left the room, closing the door behind her carefully. Fox lay back in the half dark, his eyes already closing. He hadn't realised how tired he was. As his mind swam into the dark domain of his dreams, half formed plans and thoughts rose lazily to the surface, only to vanish as sleep took him completely.

The Shadow runs west along the bank of the Lifeblood. The Land cries out in pain as the Shadow steps into the water, polluting the clear depths with dead liquid, swimming with rot.

The Dreamer moves in his sleep as the Shadow strides out. Foul water begins to overpower the river's flow. The Shadow crosses onto the northern bank, unscathed and triumphant. The Land shudders, poison threading its way into the artery of the river. The Dreamer seizes up with pain, feeling the Land's torment rolling throughout his body, even as the pollution begins to dilute.

The Land's pain sinks back and the Dreamer sinks back, into his bed.

The Dreamer sleeps.

8
Leaves And Bear-blood

It was still dark when Taneshka woke Fox and Kesta by knocking on their door. Kesta looked around the dark room before sitting up, pushing the warm blankets away. Cold air met the bare skin of her arms and she began to shiver. She kicked off the rest of her covers and quickly got out of bed, hugging herself to stop her teeth chattering as she opened the door to Taneshka, her bare feet numbed by the cold floorboards.

Taneshka grinned cheerfully at her as she stepped into the room. Fox groaned and rolled over in his bed so that he was looking at the ceiling through half closed eyes. 'It's still dark!' he protested, frowning angrily at the ceiling, 'and it's *freezing*!' Taneshka laughed.

'It's around the fourth hour. You've been sleeping for about seven. Come on! We're going hunting, remember?' Fox muttered something and sat up, swinging his legs over the edge of the bed. His covers slipped off as he rubbed the back of his neck grumpily and both Kesta and Taneshka spun hurriedly in the doorway. Taneshka pulled the door closed behind her, so that both she and Kesta were standing in the corridor. She grinned with amusement, calling over her shoulder: 'We'll wait out here for you, all right?'

'Fine, fine,' Fox answered resignedly from inside the room, trying to pull on his clothes in the dark.

Taneshka was wearing a thick, brown leather coat over dull green cloth. The inside of the coat was fleeced and looked a good deal warmer than the thin nightdress Kesta was wearing. Taneshka was wearing forest-green trousers and high, watertight deerskin boots. On her back was an oiled roll of leather, held on with a strap, where her bow and quiver were kept safe from rainwater.

Taneshka looked down at Kesta's apparel. 'You aren't planning to go hunting like that, are you?'

Kesta looked down at herself and shook her head, smiling sheepishly. 'All the clothes you brought me are in there.'

As if to confirm this, Fox's voice called out from inside the room, 'Kesta, all your new clothes are on your bed. Taneshka, do you have a spare hunting jacket? I've got the one borrowed from your father, but Kesta hasn't one.'

'Yes. Stay here, I'll run and find one.'

Kesta watched as Taneshka ran quickly and quietly down the dark corridor. She turned and knocked on the door. 'Fox? Can I come in? I'd like to get dressed. It's very cold out here.' Fox opened the door. He was still pulling on a shirt as Kesta entered the room.

Kesta went through to the balcony to change. It was far colder on the frosted boards, but it was better than changing in the room with Fox, or in the corridor. She pulled on a silk shirt and then a thicker hempen one, before wriggling into some oiled hunting leathers. She was just examining her weary looking boots and wishing she had something warmer and dryer, when Taneshka poked her head through the bamboo curtain. She was holding a leather coat much like the one she was wearing, as well as another pair of boots.

'Here, I thought you might like some better footwear. It's bound to be damp where we're going.' Kesta was about to ask where that might be, but Taneshka pulled her head back through the curtain. Kesta could hear her talking to Fox on the other side, and hurried to put on the coat and boots. Once she pulled tight the laces at the neck of the thick, fleecy jacket she felt much warmer and stood for a moment, looking out at the dark forest below, her breath coming in puffs of silver mist.

Fox and Taneshka joined her on the balcony. Fox passed her bow to her and they all stood looking out on the quiet, cold woods. Finally Fox stepped back from the rail and turned towards the curtain. 'Are we going to go, or not?' Taneshka turned.

'Yes. Where are you going?' she smiled mischievously at the bemused look on his face, before explaining. 'We're going to take the roof. We don't want Hadran waking up and telling us we can't go into the forests now, do we? Father is worried that you are in some kind of danger. It's just a feeling he has, but he doesn't want you to leave the castle. Not that he'd interfere. Not that he'll find out!'

Fox and Kesta glanced at one another, wondering how much Tiger knew about Fox and his pursuer. Then more immediate thoughts entered their minds. Fox looked out over the rail at the shadowy roof in trepidation. Kesta's expression mirrored his own. There was no sign on Taneshka's face that she was joking. She waited with eyebrows raised for one of them to say something, before swinging a leg over the rail and dropping onto the tiles. Fox grinned nervously at Kesta and followed.

The three made their way down the sloping roof to where the forest came closest to the outcrop of rock that supported the castle walls. Taneshka went to the very edge of the roof and peered casually over. Below her was a spur of the dark, natural stone that enclosed the wall, five or six feet below the eaves. Turning to Kesta, Taneshka took her bow, placing it in the leather roll on her back. Then she got down on her knees, facing away from the edge, and slid her legs over. She dangled for a moment, her feet hanging in the air, before letting go and finding the surface of the rock a few inches below.

Fox and Kesta followed with Taneshka guiding them. Soon, all three of them stood on the spur of stone. There were natural footholds down through the jumbled rock formation. Taneshka began to negotiate the harsh stone and once again they followed her, hands searching in the dark for safe purchase.

About half way down Kesta slipped, grazing the palm of her hand. Her arms shot out in different directions as she fell forwards, searching desperately for something to break her fall. She cannoned into the back of Fox who let out a muffled yell, but miraculously stayed upright. He half turned in the dark and touched her cheek to make sure he knew where she was. Kesta fought back the urge to hug him, her mind still reeling from the sudden rush of fear.

'You all right?' Fox asked quietly. Taneshka looked up, the concern on her face mirroring Fox. He squeezed Kesta's arm. 'Did you hurt yourself?'

'No. I'm all right, I just grazed my hand, that's all. Don't worry, I can still shoot!' Fox laughed quietly, relieved. They continued to make their descent as before, although Fox kept a reassuring hand on Kesta's arm, guiding her to the handholds he had just used. It was unnecessary, Kesta reflected; the going was easier now. Not that she was complaining.

They took a break once their feet met the cold hard ground. Taneshka grinned at them both. 'How do you like that for a back door?' Fox leant back against the stone.

'It's...unusual. How often do you use it?' Taneshka shook her head.

'First time. Good though. I expect I'll use it again. How are you holding up, Kesta? Is it deep?' She stepped forward to inspect the palm of Kesta's hand. It was only a graze, as Kesta had told her.

Once again they turned to look at the forbidding shape of the forest. The first trees were only a few feet away, rising up like grim and silent sentinels, branches moving slowly with the wind. Taneshka couldn't help but smile. To her, the darkness between the thick net of life was an escape. She could sink into its organic weave and become herself, truly herself. Her eyes shone brightly with excitement and she couldn't stop grinning. She turned to her two new friends and opened her arms. 'Are we ready? Come, there's no better time than now! Follow me.'

The three walked into the gloom between the trees, the hard, frost-ridden ground turning to crisp, frozen leaf-pile, and the thick matting of pine needles.

They had been walking for at least an hour when it began to get lighter. The few patches of sky that were visible between the branches had turned grey. It was very cold now, a chill brought on by the dew's damp mixing with the cold air. There had been no sight of anything to hunt since they had entered the forest, yet Taneshka surged onwards, her feet skirting the tangles of dead branches and the occasional pitfalls that lay concealed by the leafmould.

It was almost full daylight when Taneshka stopped and sat down on the trunk of a fallen tree. She leaned back and took a deep breath of the moist air. Fox sat down next to her, rubbing his hands together. Kesta joined him, pinching her numb cheeks. Her scar pained her and she rubbed it cautiously as she sat down on the rough bark.

Fox straightened his back and looked up at the lightening sky beyond the criss-crossing branches. 'So,' he started, turning to Taneshka, 'what are we hunting?' Taneshka pointed wordlessly across the clearing to a hollowed out mound made beneath the roots of an oak. There was a large hole burrowed in the side of it, half stuffed with leafmould.

'That,' Taneshka said simply. She took off the leather roll on her back and undid it, passing Kesta's bow to her. She took her own as well, selecting arrows carefully from a pouch in the soft leather satchel.

The two girls strung their bows in silence, began pushing arrows into the earth in front of them. Fox pulled his staff free from the belt on his back and looked at the hole, trying to work out what sort of animal lived there. Taneshka tried her bowstring for a moment and then, satisfied with it, checked the point of her first arrow against her thumb. Fox noticed that it wasn't a normal hunting arrow, but had a heavier, broader head. It was an arrow designed to pierce thick leather, and cause greater damage. At that moment Fox realised what they were hunting.

'We're going after a *bear*?' He asked incredulously, gripping his staff and looking at Taneshka as if she were mad. Kesta stiffened and nearly dropped her bow into the wet leaf mulch at her feet.

Taneshka nodded. 'He's just started his winter sleep. We aim for the head and neck, Kesta, and if he comes too close, Fox, give him a poke with your stick. If you can. Ready?'

'No!' Both Kesta and Fox answered, panicking. Fox frowned, the thought of killing an animal of this kind felt somehow wrong. His upbringing as a prince told him that animals were there to be hunted or tamed, yet something deeper told him that this kill was unnecessary. Aside from that, he had been told how dangerous bears were. It would be insanity to deliberately attack one.

Taneshka grinned again, the wild excited look in her eyes.

'No, wait. I don't want to do this,' Fox blurted out hurriedly, in a hushed voice. He put his staff back on his back. 'We don't need to do this, there's enough food at the castle, this is pointless. I'll not help you.' Taneshka looked at him for a moment and shrugged. She turned and walked over to the bear's burrow, her head held high. Fox and Kesta watched as Taneshka proceeded to kick the leaf pile that half concealed the entrance aside. Fox shook his head and stepped back to the edge of the clearing.

There was no sound for what seemed like an eternity. Finally the entrance was clear and Taneshka paused, peering in. Slowly, very slowly, she lifted her bow, nocking an arrow and carefully pulling back the string. Kesta tensed up. Taneshka licked her dry lips, took a deep breath and loosed the arrow.

There was a great bellowing sound. Taneshka jumped backwards, a mixture of fear and excitement on her face. She hurriedly nocked another arrow, stepping a good distance away from the bear's lair. Kesta drew back the string of her own bow, sighting along the shaft of her arrow. Another angry bellow sounded around the clearing, and like an enraged forest god, the bear lumbered into view.

Kesta loosed her arrow. The string's noise was followed by the meaty sound of the arrow punching a hole in fur and flesh. Kesta's arrow protruded from the thick folds of skin at the bear's neck, next to where Taneshka's arrow had struck. The bear rose onto its stumpy hind legs, pawing at its throat and booming out in frustration and pain. Taneshka's second arrow hit its shoulder as it turned, and suddenly the bear went forward as if it had also been fired from a bow. It lumbered forwards at tremendous speed, spreading its arms towards Taneshka.

Kesta reloaded desperately, pulling the string back and letting off a shot from pure instinct. Miraculously, the arrow struck the bear just above its eye. The creature rocked over onto its side, pawing at the shaft that was lodged in its skull. Fox gasped as Taneshka ran to the head of the bear and stood barely a yard away from it. With lightning speed another arrow was on Taneshka's string, and an arrow was buried up to its feathered flight, stuck fast in the bear's head.

No one spoke as the great animal's legs kicked feebly in the last moments of its life. Taneshka, certain that the bear now held no danger for her, crouched beside its heavy muzzle. She stroked the thick, coarse fur gently as the bear died, talking softly. She smoothed back the fur around its eyes, now matted with blood, with a sort of fondness that dispelled the brief and sudden violence that had run through her veins a moment ago.

'We never would have got you if you hadn't been asleep, eh? Rest again, old one. Rest again.' Fox turned away from the two huntresses. He had felt the bear pass on, a large, complex life energy. He was confused that Taneshka could so easily slaughter such a marvellous animal and then show such fond gentleness towards it as it died. He looked back at the bear's body, lying in the leaves, with the Tigress still stroking the great head. Taneshka looked up at him and smiled.

'I know him. I was out here in the spring, thought I'd try to take him and prove myself to the advisors. I was an idiot to try for him when he was so strong and alert. I barely got away, all I took back to the advisors was a broken wrist. Fell down on the way back! They *loved* that.' She rolled her eyes and looked back down at her quarry.

Fox and Kesta watched as the Tigress opened her leather coat at the neck. She pulled out a soft roll of leather from inside an inner pocket, and opened it. Inside there were six different knives, two of which were identical. Taneshka chose a gently curving blade and another with a serrated edge. She looked up at Kesta and threw the knives to her, wrapped up in the soft leather. Then she bent her head over the bear's carcass and began to work.

Fox sat down on the bole of the fallen tree and watched. Kesta seemed untroubled by the situation; she was a peasant by birth, at home with the concept of hunting for gain. She sat, quite happily cutting through the thick folds of fat-laden fur with the blade.

The skinning took longer than the hunt had. Fox listened to Kesta and Taneshka as they chatted quietly over their work. He let his head slip forwards onto his chest as he listened, half asleep, and content to let them think of him as truly asleep. Unfortunately, he found himself unable to slow his descent towards unconsciousness; the day grew warmer as the mists completely dissipated, making Fox feel entirely comfortable. The last snatch of conversation he heard as he fell asleep was Taneshka's voice saying how useless a prince could be if you wanted anything done, and Kesta's soft laugh in answer.

As he sleeps he dreams. Far away a voice calls, a threatening, impure howl. His enemy, veiled in endless shadow, moves at impossible speed, his touch corrupting, ending. The howl mocks and challenges, so far away, yet so potent that it sends unbearable shocks of fear through the dreamer's sleeping body. In terror, his dreaming self turns his face away. Blind, but not at all safe from the torturous gaze of the enemy, a smaller threat is felt, quite close. The Dreamer focuses intently on this threat, to avoid the stare of the Great Corruptor.

Almost able to see the minor presence that menaces him, he fails at the last and falls away into a less aware dream state. On this safer ground the regular dreams come, like a foul breath into his mind, sending a chill into his physical body, driving away the sunlight that had warmed him. A torrent of mind-breaking images flow, unstoppable and terrible. The Dreamer cries out as he always does, when this nameless terror overcomes his sleeping mind, every night, night after night, un-ending...

9
First Move At The Loop

Fox was dragged awake. Kesta was holding his hands and Taneshka shaking him, staining his leathers with rich bear-blood. Fox put a hand to his forehead as reality flooded back. 'Are you all right?' Taneshka asked, sitting down next to him.

'It happens a lot,' Kesta explained. 'Most nights he suffers with dreams. Was it bad this time?' Fox looked up at her face, stunned momentarily by her beauty, an incredible contrast to the havoc of before. Kesta sat down next to him, still holding his hand and repeating her question. He nodded.

'I don't want to talk about it. I'm sorry.'

Taneshka nodded. 'That's all right. It's your mind, if you want to keep it private, who has the right to demand a look? Are you able to walk?' Fox nodded as the two girls helped him to his feet.

'I'm well now, thank you.' He looked around for the bear and recoiled, seeing only a mound of fat and muscle. Taneshka laughed cheerfully.

'We finished while you slept. We took the pelt, the liver, the tongue, some meat and the teeth. We can eat the liver and the meat and the tongue, if we hide it when we get back. The whole castle will want it.' Fox closed his mouth. He felt sick, which annoyed him as he had seen far worse than the skinned bear carcass before, and he knew it. If it hadn't been for his damned dream, and the guilt he felt for the animal's death, he would feel fine.

'Why did we go hunting for bear, again?' He asked weakly.

'The fur mainly. It'll make a great present for Father.' Taneshka raised an eyebrow at Fox's incredulity. Fox shrugged and left his thoughts unspoken.

They left the pelt in the crook of a tree for safekeeping and turned north, following Taneshka. Taneshka said little, except that her arms ached, and that they were going to meet with one of Heron's boats at the Loop. Kesta was glad they had left the pelt behind; the day was warm now, unusually so for the autumn. The smell of blood lingered on their clothing and even though Taneshka had given her a soaked cloth to clean her hands with, her palms still felt dirty, and the liquid stung.

Fox walked a small way behind the two girls, silent and pensive. He struggled his painful way back through the memory of his dream, trying to find the moment that had left him with a particular sense of discomfort and vulnerability. His memories showed him glimpses of a place, a few indistinguishable shapes, movement, snatches of sound, perhaps voices. These came in little pockets, memories grabbed away from the backdrop of his dream: a great and immensely heavy presence, a sensation of being crushed, and pain – entirely real yet causing no physical effect – a feeling of hopelessness that continually welled up within him.

It was almost midday when they reached their destination. Taneshka led them out from among twisted and thorny trees onto a wide bank at the side of a deep, slow moving river. It was a peaceful looking spot. Across the water the other bank was lined with tall trees, smooth, silvery trunks and silver-green leaves. The trees stood proudly in contrast to the leafless bones of their nearest, deciduous, neighbours.

The bank on their side of the river was a hump of thick, richly green grass, dropping away to become a sandy shore where the clear water lapped with a gentle sipping noise. Some distance away on Taneshka's left, a man was sitting on a sharp overhang. His feet were in the water and he waved cheerfully to Taneshka.

Taneshka sat down with a satisfied sigh, as she took the weight off her feet. Kesta sat next to her, looking curiously at the man, before laying back on the grass to relax.

Fox watched them with an absent expression. He frowned as he looked around. This peaceful place was bringing back the unsettled feeling that had been bothering him throughout their journey here. Everything about the area suggested a rest, a pretty haven where he could get his breath back. So why did everything here alarm him? Why were his instincts saying *no!?*

A boat appeared around the turn in the river. A man stood at its prow, the light glancing off the blue-green shades of his scale armour. He was keeping the boat from grounding with a long wooden pole, pushing gently at the bank to keep the craft level. The man who had been waiting further along stood and called out. The boatman acknowledged him with a wave, and the oars were stowed in one fluid movement. As the boat came to a rest, its flat keel temporarily grounded in the shallows, the breeze caught the flag that flew from the boat's single mast. The emblem of a silver-blue heron on a background of green reeds fluttered in the wind.

Fox rose as Taneshka did, but their expressions differed greatly as they both began to walk towards the moored boat. Fox's expression of consternation went unnoticed. The vessel distracted Kesta, as she had never seen a boat before.

Taneshka smiled warmly and raised a hand in greeting as the three arrived by the side of the vessel. The man who had been sitting on the bank bowed to Taneshka and called up to the boatman once more.

'Watermaster! There's a Tigress to see you!' The man grinned as the craft's captain looked over the edge of the vessel.

'One moment, Highness, step back if you please, we're going to lower the boarding plank.' The man spoke seriously. The gangway was thrown down and the boatmen disembarked.

Suddenly the hairs on the back of Fox's neck rose. He had a horrible feeling that the cold threat from his dream was standing hidden in the shadow of the trees behind him. He turned slowly, his hand reaching for his staff.

A man stood by the edge of the woods, his arms folded. Fox blinked. This man was not the threat... and yet... The man spoke, causing the others to jump in alarm and spin around to face him.

'Step away from the gangway. I would like to trade with the Captain.'

Taneshka answered him with indignation. 'We're first, freeman.' She turned away, not seeing his cold little smile. The boat Captain moved to stand at the head of the gangplank.

'I'm sorry sir, but you'll have to wait a few weeks for the next boat. This cargo is intended for the Tiger family only.' The man smiled again and raised his head. Fox surreptitiously let the strap that held his staff in place come loose.

'You misunderstand, captain. I *will* bargain with you, and they *will* move aside.'

Fox understood. The troubling presence was there to give the man aid and assistance. It's wielder still stood concealed within the trees. Fox stepped forwards.

'Reveal your men, sir, and speak plainly. If you wish to take this vessel by force then make your move, don't stand there playing with the pathetic idea that I am unaware of you.' Fox managed to inject a bored tone into his voice, while in reality he stood almost trembling in anticipation and fear. There would be a fight. There would be deaths.

The waiting men stepped out into the sunlight. Fox could hear Kesta and Taneshka drawing bowstrings, and the hurried instructions from the captain to his men. The friendly forester drew a knife, glaring at the man that dared to challenge his Tigress.

Fox examined his opponents. The first man had drawn a knife and was watching, as Fox had expected, one of his comrades for instruction. The comrade in question was tall, a head above the rest. His light brown hair was cut short to his head and his green eyes gleamed with a bright emptiness. There were worms of dark coloured ink spread along his forearms, confirming Fox's fears. The marks of a sorcerer.

There was a long pause. Slow movement began on both sides, the nine enemies spreading out from their leader, eyes on the girls' taut bowstrings. Fox was aware of two of the boatmen joining his ranks, wicked looking boathooks at-the-ready.

Fox locked eyes with the sorcerer. The man did not smile, but his eyes bored into Fox as he concentrated, muttering a stream of indecipherable words under his breath. Fox felt the testing curses quest around his being like, toothless snakes. The sorcerer raised his head in realisation.

'Ah. Prince Fox. We know all about *you*, now.'

'Oh? Who have you been talking to?'

Fox kept his gaze firmly on the sorcerer's eyes, watching for the beginnings of a malicious magic.

The sorcerer smiled thinly. This exchange of words was not a waste of time, but a way of testing his opponent for weaknesses or flaws.

'News travels fast in the Sacred Lands, my prince.'

'Let me guess. You talked to someone you met on the road?'

'They say you can always rely on the help of strangers.'

'Tall *dark* stranger, was he?'

Fox's voice took on the tone and quality of steel.

'You can send him a message from me, if you see him on your journey to the underworld! I have escaped him once, and turned him aside on our second meeting. The balance of power may be shifting, to my advantage. Tell him that, son of shadow!'

The sorcerer's eyes narrowed. 'You don't know the half of it, ignorant child! You know nothing of the balance, nothing of how this works. You tipped the scales, fool! Destroying the first-to-rise, forcing my master to finish his work himself!

'Yes, you've had your luck, but while you run from castle to castle, bolt-hole to bolt-hole, he travels these lands and releases more of his servants. His power grows at every carcer stone he breaches! Great Shadows, mighty parts of the Whole, have joined with him now. All you have are your little band of warriors, the poor, lost Sons of Rashin. All they can do is rely on the protection that runs in their blood. Eventually the Master's power overcomes it! Child. I am here so that you will not live to see that final defeat.'

Fox listened, outwardly calm, his blood racing as this new information came to light. The sorcerer's men looked worried. It was clear that they knew nothing of their leader's true mission. They were a small band of saboteurs, sent by Ox, perhaps. Their leader had the same goal, it seemed, but for a different master.

Fox became suddenly aware of a presence at his side; the man who had been first to the side of the boat was standing there, trembling, but gripping his knife.

Fox made the first move. His action was almost unreadable as a steady surge of encouragement and empowerment left him, entering the frightened forester. The sorcerer failed to see, a fact Fox saw with satisfaction. Keeping his gaze firmly locked with that of his enemy, he also saw that the forester had stopped trembling.

A flicker of uncertainty crossed the sorcerer's face as the fear fell away from the forester's features, being replaced by confidence and calm. Again, the sorcerer struggled to find a weakness in Fox that he could exploit, again meeting with failure. Those cool grey eyes were beginning to disconcert him, it was becoming harder and harder to meet their gaze.

The stalemate held for a few moments more, the worried faces of the Ox saboteurs and the determination on the faces of the two Heron boatmen frozen, awaiting the inevitable break. Taneshka was the picture of calm, her fingers keeping a firm grip on her bowstring, her arrow levelled at the sorcerer's head. Kesta's heart was beating a fearful rhythm as she let the point of her arrow travel slowly back and forth between the opposing men.

The tension broke. The sorcerer, unable to take Fox's gaze any longer, released a rush of flame down the length of his arm, hurling it with a savage cry at Fox. Fox deflected the attack with a sharp wave. Kesta's arrow hit the first intruder in the forehead; he went down soundlessly, impeding the charge of his comrades. Taneshka's arrow left her bow simultaneously to Kesta's, only to be knocked aside inches from the sorcerer's face.

The two boatmen moved forwards. The swordsmen reached Taneshka, but brutal blows from boathooks killed two. The third reached Taneshka unscathed, wildly swinging his blade. Taneshka dropped her bow in an apparently helpless movement, before flowing into movement, her hunting knives somehow finding their ways into her hands. Fox ducked to avoid another blast of flame as Taneshka's gutted opponent hit the ground.

Another arrow flew from Kesta's bow, knocking an enemy onto his back as one of the boatmen made a massive sweep at the sorcerer.

The sorcerer dropped and rolled out of the way, to the detriment of one of his men, who lost most of his head in a furious rush of blood.

The sorcerer rose, the gore soaking into his clothing as he clenched his fingers into a claw gesture. Fox heard the boatman's back snap horribly.

Kesta loosed another arrow, and another, as Taneshka whirled away from the keen edge of an adversary's sword. The other boatman took the life of one of his challengers in a blind rage, before dropping his weapon as a sword nicked his arm.

Fox felt the death of the first boatman, quickly followed by that of the brave forester, who stepped forwards to intercept another wild blast of flame. The grief and anger swelled in him as Kesta's bow was smashed asunder, one of the surviving saboteurs pressing his attack. The thought of her being harmed drove him to action. He took his anger and channelled it all into one place, seeking out the shadow that resided like a coiled worm in the sorcerer's being. At Fox's sudden shout all fighting ceased. The sorcerer stopped suddenly, halfway through hurling another fireball. His fiery conjuring was a cheap trick compared to what happened next.

Stricken, he stumbled forwards, features seizing up in agony. There was a rush of light from behind his eyes and smoke poured out of his mouth and nostrils. White flame roared through his body. The girls and the boatman watched in horror as the sorcerer's burnt out husk fell onto its face.

Fox took a step back, turning his face away. Kesta closed her eyes in horror. Taneshka stood, stony faced, before turning and walking to the riverbank with upright deliberation. There she paused, before retching over the water. There was a terrible silence. The birds made no sound, a sudden contrast from the cacophony of alarm calls that had sounded above the fighting.

Taneshka straightened up, her composure never steadier. She trod her way back through the mess of bodies that were strewn across the grassy bank, coming to stand face to face with Fox.

'So. More than a prince.'

Fox said nothing.

'You know, the advisors want me to marry you. I told them it was unlikely. Well, no offence intended, my actual wording was a little stronger than that, but... Well. I wonder if they knew about this.'

'He's not a sorcerer,' Kesta said firmly, reaching out to put a hand on the Tigress's shoulder. 'He's... much more than that. He isn't like them. He isn't like *him*.' She nodded to the mess at their feet that had once been a man.

'No,' Taneshka agreed dully, 'Fox is more upright. And his face isn't... burnt off.' Kesta tried to laugh, but it got stuck in her throat. She managed to smile weakly. Fox took a deep breath.

The three of them hardly noticed as the boat captain and two oarsmen descended the gangway to administer aid to their wounded companion. A different kind of tension ruled between the three as they stood in a silence, which quickly became unbearable. Finally, Taneshka ended the strained atmosphere by breaking down in tears. She cried silently, furious at herself and the humiliation of crying. She refused Kesta's embrace, turning away, struggling to repress the pain.

'I've never killed before. I've seen it happen once, a long time ago, and I've learned how to do it, but you never think… You never think what it will be like, when you actually…'

Fox closed his eyes, sorrow taking him at the sound of her broken voice. Sorrow for the loss of innocence. Sorrow for the blood that stained the ground, slick on the grass. Sorrow for the loyal forester, prepared to defend strangers for the sake of honour. The man had fought like a tiger, just as Taneshka had fought like a Tigress. He himself had killed with fire, again, and although the guilt ached as it had last time, another part of him observed the increased efficiency this time around. No blasted earth, no burnt grass. Just an empty body, thoroughly purified of the evil that had fed within it.

Fox walked away from the carnage, to where the grass was clean. He sat down on the bank and stared into the water. How much longer would this go on?

10
Armour

Tiger listened as Fox told their story, leaving out the details of his abilities in front of the advisors. Later, alone with Tiger, the full story was told. Taneshka vouched for Fox, speaking up to say that she did not believe him to be a sorcerer. Tiger accepted this without speaking, watching Fox closely as they rejoined the advisors.

Talk turned to the significance of the intruders and what they might have been hoping to achieve.

The fact that Ox was anxious enough to attempt sabotage gave Fox heart; he was especially encouraged when the contents of the cargo were revealed. The boat captain arrived at the castle late in the afternoon. Four more boats were now moored in the waters of the Loop. Steel Fox, Fox's father, had sent steel and finished blades: swords, spearheads and arrowheads.

Tiger had been sent a gift. Steel Fox had not forgotten his family's former ally. The gift came with a letter, stating that, should Tiger choose to reactivate the alliance, Steel Fox's brother, Rice Fox would send troops to help with the offensive. The gift itself was a new bow and a hundred or so arrowheads, needle, broadhead and barbed.

'It appears that your father has remembered me at last,' Tiger said with a smile, 'these arrows will soon come to good use.'

Fox nodded in agreement, but his mind was somewhere else. His thoughts kept returning to his uncle's castle in the mountains. Would Rice Fox be able to convince the advisors to obey their king's orders? How long would the archers be able to wait, camping in the hills on the border between Fox territory and the lands governed by Ox? How had his cousin's crime been dealt with?

A fear grew in Fox's mind, a fear that the advisors would refuse to authorise troop movement. A fear that when Ox's force reached the border, there would be no one to stand in their way but a few archers and Tiger's diminutive army.

The greatest fear was that Ox was now crossing the border, unchallenged, ready to fall upon his unwary enemies. Fox took to walking about the corridors of his host's castle, deep in his dark thoughts.

Two days after the first boats had arrived, the weather took a turn for the worse. Frost cut at Fox and Kesta in their room on the morning of the third day, and they were forced to move into one of the interior rooms across the hall. The old room became a storeroom; weapons and non-perishable food began to pile up where their beds had been.

War was close, the quiet before battle increased by light snowfalls that clothed the pines in white, turning the tracks and alleyways of the small town that crowded around the keep's southern face to mud.

There were no more hunting trips into the forest, the bear pelt hung forgotten and wasted in the crook of a tree, deep within the still forest.

Taneshka was not allowed out of the castle. This was no longer to stay her from dangerous jaunts into the woods, but as a matter of practicality. The Tigress was adamant that she would be on the battlefield along with Fox and Kesta, when the time came. Tiger barely argued. His one condition was that she spent her time now in training, saying that he would not see her die in battle due to a lax training regime. Kesta joined Taneshka most days, developing her skills with the Wing-Swords and bow.

Fox did not have the heart to join them. The burden of his nation and the lives of his friends and family weighed him down.

The snow did not hold, melting away to become freezing mud. The grey skies became constant and banks of cloud on the northern horizon threatened to bring more inclement weather. Fox spent whole days in the stable with Riversteel, making sure the horse had enough feed.

He was inside, sitting on a swept leaf pile against the stable wall when Kesta came looking for him. He could hear her calling his name as she went from stall to stall. He leant back into the corner so as little of him as possible was visible, not feeling much like conversation. Kesta's head appeared above the half door.

'There you are! Taneshka has sent people everywhere looking for you. Come on, the last of Heron's supply boats have arrived. He sent a messenger to say that everything is free! There's a messenger from your uncle as well.' She looked down at him.

'Are you all right?' Her expression changed to concern as she opened the half door and came into the stable. Riversteel's head bobbed in greeting and she reached up absently to pet under his jaw, her eyes never leaving Fox.

He looked back at her, unsure of what to say. Her eyes searched his face for any clues. 'Are you well?' She came and sat next to him in the leaves, sinking into the thick pile. Fox looked up at the beams above their heads, trying to find the right words.

'I'm not ill. It's just, troubling. Not knowing what's going to happen.' He stopped to look at Kesta. 'Do you think we can do this? Win the war, I mean?' He waited for the answer with a kind of desperation. Kesta looked back.

'I do.' She said, meeting Fox's gaze. Slowly, Fox relaxed, leaning back into the leaves and returning to his study of the ceiling.

'I can't see it, I mean, I couldn't see an end to it, let alone a victory. It feels like the world is waiting for something, waiting for the war. It feels like once it begins, everything will change. It scares me.'

'It scares everyone.'

'But not you?'

'Me as well. But worrying about it won't make it go away.' She began to get to her feet. 'Come on, let's go find out what your uncle sent us.' Fox grabbed her arm.

'Don't go yet. Sit with me for a while.'

For a moment she looked at him questioningly, and then she slowly sat down again. The wind was cold outside the sturdy walls of the stable, but Riversteel's presence behind his partition and the dense drift of leaves made the space comfortably warm.

They sat in companionable silence, Fox continuing to survey the roof, Kesta watching Riversteel as he fed from his hayrack. She wondered what Fox could find so interesting on the ceiling. All she could see were cobwebs and knotty beams.

Suddenly she found herself wondering how they had come to be holding hands.

'Hey, Kesta! Why are you taking so long?' Taneshka's voice broke the peace. She walked past the doorway and started, seeing the two of them sitting in the leaf pile.

'There you are... Ah. That's what's taking you so long. You found him then?' She grinned, leaning on the half door. Fox stood up suddenly, in a shower of leaves.

'We were just sitting,' he said calmly, opening the door and pushing her, somewhat unnecessarily, out of the way. Taneshka watched him walk back up towards the keep, trying to fight the smile off her face. She turned back to Kesta.

'My, my. What would the advisors think? What would your mother say?' she said in mock disapproval.

'Nothing. My mother's dead,' Kesta said shortly, getting up and leaving the stable. Unexpectedly, she was very annoyed.

'Sorry.' Taneshka apologised quickly, looking down as Kesta passed. 'I didn't know.' She followed Kesta somewhat hesitantly, cursing her own ignorance.

Kesta slowed and turned around. 'It's all right. I don't know why I was so harsh.'

'I do.' Taneshka grinned, her disregard for propriety bouncing back. She winked at Kesta and hurried to her friend's side.

The messenger from Heron stood patiently before the table in the great hall. Tiger and Fox looked around as the two girls entered. Fox shifted his chair to make room for Kesta. He didn't look directly at her, a fact Taneshka noticed with interest, as she sat down next to her father. Tiger smiled around at them all.

'Thank you for coming so quickly.' He smiled at the joke, before continuing, 'Please, friend, no need to wait any longer. I wish to hear what Heron has to say to us.'

The messenger bowed, the green and blue hued scales of his armour rippling. He unrolled a scroll, checked its contents, and began his message.

'To His Majesty, King Tiger of the north-eastern forests. We hope the supplies that have already reached you will come in useful in your war against Ox. We have also sent similar shipments to your ally, Prince Rice Fox of the Central Plains, from his brother, King Steel Fox of the Autumn Hills. May the Land bless your soldiers with many victories.

'There are two parts to this message, my lords. Firstly, the cargoes now moored in the Loop are all free of trade or charge.

They are a combined gift, from Lord Steel Fox and my Lord Heron. Ox's move in crossing one of our rivers was a mistake. We will not trade with him, and as he has flouted the laws of the Sacred Lands. We will assist you in your fight.

'Secondly, we ask one thing of you, and one thing only. Do you have knowledge of the strange activity our scouts report along the northern bank of the Lifeblood? Twice now, patrols have failed to return. It seems unlikely to us that Ox is the source – he is too far south of the river. Any information you might have would be received gratefully.

'The final part of this message is of obvious urgency. By the time this reaches you, the first supply lines will have been moved out of the City of Lakes. In two weeks, the armies of Lord Ox will begin to arrive on the plains bellow the Twin Valley Ridge.'

There was a heavy silence. Fox took a deep breath. They had run out of time. Kesta watched him worriedly while Taneshka exchanged a glance with her father. The messenger bowed and left the room. The advisors were, for once, entirely silent. Fox found himself wondering whether the reaction of Rice Fox's advisors, and Henshin, would be the same.

Tiger broke the silence. 'Well. That leaves us four or five days for last minute preparation. Then we march, and meet with Rice Fox's warriors at the Twin Valley Ridge.' He looked at Fox, who noted the half question in his voice. So Tiger also doubted that the soldiers from the castle in the mountains would come.

Over the next few days the castle was overtaken by a rush of activity. The weapons sent by Steel Fox were distributed to Tiger's small army, as they returned in small groups from their various villages to the north. It was a cold grey afternoon when the last arrived, a band of hardy archers, one hundred strong. They filled up the main hall of Tiger's Castle, helping to gather supplies and share out the weaponry.

Kesta noted that everyone held Tiger's archers in high regard; even the King himself talked to their champion as to an old friend. The Champion of the Archers was a tall, broad shouldered man with greying hair and a serious face. The sun would break through with quick, surprising moments of humour as he joked with the other men. He was called Stavannos Karrlkebron, a northern name so unfamiliar that everyone addressed him as Stavan Archer.

'They say he can hit another man's arrow out of the air,' an awed young swordsman murmured, 'eyes like a hawk!' Kesta looked at him with a critically. She had been hanging around with him because he had no friends within his unit, and was likable enough.

'I'm named for a type of hawk,' she said, shrugging her shoulders as if Stavan's reputation didn't impress her.

'Yes, but can you shoot another archer's arrow out of the sky?' the swordsman grinned broadly. Kesta kept her expression cool.

'Not yet. But I have time, wouldn't you say? Besides, nobody can shoot another arrow in flight. That's impossible.'

The young swordsman moved out of the way as a Spear Captain pushed by, laden down with leather cuirasses for his unit of men. The swordsman made an offensive gesture at the captain's back, before saying, 'Maybe so, but the story doesn't need to be true. The fact that people say it anyway shows how good he is. I wish I was an archer, I'd love him to lead me into battle.'

Kesta rolled her eyes. 'Why don't you ask him if he'll marry you?' The swordsman grinned, but treated Kesta to the same gesture he had aimed at the spear captain. Kesta raised an eyebrow to show that she hadn't taken offence, before turning and moving off into the crowd of men, calling over her shoulder, 'I'll see you on the march, swordsman!' As she reached the table where Stavan and his captains were sitting, the swordsman called after her with his name, but she couldn't hear it over the noise of the crowd.

Kesta pushed past a soldier who couldn't seem to decide where he was supposed to be, so she could get at the table. She searched through the heaped mass of equipment for a few moments before grabbing a handful of the autumn-steel broadhead arrows for her empty quiver.

She turned to go but a voice stopped her in her tracks.

'Ho! Lord Fox's shield-maiden!' She turned to see Stavan beckoning her towards him. She hurried back to the table where he was sitting with some officers who were obviously wondering why he had called her.

She saluted him and stood silent, waiting for him to speak. Stavan stood up and offered her his hand in the greeting that she had come to expect from Tiger's men. She grasped his hand and shook it firmly. 'I'm Kesta, sir. What can I help with?'

'I talked with your liege. Prince Fox tells me that you were forced to draw bowstring in battle on the journey here.' Kesta nodded, pushing away the images of that half forgotten slaughter. Stavan smiled broadly. 'His Highness told me that you were quite good. I would like the opportunity to discuss your progress as an archer; many of my men were like you before I met them, untrained but promising. Please, would you honour my men and I with your company on the journey?'

Kesta barely hesitated. 'If my Lord Prince permits it, Master Archer. And thank you!' Spending time with the champion of so famed an archery unit would help her credibility no end. Apart from that, the better she could become at archery, the more chance she had in battle. Kesta saluted smartly. 'I will go and ask my lord, Champion. Thank you once again.' He nodded to her with the same professionalism and turned to address one of his captains.

Fox and Taneshka were in Tiger's armoury. Taneshka sat in a high backed wooden chair, polishing the head of Tiger's Fang. The long spear lay across her lap, the small amount of flexibility in the dark wood shaft allowing the spear base to touch the floor. The Tigress ran a cloth along the tapering leaf shape of the spearhead. A steel binding joined the blade to the lacquered top of the shaft.

Fox stepped over the spear pole to return a sword to its rack. He had considered borrowing one for the battle; Tiger had generously offered Fox his pick of any weapon in the armoury. They were all well-balanced blades, but Fox had found none of them to be as light or as keen as the sword he had once owned. That finely crafted piece of Autumn Steel, stronger than these others, and taking a better edge, now lay snapped and useless in the East Wastes.

Fox sat opposite Taneshka, who continued to concentrate on Tiger's Fang. Here they were, preparing for battle. He remembered the East Wastes. He remembered the feeling of excitement and apprehension on the journey. He had been made fearless by naïve ideas of honour and glory. Oh, there was honour, great honour, for the band of men and the few female archers that had stood their ground valiantly against a much larger force. And his Captain of the Guard, Branaghin, had given his life without thought.

Their deaths were not glorious. Fox winced as he remembered the sound of the heavy iron arrows hammering through the front line of defenders, splitting shields and snapping bone.

The sound of men crying out as pain and death rained from the sky.

The sickened, appalled emotion as an enemy soldier died, Fox's blade buried in his stomach.

The smell and feel of warm blood, flooding his young hands for the first time.

And the second. And the third. Again and again, until the feeling of revulsion and guilt died within him, lost to the roaring, hacking, brutal throng.

'Are you feeling ill?' Taneshka looked at him in concern, putting aside her spear. Fox lifted his grey eyes to meet her green ones.

'Have you ever been in a proper battle, Taneshka?'

'No.'

'It's terrible. Like a nightmare but far worse.'

Taneshka looked at him closely. 'I know it will be dreadful. I am afraid of fighting, of dying. But I *am* going to fight. Have you lost courage?'

'No. I cannot afford to. My nation's future rests on my shoulders.'

Taneshka stood and began to wrap Tiger's Fang in its oilskin cover. She leant the spear against the wall, thinking about what Fox had just said. Finally she turned to face him, her hand on the door handle.

'I do not fear for your nation's future, Prince Fox.' She smiled, and he returned it.

'Nor I yours, Tigress Taneshka.'

Somewhere in the castle a gong sounded. Taneshka paused with her hand still on the door handle, before Kesta came into the room, breathless, pushing past Taneshka in her haste. 'Tiger is calling an assembly in the main hall! He is waiting for you two. We have to hurry!' Fox put a hand on Kesta's shoulder.

'Thank you for telling us.' He looked at Taneshka. They both knew why the assembly had been called. Fox took a deep breath as if to prepare himself. 'We had better hurry then.'

11
Marching Songs

The early morning air was very cold. Breath rose in mist from the horses outside the stables. Fox stamped his feet, rubbing his hands together to stay warm. Kesta and Taneshka stood on either side of Riversteel, waiting as a stable hand saddled the great horse. A steady stream of soldiers was passing behind them, wrapped in cloaks against the cold, spear and sword blades catching the lamplight. Tiger was already in the saddle, his grey mare pushing her way through the marchers.

'A short autumn and a long winter this year, I fear.' Tiger looked up at the sky. The grey light of morning was masking all but the brightest stars, which sat on the edge of the sky, awaiting the sun. The mare shook her head, blowing out steam in protest at the cold. Tiger patted her neck fondly. 'It'll be warmer once we're on the march. There's no cloud cover either, so we'll get the sun, I hope. Are you ready?'

Fox nodded. 'Riversteel is just being saddled.' He looked up at the castle, sitting above them on the peak of the hill. There were no lights in its windows. 'Is no one left to look after the castle?' Fox wondered aloud.

Tiger smiled sadly. 'We'll be back to re-occupy as soon as this is over.' The last of the soldiers went past, boots sounding on the cobbles. The torchlight faded into the distance as the army passed through the gateways further down the slope.

Taneshka looked up at her father in the half dark. He seemed smaller, now, sitting on his favourite horse, with an empty castle looming above him like some terrible omen.

Fox nodded to the stable hand as the young man finished. He swung himself up into the saddle, considering what the king had just said. *As soon as this is over.*

Taneshka took the reins of her own horse from the stable hand, and mounted as the man went back into the musty dark to fetch a horse for Kesta. The four of them soon sat astride impatient steeds, each waiting for another to make the first move. Fox waited respectfully for Tiger, who didn't know why he waited, except that the moment felt like a goodbye; the fear of not returning home eating at the ageing king.

Behind them, in the stable, the young man lifted a pack from the wall and slung it on his back. In a moment he had put aside his brushes, his belts and buckles. Now a sword was in his hand.

The train of men marched along the forest paths in silence. Only when the sun rose above the level of the morose firs and stubborn pines, did conversation begin, spreading through the ranks like the sunlight. The Tiger Champions tolerated the conversation without qualm, it made everyone feel at ease, themselves included.

Tiger sat, alone in his silence, while his daughter talked with Fox and Kesta.

Even at walking pace, the horses were soon at the head of the marching men. Now and then the champions would turn their steeds back, to check up on their men, but for the most part Fox and Taneshka were able to share the journey with various Tiger veterans, all with differing opinions on strategy and tactics. Fox, trained for war, and Taneshka, a natural warrior, found conversation with the seasoned warriors easy. Kesta, however, dropped back so that her horse drew level with Stavan Archer.

'Good morning, Master Archer.' The champion smiled as she greeted him and returned in kind.

'Good morning. How did the early start fare with you?'

'I'm used to it sir. Prince Fox says that I may ride with you, unless he needs me.'

Stavan nodded. 'Good. Your company is good for morale, it shows the men that we are close to the king and your prince. How are they, do you know?' Kesta looked at him quizzically.

'Why do you ask?'

'No reason, only... I pray he forgives me for saying it, but my lord seems...distracted. His morale affects us all. I am worried that it will make the men uncertain.'

Kesta's private thoughts were that there were plenty of reasons for the men to be uncertain, but she said nothing, and looked ahead to where Tiger sat, straight as a spear in the saddle. He was keeping to himself, but that could be expected, under the circumstances. Perhaps someone should attempt conversation. Kesta's next thoughts were about the champion archer, who watched her for an answer. Why did he care so much that Tiger's attitude would affect morale? Was he paranoid that the king would fold under pressure, leading his men to their deaths? At any rate, it was clear that he did not wish to discuss her archery. She examined Stavan's expression to ascertain his intent.

The Master Archer looked ahead, and the expression he held while regarding Tiger was of worry. He cared, as much for his king's wellbeing as for that of the army, indeed, he saw the two as one and the same. Quite rightly, Kesta reflected.

'I will go talk to him. See if I can put him in a better mood.'

Stavan nodded, relieved. 'You do that. Thank you, Kesta.' Kesta nodded and urged her horse forward, heading around the outside of the marching column of men. She caught a glimpse of the young man she had befriended back at the castle. He grinned at her as she swept by, too fast for her to do anything but return the smile.

Fox and Taneshka listened to the Champion of the Sword. He was extolling the values of traps on the battlefield, while the Champion of the Long Spear waited impatiently to debate the issue.

'The key, with confrontations between unmatched forces, is to use advantages against the larger party in unexpected ways. Fire attacks, raids on the food stores, poisoning, difficult or unstable terrain, weather, even the arrogance and confidence of the enemy can be valuable weapons.' Fox nodded in agreement, but the spear champion spoke up quickly to state his own points.

'Fair enough, but these traps you describe are rarely usable, and often prone to failure. Raids and poisonings of the food require the ability to find and get close to such supplies, fire attacks rely on wind direction, which as you know, is always changing on the plains, and two can play the terrain game. Many a time, commanders can become obsessed with holding some hill or forested area, so that they forget how to best utilise that advantage. Apart from that,' here the champion lowered his voice, 'confidence often has a good basis, especially when it's being supported with the knowledge of several thousand men backing you up.'

Fox smiled wryly. The two champions looked at him expectantly and Taneshka too awaited a comment.

'If you're expecting me to reveal the plan you're going to be disappointed,' he smiled. 'Nothing is definite, not until I've talked with my own champions when we meet with my army. Don't worry though; you'll be briefed as well. This is a joint effort.'

Or we die, Fox thought to himself, but managed to keep his smile steady. The two champions moved away, discussing the effect of the weather on morale, and manoeuvres on the battlefield. Taneshka leaned in to get Fox's attention.

'There is a plan, isn't there?' He heard the worry in her voice.

'Of a sort. Divide their army, position archers to attack both armies at once, trap their cavalry and hang on for dear life.' Fox saw her expression and knew that honesty would work better with Taneshka than other measures. 'It will take more than one miracle for us to come through this. I trust your father, and I trust his men, as I trust my own, but we still haven't received a definite report about Ox's numbers. In this case, no news is probably very bad news.'

The Tigress looked away. 'I am afraid. It will keep me awake tonight.' Her eyes shone, and a fierce, sad smile crossed her features. Fox nodded grimly.

'Try to sleep all the same. Tomorrow we have further to travel before we reach our destination.'

'And I have to be fighting fit, eh?'

'Yes, for all of us.'

Kesta hailed Tiger as her horse slowed to a walk beside him. He looked up and smiled. 'And how is the prince's shield-maiden?' Kesta smiled in answer.

'I'm well, Lord King. And how are you, my lord? Your champion archer is worried for you.' Not wanting to offend him, she added, 'You are well, I hope?'

Tiger smiled. 'Quite well, thank you Kesta. I am... sorting through my life. A turning point has been reached and I must take the corner or leave the road.' Kesta raised her eyebrows.

'Very... thoughtful, my lord.' Kesta paused before asking her next question with a great deal of care. 'Where does the road end?' Tiger laughed.

'That is the question. I don't know the answer, but we'll soon find out.'

'We won't be finished by this battle, my lord. I know that as sure as my heart is beating.'

Tiger looked away and seemed to be deep in thought. When he turned back, the colour was back in his voice, and he smiled at Kesta with his eyes. 'It ends with this battle, but not for our side, is that what you mean? I do not know who will meet their end in the days to come, but live or die, it will not be the end. Death is just another road. But life? I fear for those whose ends are not met in the battle with Ox.'

Tiger took a deep breath. 'However! Today we are well and free and happy, and as far as I care, marching to victory. Let the men sing! I will ride to the front.'

Kesta let her horse slow again, until she was level with Stavan. He bowed to her, bending across his horse's neck. Then, sweeping back upright he started up a song. All the men knew it and sang enthusiastically as Kesta rode to catch up with Fox.

Fox laughed as Kesta came close. 'This is your fault I suppose? Cover your ears, Kesta, this song is not fit for the innocent!'

'Actually, I intend to learn the words. Don't we both, Taneshka?'

The Tigress turned in the saddle and called back in a mock superior tone, 'I know them already! Come on, Father intends to reach the border alone, we must race to catch him up.' The three horses broke away from the formation and cantered to the head of the line, where Tiger rode, singing along to the tune with gusto.

Fox felt that they should have marched further, but as the sun began to sink behind the trees, Tiger called a halt. Morale was high and he intended to keep it that way; all the savoury marching songs in the world would not save his men from exhaustion. Resting would. The sky was still clear, but it became cold as soon as the sunlight faded. Fires were made in the middle of the road and the soldiers camped around them, checking their weapons and sorting provisions.

Kesta walked through the camp. She was too tired from riding to feel self-conscious among the men, and by now she felt she knew them all. This wasn't strictly true, instead, they all knew her, and she was treated with more respect by Tiger's men than she had been by the rank and file at Rice Fox's castle. The rules of society meant little here in the hills and forests, and Kesta's association with Prince Fox gave her authority by default.

Walking past where the horses were tethered, Kesta saw Fox and Taneshka and went to join them.

Fox was sitting, illuminated by the flickering firelight, his staff across his knees. He was rubbing strange smelling oil into the wood, while Taneshka stared into the fire, contemplating. Kesta sat down beside him. 'What's that?' she asked.

Fox looked up.

'Hello. Riversteel has been fed?'

'I checked.'

'Good. This is to stop the wood from chipping away when I fight. It fuses the bark, gives it a kind of varnish.' Fox took a rag from the grass beside him and wiped it up and down the length of the staff. He put the rag down and lifted the staff, extending it over the flames. There was a spitting sound as blue flame spread along the wood, burning away the excess oil and sealing the bark. Kesta gasped as Fox shifted his grip to let the flame run over the wood where he had been holding it.

'Doesn't it hurt?'

'It tickles. The oil protects my hand, it burns away, but my skin is untouched. Great trick to play at banquets.'

'Did you ever?'

Fox smiled. 'Yes, when I was eleven. For some reason no one understood the joke.' He grinned at the memory and Kesta laughed, imagining the scene.

Taneshka glanced up at them and smiled, having missed the reason for their laughter. One of the foot soldiers passed the fire and threw a pack to Taneshka. 'Food for the night, Tigress. Sleep well, Sir, and you, Your Highness.' He disappeared into the dark, his silhouette passing a fire further up the road.

'What about me?' Kesta said in mock indignation. 'Don't I deserve a good night?'

Taneshka shook her head. 'No, sorry, Kesta. It's to punish you for those bawdy songs.'

'I didn't start them,' she said indignantly, oblivious of Tiger's approaching silhouette.

'No. That was my fault, Teshka. Still, I heard you singing along, so why complain?' Tiger sat down opposite Fox. 'I came to say goodnight, to all of you. We should all get sleep, even if it means having to face our dreams.' He looked meaningfully at Fox.

'How do you know about that?' Fox stared back at Tiger, frozen in place.

'Taneshka. She wanted to see if I could have a holy warrior see you after that confrontation you had by the river. However, there are none. I sent messages out, but all are missing from their homes. The watchtowers are empty as well.'

Fox felt a sudden shudder of fear. The Holy Warriors, missing? There was no good in this news, for certain. Where had they gone? Where was Rashin? Had he gone to the Twin Valley Ridge like Fox had asked, or was he too mysteriously missing? And if he was, what did that mean for the archers who waited with him?

Tiger read Fox's expression. He sat back, accepting the bread Taneshka passed to him. Sighing, he looked up at the star-strewn sky. The Sacred Lands were set to be plunged into turmoil. Tiger could see it, read it in recent events, feel it in the air. He did not consider himself a mystic, but he knew to listen to his feelings.

The talk around the fire turned to theories on the carcer stones, with Tiger telling some of the old stories about the macabre landmarks, and Fox listening intently.

The fire was burning low by the time Tiger returned to his own tent. He entered so as to remove his bedding from inside, before lying down under the sky with the rest of the soldiers.

The following day, the mood on the march was far more serious than it had been the previous day. The army had left the trees behind and the hills were easing. Some of the time the train of men marched on the Tiger side of the border, and at other times on the Fox side, the difference marked by tall poles of painted wood. Each pole served as a milestone, reminding Fox of how far they had to travel, and causing him to wonder if they would reach their destination in time.

The small hills became seas of wild grain: barley escaped from the fields to the south. Now and then the waves of gold-stemmed grass would be broken by a rise. Tiger could feel damp in the air, although there were still no clouds in the sky. The answer to the mystery proved simple, the wild barley was rotting in the fields, and nobody lived in the desolate area to harvest the crop. Fox felt a great sadness at the loss; families like Kesta's were beginning to starve all throughout Fox territory, at least on the southern plains, because too few people lived to manage and harvest the resources available.

The morning passed and afternoon began, a haze appearing on the horizon. A line of steep hills dominated the skyline, erratically clothed with patches of forest. The hills swept around from the north, to the army's right, into the west dead ahead, where the green faded and melted away against a cold, harsh sky. The army turned north towards the nearest hills, feeling the land grow steeper beneath their feet. By early evening, the horses had reached the hills.

Fox looked around. Riversteel still had some ground to cover before they reached the top, but already he was high enough to see the army doggedly marching towards his position. Tiger had stayed with the troops, along with the champions, giving his horse to a scout. Now Fox turned to call the scout over.

'Ho there! Go further up. When you reach the top, come and tell me what you see. The Tigress and I will follow at a slower pace.' The scout saluted and urged his horse forwards, attacking the last stretch of the climb. Kesta and Taneshka rode closer to Fox and let their horses slow.

Riversteel did not want to dawdle. He was tired but, like Fox, he felt the end of the journey nearing and he pulled at the bit, anxious to rush over the hill.

Fox held him back. At the top of the hill he would know his fate. Kesta smiled nervously and he replied with a grim one of his own. Taneshka looked back, to see the army starting up the slopes below.

The sky came closer, tough grass falling away. Fox heard the thudding of hooves. The scout's horse approached. Fox watched apprehensively as the man saluted, reining his horse in.

'There are a few tents by the trees. Somebody's built a temporary shelter as well; evidence suggests about one hundred people. The tents are flying your colours, my lord. On the plain there is a large force gathering, a long way out. I think they have kept their distance in case we await back here.'

Fox nodded, urging Riversteel onwards. 'That's good. That means they're not as confident as I feared.' He leaned forward in the saddle as Riversteel reached the top. The plains stretched out below.

Two valleys lay below, separated by a narrow ridge that stretched out into the grasslands. The ridge was forested, the trees growing out and around the shoulders of the hills Riversteel now stood upon. The horse bent his neck to tear at the damp turf.

Fox dismounted to stretch his legs. He walked amongst the tents that were camped on the upper slopes. The breeze was strong and Fox took a deep breath of the clean air before shielding his eyes and looking out onto the plain. Distant movements could be seen, but the yellow brown of the grass camouflaged the Ox soldiery and their camp. Fox put them out of his mind and stared around, wondering where everyone was.

The camp was empty. A cold fear began to gnaw at the pit of Fox's stomach. He turned to look back at the hilltop, stark against the sky. The first line of Tiger's soldiers appeared, dark against the skyline. Kesta and Taneshka had dismounted and were talking to Tiger, who waved down to Fox. He lifted his hand in response, turning to look at the forest. There was a moment of unexpected movement in the trees on the slope of the middle ridge.

Fox started to run down the western valley, the central ridge rose as he ran, blocking his view of the eastern valley on his right.

The movement repeated, and a spark of excitement jumped in Fox's chest. He had seen a flash of blue silk, he was certain. As he slowed to a jog, a woman broke away from the trees and ran out to meet him. Fox started to grin when he saw who it was. The Champion of Rice Fox's Archers saluted smartly. Koshra smiled back at Fox as her fist sounded off her shoulder. She was in full battle armour, lacquered leather lamellar over officer's silk. Her left arm had an officer's buckler strapped to it, a rectangular sharp-cornered shield with concave sides.

Koshra took her bow off her shoulder and nocked an arrow in one smooth movement. 'We're ready, Highness. The men are all here, we were drilling in the forest. The enemy started to arrive this morning. Oh, and your friend a...' Koshra stopped in mid-sentence, staring up at the hilltop.

'Look! The army has arrived!' Fox looked at her quizzically.

'Of course! Did you think I'd come alone?'

'No, my lord, I mean our army, Prince Rice Fox's infantry!' Fox spun to stare up the hill. Sure enough, a stream of blue silk and grey leather was spilling over the brink of the hill and down into the west valley, towards Fox and Kesta. The archers in the trees broke ranks, cheering, to wave up at their comrades.

They came! Fox felt a wave of relief. The first hurdle had been cleared. He started walking up the hill, refusing to look behind him, where a thousand obstacles gathered on the plain.

12
The Dreamer Wakes

Fox stood on the highest point of the ridge. The opening of the planning tent behind him flapped in the strong wind. With Fox stood Tiger, Renn, and the Champions Koshra, Haiken and Stavan. Below, in both valleys, tents were going up, the green and red of Tiger in the east valley, and Fox blue-grey in the west.

Long, thin banners of red stood out amongst the tents of Tiger's army. The Fox army flew flags rarely, but the distinctive bucklers could be seen on the arm of every officer. If Fox soldiers became lost in battle, grouping around the nearest buckler-wearing officer should ensure that the line stayed solid.

The sun was setting behind the planning tent. Fox stopped surveying the allied camp and turned his attention to the Champions and Tiger.

'We're here. The first step is over.' The others nodded. Koshra opened her mouth as if to say something, but stopped, unsure whether she should address Fox or Tiger. 'First things first,' Fox spoke again, looking from face to face.

'My Champions, you must treat King Tiger as you do me. The Tiger Champions are your equals, and if a dispute breaks out involving your troops and the troops of a Tiger Champion, you must cooperate. We are allies, brothers! And sisters! This battle will forge our two nations together. The Sacred Lands are changing and I would be a liar if I said all the changes are good. Together we have a chance, small as it may be, to survive. But only together.'

Tiger nodded. 'My champions understand these same rules Fox. I have already spoken with them.' Fox bowed his head. He looked at his companions' faces. Haiken, Fox's old teacher, was looking restless.

'Should we outline your basic strategy, my lords, before the sun sets?' Fox smiled. 'Anxious to get your hand on the hilt of a sword, Haiken?' He turned to stare out onto the plain, bathed as it was in the sun's last gold. 'I don't know. What do you all think?'

'We'll know roughly how many they are once it gets dark, from the torchlight. Until then all we can do is arrange our own defence.' Renn had spoken. Fox looked up, surprised. He had forgotten that Renn was an old warrior. The advisor had not fared badly, considering he had spent the beginning of autumn in damp forests on a hillside. His beard had grown, covering his scar, and his eyes were intense, burning with fervour. No doubt the murder of his brother was still fresh in his mind.

Fox nodded. 'Our defence. Solid line, three units deep, where the valley is narrowest, so that we can hold our ground. Spear, sword, spear, sword, with axe units taking up the flanks where we need to push them back.' The champions nodded in approval.

'What about special units?' Haiken asked.

'Archers on the central ridge. All being well, we can decimate the enemy, at least until we're forced to reposition. If we have linestormers, we can also bury them in the depths of the army, and surprise the enemy if their line weakens.'

'We have sixty linestormers. Will that be enough?'

'Possibly. Tiger's men will take up position in the narrower east valley. Their long spears take the flanks, your archers support mine, and then there is the same sword, spear, sword, spear line up.'

The strategists stood silent for a moment, gazing out onto the darkening plain. The sun sank behind the hills to the west. One by one, torches were lit out in the dark. Koshra and Stavan stood, silently counting the lights as they flickered into life. As the display ceased, they glanced at each other, before turning to Fox and Tiger.

'I estimate that there are about five thousand men,' Koshra said. There was a long silence.

'Stavan, how many men do we have, all together?' Tiger asked calmly.

'Three thousand.'

Tiger sighed. 'Well, we knew it wasn't going to be easy. I'm going to my bed. Is there anything else we need to discuss?' Fox nodded quickly.

'There is a weak point in our planned defence, the shoulder of the west valley against the central ridge. Without some extra defence units, we'll be overrun.'

'I can help you there.' Fox turned to see Rashin approaching, all in white. Fox gasped in surprise, and grasped Rashin's arm warmly.

'I was afraid you weren't here! By the Land, it feels right that we should be advised by one of the brotherhood, at this time.'

Rashin raised his eyebrows. 'I am here to do more than advise, my young prince. The peace vows are no longer. We were told to fight no battles, make war against no adversary, save the Shadow, where and when he appears. He has made his move, and he wants you dead. To fight him, we must keep you alive, and to keep you alive we will do anything, even die on this battlefield.'

'We?' Fox asked, looking around to see if there were other white-clad holy warriors nearby.

'Yes, we. We're all here.'

'All?' A daft hope rose in Fox. Surely Rashin didn't mean to say...

'All of us. Every last warrior of our order. All my brothers, and one sister!'

'How many?' Fox suddenly felt as if he were weightless, and made of light.

'About ninety. We'll fill this gap in the defences. For now though, I'd love for you to come join the others. We all need to see you.' Fox nodded, following Rashin without question, leaving Stavan and Koshra with Tiger and the other champions.

A large white tent sat behind the wood that swamped most of the central ridge. Smoke rose from a hole in the centre of the tent's roof. Lamps had been lit inside, and as the sun sank further behind the western hills, the light seemed all the more welcoming.

On the hill, the champions began to disperse. King Tiger still stood with Stavan and Koshra. The two champion archers had taken up vigil over the plain. The three drew cloaks closer about them as a cold wind came in from across the dark sea of grass, sweeping up the hillside, causing tents to shake in their moorings. Night fell completely, and the mass of lights out on the plain burned their way into Tiger's doubts, weighing on his mind. The odds were bad. With a sigh, he said his goodnights to Stavan and Koshra and began the walk along the hilltop to the east valley, where his daughter waited.

Taneshka had spent the evening indulging her creative side, working in secret with lumber and oil, the Master-of-Supplies and several Tiger Officers following her instructions. The Tigress had gone to her tent with added confidence in her plans, scorning the multitude on the plain.

Kesta trained. She went through all the sequences Haiken had taught her, the steel wings flashing in the dying sunlight. When night had fallen, and Haiken had come down from the strategists' tent on the hilltop, she had continued to practice, sparring with him by torchlight. He was pleased with her ferocity and intensity, and her skill was impressive. However, his own private thoughts were filled with worry for the girl. He was afraid she would fail in the press of battle. He had seen what happened to physically weak soldiers. They did not last long.

Kesta said goodnight to Haiken on the twenty-second hour. She made her way up the hill, tired, but resolute. If there was a battle tomorrow, at least she was as ready as she could be. She would fight as hard as she was able, and she would fight for Fox. With that on her mind, she stopped for a rest at the edge of the camp. A white tent shone in the dark between the nearby trees, and she made her way towards it, stopping to listen at the sound of voices.

'I'm afraid, afraid that she'll die. It terrifies me. When I dream, I dream...terrible things, you can't imagine, yet I would rather be lost in one of those dreams than dream even once again last night's.' Kesta stiffened; the first speaker was Fox.

'What did you dream last night?' It took Kesta a moment to recognise the second voice, before she remembered the holy warrior who had ministered to her after the Shadow's attack.

'I dreamt that I survived the battle. I dreamt that I wandered alone amongst the dead, searching for other survivors. Instead, I found her. She was dead, and I tried to make it better, like the time I healed the gash on her cheek. I tried to bring her back, but she was dead. I was too late, powerless. I could do nothing for her. I wished I was dead too, rather than... alone.'

Kesta's mouth opened in shock. Why hadn't she realised they were talking about her before? Fox's voice was almost broken with emotion. She crept closer, until she could see Fox and Rashin, a short distance from the tent flap.

Rashin had his hand on Fox's shoulder; the Prince was sitting on the grass, his head bowed.

'You care for her. I said it once before, remember?' Rashin sat down next to Fox, attempting to comfort him.

'Yes. I remember. You told me to be careful, that I could make trouble for myself if other people knew.' Fox looked up at the night sky. 'I didn't realise how deep it goes, until last night. I'll die if she does.'

'What about Taneshka? She'll be fighting tomorrow. Are you not afraid for her?'

'Of course, but... She fights for her country, like me, she fights for her people and for the Land. Kesta fights because I dragged her into this. If she dies, it will be my fault.' Kesta felt a touch of resentment. She had as much reason to fight as Taneshka, and she hadn't been "dragged" into the situation. She had come here willingly. Purposefully.

Rashin stood suddenly. 'We're being watched, Fox.' Kesta crouched as low as she could, hoping that they would not see her in the trees. Fox turned so that she could see him in profile, then closed his eyes briefly. When he opened them, Kesta could see by the lamplight from the tent that he had gone red. He looked away from her, before murmuring to Rashin, in tones of mortified dismay: 'It's Kesta.' Kesta saw Rashin smile to himself as he walked towards her position.

'Come out Kesta. No point in hiding!'

Kesta raised herself upright and stepped forwards from among the trees. She looked at the floor as she came forward, reluctant to meet Fox's eyes. Rashin shook his head. 'You should know not to listen in on people. It is a good thing for you that it was only Fox and I who caught you eavesdropping, another might have acted rashly.' Kesta bit her lower lip, wishing, like Fox, that she could disappear into some hole.

'I'm sorry. I heard you talking about me, and I was curious.'

Rashin nodded at her apology and clapped her on the back. 'Good. Now, raise your eyes. Fox, you as well, the blush does not suit you.'

Fox grinned awkwardly. He caught Kesta's eye. 'Um... Let's forget what I said, for now. There are other... important things to do.' She nodded, holding on to the words "for now". Rashin leaned around the tent flap so that he could see if anyone had been witnessing the conversation. Satisfied, he beckoned for Fox and Kesta to follow him inside.

The tent was well lit. A lot of people were within, some sleeping, some gathered in small groups and talking in low voices. Still more sat around the edges of the tent, awake, but with their eyes closed. They seemed very relaxed, yet vibrantly alive. All were wearing the same white cloth as Rashin. 'They are praying,' Rashin said quietly to Kesta, gesturing to the warriors involved in meditation. 'Attempting to form a deeper connection with the Land. It is particularly vital that we do so, close to a battle.'

In the centre of the tent, a few of the holy warriors were grouped around an enormous steaming pot, talking quietly. Nobody made any comment on Fox and Kesta's presence, but they moved to make a space, nodding to Rashin. After a moment, Rashin spoke.

'Thank you. The young prince is here, and his companion. It is time our order got to know the boy who has faced down the enemy.' One of the older warriors turned to call more over to join them. He smiled at Fox and Kesta.

'We've heard all about you. We're all very interested in your situation, yours particularly, Lord Fox.'

A young woman knelt down beside Kesta and leant forward to talk to Rashin. 'The others are out amongst the men, raising morale, about twenty of us, but the elders are all here. You can begin.' She flashed Kesta a smile.

Rashin rose to his feet. 'Brothers! I would like you all to meet Prince Fox, heir to the throne of the Fox family. I know that some of you, our esteemed elders, disapprove of becoming involved in the politics of the Sacred Land, and are openly opposed to our being here, preparing to fight in a war. I tell you, this war *is* a holy one. The Shadow, the Corruptor himself, is continuously attempting to end this boy's life. The question is why? Why is the Great Perversion threatened so by Fox, a prince of men?'

There was silence for a while. It was not obvious to Kesta which warriors were the elders, as they all seemed young. Then a man with white hair spoke to Fox. 'Who were your parents? I heard that Steel Fox had no wife.'

'I did not know my birth parents. One of your order brought me to the gate of the Autumn Citadel. I was found wrapped in the flag of my father, Steel Fox, who took me in and adopted me.' The man who had asked the question looked puzzled.

'There have been no holy warriors in the Autumn Hills for many hundreds of years.'

'That isn't quite true!' The young woman next to Kesta interrupted, 'there has been a tower led by female holy warriors in the Autumn Hills all these years, if some of the order were only willing to acknowledge them!' Kesta sensed an underlying, older argument in her tone and her defiant expression.

'I don't want to discuss the validity of female warriors right now,' an elder said firmly, 'rather, I would like to address the theory that young master Fox here is one of us: that none of us realised he was a holy warrior.' Fox raised his eyes to look at the elder. The man leaned closer. 'Fox. Do you believe that power runs in the Land?' Fox felt everyone's eyes on him, including Rashin.

'Yes I do.'

'Do you know why there is power in the Land?' Fox shook his head.

'No.'

'Do you remember the stories from when you were a child, about how the Sacred Lands were made – about the Maker?'

'Of course I remember. The stories say that the Maker made everything and is within everything, even the lands over the western mountains, even the southern deserts.' The holy warrior nodded.

'We believe that to be true. There are few left now who do. Even magic was not believed in until recently, with sorcerers now more frequent, mostly coming from the north. The Sacred Land was in shock when the first occurrence happened, after so long. The massacre of the last village of natives, three hundred men, women and children slaughtered through sacrifice and dark fire in one day.'

There was silence. The holy warriors all knew this history, as they had heard it before. Fox and Kesta knew less, just the occasional reference as they had grown up. The elder looked at Fox with a discerning gaze.

'The village, ironically, was founded amongst the ruins of the native peoples' past conquerors. The Valley of Stones it is called now, the ruins of the great city Dracore, capital of the Dragon family, our people's ancestors who invaded this land many hundreds of years ago. The centre of the village was built around the old Dragon temple stone. After the massacre, the bodies of the villagers were found piled on the stone. That was years back now, but even with rainfall, and snow and wind, the blood has never washed off that stone. It has never even faded. The ruins of Dracore are a dark place. Our order do not go there.

'After that, events continued, showing more and more that the old magics and the sorcerers were returning. We searched for the source. We knew when and where, and our suspicions grew as we contemplated the massacre on the temple stone. A dark doubt rose in our minds. The old scrolls were opened. The old prophecies were studied anew. And then we found it. We found the writings on the Perversion of Light. The Maker's Enemy. The Order had faced him before in its original incarnation, before the Dragon family had even crossed the western mountains. We had come in our full strength, and had faced him down.

'To stop the Seven Great Shadows from allying and uniting with the Perversion of Light, the writings say that the Order travelled throughout the Sacred Lands, seeking them out. In those times, the mergence of the Maker was still fresh, and it was with the aid of the Land itself that the Order incarcerated the Seven in various monolithic stones, cursed markers of each battle.'

Fox looked straight at the elder. 'These stones…They're the Carcer Stones, aren't they?' The elder nodded.

'Yes. Unfortunately, that truth was overwhelmed by humanity's need to embellish and exaggerate. The Carcer Stones became folklore, myth. There are seven of them, the writings do not tell us where, but within are imprisoned the greatest parts of the whole that is the Enemy, whom you call The Great Shadow. A name most apt.'

Fox nodded. 'We do know where two of the stones are, at least. One of the Seven is destroyed. Its stone was on the edge of the East Forest.'

'And the other one has been released, I saw it on my way to Castle Rice Fox,' Rashin added. 'Fox, as I told you before, was responsible for the destruction of the first.'

The elder looked at Rashin for a moment, before turning to Fox, who returned his gaze.

'Please, continue. What happened after the incarceration of the Seven?'

The Elder continued, but he was looking at Fox in an entirely different way.

'The Order came together in the great valley, where one day the Dragon family would build their great city. As the Enemy cannot pass us without contest, and our powers are equal, the Perversion of Light became trapped in a circle by over four hundred of the Order. To stop him, they gave their lives to incarcerate him within the nearby stone. The war ended. The Order slowly began to re-grow over the years, but it has never grown to the numbers of old. Now, there are only ninety of us.

'The prophecies began when the Dragon family invaded. As they subjugated the natives, the old tales of the Land and the Maker died out, being replaced by a new teaching. When the great temple was built around the Prime Carcer stone, the Order knew what was happening. We joined the resistance, and many of our number died in the ensuing fights. Eventually we escaped – the Order and some of the native tribes together – to the Autumn Hills. The nephew of Dominago Dragon, the first king, gave us refuge. This was kept quiet until Dominago died.'

'After Ferrin Dragon – the prince who gave the Order sanctuary – had revealed his association with the Order, his family formed an alliance against him. After they failed to successfully invade the Autumn Hills, an uneasy peace was made between Ferrin and his surviving male cousin, and the peace allowed their families to grow.'

'After Ferrin died, his son, who was named Rashin, established himself as a strong leader. It was he who made peace with the other descendants of King Dragon. The three families marched on the corrupt capital of Dracore, where the High Council sat in the dark, worshipping the bones of Dominago himself. The High Council were spared, against Rashin's wishes, but the temple was demolished along with the rest of the city.

'Rashin defeated his greatest adversary, causing their family to split into two. Each family took a new name, borrowing from animals they respected, discarding the title of Dragon in favour of lesser names. Rashin became the first Fox – Iron Fox, your father's ancestor. The family in the north became Wolf, probably to claim superiority over the Fox family by choosing a more dangerous animal as their namesake.

'The two plains families became Tiger and Ox respectively, and so the families of the Sacred Lands were established.'

Fox waited while the elder paused in mid-speech. He knew of Ferrin, his father's ancestor, and that one of Ferrin's descendants had been called Rashin. 'Didn't Rashin become the founder of the Holy Warriors? But...he came after their starting...'

'Yes.' The Elder nodded. 'In fact he restarted the Order after it almost died out. The High Council's offspring spread across the kingdoms, meeting acceptance as advisors to the kings. The advisory councils almost succeeded in wiping out memory of the Holy Order entirely, hoping to take their place. If it had not been for Rashin's self-sacrificing abdication, the Council would have succeeded. Even now, the descendants of the Advisory Council have a grip on the thrones of the Sacred Lands.'

'I know,' Fox said darkly, thinking of Henshin. He sighed and looked at Rashin. 'It would take someone with the strength of your namesake to win the people away from the advisors.'

Rashin looked back at Fox for some time. 'Do you really think that you do not possess that strength?' Fox frowned.

'I don't know what you mean,' he said. Rashin smiled.

'You will. Please, elder, tell him about the prophecies.'

The elder nodded. His expression became grave and he leant forwards again so that he could meet eyes with Fox. The female warrior began helping herself to some of the stew from the pot, and as the elder began, the rest of the warriors followed suit.

'It was said by Rashin, or Iron Fox, if you prefer, that the Great Shadow would not remain imprisoned forever. He made this, and other predictions on his deathbed. Not even the Order gave credence to what he said at first, until he began to be proved right. The power of the Maker began to lessen, used to keep the Enemy and his Seven incarcerated. The power of the Land dwindled, along with belief in the Maker. The carcer stones were forgotten. All this came to pass as Rashin had predicted, and out of fear, the Order began searching for other prophecies.

'They say a verse appeared, written on Rashin's grave. Some believe that when he died, Rashin's spirit travelled to his tomb and etched it in the stone. I do not know how it came to us, but it reads thus:

> *"My Enemy sleeps in stone.*
> *Thus, he waits.*
> *The Bloodline sleeps in the spirit of man.*
> *Thus, I wait.*
> *When the Bloodline wakes, the bonds break.*
> *Shadow freed, by blood. By fire.*
> *My Blood will rise.*
> *War will fall.*
>
> *Await the Land Rising. His dreams are my dreams.*
> *Await the Dreamer. His dreams are my dreams.*
> *His burden is the Bloodline. His power is the Bloodline. My champion is the Bloodline.*
>
> *The Shadow wakes.*
>
> *The Rising will find him.*
> *My Bloodline will find him.*
> *I will find him.*
> *And he will be consumed.*
> *Or all will be consumed."*

'Do you know what Rashin's last words were before he died?'

'No.' Fox shook his head. Something was stirring inside him, he could hear his heart beating, feel his pulse pounding in his head. He was aware of his vitality. And something else…

'He said: "Only the Land Rising can defeat the Seven!" and then he died. The brotherhood thought that he had been delirious, and gave the words no importance. But after the second prophecy was discovered, we understood. The bloodline, the Maker's bloodline, would one day rise. We understood that it would wake in a person, and that only that person could defeat the Seven.

'The Maker's bloodline is already present in the Holy Order. Our immunity to the Great Shadow, as you call him, is his bloodline passed on through us. As a price, we cannot produce offspring; our warriors are found through dreams. We analysed many, hoping to find the Dreamer, the person that awakens the bloodline, who can defeat the Seven and thus weaken the enemy to the point of defeat.'

Rashin raised his hand. The elder stopped, and Rashin leant forwards. 'It is fate, perhaps, that it was one named Rashin who prophesied about the Rising's coming, and that one named Rashin would be the one to find the Rising himself.'

Fox stared in shock. 'Yes Fox,' Rashin murmured gently, 'I mean you.'

13
Black Deeds On The Eve Of Battle

Fox stood abruptly. His face was blank, but a tangle of white-hot emotion surged within. His ears were ringing in the silence. For a moment he did nothing, feeling everyone's eyes watching him, Kesta's astonished gaze, Rashin's gentle smile. Fox stepped out of the circle of faces and left the tent.

Rashin put a hand on the elder's shoulder to stay him from following. The holy warrior's smile became a frown, but Rashin was not surprised by Fox's reaction. He considered for a moment what to do, before letting his eyes come to rest on Kesta, who was dumbstruck. Rashin smiled to himself.

'Kesta, you go after him. Make sure he's all right.' The girl nodded, getting quickly to her feet. Her heart beating far too fast, she left the tent after Fox.

Fox was standing on the hillside. Kesta went to him, shivering in the cold breeze. They both stood, plains on their left, hills on their right, looking into the night. Kesta moved closer to him, studying his expression. She couldn't imagine what was going through his mind. She put a hand on his arm.

Fox turned to look at her. He blinked away a few tears, looking at her caring eyes, at the scar on her cheek that he had healed. Kesta found herself holding him. His body was trembling with emotion. He clung to her like she was a rock in a stormy sea. Everything felt like it was falling away, as if he had been living all his life in a closed room, and someone had just ripped the wall away, blinding him with brilliant daylight.

Kesta felt him in her arms, remembering the rainstorm in the fields at Rice Fox's castle. She remembered the feeling of concealed energy that she had touched upon, making her release his hand. Now she felt that same, vast energy, racing in a torrent through Fox's body. It felt as though he was rooted in the universe, while she hovered at his side, a faint image. Something had to be said. If she stayed silent now, the moment would go unmarked. But what was there to say?

'Are you all right?'

She looked in his eyes as she spoke. He looked back.

He was still a boy. She could see that, although something in her also said: *But much, much more.* Fox shook his head, then nodded, then laughed, looking down.

'I don't know. This can't be. That's what my mind keeps yelling, but every time, something interrupts. If this is real, I... I don't know how to handle this, Kesta. I don't see how I can do... whatever it is they want.'

'I'll help you. Taneshka and I will. I'll go anywhere you go. *Including* into battle tomorrow.' Fox opened his mouth to protest, but the look on her face made him bow his head, accepting defeat. He looked up at her from under his eyebrows.

'I can't argue with you, can I?' Kesta smiled and took a step back, letting go.

'Don't even try.'

They slept in the Order's tent, drifting into unconsciousness, borne by the soft singing of one of the brethren. Many of the warriors stayed awake to continue their prayer. They sat silently around the edges of the tent watching over their sleeping brothers. Fox had said nothing upon re-entering the tent, and Rashin had made sure no questions were asked. The night passed, and the camps slept. Fox dreamt none of his usual nightmares, surrounded by the warriors' protection.

On the hill, the cold pair of archer champions sat in grim silence. The dark hours passed slowly, slipping by the pair's tired eyes. The scene on the plain had become nightmarish; at least, it terrified the two veterans. Since the thirteenth hour, lights had continued to flow into the enemy encampment. As far as Koshra and Stavan could see, the enemy's number had almost doubled.

Tiger stood on the hill. Stavan and Koshra had gone to steal what sleep they could, ready to be called if the enemy made a move. The sun had risen and was shining faintly in the cold sky. On the plain, the now highly visible enemy force was waking. The biting wind tugged at Tiger's cloak, which he had wrapped around him, red and green against the brown leather of his armour.

Taneshka and Kesta were talking quietly behind the king. Taneshka listened as Kesta told her what the holy warriors had revealed.

'Do you think that they're right?' Taneshka asked. Kesta looked at the Tigress for a solemn moment.

'Yes. But I don't think it's fair. There's too much for him to do, and he's only a boy.' Taneshka frowned.

'He's more than that, remember? That day at the Loop proved that. And you said yourself what he did to that creature, the carcer shadow?'

'Yes.' Kesta nodded slowly.

'So he is capable. As far as we know, capable of anything.'

Kesta considered this. If that were true, then he was far more than a boy. But she needed him to be just that, simple, Fox. There was no way for her to be close to so much power.

She was falling in love with a boy, not a god.

Taneshka returned her gaze to the east valley, where her men were rising for the day. She gave Kesta a smile, stepped forward to murmur where she was going to Tiger, and left in the direction of her camp. She still had much to arrange.

Fox walked amongst the soldiers. There was little talk, and where there was, it was loud and nervous, and soon stopped. The men were not fools. They understood the numbers they were facing. To make things worse, the wind was bringing the sound of confident voices from the plain, distant laughter mocking the allied soldiers. Fox closed his eyes. It took him a moment to find the land beneath his feet, and then he could feel it all.

Haiken watched as Fox walked among the men. The prince stopped occasionally to speak in the ear of a soldier, momentarily joining a group before moving on. The champion watched as his prince left them as braver men, finding the scared, knowing them behind their fake hardness. Slowly at first, then spreading like a flame on lit paper, an atmosphere of calm resolution spread throughout the camp. Laughter was heard again, and voices rose on the breeze.

The wind changed. Across the plain, overconfident Ox soldiers fell silent at the sound of good cheer blowing to them from their diminutive enemy's camp. An air of unease began to move throughout the Ox ranks.

With a smile and a silent salute, a watching Haiken committed his life once again to his prince, his student. 'Until I die.' He murmured solemnly, before sheathing his sword and walking toward the central ridge.

Fox stood in the tree line of the forest on the promontory. One of his officers of archery stood with him, along with Stavan's second in command. Fox took a step forward, leaving the shade of the trees. The wind buffeted against him as he stood looking out onto the plain.

The enemy were moving. Units of yellow-clad soldiers marched away from camp, not advancing, but forming up. Here and there Fox could see Ox champions riding to and fro, directing the movement. So, they did have some horse. By the looks of it, perhaps two units of cavalry could ride out against them. Perhaps one-hundred, one-hundred-and-twenty horsemen. Fox took a deep breath. His strategy relied heavily on the archers. All together there were two hundred archers available to him, and just half of Ox's cavalry would be able to tear them apart. Unless he could force them to dismount...

Fox smiled as the plan formed in his mind. He turned and walked back into the trees. Here, at least, the green aspens were growing a fair distance apart. Their branches grew from high up the trunk, unlike the beeches and birches farther in, where the branches were low and interlocking. If the cavalry could be lured in to the forest, Fox knew he could make good use of a trap.

There was no cavalryman alive, Fox knew, that would willingly charge into thick forest. But perhaps an overconfident commander would risk entering these, thinner woods. Fox walked up to Stavan's man and his own officer. To get this right, they would need the necessary resources, and the cooperation of all the archers.

'How much bowstring do we have?' The two archers were surprised by the question.

'We always carry extra on campaigns, but it's untreated. Basically silk twine, nothing more,' Stavan's officer answered, looking bemused. 'Why?'

'I want to lay a trap for Ox's cavalry. The question is, do we have enough twine?' The officer shared a slow, wicked smile with his opposite.

'How much do you need, my lord?'

Tiger listened to Rashin in rapt silence. Fox had always struck him as… different, but he would never have imagined what Rashin was now telling him. The king believed the warrior, now that he had been told; there were no doubts in his mind. He understood why Taneshka was so drawn to Fox, why he was, why his men were. They all shared a love of the Land, and now Rashin was telling him that, in a way, Fox *was* the Land.

Tiger had not completely understood Rashin's words about the Maker, but he believed in Fox's importance. He knew intuitively that his daughter would leave with the prince once the time came, and that many of Tiger's own men would also want to follow, if Fox led them through this battle intact.

Tiger did not feel threatened, as such, but the feeling that his time as a leader was coming to an end returned. Tiger was content. If Fox was the way forward for his people, then he would not stand in the way. All that mattered for now was the upcoming battle.

'Where is His Highness?' The King asked, looking about. By her red hair he could see his daughter along the hill, but Fox did not appear to be with her.

'I don't know,' Rashin answered, 'but it is possible he has gone to overlook the plains. He may be on the promontory.' Tiger nodded.

'We'll all go there, the champions as well. The enemy are breaking camp. Let us do the same!'

Rashin entered the tent. The warriors were packed into the small space, listening to one of the elders. Rashin waited politely until the older man had finished. When the elder turned to look at him questioningly, he stepped forward and spoke.

'We go to join the King and the Rising Prince on the central ridge. This is the last time I will ask the question: will you all fight today?'

There was silence for a moment, and then the female warrior spoke up. 'We will. The Land's Rising requires our help, we have no right to deny it.' Rashin nodded.

'Good. Prepare your weapons. Pray, and prepare your weapons!'

We will need both.

Taneshka watched as her men carried out her orders. She could see some of her father's champions leaving their men and heading into the forest on the central ridge. They were meeting Fox and Tiger there, to survey the enemy positions. Taneshka decided she would join them as soon as her preparations were complete. Looking up at the sky, the Tigress thanked the Land that there was no rain.

A young soldier ran up to Taneshka and saluted. 'We're finished Taneshka, sir.'

Taneshka smiled at the use of the word "sir" and saluted. 'Good. The tree trunks?'

'Filled. All the dry wood and leaves we could get hold of.'

'Excellent.' Taneshka watched as the young man hesitated, before asking,

'Um, Tigress, forgive me... I was wondering, do you know where Prince Fox's maid – Kesta – is? I wanted to talk to her before...'

'Before the battle? She's with Prince Fox on the ridge, I'm about to join them myself.'

'I'm not allowed to leave my unit.'

Taneshka did not have time for this, but the young man's disappointment moved her. 'Can I take a message to her?' He shook his head. Taneshka looked up at the ridge. She should be there by now. 'I'll tell her you asked after her. What's your name?'

'The scouts have been sent out, my lord. They're going to circle the enemy camp as close as they dare. You were particularly interested in cavalry?' Fox nodded.

'Yes. I want to make sure there are none being kept in reserve. We can't afford to be surprised.' The officer saluted and withdrew.

Tiger stood beside Fox. The man smiled and drew in a deep breath. The plain stretched out into the distance. The wind was whipping at the branches of the trees behind them.

'It's a sort of contentment,' Tiger said, stretching, and checking that his sword was at his side. 'Knowing that you've committed and can't go back. Knowing *exactly* what it is you'll be doing in the next few hours.' Fox nodded, but internally disagreed.

He did not feel content. A tumble of fears and excitements filled him, so he felt as though he might be sick, and at the same time felt the urge to take his staff and charge at the enemy. At the back of his mind rose the fearful shadow of anxiety for Kesta.

Kesta came through the trees now, followed closely by Stavan and Koshra. The three were talking, but their conversation ended as they reached Fox and Tiger on the brow of the ridge. They greeted Tiger, and Koshra and Stavan began to discuss the positioning of the ranks that their archers would be supporting. Kesta stopped next to Fox.

'What are you thinking?' she asked him.

'Everything,' he replied. Kesta laughed.

'You're afraid?'

'Terrified. You?' Fox looked at his closest friend, studying her dark eyes in that perfect, unremarkable face, unmarred to his mind, despite the scar. Kesta was shivering a little, but it was hard to tell if it was from the cold wind or from fear. Fox supposed it was a bit of both. He put a hand on her shoulder, longing to hold her, but fearful of watching eyes, remembering Rashin's advice. 'If...When we come through this, I...'

Rashin and Renn's approach interrupted him. The holy warrior was talking earnestly with the advisor, who was carrying a sword. For the first time since arriving, Fox saw Lannos, the other advisor, and Daris with him. Seeing the young advisor took Fox by surprise. The archers must have decided to keep him on, Fox supposed. Daris saluted when he saw Fox, surprising him still further. Advisors bowed, they didn't tend to salute. Lannos was carrying an officer's buckler. For a moment, Fox missed it, but when the older man passed the buckler, along with its attached blade, to Daris, Fox understood.

'You enlisted? In the infantry?'

Daris smiled. 'I am an archer. Did you think that Koshra taught me nothing while I advised her?' Fox shook his head, smiling.

'It seems like she was the one advising you, Officer, not the other way round!'

Daris nodded, agreeing. 'She is a good teacher.' He saluted smartly to Koshra as she turned to him. 'I am ready, Champion.'

Lannos bade Renn and Daris goodbye. The advisor was limping, Fox saw, as the man walked away through the trees. Fox wondered whether the advisor was relieved or frustrated, or both, at being denied a place on the battlefield by his disability. Koshra coughed to get Fox's attention, she and Stavan wanted to be briefed on the plan.

'How are we stopping their cavalry, sir?'

Fox smiled. 'Your officers are handling that now, Koshra. See?' he pointed into the near woods, which were filling with archers. Unlike the other foot soldiers, they didn't march in ranks but stepped through the trees in tight groups around their officer. A few of the archers were stretching lengths of twine between tree trunks. They operated in a concave curve, sticking to the poplars near the edge of the woods. The lengths of twine were all tied at one height; a man on a horse checked each length to make sure it was correct. In the gloom, the twine was almost invisible.

Koshra nodded, tired eyes bright with excitement. 'Very... inventive sir. Fiendish. We withdraw when they charge, and take them once they dismount?'

Fox nodded. 'If it works.' He smiled at Kesta. 'Are you ready?'

A horse raced across the plain towards the central ridge. Its rider clung to it in desperation. Blood seeped through his hempen shirt and stars darted behind his eyes from the pain. The horse began to take the steep climb of the hill, refusing to slow up. When the beast came to an unsteady stop in front of Fox and Tiger, archers ran forwards from the trees to pull the rider from its saddle. Fox knelt beside him. 'Where are you hurt?'

'My side, here, aah-that stings! Lucky spear thrust my lord, I'm sorry.'

'No, no sorries. They were lying in wait?'

'Aye, sir. Took Ralim from the saddle, I think he was alive when I escaped, but I can't be sure.'

'What about the cavalry?'

The scout swallowed. 'Two units, like you said. No more. I saw their provision chain, wagon after wagon sir. There must be enough to feed everyone on the south plains for a month or two!

My family are starving lord, it's the same everywhere, but if we could get our hands on that food…'

Fox rose. He wished he could attempt to heal the wound, but he knew he would need all of his energy for the battle. 'Get this soldier to the Holy Order's tent, there should be someone left there to tend to the wounded.'

Two archers hurried to comply with Fox's order as he turned and looked out onto the plain. There was movement at the front of the mass of yellow silk and spears. Rashin and Tiger stepped closer to get a look.

'It's Ox's flag sir.' Fox glanced at the archer who had spoken. He was right.

The flag stopped just short of halfway between the hill and the enemy. At this distance, Fox was able to see who was standing below. One of the figures was bound; green silk flowed from beneath leather armour. Two other figures were standing on either side of the captive. Fox's heart jumped unpleasantly when he realised that one of them was Ox himself. 'Oh, Land, he's here!' Fox murmured, unconsciously taking a step forward. The other of the two was young, and black haired, like his father. Prince Danakai Ox, sole heir to the Ox throne.

Fox took a step back, shocked. The confidence of Ox amazed him. His entire male family stood on the plain. Their royal guard stood behind them, fourteen muscle-bound axemen, one holding the yellow Ox flag. Fox knew that Ox was confident, perhaps overly so, but he was not stupid. Once battle was met, Ox would bury his son and himself in the depths of the army, away from harm. So close, and yet, so far.

Kesta joined Fox. 'Is that Ox?' Fox noticed that she was shivering more than before.

'Yes. That's Ox. He's probably about to offer us a chance to surrender.'

The figure on the plain took a step and began to speak, his words carrying with the wind.

'Prince Fox! Are you the runt on the hillside I can see?' Fox didn't answer. 'I received your message! Entertaining, very amusing. Your great weakness, boy, is your conscience! It's going to kill you!' There was laughter from the Ox lines. Ox paused to enjoy the moment, before continuing, 'I have a captive, Prince Fox, one of your alliance's men. The wretch serves well as an example of your families. At my mercy. Soon to be dispatched.' The man bent down close behind the captive soldier and seemed to be whispering something in his ear. As he rose, Ox smiled. 'And, due to your disrespect, Fox cub, you and he will all die in pain.'

There was silence. Fox felt Haiken appear behind him. He glanced around, seeing Taneshka with him. 'So much for the offer of surrender. Are all our men in position?' The two nodded.

Fox returned his gaze to the scene below, his face set. He anticipated what was to come with sickening anger, a righteous fire in his veins.

On the plain, Ox nodded to his son. The dark haired youth moved forward, drawing one of two sabres from a black leather sheath. As the Ox prince stood over the bound soldier, raising his blade, Kesta bit her lip in anxiety. The dark, urgent feeling in the pit of her stomach warned her of what was about to happen. Taneshka put her hand on Fox's arm. 'He's one of mine.'

'He's one of ours.'

The blade hung in the air. Sunlight reflected off the steel as the prince flexed his muscles. An almost vacant expression was on his face, suggesting nothing of guilt within. As the blade wavered above him, the soldier lifted his face. Tears of fear or pain were in his eyes, and he shook, but his voice was strong.

'For Taneshka! For Fox! Tiger! My king, Tiger! My lord Fox and the Laaaaaand!' The wind dropped to nothing at his defiant roar.

For a moment there was silence. Then shout after shout rose from the allied lines on the hilltop, spreading to the forces in both valleys, in a mighty salute. The scout raised his face to the sky, eyes closed, bathed in the war cries. Prince Ox faltered, eyes darting to and fro along the allied lines. The roar died away, but the young man was visibly shaken. Silence fell. His father took a step toward him. 'Do it! Now!'

There was silence as the scout's head rolled into the thick grass. Fox looked away, gritting his teeth in anger. Taneshka seemed to shake with it as she held back her tears. She had seen death, and taken lives, but never seen such callous disposal of human life. It was she that led the response. The girl screamed defiance at King Ox, who was walking back across the plain with his son. The roar of the army rose behind her, drowning out the cheering of the enemy. Fox turned and strode with purpose to Tiger's side.

'We go to our positions, now! Ready the lines! Champions to their posts! Stand strong, and when they come, hew them to the ground! We'll outweigh his blood with theirs, a thousand times over!'

The champions saluted, disappearing into the trees to get to their units. The archers began to line up in their place. Taneshka nodded fiercely to Fox and, gripping her spear, set off towards the east valley. Tiger called the departing Rashin back, and Kesta joined them all, drawing her wing-swords.

'Fox. I have a gift for you.' Tiger spoke, taking a wooden case from one of his guard. As the king slid the case open, steel mirrored the sun. Fox drew the gleaming blade from the case with a look of wonder on his face.

The sword was high quality autumn steel, light as air and keen as sunlight. It balanced perfectly, a beautiful, deadly double-edged weapon, with a one-and-a-half-hand grip below an elegant crosspiece. The prince swept the blade through the air. It sang as it cut the sky.

On the plain the Ox forces were hurrying into their marching positions. The movement did not go unnoticed by an impatient but polite Rashin, who waited at Tiger's side. The king smiled at Fox's reaction. 'Name her, and then Rashin can sanctify her for you. May she serve you well.' Fox bowed deep.

'I name this sword Tiger's Gift.'

Tiger laughed. 'May she fight well alongside Tiger's Fang! Rashin?' The holy warrior nodded, accepting the blade from Fox. For a moment Rashin held the blade, eyes closed. When he swayed on his feet, Tiger stepped close to steady him, surprised by the warrior's reaction.

'I have rarely felt the Land so strongly.' The warrior shook his head in wonderment. He gave the sword back to Fox. 'Use it well. As far as I can say, that blade is as sanctified as they come!' Then he bowed, nodded to Tiger, and left the hill as fast as he was able, running to join the other warriors on the shoulder of the western valley.

Tiger hugged Fox firmly, surprising the young prince still further. The king departed, leaving Fox surrounded by Fox and Tiger archers. And Kesta, who smiled bravely at him, hiding her growing terror.

On the plain, the blood of Ralim the scout soaked into the ground.

Across the leagues, the Great Shadow turned his head. His enemy stood close to death. The Shadow set himself to his task. The Rising was close to that dark border, but close wouldn't do. Until the deed was done, the Great Shadow would leave nothing in the hands of fate.

14
Thunder In The Land

Kesta struggled to breathe normally. She gulped in air to slow her breathing, to stop her hands from shaking. Her eyes darted up and down the enemy line. They were moving. Fox was shouting out orders and the archers were responding, encouraged by Koshra and Stavan.

Kesta flexed her fingers around the hilts of her wing-swords to steady them, attempting to calm herself.

The Ox army was still a fair distance away, out of range for even the best of the archers. Kesta saw Fox join hands with Stavan and Koshra, in a brief triangle of resolution. He returned to her side.

The invisible transformation she had witnessed in the village was upon him again. 'Peace. We all fear.' His hand rested tenderly on her shoulder. A feeling of calm emanated from him, and Kesta felt herself relax a little. The nausea and the trembling receded. She took a deep breath.

In the east valley, Taneshka took a moment to look back at her father's position. He was in command of the reserves, on the slope of the hillside. Taneshka herself was deep in the army's line. Her trap was concealed by their ranks, which stood out into the valley, apparently overextended. The line looked unthreatening, the badly positioned soldiers appeared ill equipped, carrying little weaponry. Taneshka smiled. It was perfect.

In the west valley, Rashin stood on the slope of the central ridge, the hill behind. The front lines were spread out below, waiting in quiet determination. Around Rashin stood most of the other holy warriors. Some stood with swords, a few with spears. The lone female warrior, Nayime, held a heavy axe head on the end of a short chain, along with a long knife at her belt. Rashin himself flexed his fingers. As they closed into a fist, the blades on his wrist snapped forward, presenting a lethal combination of cutting edges and stabbing points along his knuckles. The weapon extended along his arm, with a short, sharp spur at his elbow. The holy warrior repeated the exercise with his other hand.

Haiken waited on the hilltop. His job was to direct the entire west valley. His messengers waited in kneeling positions around him. With practised ease, the Champion picked out the Spear units who would first meet the enemy's charge, the Sword, who would hold the line, and their relief, mixed units of Sword, Spear and Axe. Buried in the middle were the Linestormers, patiently waiting their time to make a devastating counter attack.

On the central ridge, Fox and Kesta stood, awaiting the wall of yellow marching steadily towards the valleys. Koshra drew back from her position to speak to Fox. 'What if they decide to attack the hilltop?' Fox shook his head in answer.

'That would be a bad move. It's a steep hill, and they're a large, clumsy force. By the time they get close enough to hear our voices, they'd be falling over their dead. They'll use their cavalry.' Koshra nodded in agreement.

Kesta felt the air, clean and fresh, the wind refreshing on her face and forehead, the hilts of her weapons, the gliding of silk over skin, the weight of her armour. She watched, transfixed, as the archers began to nock their arrows, tilting back their bows, waiting for the order.

'The wind is still against us! Hold, we must make every shaft count!' Koshra commanded, eyes on the plain.

The enemy army was dividing. It began to peel apart, very slowly, as the thousands attempted to move all at once. The force that was intended for Tiger's valley was smaller than its partner, and as Fox turned to examine the east valley, he saw why. There was no evidence of Tiger's elite unit, the long spears, in the formation, and the soldiers in their place looked ill-equipped. Fox hoped Taneshka knew what she was doing.

'They're going to be packed in tight in our west valley!' Koshra spoke again, 'Ox is forcing everything he's got into a bottleneck. He's throwing away his frontlines!' Fox turned to stare at the western column of the enemy.

'The two forces are almost divided!' One of the Fox officers shouted. He had thrown down his buckler to more accurately loose arrows at the enemy. 'Surely they're close enough now!'

Stavan and Koshra both shook their heads. 'Not yet. Not with this wind.'

The wind seemed to have heard Stavan's voice. It turned. The banner above the Tiger archers swung to flutter in the opposing direction. A grim smile came over Koshra's face.

'Loose!' A multitude of barbed shafts rattled away into the sky. Stavan's archers waited still, unable to fire into the enemy's east column, as the wind was now against them.

Fox watched intently. Every flight of arrows struck home in the enemy's near flank, but due to the tremendous number of Ox troops, the arrows seemed almost ineffectual. They volleys were forcing the enemy's march further west. The entire Ox army, disorganised in its unwieldy size, was being pushed against the far hillside, where a tumble of loose rocks and scree jutted from the face of the hill. Fox clenched a fist at this small triumph; pushing the enemy away from the central ridge would relieve the pressure on Rashin and his soldiers on the shoulder of the hill, concentrating the Ox attack on the strongest part of their defence.

Kesta was hopping from foot to foot, excitement and fear weighed now with an impatience to get the waiting over with. Even Stavan was showing anxiety as he waited for Ox's east column to come into range.

'The west column are now full in range,' Koshra reported, as yet another flight of arrows let fly, 'and their force is almost separated.' Fox turned and looked to where the Ox army were still joined at the rear guard. They were blocking other units, Fox could see, several archery units, and, to Fox's dismay, the cavalry.

Again as if on cue, the wind dropped to nothing, and Stavan let out a triumphant cry. Both columns of the enemy were now in range, and as the first flight of arrows left the Tiger bows, the champion began to relax. Fox settled as well, at least now they were fighting at full efficiency. Looking behind him, on either side, Fox could see the two columns of Ox's army nearing the allied lines.

From his hillside, Rashin could see the Ox ranks increase their speed. The frontlines broke, and began to charge. Rashin smiled grimly. They would not break through the solid defence, not in this narrow valley. The holy warrior spoke a hurried prayer for the soldiers in the Fox front line as the yellow-clad enemy closed.

The lines met with a clash of flesh and steel. The defence held well, pushing back the enemy, and as the weight of Ox's army pushed their ill-fated front line forward, the bodies began to drop.

It looked almost as if the Fox front line were building a fortress from the yellow bodies, a wall of flesh to slow down the enemy.

On the ridge, Fox saw the meeting of the forces. Although it cheered him momentarily, a quick glance around was enough to sober him. The Ox force below was still immense, and that was without even taking into account the east column about to make contact with Taneshka's troops.

Taneshka saw the first wave coming. What pleased her was that she could see the second, third and fourth waves coming at the same time, the entire column were charging. Her troops in the neck of the valley waited for the signal as the enemy hurtled towards them. Taneshka glanced back to where her father stood. He would be able to see better than her.

The signal came. Taneshka passed it on immediately, her heartbeat racing as the attack drums began to sound. Before the Ox soldiers reached their front line, the entire forward Tiger force fell back to the narrower safety of the higher valley. They stopped and turned behind the pre-prepared, hollowed out tree trunks and bundles of dry fuel, and suddenly, as if from nowhere, each man took up a long spear passed up from the rear lines. The Tiger front now bristled death.

It was too late for the Ox east column, they were committed to the action. Their despairing front line was messily impaled on the forest of spears, driven back as far as the third wave.

From the trees of the central ridge, at a point closest to Taneshka's front line, a small unit of Stavan's men advanced. Several flaming arrows flew into the earth to the rear of the enemy's back line. For a moment it seemed as if nothing would happen, and then the oil went up with a roar. Tigress Taneshka's trap was sprung.

The fire surrounded the Ox soldiers, throwing them into a panic. The only way out was through the thicket of spears, and if they chose that way, there was no coming back. Taneshka threw back her head and howled a triumphant warcry at the sky. The sound of her men echoing her filled the valley. 'Tiiiiger!'

The enemy were now completely separate. Fox watched as the divide grew. The enemy archers were following the west column, heading for the opposite hillside. It wasn't a bad strategic move. If they climbed the difficult rocky slope they would be able to advance along the hilltop and loose arrows into the Fox defence. Fox tried to put the thought out of his mind, turning his gaze back to the plain. The Ox cavalry were coming down the middle of the gap. Fox grimaced, and called Koshra and Stavan's attention to the problem.

'Keep it up!' Koshra yelled, 'Don't stop, not until I give the word!'

Fox shook his head. 'We're going to have to time this right. If we get caught up here, we'll be torn to pieces.' Stavan stood his ground.

'Not going to happen. We'll be in those trees in no time. The Tigress' trap appears to have worked, and so will this.' Fox spun around to look on the east valley, smiling as he saw the dwindling Ox troops caught between the conflagration and a sharp place.

'Good.' He murmured. 'When they're done there, they can come around the back of Ox and make him pay for his overconfidence.'

Fox turned back to the front. Kesta tensed up, the horses were approaching faster than she had first thought, galloping at full stretch. Around her, the archers continued to loose shafts into the enemy.

'One volley at the horsemen?' Koshra suggested in a shout.

'No. Don't kill the horses. I want them alive, if possible. We *need* them. If they survive this charge, I want them to be put to use. Haiken will know what to do with them.'

A Tiger officer signalled, pointing down onto the plain. 'My lord! They kept back a unit of archers. They're moving in behind the cavalry.' The officer glanced fearfully down the hill at the speeding horses. An archer's greatest fear was open ground and armed men on horseback. Fox waved the officer away; the Ox archers were a problem to face once he had survived the cavalry. The enemy horsemen were now so close that their voices were audible.

'Last time! Make it count!' Koshra bellowed. The archers drew and released, sending their last flight into the sky. The thudding of hooves began to sound, drumming through the turf. Koshra waited, eyes wide, on the edge of her nerve. Finally, at Fox's terse nod, she gave the order.

'Now! Run! To the trees!' As one, the archers broke for the light tree cover. Fox followed them in, aware of Kesta as she ran beside him.

In the shadow of the trees, Fox and Kesta struggled to calm their breathing. Fox put his back to a tree near the edge, and Kesta did the same with another on his right. 'Courage!' Fox gasped, seeking eye contact with her. She gritted her teeth and raised a wing-sword in salute. The pounding of hooves echoed the drumming in her chest.

Fox waited, straight as a spear-shaft, head to the side as if listening, his eyes on the ground. He held his gleaming Tiger's Gift loosely, waiting for the enemy. Kesta closed her eyes and uttered a prayer to the Land, knuckles white from gripping the hilts of her swords.

The horses stormed up the hillside. With a roar from the cavalrymen, the first of them raced across the hilltop towards the trees. The front-runners raised their axes, hollering their approach. The first man, an Ox officer, spurred his horse on, pulling away from his comrades.

The first line of bowstring, taut in the trees, decapitated him.

His head spun away trailing blood, and his body galloped onwards, hands still holding the reins. The war cries became cut off screams. The first three lines of horsemen were brutally unhorsed.

The headless rider careered past Kesta, spraying her. The horse's wild eyes flashed by, and it disappeared deeper into the trees, carrying its macabre rider. Kesta's gut reaction was to hurl, but she forced it down, muscles in her jaw tightening painfully, her arms shaking. One by one, other horses came hurtling by, some with empty saddles, others with half empty saddles. Fox waited, his face impassive as the riot passed. He was not unrealistic; he knew that not all of the enemy had died on the bowstrings.

The arrival he had been waiting for appeared. An Ox cavalryman, sent berserk by the slaughter of his comrades, forced his terrified horse between the trees, axe in hand. He sighted Kesta, and with a horrific scream, drove the horse forward. Fox made a sweeping hand movement as the soldier started his axe-swing. The man was torn from his saddle by invisible arms and thrown to the ground. As he staggered to his feet, Kesta thrust her right wing-sword into his throat. Blood bubbled over the clean steel and she jumped back, firm against the tree trunk as he slumped.

The man was not the last. The remaining scores of men entered the forest on foot, leaving their terrified horses on the hilltop. The soldiers came through the trees at a run, hefting their ball-headed axes, nasty small-bladed weapons mounted on short poles.

Fox took the first soldier, stepping from behind his tree and swinging an almost laid-back attack. The target stopped at the blade, his legs kicking out as they were whipped forward by the momentum. Fox tugged Tiger's Gift free from the dead man's face, and met the next attack with time to spare, blocking an axe-swing before opening the swinger's stomach.

Kesta clung to her tree, letting some of the enemy run by her. Once she had gathered enough courage to move, she made a minimalist attack, sticking her foot out from behind the tree. The childish move worked, and Kesta forced herself to drive the blades of her swords between the young man's shoulder blades.

The enraged cry of one of his comrades alerted Kesta just in time, she spun away and her enemy's axe head buried itself in the tree trunk. As he struggled to pull it free, she turned back and slashed at him. It took a further two hacks to take the man's life.

Fox moved between the trees with the grace of a predator. Where Kesta or one of the knife-wielding archers missed an enemy soldier, he covered the gap, coming from nowhere to remove that soldier from the action with all the efficiency of a wolf among lambs. His movements were beautiful, but not pretty, his kills as messy as any other, but carried out like dance, precise and swift.

Koshra took down one of the last cavalrymen by putting an arrow through his skull from five metres distance. As he fell, the forest became silent.

In the valleys on either side, the shouts and cries of battle were suddenly very audible. Fox looked around, seeing with great relief that few of the archers had fallen. 'Round up the loose horses! Herd them along to Rashin's reserve, the swordsmen can take them.' Fox turned back to the thinning tree line, and the empty hill. 'It's not nearly over yet.'

Taneshka threw Tiger's Fang into the air, catching it with ease. Her celebration produced cheering from the soldiers around her. Save for the two long spear units, none of the small army had been tested in combat. Taneshka stood, tensed up in anticipation, wondering how long she would be able to wait before making the order for the killing blow. Her entire force were baying for blood, their blades still clean. Heart beating fast, Taneshka advanced.

The long spear were retreating, not under enemy pressure, but to make room for what was to come next. Taneshka stepped past the foremost spearmen, determined to perform this strike herself. Some of the special unit were setting alight to the bundles of dead wood as she arrived, and as the enemy rallied around their last Champion, the flames leapt into the sky. The moment the fire began to lick at the dry wood and dead leaves, Taneshka ran forward and pushed one of the trunks away. It rolled down the hillside, gathering momentum, before exploding into flames in the face of Ox's men. The last of the east column died in the flames.

Rashin was fighting a desperate battle on the shoulder of the west valley. The other warriors stood around him in a tight group, but the enemy were still piling in. Rashin raised his hands to defend himself yet again, parrying a spear thrust and stepping inside the spearman's range. He delivered a killing blow. His hands were already slick with the blood of many.

'The Tigress has fought to a victory!' Cheers rose from the archers along the hilltop. Stavan's men joined Koshra's in loosing on the main force, driving the enemy still further up the uneven west hillside.

Fox examined the damage they had done to Ox's army. Even with the east column destroyed, and minimal allied mortality, Ox still outnumbered them two to one. Fox's eyes roved across the moving, fighting mass, until he spotted what no other had seen.

'Hillstormers! Coming up the hill!'

A unit of infantry with wide, curving shields and rattan armour had broken away from the main force and were approaching the hill. They were an anti-archery unit, equipped to survive arrow salvos and move fast enough to catch the retreating targets. Their curved, hook-like swords were designed to strike around their shields, without catching the weapon or leaving themselves open.

An officer called out, 'Their archers approach! They're moving to aim at Tigress Taneshka's unit!' Fox made a quick decision.

'Send a messenger to Haiken's relief unit. Tell them we need that cavalry charge, now, we have archers approaching on the central plain. Go!'

Kesta touched Fox's bloody arm to gain his attention. 'The hillstormers are gaining ground!'

Fox closed his eyes, calling on the calm rush of the Land to steady him. 'We wait.'

Thunder rolled some distance away. At first, Kesta paid no attention, but then, as the thunder rumbled out again, she frowned. There was not one cloud above. Thunder from an empty sky?

Fox placed himself in front of the archers, hearing their shafts hissing away above his head as he looked down at the approaching hillstormers. If they reached the hilltop, the archers would be in dire trouble.

There was need of a distraction, a sudden occurrence that would throw the attackers completely. Fox swallowed, and began to gather strength. Suddenly he could feel the earth beneath his feet, the footsteps of the enemy approach, the screams of the dying. Beneath it all, stone. The Land's bones, where the Maker's legacy ran strongest, where power flowed like the blood rushing through Fox's veins.

Fox let out a cry, raising Tiger's Gift above his head. The sword mirrored the afternoon sun as it stood in salute. The hillstormers saw the prince's defiance, but did not waver. They were close now.

From the trees, without warning, mounted soldiers rode the length of the hill, down the slope and onto the plain. They went through the approaching archers easily. Fox Family blue silk fluttered from the leading horseman's spear; Ox's horses had been put to good use. They wheeled west, approaching Ox's rear flank at an angle. Taneshka, running full out, arrived as the horses passed.

Seeing Fox's blade raised, and Kesta near him, Taneshka ran forward, the long blade of Tiger's Fang lifting as she went.

Fox's cry continued like the sounding of a horn. A raw, pure sound, it seemed to ring from the steel of Kesta's weapons. Swallowing her fear, she stood beside him, facing the hillstormers down.

Suddenly Fox went silent. His arm came down, and Tiger's Gift pierced the earth at his feet. Fox felt the tip of the blade touch the stone beneath, and felt the sudden rush of power flowing up the sword and into his arm. With a swift move he pulled the sword clear, and the nearing hillstormers faltered as fire flowed across the flashing metal.

The sound of thunder rolled again, louder this time. And this time, Kesta recognised it for what it was. The thunder was in the land, not in the sky, and as the earth shook another time, Kesta felt it move her feet. Across the entire Twin Valley Ridge, the earth quaked. The Ox army stumbled as one, their attacking line again falling into disarray. The hillstormers fell to their knees. At once, the entire hillside of the west valley – with its tumbled mass of loose rock – collapsed. The Ox archers positioned amongst its boulders died in the landslide, which flowed down into the valley with the earthquake. Half the Ox force was killed immediately.

In the moment of silence that followed Koshra was heard to murmur in wonder, 'Land be praised!' And then, with a roar like a storm, battle was rejoined. The Ox army were on the point of collapse; it was only through the sheer will of King Ox's rage that his army stayed disciplined. The soldiers forced forwards by their champions and their King were severely shaken, but not yet beaten.

The hillstormers paused, unsure. As they made their minds up and started forward once more, a streak of fire-red hair and a long spear came over the hill. Tigress Taneshka struck like the tempest, killing her first of the battle, the hillstormer captain, in one spear thrust. Fox came to himself again, whirling Tiger's Gift into the nearest enemy. Kesta let the hillstormers come to her, one wing-sword sheathed on her back.

The hillside ran with blood. The archers, still loosing arrows, let out a cheer. At Koshra's command, the bows were laid down, and blades were drawn.

'Now we wait for Haiken to break their line,' Koshra told Stavan, who drew a sword in favour of his bow. The Tiger army gathered behind the archers on the central ridge like the executioner's sword above Ox's neck. Long spear soldiers came to the fore, their lances pointing down the hill at the enemy, awaiting the order.

Rashin had been given strength by the sight of the landslide and what it had done to the enemy. His warriors had pushed the Ox troops back, and they were wavering now, unsure whether to face the Fox troops, or the Tiger army on the ridge. Rashin saw that the Fox special unit, the linestormers, were marching to the front line of the west valley. The counterattack was about to begin.

Rashin pressed the advantage, attacking the confused Ox soldiers nearby. The holy warrior's white silk – painted now with blood – could be seen pushing forcefully into the yellow mass. At Ox's rear, the new Fox cavalry harried the back lines.

Ox had pushed forward to the centre of his army, to protect his son and himself from the pressing allied army. 'Curse the Holy Order! Let their blood turn to pus in their veins!' The king was panicking. 'What happened to my hillstormers? And where in the Land did their cavalry come from?'

One of Ox's guards stared wide-eyed at the surrounding enemy. 'I think they're our horses, my lord! I don't know how, but they stole our horses. They stole our horses! What… what is your will?'

Ox spat at the ground. 'Fight to the death! I'll take this bastard prince yet. We still outnumber them. Land save us!' His son looked at the ground, clutching his twin sabres tight. He had not expected to have to fight.

Haiken gave the order. The Fox defence opened momentarily, allowing the linestormers to charge through. The weapons they carried were triple-bladed axes. The Linestormers met the Ox front line with a mighty clash, the fox-heads of their axes sweeping down, through spear shafts and bone alike. In an instant, the Fox special unit were ploughing their way into the Ox lines.

'Are we ready?' Taneshka asked Fox. Her heart rate was surging, and she ached to charge down the hillside into the Ox flank.

'Almost,' Fox answered, watching the progress of the linestormers. A shout began, one of the Tiger officers banging his sword against his pauldron. The Fox officers joined in, banging their blades against their bucklers. The cacophony increased, until Fox could no longer hear himself think. He was caught along in the tide, and as the linestormers reached the middle of Ox's force, splitting them down the middle, Fox screamed out the charge. Like a flood pouring down the hillside, the allied archers and Tiger's army ran, feet flying down the steep slope.

Kesta would never have attempted to run down a hillside that steep outside of the moment. She would have been afraid that her feet would not keep up with the incline, that she would end up tumbling. Now though, with the army behind her, she flew, feet racing, feeling almost as though her wing-swords had caught the rushing air and she was flying. Fox ran beside her, bringing back his sword, readying himself for the attack. Taneshka was pulling ahead, Tiger's Fang ahead of her, steel spear-head hungry.

The two armies met with tremendous force. Kesta flung herself forward, close to the ground, to avoid the rising spears that came to meet them. She rolled upright between the first Ox soldiers, and keeping her head, swept in a wide circle, close to the ground. The wing swords severed tendons in the backs of her enemies' legs; they fell at once, to be trampled down by the long spears. Kesta joined Taneshka, joining her speed to the Tigress's range. They opened a circle in the Ox defences, allowing the Tiger archers to pour through.

Fox set off on his own. He cut a swath through the Ox soldiery, moving with increasing ease, Tiger's Gift flashing and whirling. His quick, deliberate movements opened holes in the Ox line as man after man fell. Each time Tiger's Gift cut the air, another yellow-clad soldier fell to the ground, dead or dying. Fox's movements took him closer to the hub of the action, where Ox and his son stood, surrounded by their royal guard.

'See him fight! Like a demon!' One of Ox's guards murmured in awe. 'He's coming this way!'

'Then kill him you fool! Land's sake, he is a sixteen year old *cub*!' Ox roared out a command, snatching one of his guard's battleaxes. 'If he reaches here, I'll kill him myself!'

Danakai glanced at his father. There were tears in the prince's eyes. He had just seen most of his father's mighty army obliterated, and now they were being fought into a corner. He didn't want to die.

As the nearby lines broke, anger rose to cover his fear. He stepped to the outer circle of men and drew his twin sabres.

The double action of the allied force broke the last of Ox morale. Some tried to run, but now they were surrounded on three fronts. Behind, the horsemen drove them together, until a tight circle of Ox soldiers remained around their king.

The allied forces had reduced an army of near ten thousand to less than thirty.

Fox stood on the edge of the circle of allied troops that hemmed Ox in. Breathing heavily, with streaks of blood up her arms and in her hair, Kesta joined him. Taneshka was already circling the knot of surviving Ox soldiers, spinning Tiger's Fang in her hand so that the long spear whirled behind her.

Danakai stood opposite Fox, shaking with anger. He was ignoring the calls to return to the inner circle and the Ox royal guards. It was too late now, he figured. There was nowhere on the battlefield that he could escape, and Fox had humiliated him and his father.

Fox stepped forward. The dark haired prince opposite glowered at him, holding his sabres ready. Fox shook his head. The blood of hundreds had run from his sword blade. These last did not need to die; Ox and his son could face merciful justice. But here stood the heir to the Ox crown, ready and waiting to fight to the death. Fox did not want to kill him.

Danakai Ox began to speak, and the army fell silent. His voice rang, tremulous and unsteady, edged with anger.

'I'm going to kill you. No one else interferes!'

'You can surrender. We don't have to do this!'

'No! Don't try to rob me of this! You've taken everything from me, don't take my revenge! You...*whoreson*! You've beaten us, brought my family low, *killed my men*! I'll kill you!'

Danakai ran at Fox. He slashed out first with his right arm, then his left. Fox stood motionless, expressionless. He made two small movements, barely moving. Danakai Ox was knocked away to the right by the hilt of Tiger's Gift. Fox advanced forward, ignoring the Ox prince.

One of the guards made an attempt, and Fox stepped off the line of attack, burying Tiger's Gift in the man's chest. With an exit thrust, Fox freed the blade, spinning to meet King Danashalk Ox.

With a yell, Taneshka and Kesta entered the combat, teaming up to take down two more of the enemy guards. Taneshka flicked Tiger's Fang out, letting her grip slide to the base of the spear, extending its range fully. One of the guards became impaled, and as Taneshka pulled her spear free, Kesta eliminated an enemy who had tried to take advantage of the Tigress's unbalanced position. The two fought around the edge of the circle, eliminating Ox's protection. Haiken joined them in a sudden flash of steel. The three fought a strategic battle, separating Ox's guards from the ongoing fight between Fox and Ox.

Fox faced his enemy. Ox held his battleaxe in an iron grip, face set. He spat at the ground. It was a distraction technique. Fox knew that Danakai was attempting to surprise him from behind; he could feel it through his feet. Almost lazily, Fox cut Danakai's leg as the prince passed. Blood flowed, and the youth scrambled to the side, gasping for air through a haze of pain. Fox stepped to meet King Danashalk's enraged response, parrying the blow and forcing the burly man back. Ox stumbled over a body and fell. As Fox raised Tiger's Gift, Danakai, forcing his pain to the back of his mind, rose up and attacked.

The blade pierced flesh with ease. *Something that brutal, should not be so easy*, Danakai thought. There should at least be *some* resistance. Blood spilled suddenly over trembling hands as the blade withdrew. *So easy,* thought the Ox prince, and toppled forward. Tiger's Gift shone, blade inexplicably clean, as the prince's dark lifeblood soaked into the earth. The same blood bubbled at the corner of the young man's mouth as he drew in a torturous last breath. 'S...easy.' His voice bubbled out, and he died.

Fox had felt the boy's approach and had reacted. He had felt his sword bite deep, he had heard the prince's last thoughts with startling clarity, and he had felt the boy die.

'Nooooooooo!' Ox cried out in anguish. He flung his battleaxe aside, and dropped to his knees in the blood-logged grass. His hands shook as he caressed his dead son's face, tears streaming down his own. When Ox looked up, Fox had to force himself not to retreat from his gaze. Pain filled eyes stared into his own, and another howl of grieved anger tore Ox's throat.

'Kill me! Kill me – I am yours to take! Take your sword, cleave my skull – you have already taken my life – now end it! My son, oh my son...' The king collapsed, shuddering with emotion.

Fox felt indecent, standing over his weeping enemy. He had not wanted to bring Ox this low, had scarcely considered how the battle would be won. One part of him saw what the allied soldiers saw, the final moments of a feared and hated enemy, the opportunity to end the war and feed the Land's starving. The other part of him saw the proud, arrogant man, who had lost everything, his pride, his men, his honour and his son. To kill a man in that position could not feel right.

Kesta stared wide-eyed as Fox stood over the broken king. She wondered at the torment in Fox's eyes. Taneshka made an impatient movement, everywhere Kesta looked; she could see the faces of those waiting for Fox to end it. Was she the only one who saw why he hesitated? Was she the only one who could see a man and his dead son? Her eyes found Rashin. The holy warrior had turned his face aside. So Fox's action was a foregone decision then. Ox would die, like Ralim the scout had, helpless and alone. A different victim, a different executioner. Fox.

The allied army began to beat their weapons against shields, sounding off shoulder guards as they beat in time. The rhythm built, growing and speeding up, and now men were adding their voices to the sound. A chant rose on the still air, hovering over the bodies of the dead.

'Strike! Strike! Strike!'

Fox closed his eyes as Ox opened his, hung his head as Ox lifted his.

Tiger's Gift came down; the breath in Kesta's throat caught, she looked away too late. A final word formed on the doomed king's lips.

'Son.'

The blade finished its course. The day's last sunlight shone off the wet red of the soaked grass, as light vanished from lifeless eyes. A breeze blew across the Twin Valley Ridge. It felt like relief to the survivors.

Fox's shoulders slumped. He turned away, seeing the blood run off his blade, leaving it clean. Tiger's Gift might remain stainless, but Fox felt steeped in blood. He walked through the allied lines, the men parting to let him through. Only when he had passed, and had begun to walk up the hillside did the cheering begin, resonating in Fox's ears, that could only hear screams.

15
Aftermath

The bodies of the dead outnumbered the living. Mass graves were dug below the central ridge. Many of the bodies had already been committed to the earth.

The corpses of Fox or Tiger soldiers were treated first. Fox did not omit body duty; he worked along with the others. Those with any wisdom chose not to approach him; he worked obsessively, caring little for the bloody mess around him.

Night came, and the allied soldiers returned to camp. The champions were too tired to maintain order, and Tiger soldiers joined Fox troops in their camp, and vice-versa. Fox was one of the last to return. He stood at the top of the hill, soaked in blood, desperately tired. Kesta and Taneshka joined him as the evening faded. The red sun lent them no heat as it sank behind the hilltop, bleeding faint crimson light across a landscape already stained.

'We must be done!' Taneshka groaned, sitting uncomfortably on the grass. Fox glanced at her, and wondered what she meant.

'All of our dead are buried. Are you all right?' She asked Fox, softly. He smiled at her, there were tears in his eyes.

'No. I don't think so. Are you?'

Kesta smiled sadly. She felt... fine, at least at the moment. But then, she hadn't done what Fox had done on the battlefield. She put a hand on his arm.

Taneshka got to her feet and grasped his other hand. 'I would have done it the same, in a second. Do you know what that man had been doing to his people? And his son was the same – a murderer, and worse. Don't feel too bad over their deaths.' Fox shook his head and dropped her hand.

'I thought I had seen it all. I thought that I was battle-cold. I was wrong. If they had fought me and I had killed them in the fight...that wouldn't have been so bad. For me.'

'Just as bad for them,' Kesta murmured, but immediately wished she hadn't.

'You think so? Dying over your son's dead body? With that as the last thought in your head?'

'No, of course not. I'm sorry.' She looked away. Fox sighed, looking down the valley.

The last allied soldier was found lying against the tree line on the central ridge. Kesta stared down in shock at the young swordsman. His sword was missing, but his body was miraculously whole. The terrible gash in his chest was hidden partly by his armour. Kesta put her hand to her mouth. She knew this young face, peaceful as it appeared in death. Taneshka came up behind Kesta, seeing her friend's reaction. She put a hand on Kesta's shoulder, and then withdrew it guiltily as she saw who it was that lay there.

'Oh Kesta! I'm sorry. I – I promised him I would tell you.' Kesta looked around at the Tigress.

'Tell me what?'

'That he asked after you. I forgot.'

Kesta knelt at the young man's side. She closed his eyes gently, feeling terrible that her reaction was not stronger. Could the battle have deadened her so much?

'I didn't even know his name,' she realised, standing and wiping her hand on her trousers. Taneshka put her hand on Kesta's arm. 'Tewger. He said that you could call him Tew.' Kesta swallowed. 'Goodbye, Tew.'

The camp rose to a cold day. There were some clouds now, edging into the sky. The wind was biting, and Kesta rubbed her hands together to keep them from going numb. She walked hurriedly between the tents, trying not to breathe in the thick smoke rising from the campfires, where soldiers were quenching the flames with used water. She rubbed her eyes to get the smoke out as she came away from the campsite, heading towards where Rashin stood talking with Fox and Tiger. Taneshka was a little distance away from them and she waved to Kesta as she came closer.

'Good morning! Cold today.' Kesta raised her eyebrows at this; it was unusual for Taneshka to comment on the weather. She looked at her friend's expression, reading the pain and shock behind the bright façade. Taneshka had fought like a true tiger, Kesta remembered, and she could understand the need to forget those actions. Her own hands had been trembling when she had woken suddenly in the morning, sweating from the terrible dream-memory of the previous day.

'It is cold.' Kesta smiled at Taneshka. 'What are our betters discussing over there?' Taneshka's expression broke as she laughed.

'Our betters? Speak for yourself, Kesta. Father is talking to Rashin about the next course of action. Fox is there because its relevant to him, I suppose.'

Kesta frowned. 'Everything is relevant to him.'

They stayed their distance from Fox, Tiger and Rashin, kept by their own thoughts. Kesta wondered how Fox had slept. He had only been a short distance from her where they had bedded down in the holy tent, but it was not always possible to tell that he was dreaming by watching him sleep, although that was what Kesta had done for most of the night. He had seemed quiet on the surface, tired, but Kesta had little doubt that he had dreamt.

Taneshka's thoughts were tumultuous, the remembered blood and cries of battle a background noise. It was fading now, and she was refusing to let it show, but she felt as if she had an inkling of how Fox was feeling.

Fox turned and waved the girls over. He hugged them both. To their surprise, he was smiling brightly.

'Morning!'

'You seem...cheerful.'

'Aye, we're all of us alive!'

'Not if you crush me like that!' Taneshka said, in mock indignation. He laughed.

'I apologise for being so...improper...Tigress,' he said, mischievously, 'but I'm only expressing my happiness that you're both alive.' His face turned serious. 'I was afraid for both of you. You fought well, I needn't have worried.'

Fox paused, amended his words. 'We – we all fought the best we could. "Well" is not a word best chosen to describe it.' Rashin was standing at Fox's side. He seemed a little bit like an attentive teacher standing there, Kesta thought, waiting to see what his pupil would do next.

'Tiger says he's returning to the hills. The castle needs reoccupying. Haiken is going to lead the army on, with us. Tiger says...' The prince glanced back at the king. Tiger moved, nodding to Fox and beginning to speak.

'Some of- a lot of the men want to go with Fox, to the City of Lakes. Taneshka, both armies are going to march. Without me. They don't need my leadership there, and they want to follow Fox, and yourself. You've both proved yourselves. And I have a castle to return to.'

Tiger paused, awaiting her reaction, almost breathless. The Tigress stirred slowly, brows knitted in thought. 'You're handing the army over to me?' Tiger nodded.

'It's not an abdication, not yet, but it's the right thing to do. If we return together the advisors will attempt to deny your accession. If you return from this war, in your own right, you can lead the country under our name. There will be a Tiger family yet!' She stepped forward and hugged him.

Fox breathed a sigh of relief. Taneshka turned and examined him for a moment. 'A partnership, then. The Maker's Chosen, and the Tigress of the Plains.' She extended her hand, a smile playing across her lips.

'A true alliance!' Fox shook her hand firmly. Rashin nodded gravely and spoke to Tiger.

'That was well done. You will undoubtedly have the approval of the men. You have mine.'

Tiger looked back at the smoke and movement of the camp. 'That is good, Rashin. I hope – I pray that we all make the right decisions. Something dark moves my thoughts.'

The holy warrior raised his eyebrows in alarm. He glanced at Fox, and watched Tiger's expression with interest. 'You are an insightful man, Lord Tiger. Land bless you.' Tiger nodded his thanks and stepped away towards the camp, where the tents were being pulled down. There seemed to be a new lightness in his step, and Fox was glad that the king would soon be back in his beloved forests.

Rashin stepped close and whispered with some urgency in Fox's ear. 'I will not say that Tiger is a prophet, but the Land has gifted him with sight, I am sure. There *is* some change in the Land, by what I feel.' The holy warrior closed his eyes briefly. 'Something – something is happening. You can see further than I can,' he gripped Fox's arm, 'you know how to cast your mind, and we need the benefit of foresight, now more than ever!' Fox nodded, looking around.

'Yes, but not here. Is the holy tent still up?' Rashin glanced at Kesta, who had been there last. She shook her head.

'No then,' The warrior muttered, 'the Central Ridge?' Fox winced.

'Not there. Too many bodies.'

'But they are buried,' Taneshka pointed out, 'and there is not so much blood there as there is in... other places.' She swallowed, attempting to banish the images rising in her mind. Fox looked at her strangely for a moment, and then stepped forward and passed his hand across her face. She gasped as the memories in her head were snatched away, leaving dull remnants with no real power to them. She saw Fox frown as her memories passed through him, and then he relaxed, dismissing them. They were nothing compared to the dreams.

'It can wait. I'll pray later, on the march,' Fox said, the thoughts of his dreams persuading him. Rashin looked disappointed.

'There may not be time on the march,' he warned. Fox shrugged.

'It will have to wait. There is too much blood staining this earth.' He turned away and retraced Tiger's path to the camp.

Rashin sighed. 'Keep an eye on him, Kesta. Try and persuade him, if you can, we need to know what the Enemy is doing. I'll see you later. Tigress.' They both nodded to him as he left.

Taneshka took a deep breath. 'I didn't know he could do that!'

'Do what?' Kesta asked absently; her mind was on what Rashin had told her.

'I don't know, take away your thoughts, I suppose?'

'He can't,' Kesta said after a moment, looking at Taneshka. 'He just takes away their power over your feelings.' Taneshka raised her eyebrows.

'Oh. He's done it for you I suppose?' She smiled as Kesta nodded.

'What are you smiling about?'

'Nothing.'

The army joined on the plain. With tents packed and half of Ox's supply chain in tow, the allied force began to march further out, heading north, for the high plains and the City of Lakes.

Kesta rode at the rear of the army with some of Stavan's men. Taneshka had been called away to talk to her champions, and Fox was expected to do the same.

'There is so much food here! We could feed all of us with this, for weeks and weeks!' an archer said, peering into the back of one of the wagons.

'I hope it won't take us weeks to reach the city,' Kesta replied, concerned. The archer shook his head.

'No. A few days, unless we slow up for some reason. By the Land, what my family could do with even half of this cartload!'

Many of the men seemed to be thinking similarly. It was unspoken, but clear that they disagreed with Fox's decision to take half of the supplies back to the City of Lakes. The other half, once it was divided between Tiger and Rice Fox, wouldn't spread far. The soldiers were afraid that their struggling families would not benefit from the plunder.

If Kesta's own family were not dead, there would have been no way for them to benefit, so far away from Castle Rice Fox.

The army travelled well. They were diminished in number, as the wounded had followed Tiger, or gone with Lannos back to the plains. Or else to their deaths on the way.

Kesta noticed that Renn was still with the army, riding with Fox and Haiken. She understood his choice not to return. If her employer's son had killed her brother, she would have chosen to stay away as well.

Renn listened intently, jaw set as Haiken told them about Trustan. 'He ran. Not a word to anyone, not even his father.' Haiken shook his head as he spoke. 'Apparently he already had provision and a horse ready. Of course, the council gathered over the incident, but they were careful about how they spoke to Rice Fox. It almost killed him, Fox. I hope he is all right. One moment he was in shock, or grieving, and another he could be overtaken by rage.'

Fox listened in silence, wondering where his cousin had gone. It was unlikely that Rice Fox would be able to order the correct punishment for Trustan's crime. To order the execution of his own son, would be too much, Fox knew: his uncle was too soft hearted. Fox had little love for his cousin, who had always made it clear that he was no friend, but even he would be reluctant to have him killed. It was more likely that if Trustan were caught, he would be banished, and stripped of his right to succeed the throne in the event of Fox's death.

'I don't think Henshin would want Trustan banished,' Fox said after a moment. 'He needs him to take the throne, once I'm dead. He needs his puppet king.' Renn nodded grimly.

'That's true. How did *Henshin*,' he spat the name like a curse, 'how did he react? Do you know, Haiken?'

Haiken scowled. 'He was very diplomatic. He mentioned several things, including the fact that Trustan never knew his mother, to suggest that Trustan was not in his right mind. He did, however, agree that Trustan should be brought back and punished. He suggested a flogging, possibly public, and financial repayment to the deceased's family.'

At this, Haiken glanced nervously at Renn. The advisor clenched his leather reins tightly in white knuckled fists, as he controlled his anger. 'There isn't enough money in the Sacred Lands! You hear me Fox? I want him dead.' Renn sucked in a breath to calm himself down. 'I want justice for my brother, my lord Prince.'

Fox bowed in the saddle. 'By the Land, if I can give it you, I will,' he vowed. Renn seemed satisfied with this, and he returned Fox's bow, nodded to Haiken and turned his horse, dropping behind.

Haiken looked worried. 'There's something else, my lord. Henshin left the castle, not two days after yourself. He claimed that he wanted to be the man to bring Trustan back. It made sense to the other advisors. It's no secret that the two of them were friends.'

Fox looked shocked. 'Henshin went after Trustan? That can't be good. The snake! I wonder what they are plotting?'

The day passed, and the army made good time. In the evening camp, food was handed out, and an atmosphere of content spread. Kesta passed by the holy warriors' campfire, and caught a meaningful look from Rashin. She nodded and hurried away, searching out Fox. She found him with Taneshka and a few others at a different fire, in the shadow of one of Ox's wagons.

Fox smiled at her, and covered his full mouth with a hand, polite as always. He rose, motioning for her to sit and eat. A nearby soldier dutifully passed her some food in a tied cloth. She nodded gratefully but did not sit, remembering that she needed to remind Fox of his task.

'Fox...have you remembered what Rashin asked you to do? I would hate to think that the Great Shadow is coming across the plain now, in the dark.' She shivered after she said it, but not from the cold. She had said it to persuade Fox, but now she was looking, the plain appeared to be very dark, and the wind very cold. Fox's face fell at her words, but not for the same reason.

'Don't ask me to do that now, not when everyone's relaxed.'

'Rashin says it's important.'

'Kesta, please.'

'Fine!' She crossed her arms on her chest, glaring at him. 'If you don't care about your own safety, you obviously don't have time to look to ours. Land's sake, Fox, you're the one who's supposed to be fighting the Shadow. If you won't watch out for him, what chance do we have?'

Fox stared at her for a moment, surprised at her outburst. She wasn't allowed to talk to him like that! But that thought was upbringing, social nonsense. Why was she so angry? It crossed Fox's mind that she should be, he *was* endangering everything by delaying this one task. Another thought forced its way into dominance. What about the dreams? If he looked for the Great Shadow, and saw him, then the Great Shadow would be able to look back. Fox didn't want to look into those eyes. His face betrayed his emotions. Kesta saw the flicker of fear there, quickly masked by resentment and stubbornness.

'I can do what I please, Kesta.' His voice was deliberately cool. Kesta's shoulders dropped as she gave up.

'Fine, Your Highness, do whatever you want.' She turned and walked across to where Taneshka was sitting. She sat casually and leaned in to talk to her. Occasionally, the Tigress glanced up to look at Fox, her red hair reflecting the firelight. Fox felt suddenly excluded. He walked away from the cluster of carts and tents, face to the cool night air. His back felt hot in comparison, the fire's heat almost seeming to drive him further onto the plain. It was very dark. Eyes still nightblind after the vivid flames, Fox blinked in the huge blackness.

Fox was not a child, but he felt like crying, hitting out. He was normally comfortable with his emotions, and he rarely denied them unless there was a really good reason, but he struggled now. His throat ached from holding back and his eyes stung. It was unfair! He hadn't asked to be born as the Land's own personal guardian, it wasn't his fault that the war had started when it had. It had been hard enough to cope as a prince, forced into risky military ventures and despised by half his father's household. Now he had this impossible responsibility on top of it all.

He was so mismatched with his foe. The Great Shadow was as fast as a horse, could attack his mind, body and emotions all at once, with a hideous strength. Could Fox even damage a creature of Shadow? Something deep in Fox triggered the memory of the carcer shadow and its hulking host. He had cut clean through that darkness, hadn't he? So it could be done.

Fox took a deep breath, replaying the event in his mind. The feeling of absolute *being* had been so powerful, as if his body were a song. He could almost have flown on that feeling. If that was the "Land Rising", or however Rashin had put it, then he would always need the Land to rise in him to fight the Great Shadow, or he would surely perish.

His thoughts turned back to Kesta's disappointment in him. She didn't understand how difficult it was. If he cast his mind and found the Great Shadow, then surely the Great Shadow would find him. Fox had a strong reluctance to pit his mind against his enemy's, not yet, not here. Not now.

Kesta is disappointed with me.

Yes, now. Resolution stirred in Fox, and suddenly he was determined to prove himself to Rashin, and to Kesta. If they wanted a champion, he would damn well try to be one. With this recklessness in mind, Fox sat in the cold grass. He crossed his legs, mimicking the position of the holy warriors at prayer. Feeling the pure rush of the Land touching at the edges of his consciousness, Fox dropped away into the flow. It was the first time that he had cast his mind so far without being asleep.

As his mind travels, the Rising passes over the plains. Firelight rushes by in the form of a city, lights reflecting off the surface of a lake. Further north, and the banks of the Lifeblood come into view. The Rising sees the great river, opposite bank barely visible across the expanse of water. The Great Shadow is standing on the northern bank. The water is strong here, in more ways than one. The flow is powerful, and the Maker's Legacy runs in the water.

The Rising's mind goes out above the water. On the other bank, the Shadow lifts his head. Recognition bleeds into his eyes, malice smoulders. The Enemy feels the Maker's presence in the air around him. **I am coming for you.** *The Shadow speaks. Drops of black blood dribble from the corner of his wound of a mouth, and hiss as they hit the water.* **I will not be denied, I am coming for you.** *The Shadow begins to stride deeper into the water. The Rising's mind is stayed, transfixed. The water around the Great Shadow's legs begins to boil. Smoke rises, coiling around the deathly figure as it ignores the anguish, letting its corrupted flesh touch the pure water. The Great Shadow throws back his head, letting out a roar, revelling in the harsh pain. Lurching forward, with the water evaporating around him, the cadaverous form of the Shadow reaches for the Rising's mind.*

'Come back!' Rashin's shout tore through the smoke. There was a sudden pain in Fox's head, as his mind snapped back across many leagues in an instant. His eyes burned as they came open, dark hands grasping at his face, but now fading, unreal. Distant. The dark sky around seemed to be crushing him, and then he was released and the plain was open once more. The air was cold on his fevered skin. Kesta was gripping his hand so hard it hurt, and Rashin was holding him.

'You weren't supposed to approach him! He could have killed you, as far as we know! He would have at least damaged you, what were you thinking?' Rashin's furious tirade was belied by the fear and fondness it hid. The holy warrior had an arm around Fox's shoulders, as if he was trying to keep the world away from him. It reminded Kesta of a protective parent. Fox blinked, gasping for breath. His eyes darted from face to face. 'He's coming! Oh Land, oh Kesta! He's coming for me!'

16
Liberating The Lake

The army marched with renewed vigour. Thanks to the supply wagons, spirits were high and progress was good.

Fox was subdued. Rashin rode protectively beside him, reminding him as many times as he dared, that the distance to the Lifeblood was still great, and that not even the Great Shadow would be likely to risk attacking such a large body of people. Not yet.

Kesta spent her time with Taneshka, telling her everything she knew of the Great Shadow. The Tigress listened without scepticism, although if any other than Kesta had brought the information she would not have believed them. In truth, she was worried. She was now responsible for her father's troops, and had no idea how to command them against such a thing. She caught Rashin's attention late in the afternoon, so that she could discuss the matter.

'I have faced him down before, Tigress. And there are a few other Holy Warriors still with me who have similar fortitude. For now, I think Fox is well protected.'

Taneshka looked at him shrewdly. 'But?' Her question made Rashin smile sadly.

'But the Bloodline is fading in us. It is passing into Fox, with every hour that the Enemy gains power. Soon there will come a time when we Warriors will be seeking protection from Fox, and not the other way round. The Enemy is not like a human, not like Ox, who failed due to his overconfidence. The Shadow knows the danger. He will not seek conflict with Fox once the tides are balanced. They will begin to equal one another.'

Taneshka nodded thoughtfully. Frowning, she glanced back at Rashin and asked a question. 'If they will be equal to one another, how can Fox hope to defeat him?'

Rashin bit his lip. The question was not one he knew the answer to. 'Honestly, I don't know. I pray the Land will find a way.' He bowed to Taneshka and dropped behind, calling to one of his white clothed comrades.

On the third day of the march, the clouds were gone and a weak sun shone once more. The wind still tugged and pinched at the wearying marchers, making Kesta's eyes sting. She sat on one of the absent officer's horses, Fox's silent partner. Now and then they did hold conversation, but no one could hear what they were saying. Taneshka kept a polite distance, issuing orders for the whole army through Stavan and Koshra, both now established as the army's foremost commanders besides Haiken.

At midday the sun was still low. An almost red colour washed the landscape, a crimson sea of waving grass stalks. The column of men, horses and wagons began to slow. They had not had a midday rest for the past two days, but it was obvious that every foot soldier in the line wanted one now. Taneshka kept them all moving for a little while, anxious to reach civilisation, even if that was in the form of an enemy city.

Just as Taneshka was about to call a halt, Kesta, who was still riding beside Fox at the front, let out a cry. 'Movement ahead! Taneshka?' The Tigress slapped her horse's flank and rode up to where Kesta and Fox sat in the saddle, staring out onto the plain ahead. Her jaw dropped. On the plain, appearing from the haze on the horizon was line after line of armed men.

'Land save us!' Taneshka gasped. Her eyes were wide with panic. 'How many are there, Fox?'

Fox's eyes went out of focus for a moment, and then he blinked and shook his head as if to clear it. 'Nearly eight thousand, at a guess. They must have emptied the city!' He put a hand on Taneshka's shoulder. 'What should we do, Tigress?' She stared at him.

'It doesn't look like anything can be done. We'll be annihilated if we try to fight a force that big!'

'Surrender?'

'I'd rather fight to the death,' Kesta said, sitting up straight in the saddle, gritting her teeth. Her black hair danced about her shoulders and Fox thought she had never appeared more beautiful.

'So would I.' Taneshka put her head in her hands. 'But if we do, none of these men will ever see their families again. I don't know what to do!'

Panic was spreading throughout the Fox-Tiger army. Fox closed his eyes, hands gripping the soft leather of Riversteel's rein.

He felt very calm, although his heart had begun to race. His hair, grown longer since its last cut, brushed across his face in the brisk breeze. Why did he not feel the fear of his companions? He had seen the enemy better than they could. Puzzlement growing, Fox let his mind slip back across the plain to look at the enemy ranks. He was surprised by what he saw this time.

The men marching towards him were not fearful. They did not share the stony expressions of soldiers going to war, and they were not acting like an armed unit. They were moving out of any formation, and no one was wearing a uniform. Most seemed to be farmers. There were some very young, and some quite old, and some women, more than had ever fought in a Fox army. Above all, they seemed happy, excited even. Fox shook his head as his mind returned to him. It didn't make sense.

Taneshka waved an arm to quieten the army. They did fall silent, but they were reaching for their weapons. On the plain, a horseman, one of very few, started out towards them at a gallop. 'Steady,' Taneshka called, 'let's see what he has to say.' The horse slowed as it reached them.

Kesta edged her horse closer to Riversteel, patting the creature's neck to calm him. The tension felt almost tangible.

The horseman came to a quite undignified stop. He almost fell from the saddle, landing heavily. It was obvious he had had little training. The man stared up at Fox.

'Are you Prince Fox, heir to the throne of the Fox family and their territories?'

Very specific, Fox thought. He nodded. The man broke into a smile. He bowed very low.

'Thank the Land you are alive, Lord. We feared Ox had vanquished you.' The surprise must have shown on Fox's face, because the man hurried to explain. 'We represent the City of Lakes. There has been an uprising! We brought down the home guard, my lord, and now the city awaits your victorious entry!' A smile spread across Fox's face as the man bowed.

'You're not here to fight us?'

'Of course not, my lord!' The man bowed again. 'For too long we have been rich in grain but starving to death, too long lived on a lake filled with undrinkable water. We see you as a liberator, Lord Fox. We pray you will not disappoint us.'

Fox stared down at the man. Then, without warning, he swung down out of Riversteel's saddle, and approached the messenger. He embraced the man, and cheers rose from both sides of the divide between the two armies. Taneshka relaxed, letting out a long breath.

The two armies joined on the plain, turned, and marched on as one. There was a real sense of purpose now. They were no longer marching towards the possibility of a hostile city, but to a welcome and open gate. The Lake City dwellers mixed with the allied soldiers, and food and drink was spread around, so that the massive supplies in the wagons dwindled significantly.

'There's more food, the kind that doesn't spoil easily, back at the city,' the leader of the Lake City troops told Fox. 'It was to follow up the other supplies, for when they besieged the castle.'

'Have you opened up the stores for the people?' Fox asked, his mind turning back to his own starving population. The Lake City leader looked uncomfortable.

'Not really. We've kept the stores under guard. We don't want riots over the food. With a stronger military presence we'll be able to spread it around calmly and fairly.'

Fox nodded. 'Good thinking. We had better hurry then, we can't wait here while they go hungry.' He turned in the saddle and called Taneshka. 'Tigress! Can we double our pace?' She nodded, and gave the order. As the sun fell in the sky, the army drew nearer to the City of Lakes.

The gate of the Lake City was an imposing affair. It rose out of the water on great stone pillars, supporting a network of what appeared to be clay pieces worked into a wattle and daub structure. The colours formed the Ox symbol in yellow, and the gate was drawn up, much higher than the gate at Tiger's castle.

The bridge across the water to the gate was made of stone, but seemed incomplete. Fox realised that the designers had intentionally left gaping holes in the masonry. It would be impossible to march an army across it, unless a temporary bridge could be built over the existing one.

As the army crossed in fives and tens, Fox noted the stains on the surface of the rocks. They looked like smoke stains, which probably meant that the holes in the bridge also functioned as blasting funnels, or some kind of fire defence. This gate was the only way into the city, without using boats, and the walls and defences on the opposite banks looked formidable.

Great vats of oil sat on stone jetties, with a constant flame burning in a torch bracket not far away. Fox pictured the water burning, and imagined trying to raft across the inferno. He was very glad that they were entering as guests and not invaders.

The gate swung back as the first men crossed and there was cheering as they entered the city. Fox went across with the second lot, Kesta with him. Taneshka waited to go with Stavan and Koshra; she waved to Kesta as Kesta stepped out onto the stones.

Fox put a hand on her shoulder as they crossed the threshold. She looked at his face, seeing his expression. She felt what he felt: the exultation of finishing what they had started. They had set out to enter Ox's city as victorious champions, and that goal had been achieved.

The people of Lake City were massed on the main streets. As the army gathered in the enormous square in front of the gate, Fox looked about him. Men, women and children of all ages stood and watched. There were uneasy smiles on their faces, the initial cheering had died away.

Fox understood why, in an instant. These people had been long oppressed. They were suspicious, remembering more hurts than kindnesses. And they were hungry, Fox realised, seeing the signs of malnutrition in some of the children in the crowd. There were not many elderly.

Looking up beyond the rooftops of Lake City's most dominating buildings, Fox saw the massive granaries. His blood began to boil with righteous anger. These people were starving, as bad as his own, if not worse, whilst living in the shadow of bounty. Ox was dead, and now Fox regretted that death less. The evil king had been responsible for this horrible crime. Fox waved the Lake City army chief over.

'Begin to circulate food. Start with those neediest. Do it carefully, but do it quickly. And bring the people who handled this city in Ox's absence, *bring them here*!' The man nodded solemnly. Fox looked out again across the crowd.

'Tonight you will have flour to make bread with!' His voice rang out across the square, echoing off the nearby houses. 'You shall have cooking oil, and meat. And soon we will feast, and celebrate the death of Danashalk Ox the Cruel!'

It was slow at first, but a cheer began, and soon the city began to come alive. The last of the stocks were unloaded from the wagons, and armour was removed and collected. A network of shelters was built against the nearest buildings for the soldiers to sleep under, until walking in the square was like walking inside a massive low roofed tent. Fox and Kesta joined Taneshka in the middle of it all. After the marching, and with the battle still fresh in their memories, all anyone wanted to do was sleep.

Kesta got her chance, sleeping alongside some of the weary Holy Warriors. Rashin came by now and then to hold whispered conversations with one of the elders, before disappearing for a time. Kesta drowsed, watching light filter through the gaps in the fabric shelter, casting glimpses of Rashin's white cloak as he moved.

Taneshka and Fox could not afford to take a break. Taneshka found herself consulted on every small organisational matter that the Champions could bring, and before she knew it, was off with a delegation from the camp to begin the food handouts. She saw Fox pass her as she left the bustle of the square, and they shared a moment of wry humour at the sight of each other's tired faces.

Fox was taken down dark, dirty streets. A dank smell followed them everywhere, and Fox tried to ignore it by listening to the detailed descriptions of his guide, one of the new Lake City leaders. These streets were the same as many others, houses and small shops making gloomy walls on either side. Few of the residential buildings were made from stone, and as a consequence, many of the structures were rotting. That explained the dank smell, Fox supposed.

The city was roughly circular, but the streets were not set out in any obvious pattern. A network of stone bridges and narrow canals divided it up into a maze of damp alleyways. Further in, the canals widened, and had proper walkways beside them. The buildings were sealed stonework and the drainage was better. This was where the wealthy lived, Fox thought to himself. Here and there, boats were moored at the backs of houses, and the water looked a little cleaner.

In the centre of the city, the town hall rose above everything. It was larger and more imposing than even Ox's hall on the hill behind it, which was crowned by what looked like windmills. The stonework of the town hall was ornamented with pottery shards, and there were real glass windows.

'The earth around these parts is filled with clay,' the guide informed Fox, 'and in the industrial district there are immense kilns, so we naturally pride ourselves on our pot making.' He gestured for Fox to go on, and the small group approached the building.

The guard at the great wooden door greeted them with a nod. 'They stopped shouting for help at least,' he said sardonically, 'but now I think they're planning something. You better take a look.' A questioning glance from Fox brought no response until he and the guide had stepped into the dark interior.

'This is where we are keeping the higher profile prisoners,' the guide hastily explained, 'most of them barricaded themselves in here when we rose up, so we thought we'd let them use it as a prison. The walls are thick enough!'

Many bitter and frustrated faces stared out from the shadows. The prisoners were chained to walls and pillars, hidden in the shadows. Some appeared fat, well fed. Obviously their time in power had been to their advantage. Some met Fox's gaze with aggression, some with fear, and a few offered only blank stares. They were the ones that frightened him the most.

'Don't you open the windows?' Fox asked, disgusted at the close air. The guide nodded and waved for one of the guards to see to it.

'These are all those living that watched the city in Ox's absence my lord. Do you still want them taken to the square?' Fox shook his head.

'No. Just open a window, and clean this place. It's filthy.' The man looked apologetic.

'Pardon my saying so, Your Highness, but they are imprisoned here. It isn't supposed to be pleasant.'

Fox stared at him for a moment, and then led the way out of the building. The man scurried after him. 'I'll see to it at once, Lord Fox, my most profuse apologies. I don't know what I was…' Fox silenced him with a wave of his hand.

'They probably don't deserve it,' he sighed, 'but justice is not just if those to be punished die of disease before the right time.' He looked at the guide. 'I would like to do everything I can for this place, but I am tired. If they are all of your captives, then I would like to return to the square. If you have a bed for me, then wonderful, but right now...' He blinked as a wave of tiredness washed over him. 'Right now, I could sleep anywhere.'

Fox woke with early morning sunlight on his face. The freezing air made him withdraw beneath his covers. His head hurt, and he had slept badly, but he felt somewhat refreshed. Fox pulled the cover back and swung his legs out of the bed. The cold made him shiver, and he hurried to dress. The small room adjoined the tent-covered square. A rug had been draped across the shutters to insulate the room, but it was still cold.

Soldiers were relaxing in makeshift awnings, sharing the last of the beer from the wagons. Fox walked between them, watching out for the fire-red of Taneshka's hair. Kesta found him first, and walked beside him until they had left the shelter of the coverings behind them.

'Morning.' Fox murmured, as they pulled further away from the bustle.

'Same to you,' Kesta answered comfortably. 'How did you sleep?'

Fox shrugged. 'All right, I suppose. I'm not tired anymore.' He smiled. 'Which is a new thing, eh?' He looked out to where the winter sun reflected in the lakewater. 'Something was weighing on my mind. It stopped me from sleeping, for a while.'

Kesta put a hand on his arm. They both looked out on the lake, as if searching for something. Fox glanced back at Kesta, a smile playing about his lips. 'Your hands are cold.' Kesta smiled back.

'Serves you right for holding my hand then!'

He looked down, before returning his gaze to the water. A shadow passed across the sun, and in the sudden chill, the moment was lost.

'Are you all right?' Kesta asked, noticing Fox's suddenly furrowed brow. Fox nodded, but looked up at the sky. There was a thin veil of cloud covering the entire heavens. It couldn't have been a cloud passing the sun; the entire sky seemed to be overcast. 'I need to take a walk,' Fox said after a moment.

'Why?'

'Because something in this city is *wrong*. And I'm going to find it.'

Taneshka broke away from a gaggle of Champions and City officials. All morning she had been subjected to endless questions about housing and duration of stay and trade agreements and sanitation and rightful ownership and land division and now she wanted all of them to just *Go away and leave me alone!*

She held back from shouting out in her frustration, showing a self-control that she didn't know she had. Perhaps maturity was carving her into a more stable individual. She wondered what her father and his advisors would think if they could see her now.

'Good morning, Kesta.' She joined the dark haired girl by the lake. 'Where's the incomparable Prince Fox today then?' Kesta smiled with amusement.

'Morning. He went off along the lake edge, and disappeared into those jetties, where the city meets the water. He thinks something's wrong.' Taneshka raised her eyebrows.

'Really? Well if that's what he thinks...'

'...Then he's probably right,' Kesta finished for her, 'I know. I hope it's something small. I'm tired of big dramatic events.' Taneshka laughed.

'That's all you seem to get, walking in Fox's footprints. Hah, and to think that some people wish their lives could be as eventful and dramatic.'

Kesta rolled her eyes. 'Yes. I was one of them! Nothing turns out the way you expect...'

'And?' A shrewd expression had appeared on the Tigress's face.

'Nothing. Oh, I suppose things would be nicer if the world was simpler, that's all. Do you know what I mean?'

Taneshka smiled knowingly. 'I think so.'

Fox walked along the canalways. This part of the city appeared to be deserted. Rotting wood made up most of the decrepit jetties that Fox trod, and even the stone was crumbling in places. Dark nooks and crannies between fallen masonry caught Fox's eye as he passed. Everywhere there seemed to be a dark, cold feeling, one of sadness. There was no trace of malignant evil, at least not yet.

Fox stopped in a secluded alley. The damp smell persisted, permeating everything. All was dead quiet, except for the constant sipping sound made by the water against the green stonework beneath Fox's feet. Fox saw his reflection in the still water, and leant against the slimy rail, staring into the oily depths.

The rail snapped without warning, and Fox experienced the rush of cold air and the sudden stomach clench of falling, followed by the cruel cold of the water crashing around him.

Fox panicked, imagining that hands had hold of his ankles and were dragging him down into this cold, dirty canal, away from everyone. Adrenaline pumped through him and he struggled against the water, thrashing out. His head broke the surface, and he pulled in a gasp of air. It smelt and tasted fetid in his mouth, and he kicked desperately to keep above water. His clothes were heavy and he could feel the weight pulling him down. His hand reached for land. It was much darker here, close to the water, where the only light came from between the buildings above. His hands scrabbled at the slimy stonework, finding no hold.

He dropped back beneath the surface, hands still grasping at the slippery stone around him. The light from above disappeared immediately and he was suddenly blind. His feet kicked out as he sank, trying to remove his shoes, while his hands tore at his clothes, desperate to remove the heavy swathes of material. His shoes came free, and his shirt followed. His bare feet touched against the silky bottom of the canal, where weeds clothed the stone beneath in an oily sheen. His toes curled away from the repulsive sensation, and then he forced himself to put them firmly on the bottom.

He trod in something that crumbled beneath his weight. Fox started, but concentrated on what was important. Survival. He crouched beneath the water, gathering strength in his legs to force himself upwards. His hands swept through the water as he prepared to push for the surface, his fingers brushing the sickly canal bottom. His hand pushed against something that seemed solid, and the surprise caused him to clench his hand around it as he leapt up towards the surface and air.

Fox broke clear of the dark water, clutching a putrid scrap in his left hand. With a massive effort, he was able to grab at the broken rail above. Trembling with the cold, he forced himself up and over the edge of the canal, falling back against the damp stone, his muscles aching.

His mind reeling, Fox forced himself to stare at the grim hunk of stuff in his hands. He let out a cry, and hurled it away, where it splashed back under the water, sinking to its submerged grave. For grave it was. He had grabbed a piece of bone from the sordid bottom of the canal. His mind jumped to the feeling of slight resistance as he had put his foot in something. *In someone*, he thought, sickened.

He threw up in the corner between two buildings. Getting to his feet, cramping from the cold and his panicked exertions, he stumbled back along the treacherous jetties and walkways. His mind let off alarms at every darkened doorway, every creaking and unsound piece of wood.

17
A Legacy Of Decay

'By the Land! What happened to you?' Kesta gaped at Fox as he appeared around the corner. Fox kept both her and Taneshka at arms' reach as the girls rushed forward. 'I...went for a little swim.' He began to cough violently, the taste of the canal still on him. 'Land, I feel sick!'

'Somebody bring a cloak or something!' Taneshka shouted. 'Hurry up!' A long woollen garment was passed across from the gathering audience of Lake people and soldiers. Kesta enveloped Fox in its warmth, but he shivered still, sitting on the ground.

'Come on, it's cold down there.' Rashin came through the crowd and offered Fox a hand. 'What happened?' Fox got stiffly to his feet. He glanced at Kesta, imparting meaning with the short look.

'You found it then,' she said bleakly.

'Found what? What did you find? Fox?' Fox closed his eyes as if to shut out the world.

'I found what is wrong. Why this place is so sad. Why everyone here is still afraid, even though Ox is dead.'

Rashin helped Fox to the nearest tent and proceeded to shout at everyone who had followed him there. Fox lay back on somebody's makeshift bed, mind working over the new information. Outside, Rashin made sure everyone left, or at least backed off until he was satisfied. Then he let Kesta and Taneshka come into the tent. Two of the new City Officials, the leader of the New Army, and a representative that Fox didn't know, followed the girls in.

'I'm the New City Hall Advocate. Is his Highness all right?'

'I'm fine.' Fox assured him. 'Are you aware that your city hall is full of prisoners and their filth?'

'That's only temporary, I assure you,' the official replied dismissively.

'Oh that's good,' Fox murmured as if to himself. He raised his eyes to meet the official's. 'Are you aware that your canals are full of dead people?' There was a shocked silence.

'Oh, Your Lordship,' the City Hall representative started to say, 'I'm sure that's nothing to worry about, simply an exaggeration, occasionally, people drown, most regrettable, it's a large city after all...'

The Army Chief, who had been introduced as Barna, glanced at him. In contrast to the other's false cheeriness, the military man looked nervous. 'Nothing, you say?' Fox said acerbically, 'Well, in that case, I just stepped in Nothing. Did you know him?' The representative's fake smile cracked.

'I don't know what to... surely you're not...'

'Oh, be silent!' Barna spoke suddenly. 'It's too late now! You can't hide it any longer. You'll have to live with the shame of it, and now *is* the time!' The other official stared at his colleague in shock. Then his face took on a hunted, aggressive look.

'What do you mean, *you*? We all share the shame if this comes out!'

'We?' The chief scowled, '*we*? I'm the son of a jetty builder, I grew up in the rotting tunnels of this place. I *know* you; you grew up on the hill with all the other rich ones, your father smiled and bowed for Ox like all the rest – you all had enough food! While my sisters *died* of hunger! We knew what was happening! Oh, we *knew*!'

'Knew what?' Rashin spoke very calmly. Both officials turned to him. They were both shaking, with anger in the army chief's case, but there was fear in the other's face.

Barna looked down. 'We...we knew that something was happening. People went missing, people who complained about Ox. And then the priest started calling for visitors to Ox's palace. Beautiful girls usually. Young. My little sister was one. None of them came back. None of them.'

Fox covered his face as the terror of what had taken place grew in his mind.

The city official looked dejected.

'Rumours were that Ox was disposing of them. After he'd...finished with them.' The man swallowed. 'We didn't dare believe. And there was nothing we could do if we did believe, you must understand!'

Fox lifted his head. 'Something was at work here,' he murmured, 'something not so different from the dread that is on its way.' The two Lake Citizens did not understand this, but Rashin did.

'Then we shall get to the bottom of this. I fear the feasting will have to wait.'

The foul water drained away slowly. All the locks were opened, and the gate that stopped waterflow out of the lakes to the south was removed. The level of water in the city's canals dropped dramatically. Over the next two days, the people of the City of Lakes kept away from the waterways, sticking to the city centre. On the third day, all that was left in the canals was weed and silt.

And bodies. There were hundreds, Fox saw, curled and decimated corpses lined the canals. Some had clearly floated with the current before being deposited along the course, while others had sunk to the bottom where they had met with the water. Most were weighted with nets of stone.

The concentration of bodies here was found beneath an iron bridge in the wealthy quarter. Fox stood with Kesta, Taneshka and Rashin, staring down at the macabre scene.

'Tell me,' Fox spoke to the army official in an unsteady tone, 'do the people of Lake City cremate their dead?'

The official took a step back. He was covering his mouth with the back of his hand, and looked quite ill. 'You can burn them.' He confirmed, turning away. 'If you can find a way to do so.' He walked stiffly away.

Fox took Kesta's arm and gently pulled her away from the edge. 'Come on. Do not let your mind dwell on this. We will rectify this if we can, but for now, do not tarnish your eyes with…with all this.' He squeezed her hand as she pulled away. She stared at him for a moment, brows knit in thought, before nodding slowly.

'I was just thinking,' she explained, 'that you had been in the water, and that I couldn't imagine anything worse. You are more… more…'

'Hush!' Fox put a finger to his lips. 'Rashin is right. While we are within civilisation's walls, we should not be so familiar with each other.' He smiled at her frown.

'Civilisation be damned then.' The frown was gone as she turned to go. 'Let the wilderness come, the sooner the better!' she called over her shoulder as she went. Fox laughed quietly, despite his fears. Taneshka, who had been watching with an amused look on her face, raised her eyebrows, grinning suggestively at Fox. He returned her look with a politely blank one of his own, refusing to be embarrassed by her.

He looked down at the grisly picture below, and immediately came back to earth. To think that he had almost forgotten about the dead, because he had given into a moment of warm feeling for Kesta...

'We will have to do it soon,' Fox murmured. 'Or disease will set in. Enough lives have been swallowed by this place already.'

The black pitch in the great shore defence vats had been emptied. Rashin stood on the bank, watching the lake water lap against the shore. The tarry substance was already on its way to the top of the city, where the bodies had been gathered. A procession of people followed it. There was an excitement in the air, urgent and serious. People were anxious to begin the cleansing of the City of Lakes.

Rashin was thinking dark thoughts. He had been to the top of the city, where the waters were drawn up into the canals by the windpumps. There were no dead bodies there, but the water had still flowed dirty. The windpump sails stood unmoving above the city now, and the canals were empty, but the stink of death still poured from beneath, where the pumps drew the water upwards. In the bowels of the city, beneath the streets, beneath Ox's palace, something still polluted. Rashin had not spoken to Fox about this. The prince had so much to deal with already.

The throng of people around Fox, at the head of the canal was massive. The city's army chief was organising them into crews, giving them water buckets, positioning them near buildings, particularly those with thatched roofs. Fox stood, eyes closed, listening to the shouts of the crowd, hearing the grating sound of the stone vats being dragged across the cobbles.

'My lord!' Fox's eyes snapped open. A man was approaching him through the crowd. 'My lord, forgive me for my presumptuousness. I am the city's master smith. I know a lot about the nature of fire, my lord, and well, this won't work! All the combustibles in the city won't create enough heat to destroy the bones, only a furnace, an enclosed space...'

'I know. I intend to…give the flame a helping hand.' Fox swallowed, the enormity of what he was planning to do filling him with foreboding.

'Pour in the oil!'

Rashin stepped through the mass of people, his white robes visible amongst the others. He could feel Fox tapping into the Land, the flow was immense, and the closer Rashin got to the boy, the harder it was for him not to stumble under the intense waves of power. Of all the others in the crowd, only Kesta seemed to notice the same power. She stood beside Fox, her expression unreadable.

Vat after vat of black pitch was emptied into the canals. The locks at either end of the canal section were closed. After the last vat was poured, a thin level of oil covered the entire bottom of the canal, in a slick, black coating. Fox closed his eyes once more, relaxing his hands, breathing in and out, handing more and more control over to the Land.

'My lord? Shall I throw it in?' A Lake City soldier stood by, holding a blazing torch.

'No!' Fox shouted, and grabbed out with his hand. It closed around the burning top of the wood. The flame was extinguished immediately; smoke hissing up between Fox's fingers. The crowds' noise was suddenly hushed. All was silent. The burnt out torch clattered on the stones.

'Maker help me,' Fox prayed desperately, and felt the power rush forward, enveloping him as he focussed on the heat he had felt in his hand. The crowd gasped as one, amazed and afraid of what Fox had become before their eyes, but not knowing why. There was no physical change, but now everyone could feel the power emanating from the boy.

For a moment Fox stood stock still, feeling the power take him. And then he released it all, mind focussed on the heat in the palm of his hand, memory rushing back to his battle in the East Wastes.

Fire!

There was a sudden sound that resounded around the city, the cracking of stone from intense heat, solid and oppressive, rolling off the canal. A sea of fire flowed along the length of the course, bleaching the stone beneath. Fox cried out, head thrown back, hair blowing as if in a strong wind, his arms out as the fire rushed through him. For a moment, his feet left the stonework, and he was suspended, held upright in the storm of power.

The people rushed back from the edge of the canal, to escape the violent heat. Only Kesta stayed, unafraid of the torrent of flames.

Rashin closed his eyes. 'Land be praised. The Inner Fire, Land be Praised!' The holy warrior laughed aloud, witnessing the glory of a force he had only read of in the scrolls. The Pure Flame of the Maker, channelled through the body of the boy in front of him. Visual confirmation that this boy was the Land's Arisen, the one that the Holy Order had been waiting for. The Bearer of the Bloodline. Rashin raised his arms in triumph, for he had been the one to find him.

Fox fell to the stone. The firestorm was over, although flames still flickered at the bottom of the canal. Rashin ran forward, reaching out to see if the prince was well. He was very cold. For a moment, Rashin feared he was dead, but then Fox opened his eyes.

'Did it work?'

Rashin laughed. 'The fire yet burns,' he said, taking Fox's hand and examining it for signs of damage. There were none. 'I think you have succeeded, Arisen One.' He let go of Fox's hand, allowing Kesta to come nearer. 'Suppress your emotion,' he warned her sharply, 'as hard as that may be. There are too many people.' She nodded, although frustration made her fists clench.

'By the Land, my muscles ache,' Fox complained, attempting to sit up. Around them, the crowds were dissipating, in total silence. There were no cries of congratulation. Nobody knew how to come to terms with what they had seen. Taneshka came closer, crouching at Fox's side. Her eyes were wide with awe.

'Dragon's Dry Bones, Fox! That was... incredible; I've never seen anything like... I didn't know you could do that!'

'Neither did I!' Fox gasped. 'I just, guessed. I'm all right though 'Teshka, don't look so worried!

Taneshka laughed, as much at the shortening of her name as at the relief in tension. She leaned in and kissed his cheek. 'From Kesta.' She winked at him. 'Would you like me to give her one back?' Fox laughed, wincing at the pain in his ribs. Rashin helped him to stand. Kesta looked both annoyed and gratified.

'No more experiments, Fox. What'd be the point in risking roasting yourself alive, on a guess?'

Fox smiled at her. 'Yes sir. No more experiments, sir.' He gave a mock salute. 'And may the wilderness come, the sooner the better!' He put his head back on the cold stone and closed his eyes.

'What was that about?' Rashin muttered, bemusedly. Taneshka shrugged, winking at Kesta when Rashin looked the other way.

'No idea,' Kesta said with a quiet smile. 'It was probably his exhaustion speaking.' She avoided Taneshka's amused gaze.

18
Foundations Of Stone

Rashin paused for thought, watching Fox's face for a reaction. He was not surprised. Kesta looked worried, undoubtedly considering the implications of another struggle. Taneshka looked angry at the mere idea of yet another thing to deal with. Only Fox seemed entirely composed. He nodded slowly.

'I think I can feel it. A presence beneath the city, like something has burrowed itself into the foundations. This city has had such a history, calamity after calamity, evil after evil. How long has it slept beneath, working on the dreams of powerful men?'

'Men like Ox,' Taneshka said darkly.

'Where?' Kesta asked. Her hand went to her side, to the bundle, which she had swaddled her wing swords in. Taneshka seemed to have the same question burning in her eyes. Rashin knew the answer, but he waited for Fox to speak.

'Beneath the windpumps. In the bedrock of this city, where the canal flow begins.' Fox closed his eyes momentarily. 'I think we should take our weapons, prepare ourselves and go down there. While the water is still drained. Before the winter rains force the dam open and flood the canals.'

Rashin stood and pulled back his sleeve, checking his wrist blades, flexing his fist so that the steel crept forward past his wrist, poised for the sudden punching motion that would extend them like the claws of a predator.

'Let's go.'

The four of them stood at the iron grating, attempting to hold their footing on the bottom of the canal. Taneshka had already fallen over, to her annoyance and embarrassment and everyone else's amusement. The grating was iron, old and rusty, bolted into the stone. Above, the beginning of a fortified wall rose forbiddingly.

'That's part of the original wall built by Ox's grandfather, to protect the wealthy sector from attack.' Fox said, to distract himself from the task at hand. Rashin smiled.

'Ox's curse slumbers in the foundations of the rich and powerful. How appropriate.'

It was very dark in the tunnel. It sloped, designed to allow the passage of water up to the canal, pumped by the turning of the windpumps. They had only gone a few dozen paces when running feet came echoing from behind, followed by the glow of torchlight. The City Hall Official, red faced from his exertions, came into view with two frightened looking soldiers behind him.

'Stop! Where are you going? You can't come down here! No one can!'

The man waved his hands vigorously to emphasise his words. Fox raised his eyebrows, turning to face the man.

'Why not?' His question fell into the silence. The official looked flustered, flapping his hands, as if hoping he might fan an answer into being.

'Because it's not safe, that's why! We've only been down here... we've never been down here, because no one comes down here, not since...'

'Since what? Since Ox was alive? What did he do down here, or did you all turn a blind eye to that as well, hmm? You say you've been down here, then never. Which is it?'

'We didn't...'

'You did. You came down here. I know you did, *do not* lie to me!' Fox took a step forward, so that he was face to face with the trembling man. '*Why does no one come down here?*'

The official's expression became grim as he gave up. 'The centre of these caverns is immediately below Ox's house. They called this his prayer room. Please. We must leave!' He spoke in a hushed whisper, his eyes darting around at the flickering shadows.

'His room of prayer?' Fox said aloud, as if to defy the tense atmosphere created by the man's whispering. He looked over his shoulder, down into the dark depths. 'Now what kind of prayers could run through the mind of somebody like Ox?'

A foul breeze stroked suddenly across their startled faces and the torch blew out. A sickly, dank odour came with it, making the air seem thick and heavy. There was silence for a moment. Muscles almost frozen with fear, Kesta reached out until her fingers came into contact with Fox's arm. His voice came suddenly out of the blinding blackness, a comforting sound, cautious but unafraid.

'Tell me man, and don't hesitate. What did you find down here?' The answer was an unintelligible cry, and the sound of running feet. 'The courageous man of Lake City,' Fox murmured sarcastically, 'bravest of the brave. Are we all of us all right?'

Rashin's voice answered, and Taneshka's, unusually quiet in its delivery. Fox's hand took Kesta's in the dark. 'Courage.' he murmured, like he had before the battle. 'Courage Kesta, Teshka. Let us go and see what there is to see.'

The passage continued to slope downwards, the floor smooth from years of water flow. Fox brought a little flame into being, putting it to the torch, which sputtered back into life. The going after that was easier, but they did not relax. Fox kept one hand on the hilt of Tiger's Gift, and the other entwined with Kesta's. Taneshka swallowed, angry that the dark was affecting her so much.

'The floor is levelling out.' Rashin spoke in the black. He was right, and they could tell by the movement of cold air that the space had opened up ahead. A faint glimmer of light caught Fox's eye, and after a moment's hesitation, he snuffed out the torch. Kesta jumped at the sudden darkness, and Taneshka cursed out loud. After a moment, though, their eyes became adjusted to the dark, and using the natural light beyond they could make out their surroundings.

'Don't. Ever. Do. That. Again!' Taneshka growled in Fox's ear. He smiled, putting a hand on her shoulder in a wordless apology. Rashin pointed forwards into the echoing gloom. He said nothing, but Fox understood his meaning and began to lead the way across the damp stone floor. There was silence, apart from the regular drip, drip, drip of water from the rock ceiling far above. Kesta's breathing and footfall became very present in her mind. No other sounds competed. She put her hand to her wing swords in their leather pouch, to reassure herself.

The cave was very large. Across the chasm of space, the great foundations of the windpumps could be seen, wrapped in the machinery that would keep the water moving, pumping it up the tunnel into the city's canals. There was a building of sorts, high up the rock wall, assumedly above the water line. And, rising to a similar height, towering, over and dominating the centre of the space, was a column of stone. It was disturbingly smooth, a great, inorganic monument.

The air around the monolith was very cold.

'What the hell is that?' Taneshka whispered. For a moment nobody replied. Kesta glanced at Fox's set, troubled face, pale in the half-light. She searched for his hand and clung to it, memories of the fatal day that had robbed her of her family running through her mind.

'Fox? Is that what I think it is?' Rashin's voice, steady but urgent. Everybody heard the sound that signalled the Warrior's fear, the click of his arm blades sliding forward beneath his white sleeves. Fox closed his eyes momentarily, head bowed. When he lifted his head, a fire burnt in his eyes, a readiness, a joy. Kesta recognised the transformation from the village square those months ago, and felt the same sense of inadequacy that she had felt when holding his hand in the hemp fields of Rice Castle. She dropped his hand. He was the Land's Arisen.

'That, Rashin is exactly what you think it is. Can you fight the Seven?' Fox's voice rang clear and unafraid.

Rashin shook his head. 'No. I know nothing of the Seven. Only you have fought the Carcer Shadow. Arisen One.'

Fox turned his head, surprised at the use of the title, surprised at the reverent way Kesta was looking at him, and that she had dropped his hand. 'I am still Fox, Rashin. Kesta.' He frowned, uncomfortable with the attention. 'I need to be Fox. Whatever else I am, I am still a boy, yes?'

Kesta looked away. He was wrong. He was more than just a boy. She felt it in touching his skin. It came with that dreadful sense of unworthiness, that urged her to keep her distance.

'Can we fight it? If it is released?' Rashin's question came with the same urgency. Fox nodded, eyes narrowing.

'Yes. It has a physical body but is cloaked in the shadow that animates it. Any physical form can be damaged. As for the Shadow? Leave that to me!'

Fox ran forward, to the base of the towering stone. His breath froze in the air as mist. Symbols, faint, but definitely there, lay etched on the surface. Fox began to slowly circle the carcer stone.

'It's still imprisoned. I'm not sure how they get out of these bonds the Land holds them in, but it must have something to do with consuming life-force.' He glanced back at Rashin, looking for advice. Rashin nodded.

'The old texts say that sorcerers activate and empower the shadow with sacrifice. A dead or dying body laid across the stone for the shadow to absorb would probably allow it freedom.'

Fox thought for a moment, fingertips a hairsbreadth from touching the stone's surface. The stone blocked the light from the entry lock far above, casting Fox's features in shadow. 'Seven.' Fox spoke suddenly, lifting his head in realisation. 'Seven! There are seven Great Shadows, besides the Perversion Of Light himself, am I correct? And it was one, two, three, four... yes, seven bodies that freed the one at the East Forest.'

Kesta remembered only too well the sacrifice of her mother on the stone. The other bodies must have been the four men that Fox had killed in the yard. And the one that she had poisoned, making six. Sirkor's dead body must have been the seventh, thrown on the stone by her older sister, as a simple way of disposing of them without having to dig graves. And then the thing must have come out of the stone, awakened, hungry for more.

Fox stood still, looking up at the stone. 'Once it's free, it must need constant energy to support its physical body. Didn't you say that after some time the one you tracked abandoned its host?' The question was directed at Rashin, who nodded.

Fox took a steadying breath. 'This one is still inside. Last time I was attacked in my dreams. Perhaps I can make contact while awake?'

He prepared himself for the moment when he would place his hands on the icy stone. Fox hesitated, chilled by awareness of a new sound in the silence.

Harsh, shallow breaths gasping in and out.

Fox took a step back. For a moment he was still, listening to the breathing. Then he began to walk along the side of the stone, turning the corner. Hands on weapons, the others followed.

On the adjacent side of the carcer stone, a chain hung from the top. Manacles hung on the chain, still gripping fragments of dead bones. Someone had been chained there. Kesta glanced up at the distant light filtering through the cracks of the water entry lock, so far above their heads. The person chained here must have drowned. Was he or she one of the many taken by Ox's priest? Kesta remembered the Lake City Army Chief's words and shuddered.

Hanging on the next face of the carcer stone was, something far worse than the remains: a man, naked and barely breathing. His cracked and wrinkled skin was taut, his feet barely touching the floor. His arms were dislocated from their sockets from the strain of holding up his bodyweight. A look of pure rage crossed Fox's face. With a cry, he drew Tiger's Gift and struck the rusted chains. Rashin caught the old man as he tumbled forwards.

The man gasped out in relief, then in pain, as Fox relocated each arm with ruthless efficiency. A hiss of protest at the agony came through the man's cracked lips, becoming a croaking laugh. His eyes rolled in his head, and Rashin turned his face away; the man's breath was foul. 'He's insane.' The Holy Warrior spoke with disgust and pity. Fox wordlessly agreed, sadness for the man's state stopping him from speaking.

'Who are you?' Fox asked. The man stared up at him.

'I? I am Ox's Most High, Priest of the Waters. Holder of the teachings of the Dragon! I am a true follower of Dominago-the-Mighty who's bones rest in the ruins at Dracore!' The man laughed a long, wheezing laugh.

'I am Ox's pet!' Here the man spat. 'Fool! Tell him I am no man's toy executioner! You tell him! I'm no weak magician. I am a priest! A loyal servant of the Dragon Family. I spit on his piss-streak of a bloodline.'

Fox's face went hard. 'You... you are a descendant of the Dragon Household? I was told their line was symbolic only!' The High Priest laughed derisively.

'Told? By a Royal Advisory Council, I imagine? Those thrice-damned charlatans will see their end soon, as will you all! Petty liars, seeking power in the politics of mere remnants of the true royal family. And *you*! You are a Fox! *The* Prince Fox, of the Fox, family, hmm? The only royal line that does not bear Dominago's holy blood. You are dirt to me!'

'Holy?! I've read my histories! The Dragon never had my respect, and I am glad that I have no relation to the evil man! He built his reign on the Great Shadow's Prison! No need to wonder who's will directed his actions!' Fox spat.

Rashin had to raise a hand to calm him. Fox remembered his enemy's weak state and held back, breathing through his teeth. 'Take him over to the base of the windpump machinery. I still have to destroy this One of Seven who sleeps in the stone.'

The hideous priest laughed again. 'Sleeps? Only barely, peasant! Six women have been drowned for his benefit. I was to be the seventh sacrifice, though the fools who chained me here didn't know it. They run this city now? How the state has fallen. But the Great One here has had nearly all of me. I'm breath in a corpse now.'

Fox took note of this, but still nodded for Rashin to drag the ruined man away. Taneshka helped the Holy Warrior carry the priest to the rambling network of weights and struts at the pump foundations. Kesta stayed beside Fox.

'Go with them, Kesta. This will be difficult enough as it is. If I fail, and it escapes, climb the machinery, up to that building, above the water line. I won't let you be its first victim.'

Kesta opened her mouth to protest, but the look in Fox's eyes silenced her argument. She reached out her hand, fingertips brushing his, before turning and running to the base of the pumps.

Fox turned and readied himself, whispering a quick prayer, before gripping the old chain that the priest had hung from. Then, climbing hand over hand, pulling himself up by the chain, Fox scaled the carcer stone to the top. It was hard work, but the icy atmosphere surrounding the stone stopped him from breaking a sweat. Finally, he knelt at the top.

His hand went to his sword hilt, then rejected it in favour of his staff. It had served him well against the Shadow in the village. He scrambled to his feet, took a deep breath, and struck the stone, fire rippling along the length of his staff as the Land rose in its champion.

Nothing happened. Fox felt he could almost hear laughter at his efforts.

'Very well. I shall find another way.' He knelt once more, placing his palms flat against the rock, feeling the smooth, repellent texture beneath his hands. Then he bent down, placing his forehead against the stone, opening his being as he would in seeking the Land. As Rashin did for prayer.

Awake, yet dreaming, the Awoken sees within the stone. A presence as close to him as to be within him strikes, causing him to cry out. Malevolence, a mind rises, miles deep, aeons old. A mind built to destroy, without pity, without thought, touches his own in a violation that cuts him to the soul. A voice questions him, controlled, confident; it seeks his end. The Great Shadow's being is echoed here, surrounding the Land's Arisen with insurmountable pain, his dreams, once forgotten, pouring across the pages of his mind in ceaseless torrent. A voice: YES, YES, THIS IS YOUR END! And now, suddenly, at last, the Arisen's answer to the questions.

NO!
Suddenly the Shadow is no longer in control. The Land rises in the prison, and the walls tremble as he strikes back at the dark surrounding him. The Shadow does not understand the strength that drives it back, cannot recognise the emotion that tears it down, like a light burning through the webs of hopelessness, like roots cracking brickwork. And suddenly, it is over.

Fox stood, letting out a triumphant cry as the Shadow within the stone died. The sound of the Land's thunder came, distant in the silence afterwards, as the earth quaked. Above the city, great clouds broke, covering the streets in heavy rain.

At the base of the carcer stone a crack appeared, running up the surface of the rock, splintering, splitting, crumbling. Far away, the Great Shadow cried out in a howl of pain and anger, as another of his Seven died.

19
Purgation

Fox closed his eyes and jumped. The ground cracked under the impact of his landing. Above him, the destroyed carcer stone crumbled apart. Fox spun away, fearing tumbling fragments. The monolith slumped suddenly and the great structure crashed to the floor, causing droplets of water to fall from the ceiling in a sudden shower.

Fox remained in a crouch, calming his breathing. He touched the stone floor as if to reassure himself of its solidity. He stayed like that for a moment, listening to the Land's bones beneath his feet.

'Um, Fox?' Kesta's voice floated across the shadowy cavern. 'Fox, I think we're shut in.' She was right. The fallen stone had cut off the canal-way. Taneshka swore.

'There had better be a way out!' Her false bravado echoed around the cavern. In the following silence, the distant sound of water could be heard.

'Rain,' Rashin muttered, looking up at the distant light of the water entry lock. 'We knew it was coming. Winter storms. They cause floods, out here on the plains.' He looked to Fox.

'The canals were built to protect the city from flooding,' Fox said, 'but if the windpumps are disabled... and even if they were working, the Carcer Stone blocks the outflow. This place is going to fill up and burst its walls! We need to get out, immediately!'

'Really?' Taneshka asked, a note of panic under her sarcasm, 'what makes you say that?'

There was a moment of horrible silence. Taneshka turned and in the low light from above, the tears forming at the corners of her eyes were visible.

Kesta spoke suddenly. 'The Priest said he was caught in the cellars of Ox's palace, and brought down here. Maybe the building up there connects with the cellars?'

There was a silence. Then all eyes turned to the priest. The wizened man nodded his head.

Dragging the old man up the rambling network of pipes and poles was a difficult task. Fox and Rashin's shirts had been used to make a rough sling. The priest was unconscious again, and it made the job no easier. Finally, with many bruises, cuts and lucky escapes, the four of them collapsed onto the ledge that ran along the side of the building. The sound of rushing water had grown louder.

Fox stood, legs shaking from the effort of helping to drag the insensible man up the cavern wall. He looked up at the dark doorway. Rashin joined him, reengaging the fist-blades on his wrists; he had disabled them to carry the priest's sling.

'Very old architecture. Probably as old as Darbul's reign. That was just after the schism that separated this part of the Land. Darbul was one of Dominago's sons.'

'Hence the connection with the priest? Maybe this was a temple, of sorts.'

Fox's speculation set Rashin to thinking. He had never seen the marks of the Dragon's reign, all the remaining architecture was to be found in the ruinous Valley of Stones, where the destroyed city of Dracore lay crumbling away. The thought gave the Holy Warrior a dark thrill; the followers of the Dragon were the Holy Order's opposites. Nemeses, of a sort.

Taneshka and Kesta took Fox's place in pulling the priest along in his silken sling, freeing Fox up to lead the way, a flame burning steadily in his hand. The walls of the narrow passageways were full of minor horrors, the flame lighting them as they passed, grotesque faces leering out of the stonework, blunt horns casting shadows, pooling in staring, stony eyes, bringing them to life.

Kesta shivered, attempting to tread the passageway without touching the walls. Each new doorway and arch they passed through was rounded from age, and where the bricks had crumbled around the edge, the masonry gave the openings teeth. Through mouth after mouth they walked, footsteps echoing off the walls.

The group paused to get their breath. Rashin peered ahead into the gloom, and was suddenly struck with the thought that they might have gone the wrong way.

Rashin voiced his concern, making Fox frown.

'What makes you say that?'

'Nothing I can understand. I just, really, really do not like the idea of going through there.' The Holy Warrior pointed and Fox raised his hand. The flame there flared brighter, and the group drew a collective breath at what they saw.

The next archway was big, and toothed similarly to the ones before it. In this case, the mouth-like effect was deliberate. Great, tapering globes of jet set in the wall above the mouth gave the impression of eyes, each one reflecting the flickering fire in Fox's hand. The snarling mouth was surrounded by chipped, aged ceramic scales.

Fox took a step forward. An uncomfortable feeling stopped him at the doorway. Cold air pressed on his arms and face. He paused, foot hovering above one of the shards of rock that fanged the floor. A slow, gasping laugh filled the air.

Fox turned to stare at the priest. The cackling ceased, but insane mirth still shone in the old man's eyes. 'You cannot enter. You are not worthy, little creature of mud!'

The priest shrieked, suddenly, attempting to rise, arms outstretched. 'Bastard heathen! Son-of-scum! Desecrator! Defecation!' He spat at Fox, the line of spittle falling short on the dark stone.

Fox smiled, coolly.

'You are the madman here. Dragon is dead!' This, he shouted into the opening. 'And I do not fear him!' With that, Fox stepped into the mouth. One by one, ignoring the shrieks of the priest, the others followed. To drag the old man over the threshold, Rashin kicked at the old stone fangs on the floor, breaking the face's teeth one by one.

The temple was circular. The walls were covered with faded mosaics, depicting a lithe dragon, serpentine and crowned with a circlet of bone. In the centre of the space sat a stone altar, shaped as a dragon's mouth opened wide, like the unhinged jaw of a viper, so that the two halves of the creature's mouth were almost parallel to the floor. The gullet of the serpentine creature was a sunken well in the centre of the mouth that disappeared into blackness below, surrounded by a spiralling, forked tongue.

Fox noticed dry blood on the stonework.

'We need to leave. Now.'

'What's the matter? This place scare you that much?' Taneshka said, her eyes bright, voice falsely cheery.

'No, that's not it. But we need to go!'

Suddenly they could all hear it, the rushing, surging sound of water. They ran for the opposite doorway, where steps rose into the gloom. Fox turned back, grabbing the priest's sling one handed, dragging the unfortunate man up the steps.

At the top of the steps there was a door. Its handle was another dragonhead, but when Fox reached out and grabbed the gape-jawed thing, he withdrew his hand sharply, many beads of blood welling up on his hand. The handle was covered in razor sharp crystal scales. In his panic, Fox allowed the fire to die. When it was relit, it was to see the priest reaching up, putting his hand into the dragon's mouth. There was a click, and the door slid open.

The lampless passage and gloomy palace beyond went by in an indistinct blur. After moments of exhausting terror, the four lay panting on the drenched grass behind Ox's house.

The priest, shielding his eyes from the lashing rain, leered at Fox. 'Should have let you put your own hand in the mouth. Should have watched you try to ball your hand into a fist, pull on the lever. Should have watched you have your hand torn off by the machinery.'

'What a lovely, lovely man you are,' Fox answered bitterly, sitting up. The rain pattered against his face and his bare chest. Kesta and Taneshka lay alongside one another, just breathing and relishing the fact. Rashin... *where was Rashin?*'

Fox stood, alarmed. Where was the Holy Warrior? Feet slipping on the sodden, muddy lawn, Fox retraced his steps to the cellar doors. Rashin emerged, grinning hugely, his arms filled with dusty clay cylinders. Fox breathed a sigh of relief.

'We didn't know what had happened to you! Thought you'd been left behind...'

Rashin interrupted him. 'I got them all! All of them!' Fox sat down heavily, rubbing his soaked fringe out of his eyes. Rashin laughed out loud, practically jumping from excitement.

'The scrolls Fox! The scrolls!'

'The what?'

The city escaped a total flood. A gaping crack appeared in the streets below the windpumps. Many of the deserted palaces on the hill, including Ox's own, were sucked down into a roiling maelstrom. The beautifully landscaped garden of Ox's home was flooded, water running between ornamental hills, before pouring off the edge of the stone wall that hung like a cliff over the rest of the city.

Once a fortified crown on the hill above the dwellings of the poor, Ox's estate had become a small lake, resting high above the city, fed from the pumping cavern beneath. The water overflowed the wall that bounded the palace district, in an immense cataract, falling, more or less, into the canal system below. When the rainstorm ended and the clouds opened, the sunlight reflected off the surface of the water.

The flood swept many of the decaying jetties away, along with the old water in the lower lakes that surrounded the town. The level had risen again, and over the next few days, people could be seen fishing hopefully on the shores. The grain stores and the potteries, along with most of the other important infrastructure, were left unscathed. The windpumps were torn down by the flood.

Once the waters had stilled, the people set about salvaging the flotsam. The Lake city boatyards were open again.

Fox took a break. He was sweating furiously, despite the cold weather. Nobody had thought to tell him how difficult building a dock was. Fox now remembered the knowing smiles when he had foolishly offered to help. How was he to know it would mean standing chest deep in cold water, straining to steady great lumps of wood? Wood with splinters, he reminded himself ruefully, studying his hands.

It was too late to claim prince's privilege.

'You still obsessing over your splinter?' Taneshka deliberately bumped him as she passed, entering the tent. They were taking their break in the main square.

'Ow!' Fox responded, '*splinters*, Teshka, not *splinter*. And they're practically spears, look!' He grinned as she pretended to see a horrible injury on his calloused, but otherwise unhurt hand.

'Oh, by the Land! Quick, someone call a healer, before he dies! Weakling!' Taneshka fired the last word at him, dodging a playful blow.

'Who's a weakling?' Kesta asked as she entered, grabbing a towel from the line hung across the tent.

'Fox is,' Taneshka replied, 'You'd think he'd never been to war, the way he goes on.'

'It's the prince thing,' Kesta said dryly, 'he's got no problems with fighting his way through hundreds of armed men, but he's easily defeated by the first sign of a day's work.'

Fox rolled his eyes, sitting wearily down on a wooden stool. 'It's not my fault I haven't got peasant's hands!'

The riposte was stupid, Fox knew, because his hands were as hard as Kesta's, from combat training. He felt a sudden shot of guilt, remembering Kesta's sensitivity.

Kesta's eyes darkened with anger and hurt, as Fox quickly murmured a "sorry", looking up at her, his own eyes full of regret. Why had he said that? Before, everything had been comfortable: good, hard work, easy banter. Normality, for the first time since leaving Tiger's castle. He had had to go and spoil it, hadn't he?

She stared at him for a moment, then hurled her damp towel in his face. There was a moment's shocked silence, and then they both burst out laughing. Taneshka hadn't noticed the emotional part of the exchange, but laughed along with them as Fox removed the towel from his head. His long, brown hair was damp with sweat and lakewater. It needed a cut, Kesta thought.

'Do you two know that building we helped finish yesterday? The one down near the water's edge?' Taneshka asked. Fox sighed dramatically.

'Of course I know it, Teshka. Broke my nails against every stone, remember?'

'So you did,' Taneshka continued, keeping her face straight, 'well, it's going to be a bathhouse. Barna, the Army Chief told me.'

'Oooh! When does it open?' Kesta sat upright, pleased at the prospect of being able to get really clean again.

'It's open already,' Taneshka answered casually, examining her nails with the air of somebody who couldn't care less. 'I suppose civilisation does have its pleasures, eh?' Kesta ignored this and glanced at Fox, who had gone quiet.

'What are you thinking about?'

'Barna. And the priest. Tonight.'

'Oh.' Kesta's face fell. She had forgotten. Distractions were temporary. Tonight was law, order, justice, consequence. And necessarily, death.

She could see Fox was sick of it.

Fox sat with Rashin in the small tent that had been set-aside for them. The Holy Warrior was lost in the sacred parchments he had recovered from Ox's cellar. Fox watched the Warrior's expression as the man read. Sometimes it was joyous, excited, at other times deep and intense. Occasionally, a worried frown would appear and Fox was sure the Warrior was glancing at him.

Fox was feeling the tension gather, but at least he was prepared now. His hair had been cut at the bathhouse, and he was properly scrubbed clean, for the first time in weeks.

Tiger's Gift hung naked and gleaming at Fox's belt. A blue-grey jacket kept him warm, the material falling to just above his knees. Trousers lined with a soft wool for warmth clothed his legs, of a darker shade of blue. Much to the disapproval of the Master of Ceremonies, a fussy Lakeman with a receding hairline, Fox had insisted on keeping what the man described as a "dirty stick" belted at his back. Fox would not be without his staff. His sword was beautiful, and blessed, but Fox felt a strong connection with his staff. It had once been part of the Land, a growing thing, alive.

The tent flap opened, letting in the cold night air. The Master of Ceremonies was doubled over in the gap, peering inside. 'We're ready for you now, Prince Fox!' Fox nodded tersely, first to the Master of Ceremonies, who backed out of the tent, then to Rashin, who had looked up from his scroll. The Holy Warrior nodded back, sliding the parchment roll back into its clay case.

Kesta watched as Fox emerged from the tent, looking smart and handsome, his grey eyes serious. The ceremonial garb he wore looked resplendent in the torchlight that lit the square. Taneshka shifted beside Kesta. The Tigress was dressed in soft green leathers, according to the Tiger family colours, the red of her hair completing the look. She was restless, uncomfortable with formal occasions.

As Fox and Taneshka made their way into the centre of the square, where a podium had been raised, Kesta caught glimpses of other faces in the torchlight.

Young Daris, wearing his bow over a luxurious robe left over from his days on the council.

Renn, his scar visible in the flickering light, reminding Kesta of her own.

Haiken, standing stiff and straight, exuding loyalty and pride for his pupil, his prince.

With a shock, Kesta noticed the face of one of Henshin's friends. When had he arrived? Was the Chief Advisor with him? She put the thought out of her mind, concentrating on Fox, who was standing atop the podium. The Master of Ceremonies scurried forwards.

'People of the Lakes! Honoured guests, Lords and Champions all, welcome! Welcome to this most auspicious of events. The declaring of the new Law of the Land!'

Riotous applause greeted the little man's words.

'Tonight, we rename key areas of this great city! We celebrate the rebuilding of the docks! Tomorrow, they tell me, the first of King Heron's boats will make port again at the City of Lakes! Just in time, my friends, for the celebratory feast!'

There was an even more enthusiastic applause. The Master of Ceremonies smiled, enjoying the warm attention. 'People of the City of Lakes...give due honour and welcome now, to His Highness, His Lordship, the great General, Crown Prince Fox!' Tumultuous applause met this, and Kesta joined in.

Fox rose, gesturing for quiet. 'Thank you, people of Lake City. I am most grateful, as are my men, and the men of my ally, the Tigress Taneshka, for your continued hospitality. We would be honoured if our presence here can benefit your city. We seek what is best for your people, our peoples. I formally extend the hand of friendship to your noble, independent and soon to be thriving City. May our threefold friendship be forever strong!'

More applause. Kesta noticed a scowl appear on the face of Henshin's colleague, who promptly turned and disappeared into the crowd. Fox bowed slightly to Taneshka, giving her her cue.

'We have spoken with your officials and representatives from the trades and wards. Eventually, it was agreed that the area of this City formally known as the Palatial Crown, or Ox's Town,' - booing ensued - 'shall be renamed "Victory Waters"!' cheering replaced the boos.

'However...'

The one word spread a sudden silence. The City Officials whispered amongst themselves. Fox picked up where Taneshka left off.

'However! We have come to feel that Victory Waters is not entirely appropriate. The victory on the plains was not won first for this city, for we were enemies when Ox was killed.

'There is victory here for you, people of the Lake. Once you came to know about what your lords and masters had been doing, about the bodies in the canals; then you owned a measure of triumph. But even now your leaders are lying to you.'

Fox pointed an accusing finger at where the officials were sitting. An uneasy rumble passed through the crowd, and Kesta was pleased to see Barna pale visibly.

'So,' Taneshka continued, 'the Canalways of this city will each be given the name of one of the fallen that died to make this place free, whether by resisting Ox here, or by fighting him under a Fox or Tiger banner on the plain.'

Fox nodded. 'And this square, not the lake, will be named Victory Square, for it was here you learnt the truth! The lake itself can be called Remembrance Waters. The lake has washed away the foundations of the evil that had set rot in this place, an evil instigated, I am sad to say, by men like these.'

Again Fox's hand rose to accuse the officials. One of them rose from his seat, red with anger.

'Now see here! You can't go on like that! We're nothing like Danashalk's lot! How dare...' The man suddenly sat down, quailing under Fox's stare. Kesta focused on Fox's expression. It was mainly sadness in his eyes, not anger.

'You are not like Ox's men were. That is true, for the moment. But it is what you will likely become, unless the attitude is destroyed utterly, before it can rot these brand new foundations!' Fox gestured around him, eyes shining with feeling. 'I will justify my accusation. Rashin? If you and Haiken would?'

Rashin nodded, moving swiftly away behind the tent, followed by Haiken. For a moment there was silence. Nobody moved. Then at last, the priest staggered into the square. His wrists were tied, but with silk, and he had been fed and cared for. His eyes spat hate at the officials, but when they looked on Fox, there was merely a tired resignation. He knew his time was over.

Fox examined the faces of Barna and his colleagues for realisation, or guilt. Either they were hiding it very well, or they did not recognise the man they saw before them.

Suddenly, recognition dawned in Barna's eyes. He sat back in his seat, stunned. The others still looked bemused, and had not noticed. Fox stepped off the podium, going to stand next to the priest.

'You Officials, the new order of this city! As soon as the water had drained from the windpump cavern, you committed a terrible crime. You committed it against this city and against *the Land itself!*'

Fox's bellow silenced all mutterings. Barna, trembling in his seat, hid his eyes. 'You took this man, a man who had committed great evil, yes, but *still a man*, and chained him to a Carcer Stone, leaving him to feed the Shadow within! You almost unleashed a terrible curse on this city, that would have ended everything you so earnestly sought to achieve!'

Looks of disbelief rose on the officials' faces. 'But... that's not the man we chained,' one man cried in confusion, 'he was much younger... much younger...'

'Yes! I was young, then!' The priest shouted back. 'I was fit of body, if not of mind! You stole my life! I bled away into that stone, thanks to you! Look at me now! At the feet of death!' The man stared at his wrinkled hands, tears welling up in his eyes. 'It's what I deserve,' he whispered, looking to Fox, 'no more than I deserve. I took so many lives myself. I was mad. But not truly...oh Land, what have I done with myself?'

The priest fell to his knees, weeping. Fox put a hand on his shoulder, seeing the last vestiges of something quite like the Shadow, yet not the same, disappear.

'You have only to say one thing,' Fox murmured gently. The man nodded slowly. The officials sat, stony faced and terrified, except for Barna, who wept as hard as the Priest, hands covering his face, his shame having mastered him.

The priest lifted his head. He really was terribly old, Fox saw. What he felt went deeper though; the man was clinging to life by a tenuous handhold that had something to do with what he was about to say.

'My name is Taniyan Kilner. My father was a potter. I was born here, but when my mother died, I journeyed to the Valley of Stones. I became obsessed with the remnants of the old civilisation of the Dragon Family. I found a building there, hidden beneath a grassy mound. A building marked, not with the seal of Dominago, but with a vertical line, bisected by two others, one of blue, the lower of green. The vertical line was red, and interspersed down its length were teardrops, or blood drops, I do not know.'

Fox saw Rashin shift. He was certain the Holy Warrior knew something about the symbol.

'In this building I found writings. They were held in cases of clay.'

Fox saw Rashin nod. They were the same scrolls.

'In another building, marked with Dominago's seal, I found more scrolls, written in blood, in cases of bone. They were called, respectively, the Scrolls of Song, and the Scrolls of Keening.

'I returned to this city, knowing that Ox was a covert follower of the Dragon. I showed him the scrolls. Like me, his interest lay in the Scrolls of Keening, the bone scrolls. They held prophesies, ones that mirrored the Scrolls of Song, opposite and contradictory. Some gave details on how to worship the Dragon, and thus I followed the rituals for a decade and more, willingly, at Ox's bidding.

'I lived a lie. A foolishness. A madness! Yes, I believe I became mad. Yet there is no excuse for what I did. I became bitter. I feared and loved Lord Dominago, but in dreams of him, when I lay sleeping on the top of the carcer stone, the water lapping around me, he did not love me. Could not love me. I woke with nightmares, and ran back to the temple. I did not know that the visitor of my dreams was not Dominago.

'The Dragon never knew me, and I never knew him! He never loved me, and my love for him was insanity!'

'May the Sky hear my final words until world's end...' Taniyan drew in a great shuddering breath, and Fox felt the man's life begin to slip away, as the last words came forth: 'THE DRAGON IS DEAD!' a look of freedom entered the man's eyes, and his last look to Fox was with a smile, as he died. Fox crouched beside him and undid the silk that tied his wrists, placing the wrinkled hands on the man's chest, palms open.

'The Land forgives you,' Fox whispered.

20
Guilt And Conflict

Fox slowly got to his feet. The crowd was hushed. Kesta shook her head, amazed again.

Taneshka had left the podium. She smiled at the look of pride on her friend's face. 'He's unstoppable, don't you think?'

Kesta nodded emphatically. The way that Fox affected people produced feelings between awe and fear. She had seen people reduced to tears, emotionally convicted of their shame. She had also seen men inspired to undying loyalty.

'Nothing with him is ever halfway done. Everything must be finished. All the way to conclusion.'

'Yes. That's Fox.'

The rest of the night passed in like fashion. The Lake people had never seen anything like it. Fox removed most of the officials, appointing the young soldier that had ridden out and met him on the plain as Chief, but allowing Barna to stay as his advisor.

The crowd were treated to displays of mercy and justice in equal measure; remorseful prisoners were released immediately, and sent to work under supervision of some of those that they had most wronged. This shocked many, but as soon as the words left Fox's mouth, Kesta understood the logic.

Taneshka was not quite as enthusiastic as Kesta, expecting the worst from many of the criminals. Unfortunately, she was often right. Some prisoners were defiant, violent, and some actually demanded execution. Four times, soldiers dragged prisoners away to be speared to death.

Some of them called for execution as a matter of honour. Fox treated them with respect. He forced himself each time, to remember Ox, reaching forward and stopping the hearts of the condemned with a touch. He was unable to keep from tears.

Most of the men were released back into the city.

It was late by the time Fox had finished. The crowd dispersed, once again in silence.

Fox made his way over to Kesta and Taneshka, looking weary. His eyes were red, and his hands shook a little. Taneshka glanced at Kesta, voicing both their thoughts. 'Come on Fox. Back to the tent.' He nodded gratefully, and followed them back through the bustle of tents that were being raised once more. As soon as they were within, Fox let out a loud, wordless cry.

'Aaaaaaaaggggh! Why was I born to this? My *soul* aches! Land, why so many lives?'

Kesta checked the tent flap was closed, before putting her arms around him. For a moment, he stayed as rigid as a board, unresponsive, and then he collapsed against her, letting his body become wracked with sobs. Kesta closed her eyes, pressing her cheek against his, tears wetting her hair. Taneshka sat, examining the rug at her feet, made unsure by Fox's show of emotion.

Rashin entered the tent, as quietly as he was able. His expression showed his alarm at seeing Kesta and Fox so close, but he relented and sat opposite Taneshka.

'It's not fair!' Kesta suddenly burst out, eyes dark with anger and tears of her own. 'He's still a child! You don't make children kill people!' Rashin raised an eyebrow, attempting to keep his face neutral. He had his own, strong feelings on this himself, but they were tempered with his belief in Fox's destiny.

'In many cultures, Kesta, including his own, he is considered a man.'

'Blood and Dragonfire on his culture!' Kesta roared back in response, 'it isn't fair, you *know* it isn't fair!'

'He's done as much as many men. More than most!'

'That still doesn't make him any less a boy!'

'By that token, all men are children, until they die, and it isn't fair on any of us!'

'Shut your mouth! You don't care!'

There was a shocked silence. Rashin froze over. Kesta realised she had hurt him, and felt a stab of satisfaction. Damned right. If he was going to act as Fox's father figure, then he should at least be attempting to make things easier for him.

Rashin raised his gaze. Kesta stared defiantly back over Fox's shoulder. Fox and Taneshka had both gone still, waiting to see what would happen next. Rashin spoke quietly.

'You are unfair to me, Kesta. I feel very fond of the three of you, and usually I know better than to restrict you, or to interfere. I do care, very much. More than many! But you cannot treat Fox like he is a child, no more than he can afford to treat himself that way. There is too much at stake! He has too much to accomplish, and you know that there are things he will have to do and endure that are far beyond what is *fair* for any of us!'

Kesta dropped her hands to her sides. Fox pulled gently away and sat. Kesta stood alone in the centre, still staring at Rashin. It was, she reflected, like trying to stare down a very patient, very deliberate landslide.

'But what am *I* to do?' she wondered aloud, 'I'm not even allowed to show how I feel, *remember?*' She blushed, looking down.

'Fox needs time to prepare to fight, time to learn how. *Not* a show of your feelings. How could that possibly help him against the Great Corruptor? I am sorry, but your affection, however meaningful, is rendered worthless by the truth that at some point the Land's Arisen One will be forced into battle against the Enemy! Your emotions concerning Fox *do not help him at all*!'

Rashin turned, fuming with anger, and swept out of the tent, leaving Kesta stunned in his wake. She felt as if he had just beaten her about the face.

Taneshka spoke in the stark silence. 'Well. What a surprise. Perfect Rashin is not so perfect after all.'

Fox spoke as well, his voice oddly low. 'I love it when the Land reminds you that everyone can be wrong. Even Rashin.' Kesta turned to look at him. 'He's wrong,' he said simply, a thoughtful smile on his lips.

'About what?' Kesta asked, hands trembling.

'Your feelings do help me. I'm glad for it. Thank you. It means a lot. Rashin isn't exactly skilled at supporting me emotionally, as you've just seen. He's a good teacher, but he's not my father. A good impression though.'

Taneshka stood up. 'I don't believe it! Two shocks in one day! Fox proves he's not a complete halfwit! I think my head might explode if this keeps up!' She beamed at both of them. 'Come on! Let's forget about the blabbering of Sir High-and-Mighty and just go to bed, all right? There's a feast tomorrow, and I'm *very* hungry!'

Fox rolled his eyes comically the moment Taneshka had turned her back. Kesta giggled, but Taneshka pretended not to notice. 'She's right,' Fox said, pulling back his bedclothes, 'let's just this once ignore what Rashin has to say.'

He waved a hand idly, and the candle on the other side of the tent blew out.

As he sleeps, the Arisen dreams. Foreboding grows, like a maggot feeding on his doubt. The possibility of betrayal rises in his mind. A figure. Confusion smothers him. What he wants is held just out of reach, and the closer he gets to it, the easier it is for him to fight the weight that hangs on him. A voice repeats a phrase, mocking.
You take the wrong path. You take the wrong path. You take the wrong path.
Suddenly, fire rolls across fields where the only crop is bone. Unbelievable pain, the premonition of nothingness, assaults him, and he screams into the black sun that explodes a million times behind his eyes.

Kesta opened the tent flap, letting freezing air into the tent. She changed her clothes behind the partition, before returning to sit down and watch with some amusement as the other two reacted to the cold.

Fox shivered, pulling his sheet closer about him. Taneshka woke, her cheek half on her pillow and half on the coarse rug. She lifted her head, hair unruly. The pile in the rug had etched its pattern onto her face. 'Who opened d' door?'

Kesta smiled down at her, threatening with a tin cup filled with rainwater from the table outside. Taneshka muttered something about hoping all of Kesta's hair fell out, before sitting up. 'You are evil, you know that Kesta?'

Kesta laughed, offering the remainder of her drink to Taneshka. The Tigress took it gratefully. Sipping the cold water seemed to revive her.

'What's wrong with him?' She asked a moment later, tying her hair back and looking disdainfully at Fox. 'Honestly, I have no time for people who can't get up in the morning.' Kesta raised her eyebrows at the hypocrisy.

'He had a nightmare last night, one of the big ones. *He* has an excuse.'

Taneshka shrugged, getting to her feet. 'Sun's out! Come on, wake his lordship and we can get out and make the most of it.' She watched as Kesta shook Fox's arm. After a moment or two, his eyes flicked open.

'Come on, we're going to look at the docks.'

Fox squeezed his eyes shut.

'We've seen the docks. We saw them when we builded them. Built them, I mean.' He shook his head, trying to clear it, before clambering to his feet. 'Oh fine, I'm coming. Why does my head feel like a horse kicked it?'

Kesta grinned. 'I thought I heard Taneshka moving in the night.'

'Hey!'

The lake was full of boats. Kesta stared, eyes wide. Vessel after vessel manoeuvred their way around, attempting to find a mooring post. Some had sails, catching the brisk wind. Other boats were already moored, their rigging slapping against the masts. A knife-prowed craft slewed by, sail stretching as the wind filled its canvas. A couple of rough looking characters with red skin and sun-bleached hair were on board. One of them raised a hand in casual greeting.

'They look like men from the East River Estuary,' Fox remarked with interest, 'it's said that they live most of the year on the water. Not even Heron's men go that long without stopping at the White Gates Castle.'

A lot of the boats were not as high sided, but many were more ornately designed. Big trade cogs rose and fell in the swelling water where they were moored. Their inhabitants were setting up colourful stalls as close to their vessels as possible. Lake Citizens were already running to be first in line.

'Traders!' Fox breathed. 'From the Spice River lands, by the look of it.' Kesta, who had been distracted by a strange covered boat out on the lake, turned to see what he was talking about. She started in surprise.

Wending their way between the multitudes of stalls already set up, were a group of people the like of which Kesta had never seen before. They were brown skinned, some so dark that their complexion had a rich, purple hue in the sunlight.

'Southerners!' Fox was surprised. 'I didn't realise people would come so far to trade with the City of Lakes. They must have been waiting in the waters south of here, gambling on the outcome of the war...'

Kesta walked with Fox, listening as he told her about the lands to the far south. The Spice River was aptly named. Fox told her of the fertile land around its banks, and prosperous cities that stood over the water, some as ancient as old Dracore. The exotic spices were highly valued here in the north. Every year, hundreds of boatloads of spice travelled upriver to the Central Lakes, returning to their ports laden with re-traded Autumn Steel, and lacquer work from beyond the plains.

In some of the stalls they passed there were little clay pots filled with aromatic powders, strings of chillies, strange and unknown vegetables.

Kesta lost herself in the multitude of stalls and tents. Coins in her pocket reminded her that she could buy if she wished, but for the moment she was content to look around, soaking up the spectacle of the market.

Fox took his own path through the traders and merchants, glancing from stall to stall, unsure what he was looking for. His eye was drawn to a sparsely decorated table in front of a vividly orange tent. A man with very dark skin and greying locks of thick, knotty hair bowed to Fox from behind the table of trays and urns. Fox paused to peruse the goods, offering the trader a polite smile.

'What is it you sell?' he asked.

'*Profiallechas od tea Recha de Sachard Terroa.* That, is, Noble Lord, the faces of kings sire, kings of these lands.' Fox examined one of the little clay tablets more carefully. It was with shock that he recognised the engraved profile as his own.

'That's my face!' he looked up, grinning. The man nodded, chewing on something black and pungent.

'*Tsha. Tuah profiallech,* sire. Is it a good likeness?'

Fox nodded. 'Not bad, friend, not bad. You carved this? How... how did you know what I looked like?'

The trader smiled, showing several gaps in his grin. He reached beneath his counter, before revealing a wooden engraving with a flourish. This too had the image of Fox carved boldly in the dark wood. In the writing script of Fox's people, dragonscript, was the inscription: *Fox, Crown Prince of Autumn Hills*. Fox vaguely remembered sitting for engravings at his uncle's castle.

His hair was longer now, Fox reflected, and he was sure that his face had thinned and lengthened. The Trader observed Fox's reaction and chuckled.

'Soon, Sire, it will be an older face I carve, eh? Perhaps one with a beard, no? And with few scars, I would hope. Your victory pleases me, sire!'

Fox smiled. 'I'm glad.' He picked up a tablet with his father's proud features etched on it. 'Are we well thought of in the Southlands, my father and I?' The merchant paused before answering.

'*Tsha ang tshet.* Yes and no. There is a new King in my country now. I say your victory pleases me, for it does. *Shol comirche, ban.* Good for business, lord! But this new *Recha*, he is undecided. Good news for we traders also, though!'

Fox was interested by the mention of a new Southlands King. He studied the various images in the merchant's trays, searching for an unfamiliar face that might be the new monarch. Many of the images were captioned in Dragonscript lettering, but Fox did not understand the Southlands speech, so they gave him little clue to the meaning. Only the words "Recha", which seemed to mean king, and "Sachard Terrata", which must have meant Sacred Lands, were known to him.

The face of a boy with *Recha od tea Terroa Suthe* written beneath it caught Fox's eye. So the king was a boy! Surely he was the mysterious Southlands ruler, after all, Terrata, meaning land, was similar to *terroa,* and *Suthe* looked familiar too. Fox pointed at the tablet.

'Um, *Recha od tea Terroa Suthe*? Is that him?' The Trader nodded enthusiastically.

'*Tsha, tsha! Reche od tea Terroa Suthe, tea Eqar Substices, tea Barna od Substices al tea Barna de Pretermenoor.* He is the king of the Southlands, the Spice River, the Spice Desert and the Autumn Deserts! A large responsibility for his youngness hmm? Yet he has our love, at least, while the gold flows, eh?' The man laughed, rubbing his fingers together.

Fox nodded distractedly, studying the young king's face. *He looks a similar age to me*, Fox pondered. With a quick smile he bought the tablet along with a clay engraving of his father, and after a moment's hesitation another, which depicted Tiger.

'Party! Feast! Celebration!' Taneshka yelled loudly in Fox's ear. He had been dozing in their tent after his walk in the market, but no longer.

'Why so loud Teshka? Did you think I was dead?' She laughed at his grumbling.

'The dead snore less! Come on, you need to get some good clothes on, *feasting* clothes! Kesta is already dressed and ready. You can leave your staff here, *and* the sword, this is a party, not a battle!'

Fox got to his feet. He gave Taneshka a dark look and disappeared behind the bamboo partition. A few minutes later he reappeared, wearing blue and silver cloth. He shrugged a blue silk hood on over the top, to hide the coarser weave that would keep him warm.

Taneshka was standing between him and his sword. He scowled at her.

'I like wearing my sword. And I'm never without my staff! Come on Teshka, let me take one. Please?' She laughed, darkening his scowl.

'What are you expecting? An attacker to jump out from under the food tables? Oh, fine, if you must go armed, take something concealable. It's bad etiquette to go armed to a celebration, you know!' She passed him one of her knives. Fox slipped the weapon beneath his silk overshirt.

'Never imagined you to be the one educating me about etiquette, Teshka.'

'I'm full of surprises, Fox, as you should know. Besides, it pays to understand matters of courtesy. That way you know how to get around the rules!' She held the flap of the tent for him. Fox stepped outside into the cold evening air, looking onto the main square. Firelight flickered, reflected in his grey eyes.

Many long tables had been set up around heaped blazes. Fires roasted meat and warmed great black pots, full of stews and soups. A brick oven had been built nearby, and bread was baking. Fox breathed in the scents of dough and salt and fat and a smile overtook his features. On the cold air, amongst the other aromas, was the unmistakable smell of ale.

21
Revelry Interrupted

Fox lifted the clay flagon above his head. Around him was the sound of loud conversation, and since the barrels had been breached, predominantly laughter. Kesta raised her own cup to match Fox. The firelight danced off the decorative glaze of the vessel. Foam spilled over the edge of Fox's cup as it descended, dropping to the surface of the table. More spilled as Taneshka made a swipe at the cup. Fox laughed, pushing her away.

'Get your own! There's plenty to go around. Mead, too, if you want what Kesta's drinking. It's made with local honey.'

Taneshka plonked herself into a seat unceremoniously, putting her elbows on the table. 'I've had, have already had some.' Fox rolled his eyes so that only Kesta could see.

'Really? I couldn't tell.'

Kesta snorted, spraying mead across the table as she attempted to control her laugh. Taneshka was unimpressed, her eyebrows raised, arms crossed. 'Don't make fun of me, master Fox! Rashin's been looking for you, you know. I could have easily told him where you were!'

Fox put his flagon down. 'Don't,' he said. 'I don't need his…interference tonight. I'm enjoying myself!' He said this fiercely, before lifting his cup once more to take several large gulps. Taneshka laughed, her eyes flashing in the flickering light. The laugh had an edge to it.

'It's all right. He doesn't know where you are.'

'He'll probably find us, though,' Kesta said bitterly, putting her cup down, 'although if he's sensible, he'll keep away from me. I've not forgotten our argument.' Fox said nothing, but briefly put a hand on Kesta's arm. She glanced at him, flashing a grateful smile.

'He won't, you know.' Taneshka surveyed the two of them over the rim of Fox's flagon. She had taken it when he had put it down to touch Kesta's arm. Taneshka winked at him, downing the last of the liquid. Fox shook his head, resigned to the loss of the beer.

'Won't what?' he asked, tracing a letter in the damp surface of the table, surreptitiously glancing at Kesta. She looked astonishing in the firelight, he thought, black hair shining, eyes bright, though the mead might answer for that…

'He won't find you. Rashin, I mean. I guarantee it.' Taneshka watched Fox's gaze knowingly. Fox distracted himself from Kesta.

'Why? Did you talk to him?'

'Yes.'

'And he asked you where we were?'

'Of course. He looked a bit tense. Clutching some scrolls, as usual.'

'So what did you tell him?' At this Taneshka grinned, enjoying Fox and Kesta's nervous anticipation.

'I told him that you were both celebrating over at the new dock, with the merchants.'

Fox laughed. 'That was almost cruel! There are so many people over there, you can't see the people for the crowds!'

'That's the idea. Here, I'll get some more drink, and we can toast to Rashin getting lost on the docks… Come on!' Taneshka made off through the throng. Shrugging, Fox and Kesta rose to follow.

In the cool shadow of a house on the edge of the square, Fox and Kesta waited, watching Taneshka wind her way back through the crowd to the barrels. Fox shook his head, smiling at the image before him. Amidst the raucous singing, the flowing drink and the roaring fires, there was loud and often crude storytelling, bread and meat, more drink, various ill-advised games, and yet more drink. Taneshka seemed particularly fond of the latter.

'She'll get back here with two empty cups, and the other at her lips,' Fox predicted, nodding at where Taneshka's fiery hair could be seen through the chaos. Kesta laughed easily, leaning on the lintel of the door behind her. Fox glanced at her again, as if she were too fragile to look at for any length of time. He feared he might break the golden aura that seemed to hang all around if he did.

Kesta looked back, unabashed. 'Have I lost an eyebrow?' She enquired teasingly, watching Fox's already drink-reddened face flush still further. He shook his head. Kesta shrugged. 'I only ask because you keep looking at me. What could possibly be so interesting?'

Fox moved closer, shoulder against the lintel, so the two of them were framed by the doorway. For a moment they stood with the closed door beside them.

Kesta's mind was clear, focused. She wanted him to come closer, properly close, and Rashin be damned! But she wanted *him* to move, to cross the short distance and make up for his silence. She dared not look to see if Taneshka was on her way back, in case the clearness of thought she had been gifted with was lost.

Fox felt like his mind had been tied to Riversteel's saddle and sent on a gallop. A hundred and one thoughts flew past, none worth his attention. He was vaguely aware that beer had contributed to this simplified state, and while it had not by any means removed his inhibitions, it had certainly amplified his feelings. He wanted to kiss her.

Fox moved, but stopped abruptly. A grimace crossed his face, and Kesta realised he had just walked into the door handle. For a moment she stared at his obviously pained expression, then she found herself trying not to laugh. It was *very* difficult.

'I'm sorry!' She gasped, tears in her eyes to match his as she held back peals of laughter, 'did it catch you anywhere…important?' Fox shook his head wordlessly, mouth clamped shut as he tried to stop himself from yelling out. He had a terrible urge to fold up like a piece of cloth.

'Important? – yes. Damn! I'm all right, I'm all right,' he muttered quickly, leaning against the door. 'Gah! That hurts… Did Taneshka see?'

'See what?' Taneshka asked innocently, appearing beside them. She was holding three flagons. Fox took one of the drinks without answering, and attempted to drown his pain. As he handed the empty cup back to an impressed Taneshka, he noticed that the world was shimmering and swaying slightly. Whether that was because of the beer, or the doorknob, Fox didn't know.

'Excuse me?' A small voice interrupted Fox's thoughts. Grateful for the distraction, he turned to the speaker. It was a young boy, maybe twelve years old. Fox managed a smile. 'Hello! What can we do for you, little brother?'

'Here,' Kesta took her mead from Taneshka, giving it to the child, winking at her red haired friend. The boy looked surprised, but took a sip, glancing around nervously.

'I need to talk to you, master Fox, Your Highness, Sir.' Fox smiled at the generous amount of titles.

'All right then. What about?'

'Some people are wanting to kill you, sir.'

There was a moment of uncomfortable silence. 'Tell me something I don't know,' Fox joked, but he wasn't smiling any more. 'Anyone in particular?'

The boy nodded. 'Some... some men told me to come over here and offer you a place to sleep, sir. I know them. They want me to offer you to sleep in a certain house, sir, so they knows where to go sir. They're gonna try and kill you tonight, while you're still drunk and tired from the party, sir.'

Fox sobered up immediately. It was amazing what the threat of death could do. 'Who?' He put a hand on the boy's shoulder.

'I can't point them out to you! Then they'll know I told you about the plan, sir!' the boy protested, looking frightened. 'I...just wanted to warn you, sir, only now... I don't know what to do now!' He looked close to tears. Kesta gently relieved him of the mead.

'Here's what you can do. You've been really courageous to tell us this, and all you have to do is be brave a little longer.' She crouched down beside him, as if she was mothering him.

'You run off and tell them that we've agreed to sleep in their house, and that we're very grateful for the offer, seeing as it's a cold night. When they come to kill us, we'll be ready, don't you worry.' Kesta's eyes blazed with contained anger. 'There'll be none left to discover your part in this, believe me!'

The boy nodded, face pale. Fox made a show of ruffling the young lad's hair, as if he were heavily under the influence of the drinks he had downed. The three watched as the boy ran off into the crowds.

'Good plan Kesta. Well thought out.' Fox laughed suddenly. 'Ha! Who do you think wants to kill me now?' he shook his head at the absurdity of the statement, leaning back against the house. Kesta and Taneshka shrugged.

'Who knows?' Kesta shrugged. 'We'll find out when their blood gets spilled, I expect.'

They made their way around the edge of the party, smiling and talking as best they could. Taneshka was still unsteady on her feet, which aided their act. The boy returned and was soon caught up in the drama himself, showing them the way to their night's abode as if he had never spoken to them before, at least, not as if he were caught up in a plan for their assassination.

Taneshka loudly demanded on the edge of the square that someone fetch food; she wasn't going to bed with an empty stomach. A soldier obeyed, coming to them with a small loaf of warm bread, and some hot pieces of meat carved from the spit.

The beef was slightly rare, which suited Fox fine, and the pork was more to Taneshka's taste. She tore at a piece of it, alternating bites between that and a hunk of bread. Fox shook his head. 'Unwilling to die on an empty stomach Teshka?' Her mouth was so full of food that she shook her head to delay explaining.

'I – my dear friend – am drunk.' She declared finally, taking a smaller piece of bread. 'I don't want to be falling over when our enemy attacks!'

'You're likely to kill yourself, eating like that,' Fox murmured easily, 'do you want me to help you?' There was a pause, then she nodded.

Fox raised his hand and passed it across her face. She swayed for a moment, before shaking her head vigorously and running her free hand through her hair. 'There's a useful talent! I suppose this means you never have to suffer the morning effects of drink?'

Fox laughed. 'I *never* get drunk, Teshka.'

'Liar!' She snorted in response, 'you're royalty, my dear, much of the time, getting wildly drunk is the only thing *to* do. I should know. This isn't my first foray.'

They stopped at the end of an alley. The houses were well maintained and secluded. The boy opened the house for them, and bowed before hurrying away. Kesta nervously watched him until he was out of sight.

Fox looked around the small front room. Comfortable beds were set up on the tiled floor. Fox reached across and lit a lamp with a touch. Soon the room was flickering with golden light. The tiles were richly coloured, the walls well decorated. Somebody had spent time and money on this residence. Fox shook his head.

'I think that these would-be murderers are very foolish. I think one of their number owns this house. What a waste of property! Whether their attempt succeeds or fails, he will have to go into hiding. It will be obvious the owner was involved.'

Taneshka found a name on the handle of a personal knife in the small kitchen. It was Shore, a common name in the city, but one man of that name came to mind quickly.

'Liner Shore was one of the council members under Ox,' Fox said after examining the knife's handle. 'His name is still written on the wall in the town council building.'

Kesta nodded. 'That makes sense. He probably lost a lot when Ox was killed.'

Taneshka pulled a chair up beside the front door. 'He won't be with the men he sends. He's probably hiding out in the ruins on the banks of Remembrance Waters. There are still some old houses above the waterline, or so they were saying around the barrels tonight.'

There was silence, except for the sounds made by Kesta stuffing over-shirts and extra blankets underneath the covers on the provided beds. Soon the beds looked occupied, and Kesta straightened up, looking satisfied. She joined Fox where he sat in the corner near the door. If the door were opened, it would block them from view. Taneshka leant back on her chair, nodding to Fox.

'If they come now, we'll be ready. I'll take first watch.' Fox nodded gratefully and relaxed against the wall. Kesta shifted to sit closer, so that she was resting against his shoulder. Fox raised a finger, and the lamp went out.

Taneshka kept her eyes open in the dark, purely to stop herself from drifting off. After some time had passed, deep, quiet breathing was all she could hear. Fox and Kesta were asleep. Her eyes already adjusted to the gloom, Taneshka peered into the corner. Kesta was sleeping with her head on Fox's shoulder. Taneshka smiled in the shadows, sitting back against her chair. There was still no sound of footsteps outside.

Suddenly, Taneshka was standing in a forest. Rainwater dripped from heavy, dark green branches, filling the cool, damp air around her with the sound of a mountain rainfall. Pine needles crunched beneath her feet. She smiled. She was in the woods. She was home!

A short run through the trees took her to the edge of the forest. The unending patter of water on the forest floor was a comfortable, familiar sound.

The castle wasn't there. Confused, Taneshka looked around. The rock rose in its impressive tor, dominating the landscape, but there was no masonry built into the natural stone. No gate. No walls.

No home.

Taneshka turned to stare into the face of a female tiger, her long front teeth pointing like daggers, down past her bottom lip. Wordlessly, and curiously without fear, Taneshka reached out and touched the smoothness of the tooth.

Taneshka woke with a start. Her head hurt, which shouldn't have surprised her, considering how much she had drunk. There was a terrible feeling of guilt at having fallen asleep, quickly removed by the relief brought by the obvious facts: they were still alive, it was morning, and Fox and Kesta still slept.

Taneshka stood carefully, reaching to push Kesta's shoulder. Fox's eyes snapped open. He frowned for a moment, taking in the morning sunlight that had set Taneshka's red hair ablaze. With a stir, Kesta awoke as well. For a moment nothing was said.

'We're all still alive then. That's always a pleasant start to the morning,' Kesta muttered, stretching uncomfortably. Taneshka helped her to her feet.

'They must have changed their minds.' Fox frowned. 'Maybe they realised that the boy told us,' he said slowly, climbing to his feet, 'or perhaps the boy was always lying?' A sudden thought struck him. 'You don't think this could be Rashin paying us back with a trick?'

'That's an unsettling thought!' Kesta murmured. 'I don't think so though, the boy was very convincing.'

'He was.'

'There's nothing else for it,' Taneshka said after a moment, 'we'd better go outside. Get on with the day. Find out if this business is real or not. We could track the boy down?'

Fox nodded. He turned the blanket aside where it lay draped over his fake body. Pulling his hooded over-shirt from the pile, he checked that Taneshka's knife was still there. Taneshka sighed, going to the door.

On opening the door, Taneshka received a shock. There was a man lying at her feet. Dark blood pooled from where his head should have been.

'Ah, Fox? There's a man at the door.'

'What does he want?'

'From the looks of things, his head. It's uh, a little way away. Too far away, thinking about it. To be any good to him, at least.'

There was even blood splashed across the door.

All in all, there were six dead bodies lying in the street immediately outside the door. Taneshka turned slowly to an equally shocked Fox and Kesta.

'I don't suppose you sleepwalk?'

Fox shook his head at her dark joke. He stepped forward, avoiding the puddle of gore, to kneel beside another of the corpses. It was the farthest from the door. All of its limbs were intact, but there was a nasty wound in its neck which had prevented the continuation of life in a very final way. Fox shook his head, examining the wound.

'This is strange: unlike any sword stroke I've ever seen. Come and look, Teshka, does that look like the work of an axe to you? Or a curved knife?'

The two girls approached. Kesta wondered at the deadened way she was viewing the scene; surely there should be some trauma, some effect on her emotions?

There was nothing. She was seeing the world without the veil of innocence. Suddenly, she wanted another drink.

Taneshka shook her head as Fox had done. 'No, not a knife. The main gash is thick, like maybe from an axe-blow, but there's this laceration all the way around the neck. *All* the way round. Looks like he was slashed and strangled at the same time. I don't know any weapon that can do that.'

Fox searched the dead man's pockets. There was no clue to his identity. 'What about the other five?' Fox examined the short sword the dead man had carried. 'Are they all well armed?' Taneshka looked around.

'Yes. And armoured, most of them. Discreetly, but well. They were prepared.'

'They weren't prepared for this,' Kesta stated the obvious. 'How many people did this, do you think? Who do we have to thank?' Fox frowned.

'Hmm. We might work out how many from the types of wound, and the position of the bodies. As for who we have to thank, I can't imagine! If it were our soldiers watching out for us, they would have woken us to tell us.'

Fox laughed a short, harsh laugh. 'What am I saying? This happened right outside our door! We should have heard! Whoever did this, they're professionals. Trained to kill quickly and quietly.'

Taneshka peered at another fatal wound. 'There's only one real area of damage on each one,' she said after a moment. 'The people that did this must have had the element of surprise. Every hit was fatal, and there's no blood that doesn't lead back to the bodies, so our protectors were probably uninjured in the attack.'

Kesta raised her eyebrows, impressed. 'Do they teach you this kind of thing in Prince and Tigress training, or something?'

Fox laughed. 'At home, officers in the army have some of their time taken up investigating murders. Outside of war, there has to be something for soldiers to do. That's where I first saw blood. They teach you how to identify clues, so that you can track down the killers. Of course, I got sent away before I got any real practice.'

Taneshka shrugged. 'Not many murders at home. It's just common sense, really. And a strong set of nerves.'

Kesta crouched down to join Fox and Taneshka by one of the corpses, ignoring the gathering flies. There was a hardness in her voice as she shut out the horror around her.

'Teach me.'

A voice from the end of the empty street cut across Fox's response. 'What in the Lands…?'

It was Rashin, looking unkempt and astonished.

22
Guardians And Omens

There was a long silence. Rashin looked up from his examination of the nearest body. 'This wasn't you three?' Fox shook his head.

'I left my sword and my staff in our tent.'

Rashin's face darkened imperceptibly with anger. 'Are you telling me that you were preparing to face an assassination attempt unarmed?' Fox didn't answer, instead reaching into his over-shirt to reveal Taneshka's knife.

'Fox is never unarmed,' Taneshka pointed out, retrieving her weapon deftly, 'he can do magic, if you remember?' Rashin narrowed his eyes at her.

'The term is anti-magic, young Tigress, and I'll have none of your cheek, royal or no. That is beside the point, anyhow. Fox should not be putting himself in danger when he has opportunity to avoid it! He is…'

'Too important, yes I know!' Fox interrupted, adding wearily: 'Thank you Rashin.' Rashin looked taken aback by his dismissive tone. He hesitated, looking at Fox closely. Fox did not meet his eyes.

'Am I relegated once more to the post of advisor? Prince, is this how things stand between us?' Fox looked up. A rebellious surge of feeling dictated his reply.

'You tell me, Warrior.'

The Holy Warrior's expression became unreadable. He bowed stiffly, and turned to go. A scroll fell from his sleeve as he went, and Kesta caught his pained expression as he hurriedly picked it up. He walked away swiftly, robes hanging from stiff shoulders.

Fox looked a little guilty. 'Damn it. Nothing is right,' he muttered to himself, examining the flagstones fiercely. There was a short moment where Kesta and Taneshka exchanged glances, then Fox shook his head and spoke up.

'Come on! We have to follow this. Somewhere in this city is a group of people determined to protect me. Let's find out why!' He stepped away from the pool of congealing blood at his feet.

For a moment he hesitated, then determinedly set off in the opposite direction to Rashin. This simple action struck Kesta as significant. She met Taneshka's eyes once more.

'Things don't feel right with Rashin, like this,' she said. Taneshka wordlessly agreed.

The main causeway of the City of Lakes was bustling with activity. Traders wheeled their carts up side-streets, and barrows trundled through the centre of the thoroughfare. The canal that ran parallel to the street was also full of travellers in small boats. Kesta was impressed again with how quickly the city had changed.

When an arrow came out of nowhere and plunged, quivering into a doorframe, Fox was given a shock. He was even more surprised when a high scream came from across the street, rising above the cacophony, as a man fell from a flat rooftop.

There was a moment of confusion, then general screaming rose. Keeping an eye on the rooftops, Fox ran across the street, against the flow of those struggling to run the other way.

The man on the cobbles was dead. A nasty cut from his left underarm to his right shoulder blade had put paid to any ambitions of reaching old age. In his right hand he clutched a bow. Next to him was a quiver of arrows.

Kesta shook her head. 'This is becoming a sight too common.'

'Agreed,' Fox murmured, pulling an arrow from the man's quiver. Taneshka sauntered across the street, twirling the arrow from the doorframe between her fingers. Fox took it and smiled mirthlessly as a quick comparison revealed that the arrow and its mates in the quiver were the same.

'Not a clever choice,' Taneshka remarked, 'those flights are easy to identify. A proper assassin would have chosen a plain flighted arrow. These'd catch the eye, especially in an open quiver like that.'

Fox nodded. 'We've already established that these people aren't very good at their job.'

Kesta rolled her eyes. 'Not very good? They're getting wiped out whenever they come near us!'

'Yes. Which is what is so interesting.'

Taneshka cupped her hands around her mouth. 'Hey! Mystery people! Where are you hiding? Come out and make yourselves known!' Kesta laughed.

Taneshka shrugged. 'Sometimes the direct approach works.'

Fox turned his attention back to the building from which the archer had fallen.

'It's a standalone building. It's not attached to any other, look... I wonder what's behind...?' He walked around the corner of the building.

The traders and people that remained in the street were already whispering loudly amongst themselves. After a moment, Fox reappeared from behind the building. 'Backs onto a canal. Unless they've all swum for it, they're still in the building.'

Taneshka paused for thought, looking up at the building's suddenly staring windows. 'Ha. Good thing these people are on our side,' she muttered, drawing her knife anyway. Fox waved it away.

'No need, I'll soon know...' He closed his eyes briefly. Taneshka shrugged resignedly and returned her knife to her hidden cache. Fox's eyes snapped open. He looked disappointed.

'No one in there! And there's no one in the canal up and down its length, it isn't for water traffic. I'd know if there were swimmers.'

Fox frowned, and turned the corner of the building again. The girls followed.

At the back of the building, Kesta stood looking up at the roof. Taneshka joined her, looking confused.

'Where's Fox?'

Kesta nodded at the rooftop in answer. 'He's up there. Just climbed up.'

'Well that's rude of him! He should have invited us along. Come on, I'll give you a leg up.'

After an undignified scramble, they joined Fox on the roof. He was examining a thin spatter of blood, splashed against the low wall. His footprints were easily visible in the mud that carpeted the flat rooftop. Next to his, and just as clearly printed, was another set of footprints, made by slightly larger feet.

A shout from below caused Fox to stand up. A man wearing pottery-shard armour and a broad rattan helmet was standing below, next to the assassin's corpse.

'Ho! Lord Fox sir! Would this be connected to the deaths in Stenn Street?'

'Probably!' Fox returned the shout. 'Are you from the City Guard?

The man below nodded solemnly. 'Yessir. We're looking into this one now, six murders is serious business in our city. Unsurprisingly. We got a boy in our custody says they were looking to kill Your Highnesses. Very unfortunate.'

'We weren't the ones who killed those men,' Fox called down, 'we're trying to find out who did. I wonder... would you be so kind as to remove that man's boot and sling it up here?' The guard raised a bushy eyebrow but complied. Fox caught the boot and checked the sole against the prints in the roof soil.

'Hmm. No doubt. Thank you!' He returned the boot in a more careful fashion. The guard paused, before shrugging and returning it to the body's foot.

'He was on the roof then?' he called up, 'erm, how'd he die? Well, I know why he's dead, there's a bloody great gash 'cross 'is back, but what killed 'im? Aside from the bloody great gash?'

Fox paused. 'Do you mean who killed him? Fact is, there are no footprints up here, besides mine and his,' Fox nodded at the corpse, 'and the wound looks like it was made by a blade. A kind of throwing blade could have made that, I suppose, but there is none up here! A perfect mystery.'

The guard stroked his moustache. 'Yes, well, that's me beaten. I'll have one of the men drag this one off. Good luck, Highness!' he turned to leave. Two similarly attired men with expressions of distaste removed the body.

Fox returned his attention to the rooftop. Taneshka and Kesta watched him wordlessly, sitting on the edge of the roof.

Behind them, unseen, a tall figure in brown leathers left a building across the canal, and slipped into an alley.

'All right. The man on the roof and the man furthest from our door both have the same wound. Like a heavy blade. Only the one from outside the house also looked strangulated. So... What does this tell us?'

'That we need to find out what kind of weapon can make wounds like that?' Kesta suggested. Fox nodded. He slowed his walk, thinking hard.

'We're going to have to split up. Taneshka, you can investigate up around Remembrance Waters. Find Liner Shore and make him talk. Kesta, you can go into the market and ask all the traders about this strange weapon.'

'And what will you be doing?' Taneshka asked, stopping on the bridge that led into Victory Square. Fox winced.

'I'm having a meeting with Rashin. He says it's urgent, and "vitally important."' Fox turned away. 'It'd better be.'

Liner Shore was not having a good day. He'd seen the young Tigress earlier, coming up the slope from the lower city. Every turn he made that was supposed to throw her off proved useless; whenever he looked back, she was always still on his tail. There was a young boy and a guard with her, and he just couldn't seem to shake her off his trail.

Liner turned another corner and immediately forgot his troubles.

Kesta stepped into the low building with a sense of trepidation. Smoke and heat filled the air in the little forge, and Kesta took small breaths. A wild-haired man with a soot-blackened face nodded to her, handing one of his instruments to an equally blackened assistant.

'What can I do for you?'

'I'm looking for a weapon.'

'Aye. What kind?'

'One that can cleave *and* strangle.'

The smithy looked intrigued. 'I don't know about that, miss. We make honest weapons here, see, swords, axes and the like. You're looking for something a little more...exotic.'

'So you can't help me?'

'Ah, now I didn't say that. Just because I don't make that kind of instrument, don't mean that I'm not knowing about them. Now, strangulation, hmm? Assassin's gear that, for silent work. Not usually quick though, lest you use something with a bit of bite...'

The smith paused, rubbing his thin beard. 'A length of thin chain will do that job better, if you be wanting speed, and aren't so worried about being discreet.'

Kesta nodded. 'That sounds like what I'm looking for. Only, with a blade?'

The smithy grinned. 'Oh, aye, I know of something like that, now we're talking on it. Foreign weapon. Very rare. High class assassination weapon.'

'Where can I find one then? Where are they from?' Kesta slipped a gold piece from beneath her hooded cloak. Her heart beat very fast, it was exhilarating, enquiring confidently after clandestine weaponry.

'S' that gold there? Great, very good for the memory, is money.' The smith winked at her. 'Yea Miss, it's a Southlands weapon, if I remember rightly. And used by only one group down there. If you want to hear more about them, you'd best get along to their quarter in the market; I don't even have a name to give you. Take some gold, I'd advise. And thank you.'

Fox stepped into Rashin's tent. He was sitting in the corner, reading from one of his scrolls. Fox sat opposite him. After a while, the Holy Warrior lifted his head and looked at Fox from under his blond eyebrows.

'Your dangerous journey is not over yet, Fox.'

'Well, there's an optimistic sentence.'

Rashin smiled despite himself. 'Sorry, Fox. But I feel I need to get your attention, and keep it. There's information in these,' Rashin raised one of the scrolls, 'that it would be fatal to ignore. The Arisen does not have the liberty of an easy life.'

He leaned forward. 'The Perversion is more cunning than we thought. It is not beyond him to be... obvious. His design of power through the unity of his disparate shape has been proved flawed before, when the first Holy Ones fought him, so long ago. He is making a gamble this time. He has been forced to it. And he is unlikely to make many mistakes.'

Fox frowned. 'The scrolls tell you of his plans?'

'Not directly. They are... prophetic theories, if you will. One set examines the works of my brotherhood, that set being the Scrolls of Song, and the other, the Scrolls of Keening, is based on the writings of Dominagan priests, the early Dragon Worshippers, who spawned the sorcerers. The first predicts your victory, and your rise to meet it. The latter is darker, and mentions ways that the Shadow will overcome you. They are...numerous. Here, listen to this...'

Taneshka looked at the bloody remains of Liner Shore. After a moment, she was able to vocalise how she felt. 'Damnation and dragonfire!' She turned away from the body.
Someone had broken his neck, and there was that distinctive gash in his throat, as well. Taneshka hoped Kesta was having some luck in finding the origins of the weapon.
'They got here first.' She stated the obvious to the guard that was accompanying her. The boy was waiting some distance off. Taneshka hadn't had time to warn him about the body. He had trodden on it. The look on his face said it all, Taneshka realised. There was something very different about death in civilisation than there was about death on the battlefield, Taneshka thought. Something darker, because it didn't fit with the veneer that the city presented. Like Kesta, she would be glad to get out of the City of Lakes.

Kesta walked into Rashin's tent to find Fox and Rashin in the middle of a heated argument. When she appeared, Rashin made a sudden noise that suggested he had just restrained a sudden outburst. The man spun around and presented his back to Fox, who shook his head angrily, his eyes narrowed.
'Rashin, you are a wise man, but at the moment you speak like a fool! Those scrolls are clearly open to interpretation and your view cannot be the only one! I'm interested in what you have to say but...leave me alone, on this...' here he glanced nervously at Kesta, '...this issue, all right?' He left the tent.
Kesta stood silently, watching Rashin's back. She felt a cold anger at what she imagined he had been saying. 'Were you warning him away from me, Rashin?' She was surprised at the dangerous edge to her voice.
Rashin turned around. He looked sad. 'Oh, Kesta. I have nothing against you, my girl. But I feel the burden, the need to prepare him. Do you understand? There are some writings that I

cannot afford to ignore!' Rashin's voice took a harder quality. 'Please leave this tent Kesta.'

Kesta nodded curtly. 'Goodbye Rashin. If you will pore into scrolls rather than into your friends, and what you read there is more important than us, then you have lost my friendship. Until you return to your self, I will not speak with you, except as the Prince's Shield Maiden. Do not neglect Fox on account of me though! I am sorry, but not on my behalf.'

Kesta paused in the tent doorway. Then she turned and left. Rashin sighed and sat, fingers gripping at the Scroll of Keening. 'How she has changed,' he murmured to himself. 'From peasant to noblewoman in so short a time. And not all change is good...' The Warrior's attention returned to the scroll. Muttering a brief prayer to the Land, Rashin set to work.

23
A Message From The River King

Fox and Kesta walked in silence. The sun was setting, spreading an odd, wintry light across the city. The canals shone beneath the stone bridges that arched across the waterways.

'When we get home, then everything will sort itself out,' Fox murmured confidently, looking up at the vividly streaked evening sky. Kesta nodded, thinking of her own home. It no longer was home, she realised, just a place where she had once lived.

Fox's own thoughts were full of the misty rises of the Autumn Hills, where dew would be drenching the grass below sturdy trees, limbs heavy in the Autumn, with red and gold leaves. And the blossom in the Spring...

Taneshka met them at the top of the city, at the edge of Remembrance Waters. The evening sun left a ruddy path in the lake's surface.

'You both look cheerful! Well, I'm afraid I have no good news. We'll get nothing out of master Liner Shore.'

'Dead?'

'Very.'

Fox shook his head. 'These people are one step ahead. Do you think they killed him because he was a threat to us, or because we may have used him to trace them?'

Taneshka shrugged her shoulders. 'I've no idea. How did your meeting with Rashin go?'

'Not well. Apparently, the Great Shadow intends to either defeat me through treachery, whatever that means, or through brute force. Rashin says he's not above resorting to recruiting an army.'

'Who would fight for *him*?' Kesta exclaimed.

'Exactly my thoughts. But Rashin seems to think that... oh, I don't know what he thinks! Except that I am to stop distracting myself from my purpose.'

Taneshka laughed. 'He'll have little luck there, if Kesta's the distraction. What about you, Kesta? Any news on the weapon?'

Kesta nodded excitedly. 'It's a Southlands weapon unique to the Scorpion Clan. Apparently, they're the most accomplished assassins in the Sacred Lands. Which *does* make sense...'

The three stood and considered the information for a short time. When Kesta began to shiver in the biting wind that had sprang up, Fox suggested that they leave. As the three of them headed back down towards the city, the first lights were lit against the early dark.

'I demand to speak to Prince Fox!'

The man was wearing fish-scale style armour, and was bearing a long boat-hook weapon. The insignia on his chest was of a reed-green heron standing on a pale blue background. Fox hurried to the front. He had heard the man's shouting from a street away. Panting, Taneshka and Kesta arrived behind him.

'I am Fox. Who asks?'

The man turned to Fox and a look of relief crossed his face. 'My Lord. My fervent apologies. I represent King Heron Boatmaster, Watcher of the Many Waters, Custodian of the Great Lifeblood, and Steward of the Land.' The man bowed.

'I have been here three days now, attempting to gain audience with you. Your advisors have turned me away each and every day that I sought you, and this night they attempt to do so once more! I know from my own lord, Prince Fox, that you have more courtesy than that, and most likely will wish to know wherefore I have been denied counsel with you.'

Fox frowned. 'My apologies, worthy messenger, I was unaware that I had any official advisors present in the city.'

Fox's eyes scanned the huddle of people near to the messenger. Suddenly, he recognised one or two of the faces there. 'Advisory Council? Here, without my knowledge? Explain yourselves, at once!'

The advisors looked affronted. One stepped forward, a haughty expression on his narrow features. 'We are of a higher authority than the Crown Prince, young master. We answer to the King, for only he carries the Blood that we submit to. If we wish to be here without your knowledge, then it shall be so.'

Fox's eyes narrowed. Behind him, Kesta leaned closer to Taneshka and whispered, 'He'll wish he hadn't said that.' The Tigress smiled, but it was more teeth than humour.

'I know you are here now, and my patience is short. I would like to know why this man was not directed to my tent in the first instance: he represents a valued ally! Tell me!' Fox was not smiling.

'He…refused to tell us what he wanted with you. Sire.'

'Would you open and read another man's letter, Advisor?'

'Of course not.'

'Then why hinder this courier in his business?' The advisor gaped wordlessly for a moment. Fox shook his head. 'What is your name, please?'

'Machist. Sir.'

'You are Henshin's right hand man, hmm?'

'In a manner of speaking.'

'What did you do, before you joined the council?'

'I know what you may have heard, and yes I was a Dominagan, sir. And before you ask, I was not involved in the massacre of the natives. That happened a few weeks before your arrival as a baby, sire, and I was then already in your father's service. The killings were carried out by a misguided sect of Dominagans, I have little in common with them.'

Fox said nothing for a moment. 'You were a Dragon worshipper? One of those that released the Great Shadow?'

The ex-priest looked unimpressed. 'Henshin and I are united in our disregard of your story about the mythical Perversion of Light. I'm sorry, my prince, but my mind is my own and I am not as easily swayed by your tales as these peasants.'

There was a good amount of annoyed muttering, and an angry docker at the back made his feelings known with a threatening shout. Fox himself looked dangerous, fists clenched, eyes narrowed to grey slits. The advisor seemed not to notice.

'Why, if the "Shadow" had been freed that night, then, certainly, your cousin would be dead!' The advisor said loudly and confidently, as if he were about to prove a point. 'He was born in the Valley of Stones, himself, when his mother tragically went into early labour. If what you say is true then he would surely have died!'

'Worst luck, he yet lives,' Fox snapped. 'unless he has been executed for his crime. Though I doubt that he has.'

'Master Henshin has caught up with Prince Trustan and has delivered him to the Autumn Citadel where judgement will be carried out, eventually.'

Fox raised a cynical eyebrow. 'I'm sure he will receive a fair trial. If that is all, Machist, I will take my leave to speak with Heron's man. Thank you.'

Fox turned, and with a quick nod to the messenger, departed.

Sitting in the tent, the messenger seemed more relaxed. He accepted a measure of ale and drank deeply before delivering his message.

'Thank you, that's much better. I haven't had anything good to drink since I set out. Now. The message I carry is of vital importance. It carries words of congratulations, for your victory here. It also carries a request.'

'If Heron asks it, it shall be done. I would not be here but for his transporting of our much needed resources,' Fox said firmly, as though expecting an advisor to appear out of nowhere to argue with him.

'Thank you, my Lord. Recently our concerns have grown. Patrols put ashore on the northern banks frequently do not return…well, at least, not in one piece. Sometimes remains float into the harbours from upriver…'

Fox went pale. 'Who…who is doing this?'

'We don't know. It's a wasteland on the northern banks, bordering the Ice Forest. The only king who controls any land on the northern shores is Stone Wolf, and that's well to the northwest. Until recently, he was using our heavy barges to trade quarried stone with the other families, but now all contact has ceased. Either a strong enemy has taken the lands between the Lifeblood and the Ice Mountains, or Stone Wolf himself…'

Fox shook his head. 'That wouldn't make sense. Stone Wolf may be many things, but he is not without honour. Although…' Fox remembered. 'I met Sirkor Wolf in the Southeast Wastes! He was a captain under Ox! How could I have forgotten?'

The messenger pondered this, taking a sip from his ale cup. 'I don't think that is so significant. Sirkor was in disgrace. He had been exiled by his uncle. The only one who was friendly with

Sirkor within that family was the king's middle son. I can't remember his name.'

Fox subsided, annoyed that his theory had come to nothing. Then his memory returned to what Rashin had told him. The Great Shadow was not above using an army.

'It could be that this foe is an unexpected one, and one of considerable power. It could be that King Stone Wolf's territory is already overrun.'

The messenger put down his ale. He looked up, fingers trembling. 'Who – who could do a deed so great? The armies of the north are immense – who could bring ruin to such a nation?'

A cold wind whipped past the tent entrance. The candle by Fox's chair guttered and went out. In the sudden gloom, Fox leaned forwards. 'My friend, have you heard of the Great Usurper? The Perversion of Light? The Shadow.'

'Please, stop! Please.' The messenger was trembling. In the silence that followed, broken only by the flapping of the tent flap, Fox and the messenger met each other's gaze.

'I will do what Heron requires of me. If he needs aid...'

Fox stopped suddenly, an unbidden thought halting him.

Where are Kesta and Taneshka?

He ran out into the cold. The air sliced at his cheeks, making him wince. Running through the jumble of tents and temporary structures, he focused completely on finding Taneshka. On finding Kesta...

The messenger ran behind him, slowed down by his boathook. Fox had Tiger's Gift, and his staff was on his back. He went as one running into battle, pushing surprised bystanders aside.

'WHERE ARE THEY?' Fox roared. A terrified looking advisor raised his hands in surrender.

'Who? I'm sorry, so sorry, sire, please don't do anything...' Fox pushed the idiot away in disgust. The people were hurrying away. Fox closed his eyes and sought Kesta's mind.

There was a sudden, amazing clarity. All the Sacred Lands seemed stretched out before him in one astonishing liberating moment. Heart rate surging, Fox focused his mind on the northern provinces. The wide, vital band of the river Lifeblood ribboned across the green country, and there on the northern bank, a dark swathe of malice, as wide as the river itself...

Fox forced his mind to the City of Lakes. There! He felt Kesta, she was over... over there, among the forest of dark masts and docks, above the water level... the boatyard...

Fox set off at a run. A canal came between him and his goal and he cleared it in one bound. The messenger, more than a little astonished, went for the nearest bridge.

Fox moved between struts and beams with the agility of his namesake. There was no lighting in the dark alleys behind the docks, but Fox's feet found the way nonetheless. Then, inexplicably, Fox came to a dead end. A boat had been wedged between two buildings. The dark water nearby lapped, echoing and eerie in the enclosed space. A hand grabbed Fox's arm.

'I know where your friends are.'

The hand was a dark, Southlands brown. The voice was young, but deeper than Fox's. The boy's forearm was emblazoned with a cream yellow scorpion. Fox had seen very few tattoos, save on sorcerers, and the sight made him start.

'Peace. Follow me.'

Fox could not see the newcomer's eyes beneath his deep hood. The boy reached up, grabbing an overhead beam. As the messenger came panting into the alley mouth, Fox's legs vanished up into the network of scaffolding.

Splinters bit unpleasantly at Fox's palms as he followed the stranger through the forest of wooden struts. Unlike the boy, he was not wearing gloves. Fox could see a pair of iron clubs in the boy's belt. Fox called, 'What's happening? Who are you?'

'Hush.'

They turned a corner and stopped suddenly above a disused inlet. Broken keels and junked wood lay all about, and in the shadows below, voices could be heard.

'Do you know how many those two have killed?'

'Aye, I do, and it's we who have them caught and trussed up. No need to fear them.'

'No, I suppose not.'

'All we have to do is wait until Tanner runs up from the boat to warn us the prince is coming. Then we shoot him from here in the dark, while he searches for his girl and the Tigress. Then we can present his head to the city, and see how many will take his rule then!' There was a muffled, strained sound, and then the noise of something being kicked. Fox stiffened, realising he was hearing Kesta and Taneshka, gagged and bound below.

'Ha ha! Oh yes, the mighty Tigress and the prince's wench! Not so dangerous now, eh? You're right Tavish, we got nothing to fear from them. Never did.' There was a short, tense silence.

'Tavish? Tell you who I do fear...'

'Aye, that Black Demon. All the others, gone... Makes you think. How short life can be. But we won't be found by him, not here. Here's too well hidden. Tanner will get some hints to the prince. At least he should find us...' The man was gabbling.

Fox glanced up and almost shouted from shock. Trussed up by the ankles, and passed out from the rush of blood to the head, was a man with a grimy face and rough clothes that hid armour. The stranger next to Fox glanced up too, and whispered, 'Tanner.' Fox nodded. This Scorpion branded boy had removed the spring from the trap already. Things were being done on his terms now.

The Southlander boy reached up into the dark and pulled down a heavy, long handled axe. A leather hood was pulled back, revealing a darkly shining axe head, moon shaped and keen bladed. Intricate designs had been cut into the axe head, leaving beautiful gaps in the metal to reduce weight. The stranger held it as if it weighed nothing.

With a nod to Fox, he stood, balancing on the beam. The axe head disappeared into the darkness near the hanging man's ankles, and there was the sound of a rope snapping.

As the cut rope spooled out like fishing line, Tanner was swung out above the inlet below, before being dropped from some height. There was a horrid snap as his head hit the ground, breaking his neck.

The stranger hooked the great axe into a baldric on his back, and removed a new weapon from his hooded cloak. As the horrified Lakemen below ran forward to see to their dead comrade, the Southlander swung an odd hooked blade around his head a few times, building up momentum before releasing it.

Tavish choked as a spinning blade flicked past his head, jerking back to hit him in the chest. A thin chain whirled around his neck and his life ended instantaneously, his body pulled backwards and up into the shadows. The unnamed kidnapper spun, and saw that Tavish had been used as a counterweight. The hooded figure landed easily in front of him, dropping from his high beam, holding the other end of the strange weapon.

Fox dropped under his own power, not needing a chain to let him down safely. His feet hit the ground at the same time as the Lake man's head.

The Stranger returned his bloody axe to his shoulder, and removed his hood. 'I need light.'

Fox obliged, raising both hands above his head and conjuring flame. In the flickering light, Fox saw a handsome, dark brown face, made solemn by the deed just undertaken. The boy was clean shaven, nearly a head taller than Fox, and had very short, curly hair, black, like his eyes.

Kesta rubbed her wrists, wincing. The rope that had tied her and Taneshka was long since discarded. The Southlands boy was seated comfortably on a wooden crate, but Fox hovered nervously at Kesta's side. She had already assured him she was all right. Taneshka was very angry, at nobody in particular.

'Stupid! Stupid, stupid, stupid! Why'd we follow him? We should have known something wasn't right.'

'What does she mean?' Fox asked, putting a hand on Kesta's shoulder.

'Look, I'm all right, you don't have to... she means, well, we only got trapped like this because we followed that little boy. One of the men was his uncle, remember? Turns out, *that* one, Tavish,' Kesta kicked the man's body, 'was a relative of the boy as well. Worked out what had happened and forced the boy to lead us in here. He ran off when they tied us up.'

Fox nodded. 'I hope he's all right. I thought... when you didn't turn up at the tent for so long, I didn't know where you'd both gone. I was speaking on a dark subject and it lead my mind to fear the worst.

'Thank the Land that you were here, friend, or things could have turned out very differently.'

Fox bowed to the boy. He smiled and bowed back, deeper than Fox had. The boy opened his mouth to speak, but Fox's eyes were once more fixed on Kesta. 'Are you sure you're...'

'Yes! I'm *all right*!' she shook his hand off her shoulder, and then seeing his hurt expression, hugged him close. 'You don't need to treat me like I'm made of parchment, Fox. I'm fine. Thanks to you.' This was directed at the boy. 'What's your name?'

The boy bowed once more.

'My name is Brant Mantissi, Son of Fury and Fate Mantissi, Champion of the Scorpion clan and scholar of the Scrolls of Song.'

24
Brant Mantissi

Rashin sat, eyes moving quickly between Fox and Brant. The messenger was standing at the door, listening with similar interest. When Fox finished, Rashin leaned back, fingers interlaced in thought.

'So. You are on our side then, master Mantissi?' There was a hint of a different question in Rashin's words.

The boy nodded. 'I am in Crown Prince Fox side.' His accent and phrasing made Fox smile. Rashin accepted the statement.

'Good. Then tell us your story, friend.'

'You not would know my parentage, I think. They were great warriors, famous in Spice Cities. They are hero names in my Scorpion Family. Fate, my mother, Fury, father. Our Storyteller gave them their honour for victory, many times.'

Brant paused, brow working as he struggled with the language.

'They were disgraced by murder. Un-good by orders. I cried for many night after they were executed. Four years now.'

Fox swallowed a swell of empathy. Brant shook his head as if to clear it, smiled, and continued.

'Storyteller name Shariq took me, and then I become both warrior of Scorpion and scholar. Scholar, great honour, for I given Scrolls of Song to study.'

Rashin's eyes widened with shock. He reached into his robe and revealed the first Scroll of Song. Brant beamed as if he had been given a great gift, and went down on his knees.

'I knew! I knew there were missing! You have them all? Storyteller!' He broke into his own language, a flowing, melodic tongue. Rashin handed Brant the scroll, bemused.

'I'm not a storyteller, friend, though my skills there are not lacking, I hope. I am a Holy Warrior. A Son of Rashin, who was the founder, and whose name I share.'

Brant nodded enthusiastically, close to tears as he opened the scroll. 'Yes, Rashin is a most revered hero in Scorpion, Storyteller. A hero of the north. The Storytellers in the family carried along, uh, artefacts? The scrolls, stories of the Order. I… I have lived Land's will, and am content. Coming here is right.'

Brant's legs gave way as he tried to stand. Rashin helped Fox carry him to a bed. It was not easy, he was tall and heavy with muscle and armour.

Rashin took the boy's chain-blade from his belt, as well as the pair of spiked iron clubs. He put them at the back of the tent, with the battle axe. As Rashin retrieved Brant's bag from the floor, it fell open. Scrolls bound in white leather tumbled to the carpeted tent floor.

Rashin bent and picked them up. Fox left – clearly the Holy Warrior would not be available for conversation for some time.

A cold wind tousled Fox's hair. The sun was setting in a blood red line on the horizon, above the grey green smudge of land across the steely water.

'You have to leave, Your Highness.'

Fox turned to see Rashin walking up behind Kesta and Taneshka, onto the humpbacked bridge. Fox looked surprised.

'Why?'

Rashin leaned on the stone balustrade, brow furrowed with worry, cheeks pinched red by the cold air. 'Because your infernal advisors are passing a law as we speak that will bind you to travel in their company. Naturally, if you should break this ruling, they will challenge your right to succeed the throne, as a lawbreaker. They are still discussing this as we speak, but the outcome will be as I say. You need to leave for your father's castle before they can declare the law.'

There was a silence. Fox considered the distance that had grown between himself and his best advisor. He put his back against the stonework of the bridge and formed an apology.

'You have always done your best to help me. I am sorry, Rashin.'

Rashin bowed, touched by Fox's words. Fox sighed, looking to his left, where Kesta and Taneshka watched quietly. 'I suppose we had better leave then. How did you find this out, Rashin?'

'Brant is a remarkable person. He's something of a shadow, when he wants to be. He has been spying on the advisory council for me.'

'That's resourceful. Thank you.'

Rashin shrugged. 'Brant offered to kill the council for you, but he was joking. I think.'

Fox laughed. 'That's a shame. But I suppose I don't need their deaths on my conscience. And Brant's done enough of that work already. Where is he?'

'Waiting by the dock where you saved the Tigress and Kesta. He said that he would find you a boat to cross the lake. Good luck, Fox.'

Rashin embraced him, and as he drew away, he passed a leather satchel to Fox, who tucked the satchel inside his shirt.

'Well? What are you hiding in your shirt?' Kesta asked as they made their way through the disused docks.

Fox shrugged. 'Gift from Rashin. I haven't looked yet, have I? Stop pestering, Kesta.'

'Oh, yes sir!' She saluted comically, rolling her eyes. Fox grinned.

Brant emerged like a ghost from amidst the beams.

'My prince.' Brant bowed deeply. Standing next to him was a bearded dock worker, who bowed as well. A round boat sat in the shallows, with a pair of oars resting against the side. Fox reached out and clasped Brant's hand.

'Thank you, Brant. Rashin tells me that you have served us well as a spy.'

Brant remained in a posture of respect, and kept hold of Fox's hand. 'Also I would serve you as a companion, my lord.'

Fox was surprised. 'You want to come with us?'

'Yes. I must protect your highness.'

'But why?'

'I have seen you before. There were dreams. I have my mission, I am Land-sent. Please, accept me.'

Fox saw fervent sincerity on Brant's face. He smiled and squeezed the boy's hand, releasing it at last.

'Welcome to our little group, Brant. We could use your axe-work, I think. More importantly, are you much of a cook? I'm terrible with food, and Kesta's not much better. I daren't mention Teshka here.'

Brant laughed, delighted with the acceptance. Kesta shook his hand in welcome, but Taneshka avoided eye contact with Brant, and sat in the boat in silence.

The bearded docker shook hands with Fox. 'Thank you, Highness. Just leave her in the shallows on the other side of the lake, an' I can collect her when I may. Where do you go?'

'Heron's White Gates, in the Lifeblood Marshes. I owe him a debt that I intend to repay. But be careful where you share that information, please.'

'Fox?' Kesta started, 'how are we going to be able to help Heron, if there is trouble? Is the army coming?'

'As soon as they have restocked, Stavan assures me that we will be joined at the White Gates by the whole army. He has put Daris in charge of the combined archers. Stavan is now Tiger General, Haiken serves as General for my own men. Koshra is Grand General, and will lead the whole allied force. They won't let us down.'

Fox turned back to the docker. 'How do we get to the marshes after we make land on the other side?'

The docker described woodland, a logging outpost, gorges, caves and hills, describing a route that Fox did his best to commit to memory.

'Thank you. We'll leave the boat as promised.' He turned to get into the boat.

'One thing Highness!' Fox turned back to the docker. 'Don't go past the gorge into them big old trees, the mightarchs. They're as old as anything in these lands, and superstition runs rife about the woods there. The Ancient Sisters. No one goes in. You'd best not either.'

Fox thanked the docker again, and with Brant's help, pushed the boat out into the icy water.

It was night and bitterly cold by the time they stowed the boat in the reeds and began trudging inland through the high, damp grass. The swaying stems were already crisping with frost, and Fox's cheeks ached from the knifing wind. Kesta was suffering the most. She was wearing all three of her over-shirts, but the cold still seeped through. Her teeth were chattering.

They stopped by a knotted yew which leaned out above a large boulder, offering shelter from the wind. Brant, who had never felt this cold before, was protected by a bear pelt. None of the others could have worn it, it was so long and heavy.

They knelt against the cold rock as Brant and Fox set to making a fire. The earth around the base of the boulder was hard with frost. Brant hacked some long branches off the yew tree, and chopped them into pieces, snapping off twigs for kindling. As soon as the firewood was in place, Fox winked at a shivering Kesta, and clicked his fingers. The woodpile burst into flames, and their grateful bodies were flooded with warmth.

Fox was surprised by Brant's lack of reaction. When he boy noticed Fox staring at him, he grinned. 'Anti-magic. I know that you do. Your Storyteller tell me.'

Fox wondered what else Rashin had said.

The fire crackled and spat. Kesta threaded pieces of meat onto a thin length of wood, to roast over the flames. Fox pulled Rashin's satchel out into the open, and undid the buckle. Kesta paused in her cooking to see.

Fox pulled a white scroll out into the night air. 'Oh! Rashin's given me his scrolls...but I can't read them, they're not written in Dragonscript.' Brant reached out across the fire, and Fox handed him the scroll.

'Mm. This is one of mine, Prince. Rashin has them all together, so that you will study. I can read them, I will read them to you.'

'All right.' Fox pulled a few more scrolls out of the satchel. 'And you can call me Fox, by the way.'

'Thank you, Fox. Oh!' Brant looked shocked, staring at the black scroll in Fox's left hand. 'A Scroll of Keening! I don't know Rashin had... they are *morai*!'

Fox passed the scroll to Brant, who came around the fire to sit between Fox and Kesta. Spidery writing patterned the parchment. It was in some kind of brown ink, and after a moment Fox remembered that Rashin had said the writings were penned in blood.

Brant sat, absorbed in the writing, while Fox and Kesta shared some bread. Taneshka sat at the edge, glancing back at them all periodically, with a strange expression on her face. She chewed on a strip of dried meat as if it had wronged her somehow.

After some time, Brant looked up. 'This section say how you, Fox, might be defeated. Treachery, Fox. It says someone you know well, close, will through the shadow, turn against and kill you. It is trouble. I don't like it.'

Fox nodded. A gust of wind made the flames rise and flicker, causing the shadows to dance. Kesta put her arm around his shoulders.

Fox shook his head. 'Those scrolls were written by Dominagans. Dragon worshippers! I will not trust them,' he said firmly. Brant bowed, but looked worried.

'Ha. Maybe you are too trusting, Fox.'

Fox looked up. Taneshka had spoken. Her eyes were fixed on Brant, who smiled uneasily. 'What is wrong, Tigress?'

Her lip curled in response, and she looked away. Fox frowned. He opened his mouth to challenge Taneshka's unfriendly attitude, but Kesta squeezed his hand.

'She's still annoyed at needing to be rescued,' she whispered, 'and she doesn't trust Brant, yet. I know her. She will change.' Fox made an unconvinced sound. Kesta smiled at him. 'Relax. This is it, remember? *Civilisation be damned! Give me the wild!* Well...we've got it now.' Fox put his arm around her. The wind sprang up, making him wince at the harsh cold.

'Yes. Bring on the wild, indeed.'

The Arisen sleeps. He dreams. A poison hangs in the air, and cold hands reach out to touch him. The Dreamer sees shapes, fading, inconstant. His heart beats hard and heavy in his chest. He runs, but something about his ankles is dragging, and he can only manage a stumbling walk. Icy water freezes the blood in his legs as he struggles onwards. Ahead, shapes run towards him, flailing arms and lolling heads. Turning, the Arisen sees a great wet plain, and bodies everywhere.

The Arisen's heart stops. Atop a pile of soaking corpses, a horrible, hunched **something** *feasts. Bodies tumble away as it sates its appetite. The Arisen One cries out from the horror of it. White, freezing fog rises to envelop him, and he is borne away, towards a structure, standing stark against the clinging mist. There is a body* *lying in the doorway. Everything in the Arisen's body screams as he tries to turn back.*

Let me be borne back to the creature, let me face the things in the fog, let me go to my death but do not, please do not force me there! Not there, anywhere else, I cannot stand to see...not her...

'Kesta!' Fox fought his way to his feet. His muscles burned as if he had been running, and his brow was beaded with sweat. The fire had burned very low, and in the dark, Fox panicked. Flame rose violently from the embers. Kesta stumbled to her feet, Brant and Taneshka were both upright, staring at Fox in uncomprehending fear.

Kesta tackled Fox to the ground. The fire faded, returning to glowing embers. Kesta held him down and felt his body relax beneath her. 'It's all right. Just another dream, Fox. Just another dream.' Fox stared up into her eyes. For a moment there was no sound but the spitting of the fire and the sigh of the wintry wind.

Fox blinked slowly, feeling sleep creeping back to reclaim his tired body. Kesta helped him back to the boulder and his bed.

Brant nodded to Kesta and climbed up on top of the boulder, wrapping his enormous bear pelt around him. The boy stared out into the dark, keeping watch. Taneshka watched Fox nervously for a little while, then began a vigil of her own. She did not trust Brant to be the sole watcher.

'Tomorrow, this'll just be another memory,' Kesta murmured comfortingly. Fox nodded slowly.

'My legs ache...feel like...been running... Kesta?' Fox forced his eyes open.

'Yes?'

'I should have kissed you at the feast.' And without further explanation, he fell asleep.

At the parapet of the White Gates, a guard stared down into the dark marsh. All was quiet, and very cold. The guard's breath came in puffs of steam, and he wrapped his gloved hands tighter around the shaft of his pike. Below, a voice called up to him.

'Ho! Who's on the gate? Let us in, it's freezing down here!' The guard leaned out over the edge, to see a party of five armed men, each one riding a great, horned bull.

The guard sighed wearily. 'Unit name, please.'

'Fifth Bull-riders, King Heron's Marsh Patrol. We've been on a little trip to the north bank, and have urgent news for the King. Let us in, man!'

'All right, all right. Open the gate!' The guard turned and called down to the winchmen. The great gate swung slowly open, spiked bottom edge raking through the shallow water, coated in reeds. The bull-riders came wading in, their steeds making puffy grunts, and swinging their heads from side to side.

A wooden platform, built to form a solid walkway, extended from the wall. The lead bull-rider swung out of the saddle, giving his bull's bridle to a waiting soldier.

Despite his cold muscles, the rider forced himself to run at his best speed, taking stone steps two at a time. He ran along the walltop, passing through door after door, iron gate after iron gate, soldiers hurrying to undo latches and locks at his approach.

Panting, feeling ill from the cold and damp, the man came to a stop in front of a great, lacquered entrance. A heron was emblazoned across both doors, wearing a crown, and holding a key in its bill. The bull-rider pounded on the door, glancing out to his right and the territory confined by the White Gates. In the distance, where the marshes turned back into the Lifeblood river, the king's ship was moored. There were no lights, so Heron must surely be in the building...

The door swung open on oiled hinges. The rider pushed through into the inner rooms, leaving damp footprints on the shining wood floor. Slowing to a more sedate pace, the rider paused in front of a smaller pair of doors. Keeping his head high, the bull-rider stepped into the king's chambers.

Lamplight covered everything in a warm, golden glow. The smell of polish and oil was strong; the queen was showing a young daughter how to rub polish into the surface of an already gleaming table. A young man sat by the window in the corner, fletching some arrows. The king himself was holding his baby son, lowering his head to kiss the baby. A sword was out, leaning against Heron's chair, a jar of pungent oil open beside it.

'My Lord!' The rider's feet snapped together on the boards. He bowed from the waist, removing his crested helmet in a smooth movement.

King Heron looked up, and passed his child to his wife.

'This had better be good, Rider, I am enjoying some time with my family. Could this not wait?'

'No, my Lord.'

The King looked immediately worried. 'Why? What has happened? Report!' He stood up impulsively, but at a quiet word from his wife sat back down. He ran a hand through his greying, sandy coloured hair. Dark brown eyes narrowed with concern.

'My lord, Andul Spar of the Fifth bull-riders, reporting. We were sent by your lordship to visit the northernmost fortifications. The intermediate forts greeted us warmly; they are well provided for and alert. The weather stayed clear, and as evening approached, we came near the North Forts. The wall guards were nowhere to be seen. We spurred the bulls onwards, and soon reached the armoury and barracks. They were empty.' A note of tired desperation came into the rider's voice.

'They were all gone my lord! Nothing to be found, but blood… oh, my lord, the blood, up the walls, coating the floor, red in the water around the gate. There was nothing left! And all was silent, save for the wind, and for the water eddying against the gate. They must have come and killed and taken the bodies with them.'

King Heron's face was pale. 'Who?' he whispered, clenching at the arms of his chair. His eldest son came forwards, fear written on his features. The arrow he had been fletching lay forgotten on the windowsill, and the white feathers floated slowly to the floor.

The rider looked up at his king.

'I do not know. They left no trace. The gates were locked. The walls undamaged. The weapons gone as well. All gone, my lord. All gone.'

25
Prejudice And Intimacy

Kesta found herself taking the lead. The early morning air was still but sharp. Kesta raised her collar to protect her reddened cheeks. Her pace was brisk, frost-brittle grass crunching beneath her feet.

Taneshka walked behind her, moving at an uncomfortable pace to keep ahead of Brant, who had taken up the role of rear guard.

They stopped their march on a hill. In the distance, beech woods were a brown smudge, topping the rising swell of another hill. Behind them, glittering in the winter sun, the Great Lakes were laid out like icy mirrors. The City of Lakes was hidden by distance.

Brant sat, laying his bear pelt out on the ground beneath him. Wearily, the other three joined him, although Taneshka refrained from sitting on the pelt, instead seating herself on her pack.

Brant listened comfortably to Fox's descriptions of Heron's people and their water-bound culture. The Southlander was eating an apple that he had retrieved from his bags. Seeing Taneshka sitting alone, he tossed another apple, ripe and beginning to brown. The Tigress caught it automatically. With a muttered thanks, she took a bite.

The weather did not warm as time went on. The chill led Brant to undo one of his packs, pulling a small, round, cast iron object into view. The top part was a spherical pot, attached by an ingenious screw rim to a box that sat beneath. Fox leaned in to look, interested.

'What's that?'

'It is charcoal stove. Either use it for boiling, like now, or use it for roasting, if I find the other part in the bag. Clever, eh? Charcoal in the square box, water in the pot, then we can boil, or maybe stews. Useful?'

'Very.' Fox agreed, watching as Brant began. 'How many other things do you have concealed about yourself?' he asked lightly, watching Brant's face for a reply.

Brant shrugged, with a knowing smile. 'Depend what you mean by wonderful.'

'Wonderful means full of wonder, you know, when something is really impressive?' Kesta said teasingly. She grinned as Brant rolled his eyes at her. He poured water from his leather canteen into the pot attachment, and carefully screwed it back onto the box. In seconds, the water was bubbling.

'Ah ha!' Brant raised a small leather pouch in the air triumphantly. 'Found! This, Kesta, this is wonderful.' He shook the pouch over his hand. Kesta peered at the contents with polite interest.

'Oh. Some dried leaves. How nice.'

Fox laughed at her overdone show of indifference, and Brant smiled good-humouredly. He made a face as if to say, *we shall see*, and dropped a single brown leaf into the water.

A strong, urgent aroma rose from the pot. Fox and Kesta both moved closer to breathe it in, and after a moment's hesitation, Taneshka's curiosity overcame her distrust and she came over.

'Mmm.' Kesta nodded appreciatively. 'I can really breathe now, this properly clears you up... what is it?'

'It is called Tochi.' Brant passed a little ceramic cup to Fox and Kesta, and retrieved another from his pack for Taneshka. The cups had long handles, the design making it easy to scoop up the steaming water.

Brant watched with scarcely controlled anticipation as Fox sipped at the water. But it was Taneshka who took the first real draw from her cup.

Taneshka's eyes widened, and she held the cup at arm's length, staring at it. 'What is this?! My head feels clear as ice, but I'm warmed through. Damn, this is something!'

Brant laughed. 'I love to see the first sip! Your face, Tigress, so sad, now you look slapped happy! I must laugh...'

'Yes, yes, all right.' Taneshka waved him silent impatiently, and downed the remainder of the drink. 'For a foreigner, you speak far too much. *Slapped happy?* And if you'll give me some more of that stuff, you can call me Taneshka.'

'At once, fair Tigress,' Brant said in tones of mock pomposity, but Taneshka forgave him, accepting the refilled cup eagerly. Fox and Kesta watched in amusement as she drank. When she was done, she looked up and handed the cup back to Brant, reluctantly, so that he could have some. Brant made a point of saying, 'Thank you, Taneshka,' as he accepted it. A combination of amusement and wariness danced in his eyes.

'This doesn't mean I like you, all right?' Taneshka said quickly, face turning red at Fox and Kesta's amusement. 'Certainly doesn't mean I trust you,' she added in a lower voice, looking away. 'Not just like that.' It was clear that she hadn't meant Brant to hear this, and Brant respected that by feigning deafness.

'Tochi, from Tochi-arba. We use it for medicine, when using properly. We have a saying about Tochi leaf: One leaf, this takes away the headache. Two leaves, that will give you new headache. Three leaves, you want to fight half the world, kiss the other half, and you get a really, really big headache. Four leaves, and you will see things that aren't there. You will feel like there is a hole in your head.'

Kesta raised her eyebrows. 'And five?'

'At five you will wish you didn't have a head.' Kesta laughed at this, and Fox smiled wryly as he handed his empty cup to Brant.

'I would still prefer wine to achieve that effect.'

The four of them walked on, under heavy skies. At midday, they entered the first sparse oaks and beeches of the wood. The wind was rising again, but the cold eased as they walked among the trees. Beech mast and acorns littered the forest floor. The silver intrusion of birches shone through the smooth browns and wrinkled tans of the bigger trees.

The forest was full of clearings, stumps and scraped earth showing where the loggers had been. There was no other sign of woodcutters. Fox kept an ear open for the chop of axes, or the crackle of charcoal-burners, but all was ghostly silent beneath the endlessly reaching, naked trees.

In the afternoon they found the camp. One hut remained, with a sturdy door and shuttered windows, and smoke rising from a rude aperture in the mossy roof. Fox stepped tentatively up to the door and knocked.

An old woman opened the door to him and wordlessly stepped aside. Smiling politely, Fox entered, followed by the others. 'It's cold out in the open,' Kesta remarked, to break the silence. She sat uneasily on a wooden bench. The woman nodded. Fox wondered if she was able to speak.

Brant made food ready, using the charcoal device, refilling it from reserves in his pack and emptying the used ash into the woman's fireplace. The only sounds were made by him as he moved around, and by the creak of the building in the light wind. Brant passed the first of the cooked meat strips to the old woman, and she spoke in a steady, rasping voice.

'They're not here, you know. They've all run off.' Fox froze, mouth open in the act of biting into his food.

'Who? The woodcutters?'

'Aye. All them big strong lads, tough fathers an' all. Run off from their home of twelve years an' only me, left behind.' The woman shook her head sadly. 'I can't swing an axe!' She added in an accusatory tone.

'Where did they go?'

'South. They didn't want to be going north, being that the weather is all coming bad from there. And not east, because the Lake Folk wouldn't believe 'em. They fear shame as much as anything. To leave their homes, their livelihoods... pssh!'

'Why did they leave?'

The woman looked at Fox strangely, as if she had only just noticed him. Her voice cracked as she continued.

'Howling in Ancient Sisters. Wolves were uneasy. All the beasties in the gorge caves too. Strong northern winds and the wolves come running through our camp like the very Seven are chasing them. Each as high as me at the shoulder, mark you, and plain frightened out of their wits. One stayed in the clearing for a while. We'd all hid indoors, except for the wee children who hadn't got back, and didn't know to be 'fraid. He went on howling at us for nigh on an hour, see, then gave up and ran off.

'The men saw omens. *The wolves are telling us to leave*, says they, and off they goes, running away from home. All for some foolish animals and a bit of wind.'

Fox stared, disbelieving. After a moment, Brant spoke. 'She's telling the truth,' he stated. 'Come on. Let's see if we'll find tracks of wolves. Are coming, Taneshka?' Surprisingly, the Tigress rose immediately, nodding. Fox and Kesta followed Brant and Taneshka out into the cold air.

'She must be mad,' Kesta said immediately. Brant walked slowly, in widening circles, eyes focused on the ground. Fox shrugged at Kesta's comment; he had thought that fact self-evident. Taneshka said nothing, watching Brant impassively.

Brant straightened suddenly. Then he pivoted slowly on the spot. 'You better see at this.' Fox strode over, and stopped as suddenly as Brant had. In a slick of icy mud beside an empty wooden trough, a pawprint was plainly visible. It was as big around as a dinner plate. Fox swallowed.

'She wasn't mad, then. Wolves! If I could have seen them… So big! Like the tigers were when they still lived, in your homeland, Teshka. The superstition about Ancient Sisters must have protected them. *The last ones.*'

Taneshka stared down at the print. 'What in the Land could scare such creatures?' Her question went unanswered for a moment, as Kesta crouched to examine the print. Then Fox spoke, staring into the distance.

'A wind from the north. Just a bit of wind. Except…animals can read the air. Something to the north...' Fox hefted his pack onto his shoulder. 'Come on. Let's up the pace.'

The wind whistled through the rocky gully, beating against their faces as they trudged along. The trees moved ceaselessly, high above them, bare branches swaying hypnotically, visible against the hard outline of the lip of the gorge. Fox lifted his foot clear of a puddle of icy mud in the leaf mulch. Brant had overtaken him already, his long legs providing him an advantage.

As night fell, they left the strange gorge, glad to be free of its gloomy caves and sighing wind. The dark sky was heavier than ever, with great, rolling mountains of blue-black cloud flowing, above the soft country below.

The grass was hardened and sharpened again, frost freezing the stems into miniature blades. It crunched beneath the travellers' feet.

When it became impossible to see anything other than the breathy columns of mist that curled from between their lips, Fox called a halt. Wearily they made camp, shivering uncontrollably, except for Brant, who had his bearskin. It was too cold now for sleeping out. Fox rummaged in his largest pack. After a moment, he started to search with more urgency.

'I don't believe it! There was a tent in here, I'm sure of it! A good one... agh! Dragonfire! What do we do now?' He flung the pack aside, angrily. 'Who packed this bag?'

Kesta bit her lip.

'I packed all the bags, but there's no use blaming me...'

'What do you mean? We could freeze to death!' Fox shouted, chill-reddened face reddening further from anger and panic.

'It isn't my fault!' Kesta exclaimed indignantly, putting her hands on her hips. 'You could have packed it yourself! I didn't know the tent was even there to...'

'You thought we were just going to sleep on the grass? If you haven't noticed, it's bloody freezing! Why didn't you think?'

'I never knew about any tent! And you were the one carrying the damned pack when we left! Did you never think to look?'

'You were supposed to have packed it!'

'That's not fair! Stop shouting!'

'Oh, I will, once I'm dead of cold! You...'

'BE QUIET!'

Fox and Kesta froze, shocked at the sudden joint outburst from Taneshka and Brant. Brant bowed his head apologetically, but Taneshka grinned at him, before turning angry blue eyes on Fox and Kesta.

'What are you going to achieve, fighting each other? Bloodfire! I thought you two liked one another! We'll work this out!'

There was silence. In that moment, the wind dropped. For a few seconds the world seemed better. Then the blue-black sky filled with grey. Snow began to fall, unstoppable, steady, settling thickly on the frozen grass. Taneshka swallowed her last words, a gust of wind causing snow to whirl in her face with a numbing caress.

'We better work this one out quickly,' Fox growled.

'We should better move. Nothing can be done on this hill. There is too much, how would I say... exposion?' Brant said, swinging his pack back onto his shoulders. Fox nodded, not bothering to correct his friend, and retrieved his bag without looking at Kesta.

The four of them set off, faces numbed and burning, eyes closed to slits as the wind rose once more, filling the air with thick, white death.

On a hillside lower down, Brant stopped. 'This is best. It is sheltered some by the slope, none of this will settle high, so we are stuck.'

Fox nodded in agreement; he could no longer feel his face or hands. The ground was harsh against their chilled skin, they could all feel it as they knelt low, bending to avoid the relentless wind. Kesta shouted something about groundsheets, but Fox could not hear her.

Brant came to a decision. He pulled the folded bear pelt from around his shoulders, gasping out as cold air blasted against his chest and arms. Hurriedly, the young warrior laid the bearskin on the sloping ground, falling down onto the hide to hold it still, using his body to keep the whirling snow off. 'Down!' he shouted, reaching out for Fox's arm.

Fox dropped onto the pelt as well; Kesta and Taneshka tried to follow, as the wind suddenly howled at full force. Kesta screamed as the gust threatened to tumble her down the slope, but suddenly Fox's hand was gripping her wrist, and she was pulled down onto the bear hide. As Taneshka forced herself down, hair flying about her head in a red storm, Brant reached across the fur, and pulled it over and back.

Suddenly the howling wind seemed less. The bear pelt cocooned them like a thick, coarse blanket. Immediately, it was warmer. Fox found the edges of the bearskin, where cold air still sought entry, and drew on inner strength to bring the flapping fur together.

Sealed in the warm dark, he breathed a sigh of relief. His skin was burning all over from the temperature change.

Brant was warmest, lying up against the fold of the bearskin. Fox lay with his back against Brant's, face to face with Kesta. Taneshka wriggled as close to her friend as she could, face in her dark hair. For a little while there was no sound but their relieved breathing. Then Kesta began to laugh.

Brant joined in at once, laughing quietly and uncontrollably into the bear fur. Fox couldn't help it, something required the laughter, and so it came. Taneshka put her head in her hands, gasping for breath. Finally, as the last of their relief died away, Fox spoke up.

'We should sleep. We'll be too tired tomorrow, otherwise,' he added in a softer voice. He brought his face closer to Kesta's. 'I'm sorry.' His whisper was supposed to reach only Kesta's ears, but in the close environment Brant and Taneshka both heard it too. Brant smiled into the bear fur and Taneshka closed her eyes, feigning sleep.

Kesta shivered. She shrugged, a small smile of forgiveness on her lips. Fox put a hand out and raised the temperature around her.

'I'm sorry,' he repeated, louder than before, addressing all three of his companions. 'I should know better than to lose my temper like that.' His gaze dropped again, focusing on Kesta once more. His lips formed the shapes of words, another, more personal apology, which she could just make out in the reflected light from outside.

Kesta replied to him with a whisper that the other two pretended not to hear.

Sleep came in short spells, and Fox woke to find he was embracing Kesta in the dark. For a moment he kept his eyes closed. Her body was soft, although he could feel the firmness of the muscles in her arms as well, testament to her rushed combat training. Her cheek was against his, and her hair...

Fox realised that Taneshka was awake. He could sense her alertness over Kesta's shoulder, and see her silhouette in the little light that crept in from the moonlight. Fox was sure he saw her wink at him, before closing her eyes again. Fox tried to regain sleep for himself as well, very glad that the poor light conditions hid his blush.

26
Light To Dark

Everything was still. Brant awoke shivering.

He rolled over, causing the bearskin to shift. Light streamed in, along with more cold air. Brant's nose was inches from the back of Fox's head; he could see Kesta's arms wrapped around the prince's shoulders.

Taneshka stirred on the other side of Kesta. Her wild, red hair was spread against Kesta's arm and back, and her arm was draped over both Fox and Kesta.

'A good morning,' Brant said clearly. Fox and Kesta slept on, but Taneshka lifted her head and peered blearily at him.

'Feels like a bloody freezing morning to me.'

Brant raised himself up on his elbow. 'It is that too, Taneshka.' He glanced down at Fox and Kesta, then caught Taneshka watching them fondly. She shared a warm, amused look with Brant when she realised.

'They look good together,' Brant said, a hint of a question in his voice. Taneshka shrugged.

'They've got the right idea, by anyone's thinking, they're probably the warmer for it. You'd never catch me in such a position though.'

Brant smiled. 'You'd never be catched in Fox's arms?'

'Never. Nor in Kesta's.'

'Hah! You make me laugh, Taneshka. A funny young woman.'

'Oh? Young woman, is it?'

'Am I not giving you a proper respects for your rank? Apologies, Tigress.'

Taneshka narrowed her gaze shrewdly. 'Are you making fun of me, Brant Mantissi?' Brant shrugged, keeping his easy smile neutral.

'Not much, Taneshka. Ah, they are waking.'

'Yes. Shush now, we are asleep!' Taneshka winked broadly and put her head down on the fur. Brant copied her as Kesta blinked her eyes open.

For a moment Kesta lay in the silence, listening to the sound of slow, steady breathing from Taneshka and Brant, feeling Fox's breathing against her body, the rise and fall of his chest against hers. His hands shifted from where they were clasped around her middle, and his eyelashes flickered as he began to wake. Kesta smiled, admiring the fine hairs that softened the line of his jaw, gold in the morning light. She focused on the slight movements of his lips as he opened his eyes...

Taneshka allowed them several seconds before lifting herself up onto her elbows, in a sudden flurry of movement. Fox and Kesta both jumped, moving their heads apart so fast that Fox smacked his head against Brant's. Fox looked at Taneshka with an expression that was part guilt, part anger and mainly the colour red.

'Hah! Hahaha! Oho! You kissed her – or she kissed you – who cares! About bloody time! Took an argument and a snowstorm, but you finally managed it!' Taneshka revelled in her friends' embarrassment. Brant made a pained noise, rubbing his forehead.

'Ow... I apologise Fox, it is Taneshka's idea.' Brant's own face was darkened with embarrassment on Fox's behalf.

'Damn right it was my idea! I *deserve* the acclaim for that one. Well, come on you two, don't I deserve thanks?'

Kesta began to laugh as she rolled onto her back, so she could see both Taneshka and Fox. 'You're a wicked one, Teshka. I thought you were asleep. If only you still were...' she said for Fox's benefit, turning to examine him in an almost critical way. He glanced down, cheeks still burning.

The bearskin was rolled back to let the chill air pour in on them. Shivering, they stood up in a world of white.

'Oh, Land, Waters and Skies!' Brant exclaimed, staring around in wonder. 'I'd never thought it would be so...so... oh, I cannot take the word...'

'Beautiful,' Fox murmured, although it was not clear if he was commenting on the snow-blanketed landscape, or on Kesta; his eyes were fixed on her. Brant glanced at Taneshka as he stepped forward onto the thick snow; they shared a conspiratorial smile.

They trudged through the snow for hours. The sky was a clear blue, the clouds all spent. It was bitterly cold, and occasional winds blew flurries of snow into their faces. Brant was wearing the bear pelt again, wrapped around him in such a way that he had been able to belt all his provisions to the back of it, giving him a strange, hunchbacked appearance.

Taneshka was in good spirits. Kesta walked in front, in equally good humour. Occasionally the two of them would walk close together, heads down as they talked in voices just loud enough for the following boys to hear that they were speaking, but just quiet enough to keep the information secret. Brant shook his head as he walked, a smile playing about his lips. Girls were girls, wherever you travelled.

Fox was deep in thought. Many things were troubling him, and now he had another on his mind. In the background, Fox could hear Brant break into a Southlander song with an odd rhythm and beguiling melody.

Fox frowned, concentrating on his ponderings. How would he be able to conceal his feelings for Kesta once he reached home? There were so many rules against such arrangements… *What could he do to make it work?* Brant's singing stopped.

Fox walked past Brant and the girls, and discovered why they had stopped. The last snow now drifted against spiky, frozen reeds. Snow-weighted bulrushes bobbed gently in the light wind, rising from iron-grey water. Fox stepped backwards hurriedly, feeling the icy water seeping through his boots. The spongy earth was waterlogged. They had reached the Lifeblood Marshes.

The marshlands extended as far as sight allowed to the north, northeast and northwest. The water seemed to be only knee-high, but none of them were very enthusiastic about stepping into the frigid mire. After a moment, Taneshka spoke up.

'We can't walk in that. The cold is probably bearable on its own, but if our clothes and skin get wet, we're done. We need something waterproof…' She knelt at the edge of the bog, rummaging in her pack. 'Must be a groundsheet in here somewhere…' She threw her pack down and turned to Fox.

'Have you got the groundsheets? Fox?' Fox was staring out onto the marsh, a strange look on his face. Taneshka frowned, wondering what was wrong. Kesta was instantly wary. 'What's wrong, Fox?'

'Something terrible is going to happen if we go into these marshes.' The bleak statement made the others glance at one another, anxiety growing as Fox lowered his gaze, afraid to look out onto the marshes.

'Then we won't go into the marshes then,' Kesta said simply, stepping to Fox's side. She reached for his hand but Fox shook his head abruptly.

'It'll happen whether we go or not. It's going to be so difficult... I don't know if I want to...' He raised his eyes to the horizon, avoiding Kesta's gaze.

'Was this from your dream? What did you see?'

Fox looked deep into Kesta's eyes for a second. Something hidden danced in his own eyes, but after a second he looked away.

'I tell no one my dreams, Kesta. No one.' He said softly, an echo from the past. His voice was heavy with sorrow. His eyes darted to and fro as he looked out onto the marshes, blinking back what Kesta thought might have been tears.

'Not even me?'

'Not...not this time.' Fox covered his face with his hands. After a moment his back straightened, and dry eyed and serious, he retrieved the groundsheets from his pack and handed them to Taneshka. Wordlessly, she set to work.

Wearing oilcloth to keep the water out, the four of them struggled through the sucking, clinging, icy bog. In most places, it was simply shallow water, from which rose various wetlands vegetation, undaunted by the wintry weather. In some areas decaying vegetation hid pitfalls of thick mud and slime. Fox guided them, face set, eyes hard, feeling out the solid ground ahead.

Kesta followed as closely as she could. As they stopped for a moment, limbs burning from the harsh exercise and trembling from the cold, Kesta put her hand in Fox's.

'Are you sure we should be going this way, what with your vision and everything?'

'This is what I have to do, and the way I have to go. I *will* let the Shadow see that I will meet the challenge. It's coming anyway, so I will be the maker of my own doom. This life is mine!'

He said it so fervently that Kesta took a step back, biting her lip with anxiety. He changed so quickly, she reflected. One moment, love-struck and thought-bound, the next, intent, intense and prepared for...for what?

'He...he's not here, is he?' Kesta was unable to stop her voice from trembling.

'Part of him, I think.'

Alarm crossed Brant's face. He recognised the significance of Fox's words, mind searching back through his Scrolls in Fox's bag. The young warrior said nothing, though, and marched onwards with a similar expression to Fox.

By late afternoon their legs were numb and tired. Fox sneezed loudly, stopping in his tracks. The water was surging around his legs. When he lifted his head, he saw a large figure moving towards them, just visible in the fading light. It moved with, slow, swinging strides, head swaying from side to side.

Fox made a reassuring gesture to the others, he detected no malice from the approaching animal. The creature moved with surprising speed. Soon it was clearly visible, a great, wide shouldered bull, bigger than a cart-ox. A heavy, rounded bone in its wide forehead curved round and down around its ponderous face, making a broad, blunt boss and horns. The large muzzle let bursts of steam rise into the cold air, snorting nostrils wrinkling as it caught the travellers' scent. It was covered with an immense coat of thick, shaggy hair.

There was a man sitting behind the bull's humped shoulders. He was wearing a loose scale armour, the shirt separating at the waist into two skirts that protected his legs. A coat made of the stuff was spread out in a cloak from the man's shoulders and out across the bull's back. The rider was wearing a crested helmet, the crest mimicking the curved horn of his steed. He was carrying a long, heavy weapon, like a long cleaver mounted on a pole. Fox recognised it as a voulge.

'You three all right?' The man seemed somewhat bemused at their presence. 'We don't normally get visitors here, not on foot. And through the marsh...you're not lost?' The marsh bull obeyed a click of the man's tongue, getting on its knees so he could slip from the saddle.

Fox bowed. 'I'm Prince Fox. This is the Tigress Taneshka, heir to the Tiger territories. This is Kesta, our companion, and Brant Mantissi, who is our...Guard Captain.' The bull-rider nodded, looking at Brant with curiosity.

'Your Guard Captain? Then where are your guards? And is your army coming?' There was an eager, almost desperate note in the man's voice.

'They should be only one or two days behind us. Why? Has there been news?' The bull-rider looked uneasy.

'No…not quite. That is, something is wrong – and we don't know what – the northernmost fortifications have been taken.'

'What? You've lost the northern border, but you've no knowledge of a specific threat? How can that be?'

'There were no bodies to find. No damage to the gates or walls. The torches were all out and there was blood in the water. There is no specific threat, my lord, because we cannot *find* the enemy!' The bull-rider removed his helmet. He looked tired.

'My captain, the Commander of the Fifth Bulls, was the man who brought the report back. I was with him, although I did not see the place; I stayed at the intermediary defences when the others went on. All of us from that unit have been given easy patrols, like this solo south. The King would not make us go back there.'

Fox nodded, brow knit in thought. 'I want to speak to Heron. And soon.'

'Yes my Lord. Follow me.'

The bull-rider led them through the marsh onto a slimy wooden walkway. The planks looked sturdy enough, but ice made the surface treacherous. It was faster going than the mire, and soon a great shape was rising out of the gloom. The stonework was grey with age, but the White Gates were still an impressive sight. With an army garrisoned within, Fox estimated that they were almost unbreakable.

The bull-rider left his steed with another soldier and led them up stone steps. The wind was blowing from the north, snagging at the travellers' hair and clothes, viciously cold. The rider did not seem bothered by the weather, but many of the wall guards looked unhappy. Fox saw many tired and frightened gazes.

'The weather has been northerly for days now,' the rider murmured in a low voice, turning his head to speak to Fox, 'no one remembers it being this bad, not for so long at a time, not even in the deep winter.' Fox remembered with a sinking feeling the reported reactions of the Great Wolves from Ancient Sisters, who had caught fear from the north wind.

The bull-rider left them with a swift bow at a great door, emblazoned with the Heron insignia. Another man met them there. He was wearing ornate armour and at his belt was a weapon that split down the middle, like a bladed fork.

'Prince Fox, Tigress. I am the new Commander of the Bulls. Welcome to the White Gates. King Heron awaits you within. If you would follow me?' He made a welcoming gesture and Fox nodded gratefully, stepping into the warmth.

Once in the lobby, the Commander drew them aside into a set of curtained booths. Warm clothes were laid out for them and the four gratefully changed. Fox allowed himself a moment of calm, sitting on a narrow bench in temporary seclusion. Now, whatever was coming could be awaited in calm and comfort, behind strong walls. The army would be here soon.

'Welcome, Prince Fox. It pleases me so much more than you could imagine to have you here. Commander Spar has told me that your forces are also on their way, and, if I am honest, that pleases me even more!'

Heron laughed and leaned forward to shake Fox's hand. 'Now. To business. To the dark necessity of the hour, hmm?' Heron gestured for Fox to join him at the north facing window.

The window had a wide sill, and the workings on the exterior of the aperture sheltered them a little from the wind. It was night over the marshes but some lights could be seen, a long way away.

'Those are our intermediary forts. They provide a retreat and relief station for the northernmosts, but unfortunately, as you no doubt have heard from Andul or one of his men, the north forts have fallen, uncontested.' Heron's expression was grave.

A tall young with a cascade of shoulder-length black hair approached the window. 'Father? Might I join you?'

'Mm, please do, Yann. This is Crown Prince Fox. Fox, my eldest son, Yannon Heronsen. Our only really skilled archer, and he has a great deal of fine ideas, that I am sure he will implement, once I am sailed away down the sunset river, to my forefathers.' Heron's eyes twinkled. His son seemed uncomfortable at the mention of his father's eventual death.

Fox smiled and shook hands with Yannon, before the other could stoop into a bow. The older boy smiled back, and seated himself on the sill. Heron pulled up a chair. Near the fire, Kesta and Taneshka talked with Heron's wife. Brant stood, watching and listening, his back against a nearby wall.

'What is the extent, Fox, of your – begging your pardon – *abilities*? ' Heron looked a little nervous at asking this.

Fox shrugged. 'I'm not exactly sure. I know what I already know, if you understand me, but the man that could tell you that isn't here… although Brant could probably serve just as well. He's a scholar.' Heron nodded, expression serious. He waved Brant over.

'The Arisen's abilities?' Brant frowned, dropping into a crouch. He pulled a scroll from his satchel. 'Fox has shown some controls of fire, but also, certainly he makes movement with his mind. That is,' Brant frowned at himself, and started again, 'he can make things move, or not move, through willpower. Also, because his powers are written as anti-magic, it is a theory that he could perform most things that sorcerers can, but against, yes?'

Brant paused to look down the length of the scroll. '

'Because it is Land-given, he may use element powers, fire, water, earth, air, all natural things. His power is really limits only by his imagining and strength.'

Heron bit his lip, frowning. 'Thank you, scholar, I understand you. I'll have to listen close though, to get past your accent, pleasant as it is.'

Brant looked apologetic. Fox smiled to reassure him.

'I can also see beyond my body,' Fox said, turning to Heron. My mind can leave me for a time.'

'Oh! That is what we need!' Heron looked pleased. 'Do you think we might discover the identity of our enemy through this method?'

Fox nodded reluctantly, looking out onto the black marshland.

'I think so. Give me a minute, and I will do this for you. But might I have something to drink first, please?'

Heron looked annoyed with himself. 'At once! Forgive me, Lord Fox.'

For a time Fox relaxed. It was warm in Heron's living chambers. Heron's rule was not restricted by advisors, because the council did not recognise Heron's authority. He had inherited his role not from a royal family, but through arbitration by the Holy Order, long ago. Ironically, this meant that Heron had more sovereignty than the other kings, at least, over his own extensive, watery territories.

The mood was informal, comfortable. Fox felt secure, sitting close beside Kesta, Heron and his wife across the table from them.

Heron told them he was a river-raider, of old, preying on northern farms while his father despaired of his violent nature.

'That was back when your grandfather and the other kings were sending us no tribute and war had made trade difficult,' Heron explained, 'my raids on the northern settlements were what kept us going. My banditry kept us all secure.'

Heron's wife spoke. 'I was a chieftain's daughter, in the Ice Forests to the northeast. I fought a war against Palin here,' she gestured towards Heron, 'and I lost, although I cost him dear. We are warlike in the north too, and we have to be. Palin took me hostage, but he proved worthy, and gentle enough, when war ended. I loved him. Now I am his better half and will continue to love him, until we are both sand and ashes.' She kissed her husband's cheek.

Heron returned to his conversation with Fox and Yannon, and his queen leant across the table to Kesta.

'I am still the better fighter too, though do not tell him I said that. I see your hand in his. Guard your man like a she-wolf. There is more ferocity in our blood, when we defending the cave, than in theirs, remember that. He will need you.' Kesta smiled, honoured and discomforted in equal measure by the barbarian queen's words.

Heron rose. 'Now. Let Prince Fox see what he will see.'

Fox nodded and released Kesta's hand as he stood. He took a deep breath, striding to the window. Pushing away his reluctance, Fox closed his eyes and let his mind loose.

A small sea of aggression met him at the northern bank of the Lifeblood, where the marsh turned into river, and then rock-strewn northern hillside. He could feel it there. A maddened, tortured mind, disparate and dislocated. Many, many times.

Another presence, quitter but stronger, twitched suddenly. Fox flinched. There was a sense of realisation. Of contempt. Fox felt his mind being pushed back, hard, before any details could become visible. The thing in the marsh knew he was there.

Fox opened his eyes and stepped back from the window. Heron was afraid. His wife too had a troubled expression and she drew her daughter close, reaching for her nearest child, her twelve-year-old son.

Fox stared out of the window. The creature in the marsh had called up a thick, choking fog. It travelled towards them like a wave, approaching with unstoppable, fluid motion. It broke against the White Gates and went on. The window blanked to white. The lamps on the walltop sputtered and went out. Fox closed his eyes and attempted to reach out once more. With a shocked cry he stumbled back from the window.

'I cannot see! My mind is darkened!' he turned to Kesta, holding her close instinctively. 'I cannot see beyond my body. He has blinded me!'

27
The Dark Fog

The fog stayed thick and heavy throughout the day. For most of last night, Fox had stayed awake, a sleeping Kesta's hand in his, eyes closed as he tried to see past the supernatural mist. He stayed the same through most of the morning, although Kesta sat with him then, eyes closed in prayer to support his efforts. Taneshka slept, lying in Kesta's bed on the floor of the bedroom Heron had provided for them all.

Brant paced the room's length, muttering to himself and reading scrolls, reminding Kesta of a dark-skinned Rashin. Fox broke fast at lunchtime, sitting at Heron's table, red eyed and tired. Grilled perch and a great grey eel, open mouthed and staring, were placed on the table, and everyone sat and ate.

'This mist is bad luck. We've had three people come down with illnesses today. And the number of accidents, cuts, bruises, falls…it's no natural fog, mark my words,' Heron said grimly, spreading apple preserve on a piece of soft bread. Everyone seemed to have their eyes on Fox. Yannon was wearing his bow and quiver at the table.

Fox looked at the window, which had been shuttered to keep out the mist. 'Has there been word from the middle forts?'

Heron shook his head. He put the bread down, his appetite gone. 'None. What do we do, Fox? How do we know the enemy are not coming for us now?' Fox shook his head, toying with a piece of fish.

'We'll know, Sire. This…person out there, they're the sort that like to be announced. We'll know.'

Fox pushed his plate away and got up from the table. He stumbled to the nearest cushioned seat and closed his eyes once again, straight backed and grim faced. Heron took an overlarge gulp of wine, and left the room.

Heron's wife took Kesta's arm. 'See that Prince Fox gets some sleep. What happens will happen. He has done his best.' Kesta nodded and went to sit on the recliner beside Fox.

She took his hand, and touched his cheek, so that he opened his eyes. 'Fox? You've done your part now. You should sleep. I'm here. We're all here.'

Fox looked at her blankly for a moment. 'I must be able to break through this. He can't be…stronger than me. He can't!'

Kesta shook her head. 'He isn't. Whoever he is, we'll beat him, all right?' Fox smiled, but tears appeared in his eyes. 'I'm…so tired.'

'Then sleep.' Kesta said firmly. 'Here is just fine. These people are lovely. It's like being in a family. It's been a long time.' Her voice cracked a little, but she kept her composure.

Fox shook his head. 'I can't sleep! This fog shows that he has power over my mind. If I sleep, he can make me dream… I don't want to dream, Kesta!' Kesta clenched his hand tight.

'You can damn well sleep if you want to! Nothing's getting into your head while I'm here. Just keep my hand held, all right? You and me, together, safe, all right?'

Fox put his head back on the recliner cushion. His eyes closed as he accepted sleep, gripping Kesta's hand firmly. The torches flickered and wind howled against the castle walls. Fox's voice petered out as he spoke. 'Kesta. I think I…'

Andul Spar walked the walltop, cloak swirling out behind him. The fog was too thick to see farther than a few feet ahead, and every attempt to light the torches failed. All of the Heron Guard were dressed in full gear, an under-suit of marsh-bull wool keeping the water out of their clothes, with fish-scale armour over the top. The wind was howling up a gale, but the fog never moved.

It didn't make sense. All the marsh bulls were nervy and uncomfortable, and Andul had never seen such weather before.

At nightfall Andul gave in and walked back along the wall to Heron's rooms. He had talked to the guards. They were to wait, fully armed, in the barracks. There was no point posting them on the walls. They wouldn't be able to see anything approaching.

The bull-rider entered Heron's chambers, stamping warmth and feeling back into his legs. Fox was sleeping, Kesta sitting with him still, head nodding from tiredness. Heron was deep in conversation with his wife and two older sons. Heron's daughter was at the table, watching the baby son for her mother, while Brant read scrolls at the shuttered window. Taneshka was seated on the floor, sharpening her knives.

The bull-rider sat near the Tigress, after being acknowledged by a wave from Heron. She glanced up at him, from under uncontained red locks.

'Commander. Nice weather we're having.' He laughed hollowly.

'Indeed. Nice collection of blades you have there, Tigress.' She nodded appreciatively, lifting the longest one up to see the light reflect along the steel. It was slightly waved, with a curving handle.

'This is Halver. Because it halves anything I bring it down on.' Taneshka returned it to the floor and lifted a pair of identical double edged blades. The handles of these had an odd pair of holes through them, and Taneshka showed their purpose to Andul, clipping the two handles together, so that the blades faced away from each other.

'My twin knives. I can fight with them in hand, or stop an archer by throwing them, either separate or together. And these ones,' she lifted a pair that fitted around her knuckles, and had many points set in an iron frame, 'these are for really close work. If I punch hard enough, the points make a real impression on my enemy, see? Course, they're useless against armour.' Andul winced, imagining the effect of a punch from one of those strange knives.

'I use a fork-sword, myself, or a voulge if I'm in the saddle. What's that blade there, with the edge on the reverse?'

'She's called Darker. She's an assassin blade, for quiet work. Slitting throats isn't my style though. I use a long spear called Tiger's Fang. She's in the bedrooms.' Taneshka put the slim, one-edged blade down. It's bone handle clattered on the floor.

Andul smiled. 'It is rare that I get to converse with a woman about weapons – especially one – forgive me – as beautiful as yourself. It is very good to meet you, Tigress Taneshka, Spearwoman of the Six Knives!'

Andul bowed, a smile flickering about his lips. Taneshka blushed, busying herself with her weaponry. Brant, watching from across the room, smiled to himself at her reaction as Andul moved on to talk to Yannon.

'How you like the Commander of the Bulls?' Brant asked innocently, stopping on his way across the room, looking down at

Taneshka with a neutral expression. Taneshka gave him a dark look, and snatching up her knives, walked away toward their quarters. Brant laughed quietly, eyes twinkling as he watched her go.

'You are cruel, Brant. Why did you tease her like that? You know she likes to maintain an air of unruffled...aloofness.'

Brant shrugged at Kesta. 'I have no knowing of *aloofness* and *unruffled*, but I tease because it is funny.' He went to join Kesta and Fox, sitting on the floor, beside the recliner.

'Can't argue with that, I suppose.' Kesta looking back at Fox's sleeping, untroubled face. 'I wonder how many years he is her senior though, the Commander? He's a very handsome man, with a good position but... I can't imagine if Taneshka were to marry! It doesn't seem possible.'

'What about you, Kesta?' Brant asked softly, looking up at her. 'Are you the marrying sort?' Kesta's expression froze, and she returned her gaze to Fox. For a moment she did not speak, though her expression hinted at her conflict.

'I trust you, Brant Mantissi, which is why I tell you this: without Fox I would die, and life with him, as I want it, is only proper through marriage. But I am a peasant girl. My father was a soldier, and he never married my mother. She made her money however she could, understand? My line is totally inferior to Fox's. And, inevitably, Fox returns to his kingdom, where rules matter.

'Fox thinks always of going home – he is brilliant in many ways, but as Teshka always points out – he is not very clever, when it comes to these matters. He wants to go home, and he wants me too, I think, I hope. I pray. Does he ever wonder which is more important? Or that there will be conflict between the two?'

Kesta looked at Fox's sleeping face, tears caught in her eyelashes. 'I don't think he does.' She turned back to Brant, who sat, solemn and attentive. 'Sometimes, Brant of the Scorpion, I believe that the only way for us to be together is for us both to die in battle. But again, I am separated from him in this! He is the Arisen...I... Oh, Brant, he cannot die, he is too important, to the Land, to everyone, but I...I can die. Alone.'

Brant reached out and rested his hand gently on Kesta's arm. 'Live. He will not forget you.'

One by one, everyone went to their beds. After the last candle was put out, Kesta woke Fox.

'Fox? No, nothing's wrong. Everyone's gone to bed. Come on, Brant and Teshka are already there.' Kesta helped him to his feet. He smiled at her, bleary eyed but a little refreshed.

'Thanks Kesta.' He kept her hand in his. For a moment, Kesta considered asking him what he had been about to say earlier, before he slept. She didn't. They went through the silk curtain into the guest bedrooms.

They laid down between Brant and Taneshka's snoring forms. Fox made sure he was still holding Kesta's hand. 'It'll be cramped in the morning!' Kesta pretended to complain, changing hand so that she could lie comfortably.

Fox smiled, eyes already closing. 'It's working though. Goodnight, Kesta.'

Heron pushed a bowl of honeyed porridge across the table to Fox. 'At some point today, you expect your forces?'

Fox nodded in answer. He was never far away from Kesta, the king noticed, and seemed nervous when she went too far from him.

Heron settled back in his chair. His nervous and troubled visage contrasted with his wife's calm exterior. She placed a calming hand on his arm. 'If Lord Fox says they will come, Palin, then they will come.'

Commander Spar had joined the morning's breakfast. He sat, eating somewhat self-consciously, aware that he was with his king's family and guests. His attention was held by the question relating to Fox's army. He needed confirmation of their coming as much as his master, after all, he would be leading on the front line, if the forces to the north ever revealed themselves.

'I thought, perhaps,' Andul began, in the brief silence that followed the Queen's words, 'that I could show your guests the bull-keep and the barracks. Particularly as they are here in a partly military role. It would be good for the men.'

'Yes of course. You have my permission, Commander, assuming that all here are happy with this arrangement?' Heron looked around the table. Fox nodded, smiling to the bull-rider.

'Thank you for the offer. I think it will be good for me to get outside for a little while.'

The fresh air was not so much fresh as it was damp. Fox wore a scarf around his lower face, mimicking the commander. Kesta and Taneshka followed suit, but Brant stayed indoors. The climate did not suit him at all, and he looked a little ill.

Fox and Kesta descended the stone steps, a few paces behind Kesta and Andul. Fox, Kesta and Taneshka had been given infantry issue marsh-wear, lightly armoured trousers of marsh-bull wool, that kept the water out more effectively than their improvised oilskins.

The commander was very courteous and somewhat awkward. Taneshka had found her feet and began to tease his formal style as they walked together.

The bull-keep was a great wooden structure near the wall. The doors swung open, creaking in the still air. The thick mist still clung to everything, although at least in the daytime visibility was improved, and the wind was quiet.

A score of marsh-bulls greeted them, lumbering forward, creating swells in the frigid water. Kesta reached out to pet the wrinkling snout of the nearest bull. Its tongue, very hot in contrast to the air, wrapped briefly around Kesta's hand, rough and gentle. The bull's great liquid eyes stared dolefully at her as she ran her other hand through the hair above the boss of its great horn.

'They're amazing!' Kesta breathed, vapour rising from her lips. Her eyes shone as she patted the creature's broad neck. Fox voiced his agreement, tracing the curve of the bull's horn with his fingertips. Andul smiled appreciatively, greeting the bulls by name in a soft, controlling voice.

'They're not really bulls, of course. They are a bit like oxen, but have more in common with the giant goats you find in the Ice Mountains. They're similar too to the aurochs that you find in the hills of your homeland, Fox. They're an old species. As old as the great wolves perhaps, or the tigers of your land, lady.'

Taneshka nodded, keeping her distance from the bulls out of wariness, but feigning disinterest. Andul brought one close to her; it stamped through the soggy shallows, swinging its head as it moved.

Fox pulled Kesta aside as Andul talked with Taneshka. 'I need to sleep some more,' he said. 'I have a sense of foreboding... I need to prepare for the worst.' Kesta frowned, her hand automatically reaching for his, but stopping to correct the collar of his silk undershirt where it appeared from the bull-wool armour.

'What do you mean, the worst?'

Fox did not answer immediately, turning to stare past the wooden wall of the pen, in a southern direction. Towards the City of Lakes, and the Allied army.

'They will come, won't they, Kesta?' he asked in a small, almost childish voice. 'They wouldn't let me down, would they?' The wind rippled suddenly into being, and the bulls grunted amongst themselves, agitated by the sudden change.

Kesta shivered. 'They'll come,' she said firmly, but even as the words left her mouth, a feeling of doubt and fear rose. She bit her lip, brow furrowed with anxiety. She squeezed Fox's hand. 'It will be all right.'

Yannon Heronsen was in a very bad mood. His request for a scouting mission had been denied, very emphatically, first by his father and then by Fox. Yannon was older than Fox, and though he understood himself to be lower in rank than the western prince, the refusal still rankled. Yannon was a practical person, and waiting around indoors for something to happen was not his way of doing things.

Fox found the Heron prince in one of the little corridors leading off from the bedrooms. The elder boy was leaning against a wall, scowling ferociously and thumbing the curved tip of his bow. Fox leaned against the same stretch of panelled golden wood, quietly sharing the prince's frustration.

'I apologise for being so blunt earlier. I feel that I have a greater sense of who we are facing than anyone else. He is the kind to lie in wait. Playing into his...hands would not be a wise move. I'm sorry. I wish we had some course of action to commit to as well.' Fox glanced across at his counterpart. The black-haired prince accepted the explanation, scowl gone.

'You're smarter than I, Lord Fox. Or maybe just better informed.' He laughed quietly, and Fox smiled, turning to face the boy more squarely.

'We will get to fight. That is certain. Your bow, and my sword, yes? We shall drive them back together!' Fox offered Yannon his hand. The prince considered for a moment. Then he shook back his mane of dark hair and accepted Fox's hand.

'With this clasp, I bind my allegiance. To whatever end, brothers in war. Agreed?' Fox looked slightly troubled by this, but he honoured the young Heron's proposal with a bow.

'You should not swear allegiance to an external power, my friend. One day you will represent your father's household, and you may regret casting off your neutrality. My household is prone to conflict,' Fox said seriously, running a hand through his brown hair. It stayed ruffled, giving him a slightly comical appearance which belied the solemnity of his words.

Yannon shook his head. 'I will never stand for my father's house. I am not bound to rule as Heron.'

'What do you mean?'

'I just know – I have always known, I think – that I am not to become Heron. There is a fault in me that cannot be overcome.' Yannon did not qualify the statement with further explanation, and Fox simply accepted the words without question. The boy looked uneasy as he went on.

'Fox. I must know, do you feel that our immediate future is a good one? Are we set for victory, or…or defeat? Will your armies come to our aid?'

Fox ignored the silent shout of alarm at the back of his mind. 'I am no fortune teller, my friend.'

'Please, do not avoid the question, brother. I need to know how you perceive things.'

'Then…know that I do not know, but my stomach churns with worry, and my mind reels with doubt, and I cannot control it. Never have I felt more contested. I am fighting a war, as we speak. I do not know if I am winning. I fear the opposite.'

Fox watched his new ally carefully for a reaction. The Heron prince seemed somehow calmed by this.

'Thank you for your honesty, brother. I will see you at dinner. Perhaps your men will be here by then! Until then, Fox.' Yannon bowed and began to walk away. Fox smiled, the thought giving him hope.

'Until then, Yann!'

Heron's twelve-year-old middle son sat alone at the dinner table. The used plates had been cleared, and a candle placed in the middle. It was by the light of this that the young boy polished the blade of a long, narrow dirk. The handle was wrapped in black leather. A crown formed the shape of the hilt's pommel, and the crosspiece was designed to resemble a pair of heron heads, back to back, the beaks forming the cross. Alongside the dirk lay a round, bladed buckler, with the Heron insignia embossed on it.

Kesta came and sat down next to the boy. She passed him a smooth oilstone, so that he could sharpen the blade. 'I don't know your name, sir, but I thought I'd come over and talk to you. The others are so tense that I couldn't stand it anymore.'

The boy looked up and smiled, passing the blade's edges along the oilstone. 'You don't have to call me sir, mistress Kesta. Ma says you're a barbarian queen, like her. You just don't know it yet, she says. You have black hair like Ma, so maybe she's right.'

Kesta smiled. 'Thank you. Your mother is very kind, and so are you.' She watched the blade. 'You…you're not going to fight, are you?' she asked nervously, the cold shine of the steel reflected in her eyes.

The twelve year old looked at her solemnly. 'These are dark times,' he said simply, and slid his dirk into a sheath at his side. He began to rub polish into the buckler's surface. Kesta shook her head, feeling tears rising. Was this what the world was like? Even those children younger than herself, considered warriors? Dark times. *Dark times*. The phrase repeated itself in her head.

The others returned from the walltop. They unwrapped themselves from their protective garments, wincing as their bodies adjusted to the warmth. Fox was with Yannon, and both looked grim. Heron seemed confused and worried. His wife kept her composure, although the muscles in her jaw looked tighter than usual. Andul Spar did not remove his weather-wear, and with a face sick with worry, he returned the way he had come, along the corridor.

Heron sat down heavily. 'Well. They have not come this night. Let us hope that they come in the morning. The mist was less earlier, and the guards could see the intermediary forts. The lights were out. No messengers have come thither.'

There was a long pause, as Heron's eyes, shining with emotion focused on the face of his twelve year old son, who stood readily dressed for battle.

'Bring me my trident!'

28
The Howling Of The Husk

They went to their beds, armed and tense to the point of breaking. Fox and Kesta had the bedroom to themselves, because Brant and Taneshka were both incapable of proper sleep, and had chosen to take watch on the walls. This was a pointless activity once more; the unholy fog had returned in full. It seemed to leech what light there was out of the castle's rooms.

Kesta stayed awake until Fox's breathing deepened. Her hand was once more a part of his, and his expression was peaceful. Slowly, Kesta began to nod off.

A voice dragged Kesta to consciousness. It was a cold awakening. She shivered, sitting up in the bedclothes. Taneshka and Brant were standing there, faces worried and filled with urgency. In the doorway, Heron's middle son stood.

Taneshka spoke. 'Kesta! Come and listen to this – a noise has started out on the marshes and Brant thinks he knows what the enemy are. There's a council of war in the dinner room.'

Kesta shook Fox to wake him. He sat up, blinking furiously. 'What...? I... What time is it? What's happened?'

'Nothing,' Kesta soothed. 'There's an emergency meeting with Heron, because Brant thinks he knows what's out there. You look so tired...'

Taneshka put a hand on Kesta's shoulder. 'You can come alone, Kesta, Heron said to let him concentrate on building his strength. You can give him the details afterwards.'

Fox nodded blearily. 'Mm. That's a good idea, Kesta. 'S'all right. I won't go to sleep.' Kesta nodded, satisfied, and rose to join Taneshka and Brant.

'The scrolls describe many creatures that the Great Shadow, as Fox calls it, might call to being.' Brant read directly off the scroll, which improved his pronunciation and grammar. 'This one, I have found. An account of a collection of creatures, of terrible aspect. "A howling, maddening mass of humanity, twisted into weaponhood." That is what these words say. Men – but without soul nor consciences.' Brant looked up. The assembled people, comprising of Heron's family and a few senior officers, regarded him with grim expressions.

'These things may have no sense of pain, or fear. These things not avoid death, but live in pain and destruction. They feel hunger. Rage.' Brant swallowed, and placed the scroll on the table. 'Me and Taneshka were walking on the wall, because we weren't sleep. We heard a noise. Heron, if you please, Sire, open the shutters on the window north?'

Heron went across to the window and unlatched the shutters. The sound of the wind howling against the stone walls was immediately audible. Taneshka and Brant exchanged grim glances.

'I hear the wind,' Andul muttered. 'nothing else.' Brant leaned forward on the table, hands clasped in front of him, head slightly bowed.

'Listen close.'

For a moment, no one spoke, then Heron's wife cried out in revulsion. 'Agh! Those are cries! Howling! Hear it now?' And suddenly Kesta could hear it. The sound was not the wind. The sound was horrible, inhuman. No, it was human. It was an empty, despairing sound. A cry of terrible, violent pain. It was cast by many voices, a keening sound that chilled Kesta to the bone.

Kesta shuddered, standing up. She could feel the cold more now than before, and her head ached from lack of sleep. The howling echoed through her mind, making her feel sick. Heron's younger son clutched convulsively at the hilt of his dirk.

Heron stood. 'We arm ourselves. We cannot afford to sleep. Not here, while the men wait on the wall!' He walked decisively to where his chosen weapon rested. The great trident cut the air as the King turned.

'This is *my* river, my marsh!' he muttered fiercely. His wife looked at him with a strange expression for a moment, then turned towards the royal bedroom. She disappeared behind the curtain for a few moments, then reappeared. She was holding an old armour shirt in one hand, and in the other a black, iron mace, starred with bladed edges.

'My old friend,' she murmured, looking at the ugly weapon. She looked up at her husband, eyes fiery. The pre-battle excitement was rising. 'Help me on with this, dear one.' He strode towards her, and assisted her with the heavy armour. When he drew back, a savage smile parted her lips.

'Like stepping into an old skin! Come, we will take our tools to the walltop. There is a room there, in one of the towers. We'll be closer to the men.' She led the way, black hair poured over the tarnished metal.

Brant followed, bowing to Heron as he snatched up his pack, and his hooded axe. 'I will follow, King.' Heron left the room, the Southlander in tow.

Yannon took the queen's youngest son from his little sister's arms. One of the officers took the babe from the prince. Yannon turned to his little sister.

'Go with Dankel. Look after your little brother.' Turning to the officer, he added, 'take them to the Westward-last Fort. Hurry.' The boy watched as his youngest siblings left the room.

Yannon steeled himself and looked down at his younger brother. 'Ready for it, Salaben? A strong arm, and a stronger heart, yes?'

Salaben nodded, his black curls, nowhere near as long as his brother's, bouncing with the movement of his head. He swallowed, trying to hide his fear as his brother spoke again.

'Good. Then you will go with Bardock's men and defend the Middle-last Fort. Land with you, and my prayers!' The twelve year old made a clumsy salute, and accompanied by Captain Bardock, left the room. Yannon's eyes filled with tears, but he dried them with the back of his hand, embarrassed and ashamed to let Kesta and Taneshka see.

'Where is Fox? Surely he has heard us moving out?' The River Prince made an attempt to distract them from his condition. Kesta's eyes widened with alarm, and she ran for the bedroom.

Taneshka put a hand on Yannon's arm. 'Just so you know, I've never been in a battle I haven't won. Does that help?' She smiled encouragingly. Yannon looked at her seriously.

'I am not afraid of dying, Tigress.'

'Oh? *I* am. I just don't care about what comes after. But I suppose that's what you meant. We'll bring Fox after you, if you want to go ahead to your parents.'

Yannon nodded, smiled. 'Yes. You've never lost a battle, you say! Very well. Follow on quickly, Tigress.' He strode away. Taneshka smiled to herself, gaze returning to the curtain.

'There's a first time for everything,' she muttered dryly. She shook herself and went to retrieve her spear from the bedroom.

Kesta ran into the bedroom to find Fox, awake, but sweating and staring, gasping for breath.

'Kesta!'

She dropped to her knees in front of him.

'You didn't...! Fox, you were supposed to stay awake! Did you dream?'

Fox nodded. 'He pushed too hard for me...I buckled, Kesta, I'm sorry. He threw my own dreams back at me. He's trying to control me through my fears. This time though...this time I won't be cowed!'

Fox jumped to his feet, pulling his shirt off and reaching for another. Kesta helped him pull on his undershirt of marsh wool, sealed tight about his wrists and neck. As he changed his bottom half she stood with her back to him, wondering fervently what was running through his mind. His defeat at the mind of their unseen enemy had, if anything, revitalised him. Why?

Fox squeezed her shoulder briefly to let her turn around. She helped him on with the final layer of steel-studded and lacquered leather armour. 'We're supposed to do this in the walltop room,' Kesta said softly, buckling the armour tighter about his chest. Fox touched her cheek, then rested his hands lightly on her shoulders. He was almost a head taller than her now, she realised. He had grown in the last weeks.

'Shall I help you with your clothes?' he asked lightly, eyes sparkling in the low light.

Kesta smiled, despite herself. 'They'll be wondering where we are...' she said, leaning against him in the dark room. Fox opened his mouth to say something, but someone spoke first.

'*I'm* not wondering. But I *am* eager to get at my spear, could you move over?'

Taneshka grinned at them as she walked across the room. Wordlessly, Fox handed Tiger's Fang to her. She manoeuvred the long spear out through the door, grinning at Kesta. Fox turned away, scowling. Kesta looked at the floor and waited for her friend to leave.

Fox strapped his sword at his waist, and checked that his staff was secure against his back. Kesta hurriedly changed in the corner.

The air was cold, even here, and she was glad of the warm wool. She fitted on her adjusted Fox Army armour, and took a moment to belt her Wing Swords to her back, so that she could swing them off her shoulders at short notice. Her gloves went on last. Turning, she met Fox's eyes. He was staring at her with a fierce, protective intensity.

'I'm not going to let you get hurt. I swear it!'

Kesta frowned, taking a step backwards. 'Why say that?' she asked. Fox smiled, his expression changing again.

'Just letting you know.' He slapped his gloved hand on her shoulder-pad. 'Come on, before Taneshka gets the chance to gossip with the others.'

He followed Kesta out of the room, struggling to keep his expression normal as images from his dream flashed through his mind. Always the same picture. *Well, nothing was going to happen to her.* He was here, and a mere dream would not intimidate him that easily. *No.* This fight would prove that! Face set with determination, Fox walked to the walltop.

Outside the open door of the tower, armoured men paced, casting shadows into the small arming room. The Queen sat with her face to the window. Kesta sat behind her braiding the imperious woman's hair as instructed, into eighteen individual braids. Each one represented one of the woman's ancient, lost, northern gods. Little runic blades attached to bands of cloth made the tie-offs, and Kesta had to be careful not to cut her fingers.

Fox sat on a high backed wooden chair, tracing the blood channel of Tiger's Gift with his fingertip. Yannon watched, eyes barely open as he dozed against the opposite wall. Fox gently slit the end of his finger, causing Taneshka to raise an eyebrow in surprise, and Yannon to jerk upright.

'What are you…?'

Fox raised the finger so that Yannon could see it. The cut was healed, but the drop of blood still rested on the fingertip. Fox let it drop onto the blade. It hissed, and turned to nothingness on contact.

Fox smiled. 'Just showing off.' He slid the blade back into its sheath. Yannon shook his head, impressed.

'That's a wondrous blade, brother. Order blessed?' Fox nodded in answer, looking curiously at Yannon's half-halberd.

'Is that halberd supposed to be so short?'

'Yes!' Yannon grinned, hefting the weapon in his left hand. 'For closer work. It's not really much more than a pointed axe.'

'What's wrong with axes?' Brant asked mildly, drawing the hood back from his own. The round metal shone in the small space. Yannon raised his hands, shrugging.

'Nothing at all.'

Heron was quiet, Kesta noticed, as she switched around on her stool so that the queen could braid her hair in return. The king stood with his back against the wall, staring into space and holding his long trident. The serrated edges and the triple points glinted menacingly. A bladed club counterweighted the trident's head at the bottom.

'He's trying to recall the self-peace lessons he learnt from his father, years ago.' The queen explained quietly. 'His father taught him to calm his temper, hoping it would curb his love of war. Palin used it every time he went into battle against my people. It has never yet failed him.'

'Do you use it?' Kesta asked, trying not to wince as the warrior queen's hands pulled her hair tightly back off her forehead into the final braid.

The woman shook her head. 'No. I avoid the traps of fear and doubt by focusing on my rage. Palin and I, we are opposites. Like winter and summer.' Kesta smiled at the description as the queen finished. 'I've put twenty three braids in. You're not a northerner like me, so you shouldn't pay blood homage to my gods. Nor, as Fox's expression seems to say, should I. But old habits die slow. Each braid in your hair represents one of the original tribes of these Lands. You're almost certainly descended from native folk, Kesta. The colour of your hair, the shape of your eyes… Even Fox, for all that he is, is descended from a visitor to this realm. Take pride in your blood!'

Kesta rose, touching the thin braids that fell onto her shoulders. 'Thank you.' She let the queen embrace her.

'I would that my daughter grows to be like you, Kesta Shieldmaid.'

Kesta, embarrassed, looked out into the mist.

'It's nearly morning. Why haven't they made their move yet?'

Fox stirred. 'He, or they, are waiting for something. I don't know what. It may be that they won't attack before tomorrow nightfall. Another day.'

'That's good! The army should be here by then!'

'Yes.'

The rest of the night passed in the same way. Everyone except for Fox slept. Occasionally, apologetic walltop guards dropped by for supplies, and Andul Spar was a regular, if silent visitor. He stood beside Taneshka whenever he entered, but never spoke.

The morning was mostly gone when Kesta woke from her most recent doze. Fox was quite tense, and as Kesta rose, she realised why.

Heron entered. He had slept earlier, but now he was wide awake. He stopped in front of Fox, looking down with a tight expression. 'The south patrol has returned. It's midday, they say you can see the sun at the edge of the marshes. It is high in the sky. And there is no army.'

Fox closed his eyes as if pained. 'I don't understand,' he said honestly, looking up at Heron with a calm expression, 'they assured me they would get here. Something must be wrong.'

'You're telling me! We have no aid, and have no idea how many we are facing, but we know that they must be powerful, seeing as they can control the bloody weather!'

Heron retreated to his chair in the corner. Fox looked down at the floor regretfully. He knew that Heron was not really angry with him, that the man was just expressing his fear and frustration. Yannon met Fox's eye and gave him a reassuring smile. Fox returned it gratefully.

Taneshka and Brant rose and went for a walk on the fog-shrouded walltop, to look for Andul Spar. The afternoon crawled by. Servants came in with food, but were sent packing by an angry Heron, who wanted them to retreat to the Last Forts.

The dark began to return. Fox stood, went to the door and looked up into the white thickness.

Hours passed. A guard came in to report that all non-combatant personnel had retreated to the last forts. 'Salaben is in control of the Midway Last Fort, my Lord King, and Captain

Bardock is with him. Your daughter and your youngest child are in the Westward fort. They'll be safe there.'

Heron waved the man away. It was very dark now.

Fox shifted uncomfortably in his chair and felt the first stabs of aggression at the back of his mind. 'Ah,' he said, rising to his feet and smiling grimly. 'At last. They're on their way.'

The wind rose in a steady howl, though the mist did not move.

Andul Spar met them on the walltop. He was wearing his fork-sword at his side and holding a recurve bow. He saw Fox's expression and understood immediately. 'Can they scale the walls?' he asked seriously, taking hold of Fox's left arm to get his attention.

'I don't think so.'

'This damned mist will spoil our arrows. It would be better to take up positions on the walkways behind the gates, and when the doors break in, let fly then. There is greater visibility at ground level.'

Fox nodded in agreement. Heron gave the order and the group descended the steps, treading on the creaking wooden walkway. A hundred or so men stood there in total, gripping pikes, voulges and bows.

Heron smiled as he walked faster, intent on meeting them first. He embraced the nearest soldier. 'Brother! We will not fail each other, believe me, men! This battle will be ours!'

Fox tried to enjoy Heron's bravado.

Howling rose on the air. Shrieks and haggard bawls. They were close. The time for smiling was over.

Heron stood calmly, face impassive, eyes watching the gates closely. His wife stood beside him. Her face was painted with angular black stripes that spread out across her cheeks from her lips, which were painted black as tar. The head of her mace made a steady slapping sound against her gauntlet. It was a good sound, Brant thought, swallowing his fear. Like the battle drums of his last great combat, in the south. They brought calm: a slower heartbeat to affect the one hammering in his chest.

The howling intensified.

'Like demons!' One soldier breathed, terrified. Fox wanted to lend him some courage, but knew that he would need it all for himself. The enemy were upon them.

The gates creaked loudly, and moved under sudden impact. The horrible keening was unending, and louder than ever, as the gates shook.

Suddenly Commander Andul Spar was running forward, wading through the shallow water. He swore loudly, striving to reach the door of the bull-keep.

'Why did no one set them loose?' Fox muttered angrily, echoing Heron. Soldiers gripped the handles of their weapons, teeth clenched from the strain of watching their Commander struggle with the gate beam on the pen, while the nearby gates began to buckle.

'Andul! Come back at once!' Fox shouted out. His voice carried command, and immediately the bull-rider turned and began to wade back to the walkway.

'Ready the bows!' Yannon called, voice cracking as he raised his own, arrow nocked on string.

There was a splintering sound. Yannon almost let fly, but realised in time that it was the bull-keep that had lost its gate. As the wooden structure collapsed into the marsh, the bulls surged out in a snorting, terrified stampede, before fleeing southwards, as the great wolves had, days before.

Fox relaxed momentarily. It had not been so draining for him to break the bonds of the pen's gates. Now the real work was coming.

The famous White Gates gave at last with a terrible, groaning crash. Ripples spread, breaking against Andul's legs and passing him. A pair of pike-men ran forwards to help their Commander, who had stumbled, foot caught in hidden reeds. He was nearly at the walkway.

Yannon cried out, 'Loose!'

A flight of arrows flew into the vague, shambling mass of figures, which were still hidden in the mist.

There was a bellow, barely audible beneath the cacophony of screaming emanating from the enemy. One lone marsh-bull had returned. Bellowing its territorial warning, it settled beside Andul, who frantically clawed his way onto its back. In four quick strides, the mounted Commander was beside the walkway. Another flight of arrows left the bows.

The two men that had gone to help their commander were now stranded, Fox saw, with a sick wave of terror in his chest. The two soldiers floundered in the water.

The first figures came hurtling out of the mist. They were human, sinewy and scrawny, with torn skin and crazed, empty eyes. Their lips were tattered and their skulls bald. Grim, gaping mouths with jagged broken teeth were set like caves in lolling, senseless heads.

They fell upon the struggling soldiers and tore them apart. Internal tissues poured into the water from the stricken victims, as with tooth, and nail, and raw, mad strength the creatures killed. Two human screams briefly joined the deafening choir of shrieking voices.

Kesta fought the urge to run, her heart pumping in her chest, reminding her of her fragility. Fox's face was suddenly overtaken by a look of pure rage.

He roared, his voice causing ripples in the mist. He tore the gloves from his hands, his fingers curling into casting positions. His hands clenched, and the spines of the forerunners snapped. The empty bodies fell into the water.

Brant hefted his axe, moving forward to stand beside Fox. 'These are Husk,' He said, setting his feet apart in a stance. 'Dismember them, disembowel, these will not stop. You must behead them, or cut them in two.' Fox raised his sword in answer. As the last flight of arrows sped to their targets, doing little, Fox raised his left hand once more in the casting form.

'You *will* be ended, abominations.' Flames flickered briefly up the length of Tiger's Gift. The archers withdrew behind, taking up pikes and swords. Kesta pulled her wing-swords free of her back. Taneshka, jaw set and eyes alight, brandished Tiger's Fang with stubborn bravery.

The first wave broke.

'MAKER'S FIRE TAKE YOU!' Fox roared, swinging Tiger's Gift in a great arc. Flame soared away in an expanding arc, cutting through the nearest husk. It was surprisingly ineffective. The panicked thrusting of the pikes and voulges held the enemy off. Grasping arms snatched out at Kesta, but Taneshka's spear impaled the skull of the attacking creature.

Kesta gasped from exertion as the entire defence force backed off. Brant shook his head, returning his axe to his back and drawing Fate and Fury, his iron clubs. 'They will overrun us!'

Kesta's lip curled in a sickened snarl as she fought the husk. There was no one inside the people that clawed at her now, no one behind the eyes. The sharp tang of blood hung in the air.

'Retreat!' Andul roared, turning his bull as he brought his voulge down on the nearest husk.

Heron buried his trident in a skinny chest, making the thing spew blood. 'Never! We'll lose the White Gate Castle!'

'It must be done! Let them have it! Let us keep our lives!'

'No! It is my duty, the Lifeblood River is mine! I cannot!'

The men were already retreating, though, leaving the four children to defend the King and Queen, along with their son Yannon. Fox felt defeat creeping, like cold from the freezing water, as the husk horde began to surround them. Flashes of his dream hit Fox then, making him reel. A voice at the edge of his mind began to laugh, satisfaction layered thickly, filthy, guttural.

Fox raised his left arm again, focusing on the husk that together represented the greatest threat to Heron. One by one, Fox felled them, aware that the press was not heavy around him; he and Kesta were being ignored. Brant and Taneshka, who were closer to the King, were in the thick of it. *They're being driven!* Fox realised, as a sweeping motion of his sword beheaded a husk some distance away.

Fox felt out with his mind and found what he had been expecting. The enemy mind was indeed directing the husk movements. Fox felt a great surge of aggression against Heron, rising from the creature's mind. Heron was a tall, defiant figure, back to back with his fearsome wife, surrounded by more than thirty mindlessly clawing husk.

A sudden charge separated the King and Queen from Andul, who was circling the fight, and from Brant and Taneshka. Brant's clubs flailed out ceaselessly, his handsome face spattered with blood. He struck out with practiced violence, braining or crippling each of his targets.

Taneshka's spear was slung, her twin knives out, and she was coming close to being brought down. Kesta's bow was up, releasing arrows into the small pack of husk around Taneshka, easing the pressure on her. Fox set off towards the main throng.

'Fall! Fall! Fall!' Fox snarled out as husk after husk turned away and came for him. Power-assisted blows sent them flying, cracking the air like thunderclaps. One scrambled past its neighbours, and Fox punched it in the face with his free hand. Flame and blood shocked suddenly upwards in the creature's destroyed face, lighting up the area as the skull exploded and the body fell away.

Brant ducked out of the action, a windmill of battering, iron death. With a gasped out thanks to Fox he ran towards Kesta, keeping his head down as arrows flew past.

'The others have retreated!' Fox shouted at Heron, drawing the Holy Order's symbol in the air, and sweeping the flame down on the backs of the nearby enemy, palm jutting out and down. Flames burst forth from the cages of their ribs, but they struggled on, shrieking horrifically, eyes rolling madly in their skulls.

Heron turned and saw that all his men had run. His wife brought her mace down on a struggling husk so hard that its neck, knees and back all broke at once. She turned to see what her husband saw.

'Cowards! Come, my love! Death! Death! Death, and the black storm of the Ice Waste! Death!' She strode forward, husk already grasping at her face and arms. Her husband roared out her name, lost in the sound of the enemy, and ran forward after her, into the churning press.

Horrified, Fox stopped short, seeing the horde break apart and stream away, picking new targets. Their task had been accomplished. For a moment, Fox thought he had seen Heron's proud stare, his wife's black hair, glimpsed through the crush. But they were gone. Blood curled like smoke in the water. Heron and his Queen were dead.

29
Bloodgrim

Fox let out a cut-off yell. There were fewer husk. Many had run on, past Brant and Kesta, seeking the escaping soldiers.

A cruel laugh echoed in Fox's head.

Yannon was fighting like a demon, hair flying about his face as his half-halberd carved a swathe through the remaining husk. He turned to Fox, opening a husk's stomach as he did, before driving the point of his weapon through the back of the creature's head.

'I cannot get to the Tigress! There are still too many!' his face was pale with fear. Fox turned to look at where Taneshka struggled on, red hair flying out behind her as she wielded Halver two-handed.

Suddenly Andul Spar went by, his bull kicking up the water, lowering its head to the charge. It bellowed out as husk tore at its face. Half-dead husk gripped at the bull's stomach, tearing maniacally at the soft flesh as they were dragged through the water.

The bull's legs buckled and Andul made a controlled dive into the water, rolling and rising immediately, delivering a wheeling blow to the nearest of many enemies. Taneshka cried out in relief as he joined her, forcing a way back.

'Taneshka! Go with the princes! Fox and Yannon! Run! Run, they will separate...lesser numbers then!'

Taneshka did as she was told, stumbling to where Fox and Yannon fought. She turned in time to see Andul brought down, his cry strangled.

'No! No! Fox, do something!'

Taneshka started to run back, feet churning the icy water. Fox brought three more husk to their end, and Yannon, bow drawn, took down another pair. But it was too late. The remaining husk piled in, some tearing at the ill-fated bull, others at Andul himself.

Fox grabbed Taneshka's arm and looked into her eyes. 'Teshka. Run!' She did as he said, and all three of them went, using Andul's distraction to put distance between themselves and the enemy. They joined with Brant and Kesta, and kept going, feet slapping at the frigid water, sinking in the hidden mud.

Finally, Fox raised a hand. Howls still sounded all around them, but none of the husk were visible. Yannon and Taneshka were in shock. Taneshka kept shaking her head, gasping for breath as she bent double.

'Stand straight, you'll fill your lungs easier,' Fox ordered. He was breathing easily himself, but grief was heavy on him.

'He died for me...' Taneshka moaned, standing up, and pulling her spear free. 'He died for me.' Fox put a hand on her shoulder.

'We need to ready ourselves, and use the time he has given us. There is a second wave coming and we have already been routed.'

'What!' Taneshka stared in panic. Brant and Kesta's expressions were the same. Fox nodded grimly. For a moment, his mind searched the dark marsh around them.

'Some of the first wave are regrouping. They are heading southwest.'

Yannon frowned. 'There's no strategic advantage there.'

'These are husk. They don't care about strategic advantages!' Fox reminded him. Then it struck home. Yannon's eyes widened.

'My sister! My little brother! Oh Land, no!'

Brant looked up, gripping the hilts of his clubs.

'I will go.'

Yannon spun to look at the Southlander. 'What?'

'I will go to defend the Westward-last Tower. I know where it is, your father show me the maps. I can run faster than all of you, except perhaps Fox.'

Fox nodded. 'Go. Land bless you Brant. Go!' Brant bowed, and set off, moving at a considerable speed despite the clinging mire. His form disappeared like a fading illusion. Fox stared after him for a moment. Then he turned to face the north.

'Here they come again.'

The wailing on the air rose. *At least the mist is thinning*, Kesta thought, nocking another arrow. Yannon copied her and they stood, one on either side of Fox. Taneshka stepped up on Kesta's right, Tiger's Fang held firmly in her hands.

Fox counted the numbers as they came running, as yet unseen, through the fading mist. There were so many. So many.

'I will end this.'

He lifted his head, eyes hard as ice chips as he focused on the first figures, fading and inconstant, barely visible in the gloom.

Suddenly, the shambling, howling horde stopped. They stood, swaying, staring out of the mist. He felt a dark presence flowing forward, taking prominence in his mind. The ranks of husk parted.

So you have come then.

Black fluidity stepped towards the small group. Its shoulders hunched up and down as it moved, an odd, sinuous stalking motion, head swivelling from side to side as it surveyed them. It had an ill-defined shape. The body as of a man, very tall and broad shouldered, but with an odd, dislocated look to it, as if all its joints were reversed or twisted.

'Ah. The Land's Arisen. At last, face to face. In the way of men, we shall conduct this prelude to your destruction. Conversation with the enemy, so rare, yet so noble.' The creature laughed, a horrible gurgling sound. A hiss trailed off at the end. Fox stared the monster down.

'What are you?'

'I am the Bloodgrim. The First Bloodgrim. I am the pinnacle of sorcery, the Great One's creative triumph. I have come as assassin in his service, little man.'

The creatures face was still veiled. The black shroud hung about its shoulders like a cloak, and as the material shifted Fox saw the curve of a leg, covered in hide, with the knee bent backwards.

Suddenly, the Bloodgrim withdrew into the mist, sweeping away with frightening speed. Its horrible voice floated back to Fox, along with the image that he so feared.

Kesta!

'Your first trial, Risen One. Fight my husk. Yes…your fear tastes good! Let it build! You can't prevent the inevitable, little boy.'

The husk stirred, the power of their limbs returned to them. Fox gathered his strength. A little voice, his own, this time, told him that he would never be able to destroy all of them. Not without standing on stony ground.

I will try nonetheless. Fox sheathed Tiger's Gift and raised his hands. The husk scrambled forwards, desperate to bloody their teeth and Fox let out a long, loud cry.

'WATERS TAKE YOU!'

A hundred or more came for him, tripping and stumbling. The water withdrew beneath them and the mud caught at their feet.

Fox stood, eyes narrowed with concentration. The water all around ebbed away.

The first flailing figures were within a few yards of Fox when the water returned. Fox guided the flood, so that the wave took out the greater number of the husk, breaking the charge. The return wave carried them backwards. Fox threw back his head, breathing in as he prepared to deliver the final blow.

Some small barrier within him broke, and suddenly the world was made naked to him.

Fox's hair whipped back from his face. Energy crackled across his knuckles, around his hands, lightning dancing up his arms. The uncovered reeds and marsh grasses about his feet were bent outwards, as if under the force of a gale. The flash flood peaked and Fox flung his arms forward, letting the power leave him in torrent.

Lightning leapt from his hands into the swell of water. The struggling husk were stricken, and then destroyed, as a second fork of white energy lanced upwards from the marsh water into the sky. Charred flesh floated in on the returning swell. Blank, torn faces stared upwards. The mist was clearing.

Fox clenched his fists. Little aftershocks of energy darted away from his body to ground themselves in the soggy marsh. Slowly and deliberately, Fox drew his sword. Green flame licked up the blade, and the movement of the sword left trails of fire in the air. Behind Fox, the few husk that had escaped the wave fought with Kesta and Yannon.

Fox turned, sweeping his hand out. Yannon found himself surrounded by an invisible dome; whenever husk tried to strike him, the offending limb exploded, broken by white light. Kesta slew her last husk, arms burning from the cold and exertion. Taneshka was in a similar state.

'Are there more?' she asked Fox, leaning on her spear. Fox nodded. His eyes were watching the shape of the Bloodgrim, returning slowly, taking his time.

Yannon made a decision, eyes staring into the distance, hands gripping his half-halberd. 'You two should make for the Middle-last Fort. Salaben is there, and there should be a few soldiers too. I'll stay and finish this with Fox.'

Taneshka opened her mouth to protest, but fell silent after only a word, realising that she would die if she was forced to continue.

'What does it look like, this fort?' Fox asked Yannon, eyes still watching the Bloodgrim's shape. *It knows what we're saying. It knows what I'm thinking.*

Yannon shrugged, wiping blood off his cheek. 'It's a small tower with a battlemented roof.'

The Bloodgrim's distant shape moved suggestively. Fox saw an image of a tower, stark against the mist, pass across his mind's eye. It was straight from his dream.

'Not the tower. The Bloodgrim wants you to go there. Where else is there?'

'There is nowhere else, not unless you want them to run all night for dry land!'

Fox bit his lip. That would be preferable, he thought, watching the Bloodgrim. Suddenly, the figure made a showy gesture, like a conjuror. And Fox became aware of another wave of husk, moving in from the south. Soon, they would cut Kesta and Taneshka off from the tower and any hope of safety.

The Bloodgrim moved closer. And now, with the mist all but gone, they could truly see him.

His head was framed by curling horns, similar to those of the carcer beast, from all those months ago. His legs were reverse-jointed, and he walked with an odd, predatory gait. His mouth was a jagged tunnel, constantly changing shape to fit his dread face. Dark, soulless eyes stared out of the gaping visage. *Spider's eyes.* Long, clawed fingers ended long, sinewy arms. The ribcage, partially covered by the creature's membranous cloak, was just that, a starved exoskeleton, a cage for the monster's innards.

'*Not the tower. The Bloodgrim wants you to go there. Where else? Where else? Where else?*' The creature's mocking voice floated across to them. Fox swore, and made his decision.

'Kesta, Taneshka, run to the tower like Yannon says. Hurry, or you'll be cut off. Run fast, as fast as you can!'

The girls turned and ran. The Bloodgrim watched Kesta go, gaping, tube of a mouth contorting into a smile. '**Maybe you should run too, little boy.** *Run fast, as fast as you can!* **Hahaha!**

You can run faster than her, can't you? You could overtake her easily.'

Fox ignored the taunting. 'Are you here to fight, monster, or to talk?'

'**Both. I would like to introduce myself. You asked what I was. I am nothing if not polite, let me answer you.**'

'What are you?'

'**A baby.**' The Bloodgrim laughed thickly, bowing a little. Fox spat into the water, disgusted with the comparison.

'**No, but it is true, Fox. I am very young. Once I was a man. A sorcerer. Now I am reborn! I am Bloodgrim!**'

'You'll die just the same.'

'**Ha! Will I? When I can do this?**' The Bloodgrim darted forward, horrible head jerking out like a blade. Fox jumped forwards to meet him, but the creature drew a sword and struck. The impact on Tiger's Gift was so hard that Fox was thrown into the bloodied marsh water. He got back up, too late.

The Bloodgrim swooped down on Yannon. His hands gripped him fiercely, pincer like, holding him upright. The Bloodgrim's spine extended and his neck bent so that the terrible, cavernous mouth came down over Yannon's head. Fox let out a cry, throwing out a hand to use his gift, intending to knock Yannon out of the monster's grasp.

Another pair of clawed arms snaked out from beneath the Bloodgrim's ribs. They transfixed Yannon completely. The spider-eyes bored into Yannon's terrified face, then turned to Fox above a horrible grin.

The mouth stretched, wider than Yannon's shoulders.

It bit his head off.

Fox screamed. 'Nooooooooo! Land no, *please* NO!'

The Bloodgrim cast Yannon's carcass aside. '*No! Please no!*' He mocked Fox, his head swaying from side to side on his hunched shoulders. The second pair of arms withdrew. Once more, images from Fox's dream flashed violently through his mind. The tower. The doorway. Kesta in the doorway.

'**Do you know how I became this way, little boy? I knelt before Shadow Incarnate, and He made me sacred with a touch. I knelt on the altar. Six animals I chose for myself, to fuse to myself, their energies with mine, one power! Ram!**

Wolf! Spider! Eel! Crow! Flesh-fly! One by one, I drank the blood of each. Oh, I know what you're thinking, what blood is there to be had from a spider, or a fly?'

The Bloodgrim opened its mouth, the tunnel changing to make a more wolf-like maw. It mimed chewing, and then an exaggerated swallow.

'Hahaha! Don't judge until you've tried it, Risen One! Oh yes! My jaws, wide as an eel's, the strength of the wolf! Imagine what they could do to the little girl's skull! Kesta, am I right? Imagine how pretty she'd look with her scar opened up...'

'Don't you say her name! Don't you dare, I'll kill you!'

'*I'll kill you! I'll kill you!* Hahaha! Will you? You've seen how fast I am. You saw what I did to your pitiful friend. What makes you think I won't do the same to Kesta?'

Fox stood, shaking from head to foot. Tiger's Gift reignited in his hand.

'Because I'm not done yet, demon! You know what this water is that we stand in? I may not be standing on rock but if the rocks are the bones of the Land, then the water is its blood! *Maker take you*!'

A torrent of Maker's flame poured forth. Fox's eyes filled with tears from the effort. The water rose away in steam. But when the surge of fire ceased, the Bloodgrim stood.

'*How?*'

'*How?* How? Haha! Little boy, Maker's fire cannot hurt me! Your *anti-magic* will not harm me! I have been touched by the Great! Part of his essence is in ME!' The Bloodgrim's voice quietened, and he began to prowl again, in a tightening circle. 'Where were we? Oh yes, considering my great speed and strength, not to mention my diabolical hunger for human meat, haha, what is there to prevent me from killing Kesta? Obviously not you.'

Fox smiled wearily. 'It doesn't matter. She has almost reached the tower.'

'Yes. Almost.' Another horrible grin split the Bloodgrim's face, and briefly the hoary mouthparts of a spider curled away from the clean air. '**But, little boy, she's not there yet. You're faster than her, remember? Haha. *Run fast, as fast as you can!* That's** what you said to her. But you could've overtaken her easily. You're faster than her.'

The creature's shoulders hunched even more, and it's feet, hooves, but cloven into four parts like a wolf's pad, spread out on the ground, like a runner at starting blocks.

'Fox... You're faster than her. But I am faster than you.' And in a rush, the Bloodgrim went. He moved away, faster than almost anything Fox had seen, quick as the Great Shadow. His feet barely touched the water as he sped away. The laugh echoed in Fox's ears. Fear stabbed his heart. Kesta was not yet at the tower! He could sense her, running still, just behind Taneshka.

With a terrified sob, Fox began to run. His feet pounded the soggy marsh, splashing through the shallows. He ran faster than he had ever run before. Ahead, close, but always still ahead, the Bloodgrim surged onwards.

The race made Fox's heart rate triple. His legs began to burn from the pain, and in response he pushed himself harder. He could not let the monster reach her! There, ahead was the tower. Beyond the Bloodgrim's fluid shape, Fox could see the silhouette of Kesta, twenty yards from the open doorway. Soldiers were taking Taneshka's weapons so that she could stumble inside, and now they too were backing away from the speeding shape of the Bloodgrim. Only Kesta was in the open.

Fox put on an extra burst of speed. His feet beat the ground in a desperate rhythm, he was almost there; not ten yards behind the Bloodgrim...

Who caught her in the doorway.

She froze, feeling the claws on her shoulders. His face lowered down beside hers, leering. Two soldiers made to attack, but hissing, the Bloodgrim used his second pair of arms to knock them back through the doorway.

He spun to face Fox, holding Kesta's terrified form tight. Her eyes met Fox's as he stumbled to a halt, heart and lungs burning, too short of the doorway. Too far away to save her.

The Bloodgrim drew a claw cruelly across her cheek. She cried out as her scar opened, and blood began to trickle down her face.

The Bloodgrim opened his mouth.

Kesta fell into the water as the Bloodgrim jerked away, a rattling hiss breaking from his mouth. In the doorway, Salaben Heronsen stood, dirk in hand. Black blood dripped from the blade. The twelve year-old's face was a picture of terror and stubborn courage.

Fox ran forward, scooped Kesta up, and rolled in through the doorway. The soldiers slammed the heavy door, and brought down the locking beam with a crash.

Fox gasped out his pain, tears of relief streaming down his face as he held Kesta's live, breathing form. She was crying too, and holding him as tight as she was able. Taneshka, wide eyed, helped them both to their feet.

'He's still out there?'

Fox nodded wordlessly. He sat on a chair, and struggled to control his breathing. Salaben looked around, confused.

'Where is my brother?'

Fox looked at the young boy, his heart breaking. 'He died, Salaben. Died fighting.' Salaben stood stock-still, staring at the black blood on his dirk.

'Then you are my brother now. I have no others, then.' The boy turned and walked across the room to a ladder, which must have led to the roof. Fox frowned, turning to the nearest soldier.

'What does he mean?'

'Sir, he means that his younger siblings are also dead, sir. One of the men from the Westward Tower escaped a massacre there. He said that the husk moved on, and when he went back, there were none alive. The babes must have perished with the rest. We lost Captain Bardock too...'

'But...Brant was out there! Land, no!' Fox put his head in his hands. Kesta slumped against the wall, stunned. Taneshka turned away, tears pouring down her face.

Fox raised his eyes to stare at the barred door. 'He will die at my hands, he and all his husk, I swear on my own blood. Brant will not go un-avenged.'

Taneshka turned back, fear mixing once again with her sorrow. 'You can't mean...? Surely he has given up! I thought we had killed them all...Is this not over?'

Fox stood, reaching for his sword.

'No. It's not over.'

30
Last Stand

The glorious last stand, Fox thought grimly. Two Heron voulge-men. One twelve-year-old prince. And three teenaged warriors, tired both mentally and physically. All against the last few Husk, and their unholy captain. *This,* Fox reflected, *will be a fight to remember, if any live to do so.* He turned to Taneshka.

'Hold this room. The door is unnecessary, they will break it down and stay unharmed throughout. Take it off its hinges and barricade the way in. Use the table, the chairs, anything! You two!' He turned to address the two soldiers. 'Take up bows. Loose into them as they try to come over the barricade. The Tigress will take down the ones you miss.'

'I shall.' Taneshka straightened her back wearily, pulling her hair back from her face. Fox took her right hand and began to rub up her arm, flooding her burning, fatigued muscles with warmth and vitality. He repeated the task with her left arm, and then did her shoulders and back. The soldiers watched as Fox turned and began to do the same for Kesta. Taneshka now stood tall, as she had done at the beginning.

'Where are you going to go?' Taneshka asked, looking at Fox with red eyes. Her voice was harsh with thirst. Fox glanced up at the ceiling. 'Onto the roof, with Kesta. Everybody, prepare. They are coming!'

The soldiers rose, faces set with new resolution. Kesta went up the ladder two rungs at a time. Taneshka helped Fox tear the door off its hinges and lie it across the doorway, held in place by the table. Fox looked out into the black sky and shadowy wetland. A thin, reedy howling was rising again. The last of the husk were regrouping.

Fox climbed the ladder onto the roof. Kesta was sitting with Salaben. They were both looking out over the marsh. Kesta's bow was in her hand. She rose.

'How many are left?'

'A dozen, maybe. More importantly, he is still out there. I think you but wounded him, Salaben. Where did you stick him?'

'In his right leg. He didn't lift it at the knee as he moved away, I saw.' Salaben answered matter-of-factly. Fox nodded.

'Good. If you would descend the ladder then, Salaben, and help Taneshka keep the room clear of husk.'

'Yes, Fox.' The boy went to the ladder. Fox smiled after him, and reached to take his hand.

'Thank you for saving Kesta, Sala. Thank you.' The boy smiled a thing that seemed impossible now, like sun cutting through cloud. Fox released his hand.

'Now.' Fox turned to the parapet. 'This is almost over, one way or the other. Have you any arrows left, Kesta?'

She nodded, and nocked one to the string of her bow. Fox took the quiver from her and laid it on the parapet. He touched the arrowheads, one by one, then the arrow that she already had ready. The points glistened.

'For speed and accuracy. Don't miss. Here they come!'

He was right. Coming in one final charge were a dozen husk. They came like macabre escaped lunatics, naked, smeared and caked with blood and mud. Kesta raised her bow.

Fox glanced around the small rooftop. His eyes alighted on a jar in the corner. He strode to it, removing the lid and dipping his finger in. Sealing pitch. Fox's eyes narrowed as he lifted the jar, replacing its lid.

Kesta loosed an arrow, it sailed out across the marsh, before removing the head from a husk in a shower of bone. She gasped, shocked at just how effective Fox's alteration was.

Fox hurled the jar out over the battlements. It landed with a heavy, wet sound in the marsh water some way out. Kesta nocked another arrow. She glanced at Fox over her shoulder, and saw his fingers twitch. The jar shattered without warning. Understanding, Kesta changed her aim, and released another arrow. It lanced down from the rooftop, bursting into flames halfway to its target. The pitch went up, fire burning fiercely in the water.

Some of the husk ran straight through it, burning pitch clinging to them, lighting them up, easy targets for the Heron archers in the tower. Kesta killed another four, while Fox watched, conserving his energy, and studying the gloom around the tower, searching for the Bloodgrim.

In the tower room, the bows sang twice more, before two husk sprawled in across the barricade. Taneshka ran one through, driving its still kicking body against the wall. Salaben stepped forward and hacked at a knee with his dirk. One of the soldiers put his voulge through the creature's neck.

And then it was quiet. Taneshka and Salaben stood side by side, breathing heavily. On the top of the tower Kesta allowed herself to stop, unstringing her bow and returning it to her shoulder.

She turned to look at Fox. Her eyes brimmed with emotion. He smiled at her, and gently moved one of her braids out of the way of her face, tucking it behind her ear. 'You're beautiful,' he said.

She closed her eyes to stop the tears, and raised a hand to touch the bleeding gash on her cheek. Her other hand ran through her hair, and came back with blood staining the fingers. She looked away.

His hand touched hers. 'Even so. Bloodied face or no, scar or no, marks of battle or no, you are still beautiful.' He stepped up onto the parapet and let her hand go.

She stared up at him. The sun was rising, away to the east. The dread mist was all but gone. One last well of shadow waited out in the mire, concealing the Bloodgrim, yet now giving his position away. Fox turned to look, heart beating faster.

'Strike him down for me,' Kesta said, bowing her head.

'Aye. And for Brant. And for Heron and his Queen. For Yannon. For Andul Spar.' He looked back at Kesta. 'I love you, Kesta Shieldmaid. And I will come back to prove it.' He dropped off the parapet.

Kesta rose, and saw him stepping out, steady and straight. He drew his sword as he went.

'Oh Land! Protect him! He's mine as well as yours!' Kesta prayed, hands gripping the stonework.

The Land's Arisen stepped into shadow, and waited for his enemy to approach.

The Bloodgrim came out of the shadows, intending to take Fox by surprise. They exchanged jarring sword strokes, and the monster wheeled away, making that horrible hissing in his throat. His eyes glinted at Fox out of the coiling, curling mist, and the mouth, part lupine, part arachnid, snapped viciously. The humiliating failure to break Fox's spirit had reduced the

Bloodgrim. The soldier of darkness was gone, all that was left was the beast.

Fox smiled, though his heart pounded from fear. Now he had the advantage of self-control. Again they skirmished, parrying and striking out, Fox's mirror clean blade against the Bloodgrim's black sword. Fox's feet danced through the water as he moved to avoid slashes at his head and neck, the Bloodgrim's cloven hooves stamping through the bog with belligerent persistence. The spider-eyes leered down as the creature grew slowly, its spine stretching to give it a heavier attack on the downswing.

'You can't fight me like this forever!'

Fox didn't bother answering, spinning away from another powerful swipe, aware that he was tiring. Yes, the Bloodgrim's injury was making him slower and less agile on his feet, but he still had a strength and endurance that far surpassed Fox's. His muscles, already tired, were beginning to ache with a draining insistence. Each stroke of the black sword was coming closer.

Fox stabbed out at the creature's stomach, and pushed a little with anti-magic to hinder the Bloodgrim's return blow. This gave him enough time to whip his sword up and across, aiming to strike the head. The Bloodgrim jerked back, ram's horn shorn off by the sudden attack. A bubbling hiss sounded as the monster stepped back, shaking his head in agony.

The second pair of arms snaked out from beneath his ribcage. The black sword was thrown from hand to hand, as the Bloodgrim stepped forward again, confidence returned, head lowered. Fox's heart fell. He would not be able to fight off every blow, not from four different angles. As the monster rushed in, he reacted in desperation. Maker's fire rippled along Tiger's Gift, and a lucky strike snapped the black sword in two.

The Bloodgrim went into a blind rage, four arms slashing out, spidery hooks forming in the place of hands. One snagged at Fox's armour, tearing through the steel-studded leather with ease. Once again, Fox was retreating, blocking desperately, unable to defend himself fully…

'Aaagh! Get back!' Fox roared out in frustration, using anti-magic to physically hurl the creature backwards. It rose, laughing, and came for him again.

Enough.

Fox threw his sword down, and extending both arms out in front of him, released all his energies into one purpose. Pure flame roared suddenly from sky to earth, briefly passing through Fox, then blasting into the ground where the Bloodgrim stood, still laughing in the midst of the inferno.

'**You cannot hurt me this way! Hahaha! Pitiful. This doesn't even hurt, little boy!**'

Fox ignored him, pouring more flame down. The water had boiled away and now the thick, black mud was drying in the heat. The pillar of flame could be seen all across the marshes. Silently watching from the roof of the tower, Taneshka and Salaben stood with the surviving soldiers, Kesta slightly apart from them, hugging herself as she silently prayed for Fox's safety.

The flames stopped abruptly, leaving a smell of burnt air. Fox stood there, breathing heavily, his sword lying on the flat, hard-baked ground. The Bloodgrim smiled, sickly.

'**A waste of time, Risen One. What next?**'

Fox looked down at the ground, where the Bloodgrim's feet were sealed securely in the fired clay. He smiled back at the monster, bending to pick up his sword.

'Next I'm going to ask you to look at your feet, foul one.' The Bloodgrim's demeanour flickered, and his eyes rolled down to look at where his hairy, hideous shins emerged. From clay. Thin cracks were spreading across the surface, but as he tried to move his feet, he found they would not respond. The Bloodgrim looked up at Fox, silent and shocked.

'Didn't hurt, eh?'

Tiger's Gift suddenly became a firebrand, a firebrand with a very sharp edge. Fox lifted it casually to his shoulder, hair flying about his face in the morning breeze. The sun was all but up.

'Does *this* hurt?' He stabbed the Bloodgrim in the ribs. An inch of the burning steel cut into him, making him writhe and splutter with the agony. Fox grinned savagely, thinking of Yannon, and of Brant.

'No?' Fox removed the blade, a look of feigned surprise on his face. The Bloodgrim spat at him, rocking from side to side as black blood trickled out over his ribs.

'**Just kill me and be done, Risen One!**'

Fox smiled.

'Yes.'

He brought his right arm back, and cut the Bloodgrim's head off. It landed with a soft *thunk* some feet away. A fountain of blood spurted intermittently from the gaping neck, and then the body tipped, fell.

Fox looked down at Tiger's Gift. The Bloodgrim's gore smoked on the blade for a moment or two. When he looked again, the blade was clean.

Fox let out a sigh of relief. Feeling came back to him, along with his grief at the night's events. He kicked the Bloodgrim's corpse savagely, letting out a howl of anger and rage at what he had been put through. Then he walked over to the head, picked it up, and strode back to the tower.

'There it is.' The head landed on the stone floor, making Kesta and Taneshka jump back. Salaben examined it, then bowed deeply to Fox.

'Thank you.' He said nothing else, but his eyes shone with tears.

'Thank *you*,' Fox replied. 'If you hadn't wounded him when you did, not only would Kesta be dead, but I would be too. He would have easily beaten me. So, thank you, Heron.' Salaben's head jerked in surprise.

'What did you call me?'

Fox bowed deeply. 'I called you by your title, Highness. I give tribute with this creature's head, to King Heron Boatmaster, Watcher of the Many Waters, Custodian of the Great Lifeblood, and Steward of the Land. Long may you be arbiter of these marshes.' Fox rose, face solemn. Salaben looked down at the floor, stunned.

'I am alone in this. I wish my Da were here to show me how...'

Kesta put an arm around his shoulders. 'You will make a good king, Salaben.' She looked up at Fox. 'Are you all right?'

He nodded, breaking into a weary smile. She rose, and went to embrace him. Taneshka joined her, throwing her arms around them both. Fox couldn't tell whether they were laughing or crying, or both. One of the soldiers was weeping as well, but his companion, grim faced, raised his voulge.

The Bloodgrim's head rose once more. This time though, impaled on steel. Blood stained the pole, but the soldier raised it at the door to the tower, a symbolic gesture to the dawn. Morning sunlight hit the contorted face. It was over.

Fox turned in the doorway, letting his mind travel the marshes. There were no husk left to the north, or to the east. But now, coming from the south, he could sense the army.

Silently he went to the ladder. He climbed onto the roof, and turned. There, at the edge of the marsh, lit up in golden winter sunshine, were the blue, green and red banners of the Lake Alliance.

31
Farewell

The White Gates Castle was filled once more with voices. A Heron boat had been commandeered to ferry the soldiers of the Alliance around the marsh to the East Watergate. Now the wall was secured, and most of the army were relaxing. Fox sat with Taneshka and Kesta at the dinner table in Heron's chamber, surrounded by officers. Each one of the three had a stony expression.

It was a mere four hours into the day.

Rashin approached with some caution. He put a hand on Fox's shoulder. 'What you have done, Fox, what you have done is incredible. You have cleansed the marsh of these, these *husk*, and destroyed the Perversion's assassin. No other could have done that.' There was a pause, and then the Warrior met Fox's eyes.

'I am so glad you are alive, Fox.' Fox smiled at him, but it was brief. The reason that his expression had suddenly darkened once more approached across the hall, dressed in silk robes. Fox stood. The advisor bowed deeply. As he did so, Rashin moved forwards to whisper in Fox's ear; it was Machist who had delayed the army's march.

'My lord Fox! You are…'

'Alive?' Fox growled. 'Are you surprised?' Machist looked taken aback. Fox sneered at the act. 'This is the last time, advisor, that you try to kill me. If it happens again, I *will* kill you.'

An ugly expression spread on Machist's face. 'What is this doggerel? I come here to greet you, congratulate you on your victory, glad that you are alive…'

'Victory! Victory? You liar! This is no victory, *fool*! This is defeat you look upon! Heron is dead, along with most of his family! I have lost good friends, you *serpent*, and it is all your fault! I would cut you down where you stand, if it would not dishonour my host!'

The advisor took a step back. The tone of his voice changed.

'Less of that, my prince. You are dangerously close to being reported for your insolence. And what host do you speak of? This castle is now under the Alliance, though negotiation is under way to decide whether the lake people really deserve…'

Fox's control snapped, astonished as he was that the council would seek to exploit the Heron family's loss. He punched the man in the mouth. Machist went down in a confused jumble of silk and soft fabric, his mouth bloodied. There was sudden silence in the crowded hall.

'Arreft 'im!' Machist gasped out, holding his jaw, staring up at Fox. Another voice echoed out in the hall, and the great doors slammed close.

'Arrest that man!' Salaben stood there, dressed in full Heron regalia, his hair and face washed clean. He was pointing at Machist, who scrambled to his feet, panicking.

'What? No! 'e punfed me inna fafe! *Arreft 'im, 'ot me!*'

Salaben marched up to the advisor, flanked by the two surviving soldiers, who were wearing bull-rider armour. Salaben's eyes narrowed as he looked up at Machist.

'Sir, you have challenged my sovereignty as king of this court and this territory. Under my rule, that is an incarcerable offence. I am handing you over into Prince Fox's custody. Good day.'

Machist was dragged away shouting angrily over his shoulder. Salaben smiled, but it was a tired smile.

'Taneshka, I found my father's testament. It states that in the event of rule passing to a son of his, of lesser age than fifteen, then stewardship of the Land's waterways is to be handed to Tiger. He is deemed honourable and responsible. As your father's military representative, Tigress, that makes you my Steward until I come of age, unless you wish to appoint another.'

Taneshka's eyes widened. For a moment she looked up at the high ceiling of the room, where the wooden beams crisscrossed the gap between the polished, panelled walls. For a moment she considered it; a place to stay, with food and rest always at hand, behind strong walls. She would be not that distant from her father then, a week's journey down the river on a boat with broad sails, and she could see the soft, damp green of the firs and pines again, the ruddy walls of her home, the bamboo standing tall and strong, swaying in the rainy breeze...

And again, Taneshka remembered the great tigress from her dream, alone and homeless.

She could not go back.

Fox looked at her shrewdly. Taneshka, like Kesta, began to get the feeling that Fox could see her thoughts.

'I am carrying on to the Autumn Hills, as soon as I am ready,' he said, watching Taneshka for her reaction. She bit her lip, torn still. Seeing Kesta, she saw that the girl's face held no indecision: Kesta would be going with Fox. That was certain. Taneshka thought of the blood that still tainted the waters of the marsh, and of Brant's body, four or so hours dead, lying out somewhere in the frigid water...

'I'll come to the Autumn Hills.'

I don't want to stay here.

Kesta beamed, happy at her friend's decision. The movement of her face caused fresh blood to trickle down her cheek. Taneshka stepped forward and wiped it away, smiling back. 'I'll come with you both. Land knows, you'll need me!'

Fox grabbed her shoulder in an affectionate gesture. 'I know we will! Come on Tigress. Let's prepare what we need. I will stay here no longer. Too many here have failed me!' He said this in a hard voice that carried around the large room. The Officers and Champions glanced away, or examined their feet in shame. The young Heron stood by, watching patiently.

Haiken came forward, anguish written on his face. The other Champions gathered behind him, hiding behind each other, afraid to meet Fox's blazing eye.

Haiken dropped onto his knees. 'Forgive me, Lord!' He drew his wide, tapering cleave-sword from his belt and laid it at Fox's feet. 'Demote and shame me, my lord. I am unworthy of my Championship.'

Fox raised the man up. 'Never will I shame you, Haiken. You are my teacher, and I love you, as I love my friends. Though they have been steadfast, while your strength failed.' Haiken bowed his head.

'It has. I am truly sorry. I could not...I did not argue with the advisor, for I feared I would lose my position. Which I will gladly give up in penance, my lord!'

Fox shook his head. 'You are still my Champion, my General. Go, put aside your shame and see to the stocking of the army. They will need to march across the Lands to the East Gate of the Autumn Hills, come the spring.'

'Yes, my lord.' Haiken beamed, and kissed Fox's hand before hurrying away.

'As for Machist…' Fox paused, striding past the other Champions, allowing them each a small, forgiving smile. For many it was like a pardon to a condemned man. Their love for him was reaffirmed.

Kesta and Taneshka followed Fox through the corridors of the White Gates Castle. They had not ventured this way before. They came to a broad, heavy door in a well-lit passageway. A tableau extended all down the wall, made from small wooden tiles set in a dark, polished frame. It showed a legend in the Dragonscript, above a field of battle, showing a defence against northern tribes. Kesta wondered what Heron's barbarian queen had thought of the image.

Before the door stood two Lake Alliance guards, one wearing a blue silk undershirt that showed at his neck and wrists, marking him as a Fox soldier. The other wore armour augmented with pieces of hard baked clay, which gave it a light, orangey red colour, similar to the bright red scarf of silk that wound the soldiers neck.

Fox greeted them warmly. 'It is still good, after all I have seen, to see two men that might have been enemies stand as brothers. The freeing of the City of Lakes was a great thing!' The two men bowed deeply, moving aside.

'The door is not locked, my lord. He has not the strength to break out,' The soldier explained briefly, turning the handle for Fox.

Fox and Kesta entered the room and Taneshka followed, closing the door. In the corner, Machist sat. He rose, already sneering. 'So! You have wisely changed your minds then, about allowing the upstart to imprison me.'

'Not at all,' Fox answered calmly, 'It is his right to do so.' Machist's eyes were hot with anger.

'You will regret this, you false and bastard son! When Henshin hears of this…'

'Where is Henshin?'

'He has been tracking down your cousin, to bring him to justice, as you should know. Do not think that you will escape justice yourself! Henshin's influence is strong!'

'Henshin is a serpent. He lies and seeks to further his own agenda. When I find out what that is...'

'I can tell you that, and gladly, *peasant*!'

Taneshka and Kesta both raised threatening hands at this, but Fox waved their aggression down. 'Good. Do tell, Machist.' He sat. The advisor's eyes brimmed with malice and he began to talk, his voice thick with spite.

'Henshin is set to the noble task of purifying the bloodlines of the families. One day, one glorious day, a king will be found with the strength to unite the lands. Superstition will be done away with, the so called Holy Order removed, replaced with men of order and reason. The glory of the old days will return!'

'The old days. The days of the Dragon.'

'Exactly! Then civilisation was truly great! They knew things then that have long been forgotten. It was they that learned how to fell the mightarchs, the great trees that left these lands wasted under forest! They made vast farmlands...'

'Wastelands! The reason that our people starve is the Dragon's legacy!'

'...farmlands, and forges, and armies that controlled the rebellious natives...'

'Massacred them, you mean!' Fox rose, angry. 'And do not forget, Machist, the other legacy of the Dragon! They built their capital on the sleeping place of the Shadow, and their priests, *your* old kindred, learned sorcery there in the ruins long after the walls of Dominago's keep were brought down!

'The reason so many servants exist to do the Shadow's work is the folly and darkness of the Dragon family! There will *never* be a return to those days, not whilst I live!'

Machist's lip curled. 'I agree with that at least.'

Fox's eyes narrowed, and he resisted the urge to hit Machist again. 'I am not about to die, Machist. Henshin would do well to know that; I am not going away.'

'Problems can be made to go away!'

'Not. This. One.' Fox bit down on each word. Then he turned to go. In the doorway, he stopped as Machist spoke again.

'Your Great Shadow nonsense will not help you, Fox. We are the learned ones, we are the ones that know of the old technologies, the ancient wisdoms. We have tested all. The Shadow, as you call it, does not exist. It is a lie. A falsehood, a superstition!'

Fox looked over his shoulder at the advisor. His expression was sad. 'Your certainty has blinded you, Machist.' And with that he strode out of the room. Kesta offered Machist a last look of enmity, which he returned. Then the door was closed, leaving him alone in the comfortable cell.

Fox stopped to say a few words to the guards. 'Spread the word: resist any attempt that any of the other advisors make to free him. He must be brought to justice at the Autumn Citadel, in the spring. Be strong, and do not fear them. They are toothless snakes. Your places are safe under my banner.'

The guards bowed low. If the advisors were to break Machist out, it would be over their dead bodies.

Fox, Kesta and Taneshka packed in silence, wearing their weapons beneath cloaks. Once again they stepped into marsh gear to cross the marsh, intending to discard it afterwards.

At the sixteenth hour, they stole out of the castle. The sky was clear and the air cold, but the journey beckoned to them. Fox felt that he was leaving behind his bitterness, and his army's failure.

Taneshka was happy to leave Stavan in her place as Steward.

Kesta ached to be away from civilisation, for her own personal reasons. The three of them all kept their main motive secret. The need to put the Red Marsh behind them was very great.

Fox pointed west. 'We'll walk along the Lifeblood once we leave the marsh to the west. Then we'll enter the Autumn Hills through the mountainous north gate. It's a little too close to the north for the army to safely pass that way in the spring, but the three of us should be fine.'

The sun was sinking ahead, making a silhouette of the Westward-last Tower, standing a few hundred yards away, off to the right of their path. The grass beneath their feet was crisp with frost, and they walked on firm, dry ground.

Epilogue

The Westward Last Tower is still surrounded by its dead. Many of them were Heron infantry, but most are husk. Their twisted bodies are headless, and hewn with great axe strokes.

The tower is empty, save for the corpses of the last few Heron guards, lying dead around a door within the structure itself. The door had been locked, but despite its stalwart defenders, it has been knocked in.

Inside the room, blankets and curtains are strewn about. A mattress is lying against the wall, in tatters, the bed frame broken. A baby's cot lies in in the corner of the room. It is smashed in, the blankets spread with the rest of the carnage. Many husk are within the room, but all are dead. The smashed cot is empty, as is the destroyed bed. The only bodies there are husk.

Further into the marsh, where night has almost fallen, a single husk staggers on. It is the last of its spawning, and the single dark consciousness that had driven its brothers as one is now so fragmented that the body is barely functioning. Suddenly, a familiar smell hits the husk's nostrils. It turns, and begins to flounder through the water, towards the vague shape ahead. Its failing eyes cannot make out the shape, but the nose tells it in plain terms that it can smell blood, and blood is good.

Without warning, an object flies past the husk. A long, thin chain hits against its neck, and suddenly it is choking as the chain wraps around its throat. The creature scrabbles at its neck, and then its life ends as a hooked blade slams into its face.

On the other end of the chain, cut in many places, but standing straight and tall, is a warrior. On his back is a great battle axe. His skin is dark brown, stained red with blood. In his free arm, he is holding a baby, swaddled in its last blanket, as carefully as the kill was brutal. By his side is a little girl, dressed in marsh garb, but cold and frightened.

The warrior makes a sling for the baby, and puts it around his neck, so that the baby is against his broad, muscular chest. He removes his axe from its belt, and holding it in his right hand, he crouches so that the little girl can climb onto his shoulders. Then he turns and begins to march through the marsh towards the distant castle.

The warrior is in pain, but there is a euphoria in his chest. He has succeeded. Breaking into a run, Brant begins to smile.

The Maker's Bloodline

Will be continued in:

The Maker's Bloodline:

Hunter's Path

Michael-Israel Jarvis started out telling stories to his friends, both real and imaginary, and things just followed on from there. He lives in Great Yarmouth, in Norfolk, a very Sacred Land indeed.

The Maker's Bloodline: Land Rising is Michael-Israel's debut, now edited and released for the first time on Amazon.

Michael-Israel Jarvis is also the author of **Gravedigger**. You can find him through social media on both Facebook and Twitter.

www.facebook.com/michael.israel.jarvis
@JarvisAuthor

Printed in Great Britain
by Amazon.co.uk, Ltd.,
Marston Gate.